THE ALPINE WINTER

An Emma Lord Mystery

Mary Daheim

CHIVERS

British Library Cataloguing in Publication Data available

This Large Print edition published by AudioGO Ltd, Bath, 2012.
Published by arrangement with Ballantine Books, a division of Random House Inc.

U.K. Hardcover   ISBN   978 1 4458 9169 9
U.K. Softcover   ISBN   978 1 4458 9170 5

Copyright © 2011 by Mary Daheim

The Alpine Winter is a work of fiction. Names, characters, places and incidents either are the products of the author's imagination or are used fictitiously. Any resemblance to actual events, locales, or persons, living or dead, is entirely coincidental

Printed and bound in Great Britain by
MPG Books Group Limited

For Jean Hopkins, whose dedication to high school students and patience with their parents' tardy tuition fees has made her a lifelong friend beyond Bishop Blanchet High School.

AUTHOR'S NOTE

The action of this book takes place in December 2004 and concludes January 1, 2005.

ONE

My brother Ben was driving me insane. He'd missed my early November birthday, but sent a gift just after Thanksgiving. When the package arrived, I didn't open it. I was mad because he'd canceled his plans to join me for Turkey Day.

Then life took a weird turn, hurling me into a personal and professional crisis that made me forget about his present. But a few days before Christmas, I remembered that I'd ditched it in the back of my closet. It was a cell phone. Not having updated my ancient model and being high-tech impaired, I didn't know how to use the new one without directions. Ben told me there weren't any. He'd gotten it from an incarcerated drug dealer. I accused him of taking a bribe, but he insisted it was a thank-you for visiting the inmate who owned it. I believed him. Ben, after all, is a priest.

Thus, the Wednesday before Christmas, I

showed the cell to Kip MacDuff, my tech wizard who runs the *Alpine Advocate*'s back shop.

"This is the latest type," he said, his still-youthful thirtysomething face envious. "I thought drug dealers only used cells they could toss."

"I don't care if they use two tin cans and a string," I said, sitting in my ad manager's chair in the newsroom. "Teach me to use it."

Kip hesitated. "I'll give it a run-through first." He picked up the device and fiddled with it. "Wow. It has all the latest gee-whiz features. Download music, access email, text . . ."

I held up my hand. "Stop. My son texts from St. Mary's Igloo. He's nagged me to get one of these so we can text each other. Phone connections to Adam in Alaska are dicey and email's too slow. I figure he and Ben conspired about this. Why do I think it'll drive me nuts?"

"It's easy, just tap in the words. You don't have to spell right. In fact, you shouldn't. You can only enter so many words."

I glared at Kip. "You're telling me — Emma Lord, your editor and publisher — that I can willfully screw up the English language?"

Kip grinned. "It makes communication faster. Don't you want to be in instant touch with Adam?"

"Not necessarily, since he took a vow of poverty. The kind of 'touch' my son puts on ol' Mom indicates he's trying to impoverish *me*."

"I thought Adam and Ben were coming for Christmas," Kip said as my House & Home editor, Vida Runkel, stomped into the newsroom.

"They are," I said hurriedly, aware from the look on Vida's face that she was about to make a pronouncement.

"Bones!" she exclaimed, whipping the plastic rain bonnet from her green derby hat. "I am so sick of bones!"

"What bones?" I asked, getting out of Leo Walsh's chair.

"Who knows?" Vida retorted, hanging up her tweed winter coat. "A bear, a deer, a gopher. . . ." She shook out her rain bonnet onto the radiator. "When any bones are found around here, the Eversons go wild. It's been sixteen years since Myrtle Everson disappeared. Why can't they let her rest in peace?"

Kip correctly assumed this wasn't the right time for a cell phone tutorial. He was moving toward the back shop, but paused

11

at the door. "That Mrs. Everson thing happened not long after my high school graduation. Tina Everson was in my class. When her grandma didn't come back from berrypicking, Tina got us grads to search for her. We spent three days going all over the woods. I fell into a bunch of devil's club and practically itched to death."

Vida gazed at Kip through her new silver-rimmed glasses. "From what I heard, very little searching occurred. Beverly Tomlinson and Jeff Dahlquist had an unanticipated wedding in October. Their baby was born on April Fool's Day. Jacqueline Munson sprained her ankle running away from Terry Caldwell's amorous advances. Coach Ripley complained that when four of his seniors came to collect their sports memorabilia after supposedly looking for Myrtle, they were high on marijuana."

"Hey," Kip said, laughing, "we felt like we were out of jail."

"That's no way to talk about an education," Vida huffed as she sat down at her desk. "You're fortunate to have a marketable skill."

Kip made a little mock bow. "You're right. To prove it, I'll get to work." He exited the newsroom.

"Cheeky," Vida murmured affectionately.

"If Kip doesn't have time to teach you how to use the cell, Ben can."

I sank into her visitor's chair. "True. I'll be able to text Adam."

Vida barely glanced at the cell. "Roger's texted for ages. If he joins the Marines," she added pensively, "he can chat with his chums."

I tensed, as I often did when she mentioned her grandson. Roger had finally gone off the rails in October, ripping the blinders from his grandmother's doting eyes. "Roger's taking Buck's advice?"

"Well . . ." Vida rested her chin on her hand. "It's either that or getting his grades up to attend Western Washington in Bellingham."

I had no idea how many credits — if any — Roger had earned in his sporadic career at Skykomish Community College. I was more interested in the status of the child he'd had by a local hooker who was doing time for offing one of her other customers. Vida was mum on the subject, although I assumed the toddler was being cared for by Roger's parents, Amy and Ted.

"As a career air force type, Buck believes in military life," she said, referring to her longtime companion. "But Roger could end up in harm's way. That terrifies me." She shuddered. Vida is a big woman, tall and buxom. I could've sworn the aged floorboards creaked under my chair.

She paused as Leo Walsh entered the newsroom. "Emma! Duchess!" he cried, freezing in place. "Duchess? Are you okay?"

Vida bridled a bit at the nickname she claimed to despise, though I sensed she secretly relished it. "I was considering the lack of peace on earth. Isn't that what Christmas is about?"

Leo went to his desk, a few feet away from Vida's. "Backslider I am, but I bring glad tidings of great joy." He propped his ad portfolio against the wall and removed his raincoat. "I sold six full-page ads, plus a four-color coupon for Pete's Pizza. And I conned the merchants who can still breathe without a ventilator into a double-truck New Year's ad. Isn't that jolly *Advocate* news?"

"Splendid, Leo!" Vida cried.

I leaped out of the chair to kiss Leo's weathered cheek. "You're a wizard! And you still have one more day before heading to California."

"I'll have everything set before I leave in case I don't get back by deadline. You can get bumped from a flight during the holidays."

14

"I should start next week's editorial," I said, backpedaling to my office cubbyhole. "Ben and Adam's visit may cut into my work hours."

"The priests," Leo remarked. "Where are you putting them?"

"Ben's staying at the rectory," I said. "He's relieving Dennis Kelly. If you'd go to Mass, you'd know Father Den is spending Christmas with his sister's family in Houston."

Leo wagged a finger at me. "Hey — I'll go to Mass with Liza and the rest of my family. I even know the liturgy isn't in Latin anymore."

"Good for you, Leo." I heard my phone ring and dashed to take the call before it trunked over to our temporary front office manager, Alison Lindahl. I barely said hello before Lori Cobb, the sheriff's receptionist, interrupted. "I've got bad news, Ms. Lord," she said in a tremulous voice.

I stumbled over the wastebasket and just managed to catch myself on the desk. "What?" I all but shouted, steeling myself for the worst.

"My grandpa died about an hour ago," Lori said, and paused.

I collapsed into my chair. "Oh." My voice was a croak. I cleared my throat. "I'm sorry,

15

Lori. It must've been sudden."

"It was." Lori sniffled a couple of times. "A heart attack, I guess. He'd finished lunch and was sitting at the table and fell into his cake plate. Grandma called 911, but it was too late."

"Are you at work?" I asked.

"Yes, but I'm leaving soon." Lori paused. "My folks are with Grandma now. Mrs. Runkel will write the obituary, but I don't know when the funeral will be held, because of Christmas. I hate taking off from work when we're shorthanded, with Doe Jamison on vacation and the boss man gone."

I didn't need a reminder that Sheriff Milo Dodge was out of town. "He can't stay with his daughter forever," I said, trying to keep the lead out of my voice. "She's on the mend."

"Physically," Lori said, "but mentally, she's a mess. Who wouldn't be after getting shot by their fiancé before he killed himself?"

"Yes, very hard on Tanya. Her mother, too." *And Milo and me.*

"There's the other line — got to go." Lori hung up.

Vida, her nose for news at work, stood in the doorway. "Well?"

16

"Alfred Cobb died," I said. "Heart attack."

"It's about time," Vida declared. "He was ninety-two and gaga for ages. I wonder if Lori will take his place on the county commissioners' board."

"I doubt that's a high priority for her right now."

"Probably not," Vida conceded, moving closer to my desk. "Did Lori say anything about the bones?"

My mind had gone blank. "Bones?"

"The bones that were found." She scowled at me. "Are the Eversons insisting they be examined by the sheriff's office in case they belong to Myrtle?"

"Lori didn't mention it," I replied. "She was pretty upset."

"I suppose." Vida drummed her short fingernails on my desk. "The Cobbs attend the Baptist church. Actually, Alfred only went at election time. Still . . . that's where the funeral will be." She stood up straight. "I'll get his file out so I can write a draft while I have time." She started to turn away, but stopped. "Where's Mitch?"

It was almost three-thirty. My news reporter had left before lunch, saying he'd be back in a couple of hours. "He's shooting photos for our New Year's greeting. He said

17

he'd wing it. I trust him, he's an old hand."

"A vast improvement after Curtis Mayne," Vida declared. "All those big ideas about going global. This is Alpine. What was he thinking?"

"He figured he'd get a Pulitzer after he got his college diploma."

"Curtis thought *he* was the story," Vida said. "Making a false homicide confession to write about the experience was the last straw. It's a good thing he didn't get charged with impeding justice. Milo was too lenient not doing any more than holding him overnight after he told such outrageous tales about shooting people."

"Milo couldn't stand having the little jerk around, either," I declared, as the screwups, missed appointments, and unreturned ASAP phone calls to Curtis came back like a bad dream. "All I wanted was to have him gone. Luckily, Mitch was available."

"I thought the Laskeys planned to visit family for the holidays," Vida said.

"They're waiting for better weather in northern Minnesota, where one of their sons and his family live. Being Jewish, Christmas isn't so big, except for Brenda filling gift orders with her weaving. Her shuttle broke last week, but she's found a local supplier for spare parts."

Vida nodded. "Yes, Dee Krogstad. She also weaves."

"Cut the Laskeys some slack," I said. "Having a son in jail at the Monroe Correctional Complex isn't easy."

"True," Vida agreed, "but Brenda strikes me as standoffish."

I stifled a smile. Vida's attitude really meant that the Laskeys were disinclined to reveal family secrets into her eager ears. A sudden commotion in the newsroom caught our attention. Vida blocked my view, but when she moved out of the way I saw the local postmaster, Roy Everson, at Leo's desk. An orange crate was next to him on the floor. Alison, looking puzzled, hurried to join me in my office doorway.

"Is Mr. Everson okay?" she whispered. "He's talking about bones."

"Don't get excited," I said softly. "It's not a crisis."

Reassured, Alison smiled and headed back to the reception desk.

Meanwhile, Leo was trying to give Roy the brush-off. "Don't ask me. Here's the expert," he said, pointing to Vida.

Roy turned to my House & Home editor, who, at almost six feet in her sensible heels, towered over him. "This could be Mama," he said, gesturing at the crate. "Why do Jack

Mullins and Sam Heppner think it's a joke? Just because Dodge is away, his deputies sit around drinking coffee and wasting taxpayers' money. And some people say the *post office* isn't efficient! I knew you'd tell me I'm not crazy."

Vida cast her gimlet eye on the wooden box, apparently taking Roy's statement about the deputies as a challenge. "I'm always open to possibilities," she said. "Can you show me what's in there?"

"Sure." Roy picked up the crate. "I'll put it on your spare chair."

I was halfway across the newsroom when Leo started for the back shop. As Roy carted the box to Vida's area, my ad manager went by me, murmuring, "It's not heavy, it's my mother."

I managed not to laugh. Judging from Roy's earnest manner, this was serious stuff. I'd never paid much attention to the missing woman's saga. She'd disappeared before I arrived in Alpine.

I was refilling my coffee mug when Mitch arrived, a weary expression on his lean face.

"Whoa," he said, espying Roy. "We rate personal delivery? Who sent us oranges?"

I joined the others at Vida's desk. "Not even close," I murmured. "How did the photo shoot go?"

"I need more snow and less rain," Mitch said. "Days are too short, clouds too low, no mountain view." He stared at our visitor.

"It's a femur," Roy announced, holding up a large bone. "Human." He set it on Vida's desk, oblivious to her annoyed expression. "Two ankle bones," he said, showing off what looked like chicken drumsticks. "Aren't these worth testing at the Everett lab?"

"Where were they found?" Vida asked.

"Downriver on the Sky," Roy said, turning over the two smaller bones. "By the campground and the ranger station. A family heading over the pass last Sunday with their little boys stopped there. The kids were horsing around, digging up rocks along the riverbank. Their parents are into that geocaching thing. They found these." He carefully placed the small bones next to the larger one. "Human, right?"

"Perhaps," Vida conceded. "How did you get them?"

"The kids' folks took them to the ranger station. Wes Amundson heard about it and called this morning. He and the other rangers always let us know when they find something that might be Mama."

"Indeed," Vida said noncommittally, glancing at the bones. "I have no idea about

21

anatomy. I assume you intend to have them tested?"

"Sure, but the sheriff has to get approval from SnoCo's DNA experts. Can you talk Doc Dewey into taking a look as our coroner?"

"Given that Doc's overworked and Milo will return soon, I suggest waiting," Vida said. "If the bones are your mother's, why rush?"

Roy's shoulders sagged. "We've already waited too long."

Vida touched his hand. "A few days won't matter. Wouldn't it be nice to take the bones home and have Mama with you for Christmas?"

I couldn't look at Leo or Mitch. Instead, I backed away from the little group and managed to keep a straight face.

"That's a great idea," Roy said, brightening. "I knew you'd help."

"Any time," Vida said rather grandly. "Merry Christmas, Roy."

He reverently repackaged the bones. "A happy new year to all!" he called, moving briskly from the newsroom.

"Ninny," Vida muttered, using a tissue to wipe off her desk where Roy had put his treasured remains.

"Dare I ask," Mitch said, "what that was

all about?"

Vida emitted a huge sigh, her bosom straining the buttons of her candy-cane-striped blouse. "Must I? It's a tiresome story."

Alison was standing in the newsroom doorway. "Oh, please, Mrs. Runkel! I grew up in Everett, so I don't know much Alpine lore."

Leo was back at his desk. "This isn't the first time the Eversons brought in bones. Were they all supposed to be Mama?"

Vida looked resigned, though I suspected she was dying to tell the story. I vaguely recalled an occasional find of bones and a couple of skulls, but after DNA testing, they were found not to be Myrtle's. In fact, some had been from four-footed animals and at least one owl.

"Oh, very well." She straightened the bow on her blouse and settled in to relate the mystery of Myrtle. "It was August 1988, wild blackberry season in the second growth after a timber parcel had been logged north of Carroll Creek. Myrtle was a widow in her early sixties living out on the Burl Creek Road where Roy and Bebe Everson do now. She'd told her daughter, Joyce — Joyce had just married Lyle Rhodes — that she was going to pick berries near Carroll Creek that

23

afternoon. Joyce worked at . . ." Vida bowed her head, as if she kept notes in her lap on every Alpiner, past and present. ". . . the Sears catalog store. She talked to Joyce on the phone just before noon. Around two, Myrtle came to Edna Roberson's house, asking where she — Myrtle — lived. Edna was startled. She told Myrtle her house was right across the road, saying, 'Don't you know that?' Myrtle nodded and left. Edna assumed she was going home, though she'd noticed the bucket was empty. That evening Roy stopped by to deliver a parcel for his mother. The door was unlocked. Myrtle wasn't there." Vida paused to sip her hot water.

"Early Alzheimer's?" Mitch suggested.

Vida shook her head. "If it was, no one recalled Myrtle showing any symptoms."

"Good weather?" Leo asked.

"Yes, a fine August day," Vida said. "But no one ever saw Myrtle — or her bucket — again."

Alison shivered. "That's awful. You think a bear ate her?"

"Dubious," Vida said. "It was the first thing people thought of when the search parties found no trace. Bears and berries go together. But Myrtle was wearing a wrist-watch, a large one, being farsighted and un-

24

able to see small numbers without glasses. The elder Dr. Medved — he hadn't yet retired as a veterinarian — said that while a bear might eat an entire person, bones and all, the one thing the animal can't digest is metal — such as belt buckles, buttons, and watches."

"Yuck," Alison said, grimacing. "That's gruesome."

Vida shrugged. "It's Nature, dear. We live so close to it in Alpine."

"So what about dem bones?" Mitch inquired.

Vida sighed. "The family became obsessed with finding out what happened to Myrtle. When any unidentified bones show up, they insist on DNA testing. This wasn't possible until the last few years — except for the skulls. They'd check dental records. Don't you remember, Emma?"

I nodded. "It was always a nonstory, at least regarding Myrtle. One skull showed up when Carla was our reporter," I said, referring to the ditzy young woman who'd almost unhinged me with her typos and idiosyncratic approach to news. "I envisioned her headline, 'Myrtle's Still Lost Her Head,' following up in the copy with 'skullduggery.' "

"Too true," Vida declared. "No doubt this

time is no different."

"Maybe they'll give up," Leo said. "Is it a hobby or a fixation?"

Vida sighed. "Both. It's the end of the year. I wish it was the end of Myrtle."

Leo chuckled, Alison was still dismayed, and Mitch looked bemused. I returned to my office, never guessing that this was far from the end of Myrtle's saga.

Thursday was busy. Leo plunged into ad copy and mock-ups, skipping lunch before taking the fruits of his labors to our merchants for approval. He finished by four, heading to Sea-Tac Airport to catch an evening flight to California and his no-longer-estranged family.

Mitch's hard news shrank the week before Christmas, with meetings postponed and guest speakers replaced by holiday parties. The sheriff's log listed minor vehicular accidents, three burglaries at the upscale neighborhood known as The Pines, two prowlers, and the theft of Rudolph the Red-Nosed Reindeer from Old Mill Park. Mitch wrote a droll piece on Rudolph's adventures after leaving his spot by the picnic tables.

I asked if there was any progress nailing the maple poachers who'd recently hacked down trees close to town. Mitch said that without the sheriff cracking the whip, there was nothing new. The poachers seemed to be lying low, perhaps scared off after our artist recluse, Craig Laurentis, had been shot near the site of the latest arboreal carnage.

"What about those burglaries?" I asked. "The Pines is our version of . . . what in Detroit?"

Mitch laughed dryly. "Royal Oak is nice and so are some other suburbs. But after seeing Seattle real estate prices, how does anybody afford to live there? I saw an ad for a shack that cost a quarter of a million dollars. Heck, even The Pines was out of our price range."

"That probably wasn't a shack," I said, "but a garage. And you know what? As ugly as it was, I bet Casa de Bronska would've sold for six times as much in Seattle than what Ed Bronsky got for it here in Alpine."

Mitch shook his head and walked away.

Vida wrote the background for Alfred Cobb's obit, leaving space for funeral information. She was still receiving Christmas party news and photos from various social clubs for her section. Last but not least, Vida dealt with her advice column. Several queries came from people who didn't want to spend the holiday with

27

certain odious family members.

My tasks were easy. I wrote two editorials, the first lauding Alfred Cobb for his long service to the county. The second hit Sky-Co's highlights since January, ending with a wish for the new year to treat our readers kindly. I could've typed that one with my chin. I'd done the same thing every December since taking over the newspaper.

When I left the office, it was still raining enough for me to keep the windshield wipers on. I headed for the Grocery Basket to stock the larder. There was already a twenty-pound turkey jammed into the freezer; I'd purchased it for Thanksgiving before Adam and Ben canceled.

The store was busy, forcing me to circle the parking lot twice. Betsy O'Toole, the wife of the owner, Jake O'Toole, was helping an addled Grace Grundle with the cash machine by the door.

Betsy saw me and forced a tired smile. "Hi, Emma," she said, abandoning Grace. "I'm glad your family's coming for Christmas." She glanced at the produce section, where her brother-in-law, Buzzy, was unloading a pallet of Idaho potatoes. "It's a tough one for us."

I nodded. "How are Buzzy and Laura doing? I've hardly seen them since Mike was killed."

"They keep a low profile," Betsy said, stepping aside for a young woman pushing a toddler in a grocery cart. "Especially Laura. She's always been quiet. I put her to work in the storeroom. She needs to stay busy and not dwell on the truck accident."

"Good." I saw Grace chewing on her fist and staring helplessly at the cash machine. "Kenny's still working for you," I said, referring to Mike's younger brother, who was carrying out an elderly couple's bags.

"Kenny's a great kid," Betsy said. "Speaking of kids, is Ginny coming back to work for you or is she serious about being a stay-at-home mom now that they've got the new baby and two other little boys?"

I shrugged. "Ginny's mulling. Alison goes back to teaching her cosmetology course right after New Year's. If Ginny opts out, I'll ask Amanda Hanson to take over. Once Amanda settled in, she did very well. She should finish her temporary post office job by next week."

"Amanda's changed," Betsy said. "She used to be so flighty, not to mention a bit of a . . ." She stopped, apparently seeing my eyes widen as I looked beyond her to Grace, who had taken off one of her sensible shoes

29

and was whacking it against the cash machine. "Oh, Holy Mother!" Betsy exclaimed. "Gotta go!" Whirling around, she rushed off to save the money dispenser from destruction.

It was six-thirty when I got to my little log house. The phone rang just as I carted in the last grocery bags. Racing into the living room, I grabbed the receiver before the call went over to voicemail.

"Why haven't you texted me?" Ben asked in his crackling voice.

"Because . . . ," I said breathlessly, just then realizing I'd left the cell at work. "Because I don't know how."

"Oh, for . . . Emma, you really are a moron. It's not astrophysics. Any six-year-old can use those damned things."

"Hey — we've been so busy that I forgot. I showed it to Kip yesterday, but we were pulling things together so I can entertain you and Adam without neglecting work. And did you forget I almost got killed?"

"No," my brother said, "you alluded to that in an email. But your recent news has been brief except for nagging me about not standing you up again. We haven't spoken for a while."

"You've been busy, too. Are you canceling again?"

Ben chuckled. "No. How long could you put up with me beyond the five days I originally scheduled?"

His query was disconcerting. "What have you got in mind?"

"Den asked if I could stay through New Year's. He wants a few extra days to go from Houston to see his brother in Pittsburgh. I need a break, so I asked for a six-week leave. I should get it. I haven't had much time off in five years."

"You're burned out?"

"Not as a priest," he replied, sounding more serious than usual. "But I am burned out with city life. Ever since I started doing temporary assignments, I've been sent to big cities. I miss the desert, I miss the Delta. I need to reconnect with the first thirty years of my life serving the Church. I want to see the sun baking on adobe, listen to blues by the Mississippi, see my old parishioners, and air myself out. I might even go up to see Adam's frozen world in Alaska."

I understood. "That's wonderful. How long would you stay in Alpine?" I asked after only a faint pause.

"Why? Will I cramp your style?"

"No," I fibbed. "I just stocked up on groceries. I'm thinking about food over the long term."

Ben's pause lasted long enough to make me more uneasy. "I don't plan to impose on you. Why are you fussing over menus? You're a lousy liar, Sluggly."

The childhood nickname annoyed me as much as the accusation. "Okay, Stench," I snapped, calling him what I always did when he was making my life miserable, "I do have a life outside of the *Advocate*."

"Is it that AP guy who took off for a Loire Valley *petit chateau* or did you finally succumb to Mr. Radio's feigned indifference?"

"Oh, God, you *are* evil!" I slid off the sofa onto the floor. "I haven't heard from Rolf Fisher in weeks, and Spencer Fleetwood may seem like a dream walking *and* talking, but I do not find him appealing. The thing is, Vida will want to invite you to dinner and she'll pester me until I give her your schedule."

"Stop!" Ben cried. "Don't threaten me with Vida's ghastly exploits at a stove. I was thinking of leaving a few days after New Year's, maybe. I don't have any plans beyond getting to your little log cabin on the Sky. But I connect with Adam tomorrow at Sea-Tac. His flight arrives an hour after I do, so I'll rent a car and try not to get cuffed by security while I wait for him."

"Maybe if you'd wear your clerical garb

and not look like a reject from Nirvana's heyday, you'd get some 'spect, bro."

"You've ruined my self-esteem. See you tomorrow, Sluggly."

I smiled as he rang off. My brother could make me smile even when he made me mad. Or, in this case, uncomfortable. I knew I had to tell him what was going on in my life. Or *not* going on, at the moment.

Hauling myself up from the floor, I turned around to gaze at Craig Laurentis's painting, *Sky Autumn.* The rushing waters over rocks and under fallen branches seemed to flow right off the canvas. I never looked at Craig's work without marveling at how he could create such magic. Yet in recent weeks, I'd been afraid to look at all, fearing he might never paint again. After he'd been shot near the tree-poaching site, his life had hung in the balance. But he'd rallied, returning on a pale December morning to wherever he lived in his mountain aerie among the other wild, untamed creatures. If that's what it took to create genius, so be it.

After dinner, I added the final touches to my holiday décor. I'd put the tree up on Sunday, but had overlooked a box of candles for the mantel. Many of them had belonged to my parents. I set them out, then I placed the painted resin figure of Mary next to Joseph in the wooden stable. The ritual was carried out one piece at a time, with Baby Jesus settling into His crib on Christmas Eve. I always offer a prayer and on this night I said one for my kinsmen's safe journeys.

By the next afternoon, only half of my prayer was answered. Ben called from Sea-Tac around three to say he'd heard from Adam, who couldn't leave the village because of a whiteout. "He may make it tomorrow," Ben said. "There's no point waiting here any longer."

"Damn!" I slumped in my chair. A white-out was a snowstorm that didn't just snarl traffic, but prevented more than an inch or two of visibility. "Why didn't he call or send an email? I'm his mother."

"He can't go online. He texted me because *he* can. I'm hanging up so I can join the other bad drivers on Highway 2."

I cringed. The road to Alpine was called the Highway to Heaven because it was so dangerous, and my brother was reckless behind the wheel. Maybe it was his way of defying fate after our parents were killed in a car crash on their way home from his ordination.

"You're glum," Vida said when I entered the newsroom. "Why?"

I told her about Adam's delay. "What if

he never gets out?"

"Oh, heavens!" Vida cried. "He'll be here. Who's taking his place?"

"I don't know — a Jesuit from the northern Alaska diocese, I think. But if Adam can't get out, the other priest can't get in."

"But Ben's going to be here," she said in reassurance. "I must invite him to supper. It'll have to be after Tuesday, since our family's gathering in Bellingham at my daughter Meg's tomorrow after church." She frowned. "It'll give Roger an opportunity to see the Western Washington campus. His old chum, Davin Rhodes, likes it there."

"Could Roger enroll for winter quarter or is it too late?"

Vida straightened the red vest she wore over her white blouse. "Oh — I don't know. He hasn't gotten his transcripts together. Amy and Ted won't nag. I wish Buck hadn't left town to be with his children and grandchildren. I'd hoped he'd come with us to Bellingham and see what a nice campus they have. Very woodsy and not unlike Alpine, though larger. Viewing the lovely setting might make Buck forget the Marines."

"The school's grown since it became a university," I remarked as Mitch entered the newsroom. "Any luck with New Year's photos?"

Mitch ignored me, briskly walking to his desk. He acted as if I were invisible. "Hey, Laskey," I called good-naturedly, "you deaf?"

My reporter waved an impatient hand and picked up the phone. He remained standing, his back turned to me. I looked at Vida, who was regarding him with fiercely curious gray eyes. "What's this?" she hissed.

I shook my head. Mitch was speaking into the phone, but so softly that we couldn't hear what he was saying. He paid no attention to Kip, who'd arrived with what looked like Photoshop art and was standing a few feet away, apparently waiting for Mitch to hang up.

Kip noticed that Vida and I were frozen in place. Alison had come from the front office, also acting bewildered. She motioned at Mitch, looked at me, and held out her hands as if to ask what was going on.

I shook my head. Kip backed off, moving toward Leo's vacated area. I signaled for Alison to follow me into my cubbyhole. Before we could take more than a few steps, Mitch put down the phone in what seemed like a difficult act of self-control.

"Sorry," he said. "I have a family emergency." He took a deep breath, his face pale. "I'll be in touch." He grabbed his laptop

36

and practically ran out the door, his black raincoat flapping at his legs.

"Well now!" Vida said, fist on hips. "What's that about?"

Kip shook his head. "I haven't heard sirens. It can't be medical."

"It has to be Mrs. Laskey," Alison said. "Didn't he say 'family'?"

We all agreed. Vida drummed her fingers on the desk. I knew what she was thinking: Who among her vast network of relatives could help? "True, Kip," she said after a long silence. "What does that leave?"

"Mental? Emotional?" I suggested.

"Possibly," Vida allowed. "Didn't I say Brenda's odd?"

"It's Christmas Eve," Kip blurted, then shook his head. "I forgot, the Laskeys are Jewish, so they shouldn't be in a holiday funk."

I asked Kip if we were close to being done. "I'd like to shut down early in case Ben stops at my house before he goes to the rectory."

Kip clasped the Photoshop art. "I wanted to ask Mitch about using this for our New Year's greeting. Did he take any more pictures?"

"I don't see his camera," I said. "He must've left it in his car."

"Then I'm almost finished," Kip said. "Chili's mom called last night about Roy and the newest batch of bones. What's up with that?"

Vida grimaced. "Nothing new until they're sent to the Everett lab."

Kip's wife was related to the Eversons on her mother's side. "Is Chili caught up in that, too?" I asked.

"No," Kip said, "but her mom is. Chili likes to think her grandma ran off with a man. Like that would happen at her age."

"She was only sixty-two," Vida huffed. "Love is ageless."

Kip shrugged. "Well . . . sure. I'll tell Chili that. It'll make her feel better about the whole deal." He headed for the back shop.

Alison had lingered. "I'll stay until five just in case."

I shook my head. "You have to drive home to your parents' house in Everett. That's not going to be any picnic. Take off now."

Alison smiled. "Okay. I'll clean up and go. Merry Christmas!"

"Such a nice girl," Vida said softly. "So chipper compared to Ginny when she mopes. If they straighten out the bank mess, maybe Rick will be promoted and Ginny won't have to work. Marv Petersen doesn't seem inclined to sell the bank to outsiders.

I'm not sure he knows what happened. I hope he's too addled or the Arizona sun has shriveled his brain so he can't take in the disaster he left after retiring as president."

Rick and Ginny Erlandson had been spared the worst of the bank's recent tragedy. But the Petersen family had been decimated in the past ten years. The last funeral had been held only two weeks ago. I, too, had suffered from what seemed like the Petersen family curse. I'd awoken in the middle of the night at least twice thinking it was happening all over again. I was falling, down, down, down. Then . . . nothing, just my dark bedroom, with chilly rain splattering the window. And Milo not there to comfort me.

"Drat," Vida said under her breath. "Dare I call Brenda?"

"Bad idea," I said. "Whatever it is, it isn't good."

"It's the not knowing that bothers me," Vida said.

If there was one thing Vida couldn't tolerate, it was *not knowing.* "We'll find out eventually," I told her. "Are you almost done?"

"One more letter." She tapped a sheet of stationery. "Pastor Purebeck's wife, Selena, thinks he's strayed."

39

My jaw dropped. "Your pastor? Did she sign her name?"

"No, but I know her handwriting. Pastor Purebeck is a most virtuous man with a spotless reputation since coming here in 1985."

"Does she offer proof?"

"Only suspicions. Not being where he said he'd be. Coming home late with flimsy excuses. Remarks by other church members."

"What will you tell her?"

"To proceed with caution — and trust. Selena insists it started in October. If so, I'd have heard. Of course, I can't say that in print."

"Too bad," I said. "That'd convince me."

My phone rang, so I left Vida to handle Mrs. Purebeck. I heard Spencer Fleetwood's mellifluous voice at the other end. "You're still working," he said. "I'm halfway to Seattle for the holiday. Did you get the sheriff's news?"

"What news?" I asked, falling into my chair. "What's happened?"

"Calm down," Spence said, amused. "I'll clarify — the sheriff's *headquarters,* not the great love of your life. He and I are not close."

"You are a real jackass," I said, sitting up

straight. "What is it?"

"Maybe I should hang up. Now you're mad . . ."

"Just tell me. I'm busy."

"There was a prison break in Monroe this afternoon." He paused for a single beat, just as he did before breaking news on the air. "The escapee is Troy Emory Laskey. Merry Christmas, Emma."

Two

I spent most of Christmas Eve alone. Ben had to say two Masses — the children's Mass at seven and the midnight Mass at nine. The latter ran for almost two hours. My brother couldn't eat in between because he had to take communion at both liturgies. He'd gone straight to the church and didn't reach my house until eleven-thirty. Not having eaten since grabbing a pastry at the airport, he was in a grumpy mood and expected to be fed upon his arrival.

"You never gave me details," I yelped at him while he searched the fridge for edibles. "You didn't call me until almost eight."

"I didn't have time," he shot back. "I thought you'd have dinner ready when I got here."

"Why would I make a big dinner at this hour? It's three a.m. in your time zone. I thought you'd be dead on your feet by now."

"The trip up here sucked scissors. Drivers

go fast, go slow, can't make up their frigging minds. They leave their brains in the garage."

"You are one uncharitable priest," I said, trying to push Ben out of the way. "I'll make scrambled eggs and ham. Sit down and shut up."

Ben gave in, falling into a chair. "It's been a long day."

"I know. Fasting was never your strong suit. How many eggs?"

"Three." He sighed. "It's a good thing I only have a ten o'clock tomorrow. I assume you'll be there."

"Maybe." I put a ham slice on to cook. "How long's your homily?"

"Six minutes." He stretched and yawned. "Not my strong suit."

"I can endure that," I said, breaking eggs into a bowl. "Den keeps his short, too. Neither of you exactly electrify your listeners."

Ben yawned again. "It's a dirty job, but someone's got to do it."

"You two have other gifts. He's a good manager and down-to-earth. Parishioners love him — once they got over realizing he was black."

Ben nodded. "Den can't change that. He's a fair theologian, too."

43

"Say," I said, flipping the ham, "can you say a special prayer for Mitch and Brenda Laskey? Their son escaped from Monroe today."

"The town off Highway 522? What's wrong with Monroe?"

I realized Ben still didn't know all the local references. "The state correctional facility that used to be known as the reformatory," I explained. "That's why the Laskeys moved here from Royal Oak, outside of Detroit. Or so we've gathered. They're Jewish, but . . ." I shrugged.

"What the hell. Sure, I can do that. You got a beer in the fridge?"

Ben's lack of curiosity about Troy Laskey indicated he was really tired or had seen so many slices of life on the raw that nothing surprised him. The eggs sizzled, the toast popped up, and I got Ben a bottle of beer.

"Glass?" I inquired.

He shook his head. I dished up his meal. He wouldn't eat again until after the ten o'clock Mass. I sat down, but neither of us spoke for a few minutes. It was a comfortable silence. It could've been forty years ago and we were sitting in our parents' kitchen.

"What are you smiling about?" he asked.

"Us — as kids. Our folks." I leaned closer. "Except for being tired of city life, are you content with who you are and the choices you've made?"

Ben was unfazed by my random question. "Yeah, for the most part. I'm okay with it." He ate some toast, chewing and swallowing before speaking again. "And you?"

"I'm getting there."

The brown eyes so like my own gazed back at me. "Don't tell me now. If you run off with Crazy Eights Neville, I'm too tired to care."

"I didn't intend to," I said. "And it's Crazy Eights *Neffel.*"

"Emma Neffel," Ben murmured. "Eme-nefel." He shook his head. "Why am I thinking 'Heffalump'?"

I laughed. "Because when we were little, Mom couldn't read that part in *Winnie-the-Pooh* without literally wetting her pants."

Ben laughed, too. "She'd start giggling, try to go on, giggle some more and fall apart. I didn't know what happened to that Heffalump until I learned to read."

We spent the rest of his brief visit talking about our favorite childhood books. I mentioned *Heidi* and *Heidi Grows Up;* Ben confessed that he'd reread his own favorite, the classic *Robin Hood,* only a year ago. He left for the rectory shortly before one o'clock. I told him I'd see him in church.

■ ■ ■ ■

Spence's stand-in — a woman named Rebecca — gave the local news Christmas morning. She reported that Troy Emory Laskey had escaped from Monroe the previous day and was still at large. Law enforcement agencies in SnoCo, SkyCo, and KingCo were searching for him. There was no mention of his parents living in the area. I considered asking Kip to post the update on our site, but decided against it. I didn't want to bother Kip on Christmas, nor did I want to add to the Laskeys' misery.

Before going to Mass, I checked to see if Adam had emailed me. Nothing. I left early for church. I wanted to ask Ben if he'd received a text from Adam. While putting on his red liturgical vestments, he told me he hadn't. I went into the sanctuary to find a seat close to the altar — and far from Ed and Shirley Bronsky. I needn't have bothered — my former ad manager and his brood weren't in attendance. Ben told me later that they'd been at the evening service.

"Fat and fulsome as ever," he said upon arriving at my house around noon. "Are Ed and Shirley really living in a shallot on the river?"

"Oh, good Lord! He probably meant 'chalet.' It's a decent house, if cramped. I don't know why their older kids haven't moved out. They're as lazy and unmotivated as Ed. The villa formerly known as Casa de Bronska before Ed blew all his money is opening soon as a rehab center."

"For Ed?"

"Too late for that."

We were in the living room. I'd put the turkey in the oven before he arrived. Neither of us had heard from Adam. I was getting nervous.

"You did text him, didn't you?" I asked Ben.

"Twice. No response could mean he's airborne."

"If he is, I wish he'd let us know."

"Give him a break," Ben said, lounging in the armchair across from the sofa where I was sitting. "You've never been up there to St. Mary's to see what it's like, and I can only tell from what he says and the pictures he sends. Adam has to get out by bush plane to Nome, then fly to Anchorage and on to Sea-Tac. That's a long haul. Throw in lousy weather and the holiday, and he'll be lucky if he gets here tomorrow."

"But once he gets to Nome, he could call me or text you."

Ben smirked. "He could text *you* if you weren't such a dolt. I'll bet he's still stuck in St. Mary's. The presents and the leftovers can wait." He glanced at the dozen pretty packages under the tree. "Let's make drinks. Then you can tell me about your journey to self-discovery."

"Oh . . ." I dreaded this moment, but I had to face it. "Let's see how many drinks I need before I can talk about it."

Ben grimaced. "It sounds worse than I thought."

"It is and it isn't." I went into the kitchen. Confronted with the small stash of liquor in an upper cupboard, I stood like a lump. Ben would drink just about anything, including kerosene, so I got down my favorite Canadian whiskey and managed not to spill any liquid or drop the bottle. After adding ice and water, I checked the turkey, taking my time to baste the beast. I decided we needed coasters. I had a set with a Currier & Ives motif in the towel drawer — or so I recalled from seeing them circa 2002.

"What are you doing?" Ben called. "Drinking all the good stuff?"

"I'm coming," I yelled back, finally giving up. Unless, I thought, they were in the junk drawer . . .

They were. I emerged from the kitchen. "I

was looking for these," I said, placing a coaster on the table by Ben's chair. "Nice, huh? I got them from Edna Mae Dalrymple at a Christmas bridge club gift exchange. I never remember to use them. Is that enough ice?"

"Why are you talking so fast?" Ben inquired. "You haven't offed somebody, have you?"

I scowled. "Not intentionally. But that's a side issue."

"Wow. Guess I'll pretend I'm in the confessional and nod off."

"I wish," I muttered, taking my glass over to the sofa.

The phone rang, causing me to slosh my drink on the rug. I set the glass on the coaster and grabbed the receiver. Maybe it was Adam.

"Merry Christmas," Milo Dodge said, devoid of any kind of cheer. "Whatever you're doing is more fun than what I'm doing. Some holiday. Everything okay with you?"

I sat down, trying to act unruffled. I hadn't heard from Milo in almost a week. "Yes," I replied, "but Adam hasn't arrived yet. Ben got here last night."

"Is he there now?" Milo asked, sounding wary.

"Yes." I glanced at my brother, who was trying to appear disinterested. "We're having a drink. How are things with you?"

"What you'd expect. Tanya's coping a little better. At least she only woke up twice last night."

"And . . . Tricia?" I inquired, using his former wife's real first name for once.

Milo uttered a tired laugh. "Mulehide went to the store — if she can find one that's open. She ran out of orange juice. That's about all Tanya drinks for some damned reason."

"How about the rest of the family?" I avoided looking directly at Ben, who'd fetched a magazine from the rack by the fireplace.

"I haven't had to throttle anybody yet," Milo said. "Jake the Snake showed up today, making nice with Mulehide. I couldn't say hello to the bastard without wanting to deck him. I'd like to blame him for screwing up my kids while he was screwing around, but Mulehide should've figured if he'd cheated with her while they were both still married, why would the S.O.B. change?" He paused. "Hell, I blame myself, too. If I'd spent more time with the kids, maybe it'd be different. Who knows?"

I certainly didn't. "Do you think Jake

wants back in?"

"I don't know. Don't care, either. Hey," he said, his voice taking on a brighter note, "Sam Heppner called last night to tell me the Laskey kid broke out of Monroe. Anything new on that?"

"Not as of this morning," I said, aware that Ben was pretending to concentrate on an issue of the *National Geographic*. "I haven't talked to Mitch since he took off yesterday in a tizzy. He didn't even tell us what was wrong."

"Can't blame him," Milo said. "God, what's wrong with this younger generation? You sure you're okay? You sound . . . strange."

"I am," I admitted. "Do you know when you'll be back?"

"Maybe Tuesday. I hope." He'd lowered his voice. "God, I miss you. If I stay here much longer, I'll even miss Sam Heppner."

"I imagine you miss work, too," I said.

"Not as much as I miss you. Well . . . you know what I mean."

"I do." I did. "I'm the same way."

"I hear Mulehide. Got to go. Oh, shit, here comes Tanya, tears running like Deception Falls. Shit!" The sheriff clicked off.

Ben waited a moment or two before closing the magazine. "Want me to get a rag to

51

mop up what you spilled on the rug?"

I looked down at the carpet. "No. This rug needs cleaning. I didn't slop that much anyway."

Ben nodded absently and took a swig of his drink. "I thought that might be Adam calling," he remarked.

"I did, too," I said, fiddling with the lampshade on the end table, hoping my brother wouldn't notice that it didn't require my attention.

"Well?"

I shook my head. "Never mind." I waved at the lighted Christmas tree in front of the living room window. "It's the wrong day — the wrong time of day — to talk about deep things." I pointed to the mantel. "Do you remember those little candles from when we were kids?"

Ben turned to look toward the fireplace and chuckled. "Snowman, streetlamp, choirboy, Santa, tree. They came from a gas station, right?"

"Freebies," I said. "Imagine — coaxing people to buy gas."

Ben had gotten up to study the candles more closely. "I never took much of Mom and Dad's stuff. I couldn't. I've always had to travel light."

"I didn't take a lot, either," I said. "All I

could do at the time was try to keep from going crazy and stay in college."

"Yes." He stood very still, a taller, broader, more stalwart, masculine version of me, staring at the candles. Staring inwardly at memories. Staring into the reality that, in the end, is all we have.

I got up and went out to baste the turkey again.

I was mashing potatoes when Adam called from Nome. Ben answered, but gave me the phone when I rushed into the living room. "Hey, Mom, don't return my gifts," my son said before I'd barely said hello. "I'll see you tomorrow afternoon if I find space in the baggage section."

I was too elated to ask why he hadn't contacted me or his uncle until now. "At least you'll be here. Oh, Adam, I'm so happy! But you'll have to rent a car. Have you got money?"

"I can roll a couple of Christmas drunks when I get to Sea-Tac," my son replied, typically sounding more like Ben than his father, Tom. "Or cadge a loan from a hooker working the main drag by the airport."

"Just don't take any detours," I said. "I can't wait to see you."

"Good. Then maybe I'll use your credit

53

card for the car. Got to go — people are lined up for the phones. My cell's dead."

Ben regarded my smiling face. "Feeling the Christmas spirit now?"

"Definitely," I said. "My appetite's back."

"Mine never left," Ben said.

After dinner, we sat in the living room, chatting easily and listening to music. Ben hauled himself out of the armchair just before nine. I assumed he was leaving, but I was wrong. He threw another log on the fire and sat down. "Let's hear it. Once Adam arrives, you'll shut down."

"I want to talk, but I'm not sure you'll like what you hear."

"That's a given," he said, folding his hands in his lap as if he was about to hear a confession.

And that, of course, is what it was.

It took twenty minutes to relate what had happened in recent weeks and how I felt about it. When I finished, Ben stretched and yawned. "Sluggly," he began, gazing at the ceiling, "you're a smart Catholic woman. You know the rules." He looked like he did at twelve when he told me why a ten-year-old girl couldn't play baseball with him and the other boys on the vacant lot at the corner. The lot was gone. So was our youth.

"Have you been to confession lately?"

"Yes," I informed him, on the defensive. "I won't go to St. Mildred's. Too many people lurk outside the confessional and I'm always afraid they'll overhear something. Last Saturday I went shopping at the Everett Mall, so afterwards I drove over to St. Mary Magdalen's."

"St. Mary Magdalen sounds about right, given what you told your confessor," Ben remarked. "Did he have anything to say?"

"No," I said. "He seemed bored."

"He probably was. Adultery's not very interesting to a third party."

"Hey — it's not as if Milo and I are married to other people."

"He still is if he got married in a church. Any church. That's the way it is. I figure he did. That counts."

"He's never really talked about his wedding. I assume they got married in a church. They had a reception. He mentioned it recently when he thought his daughter was getting married this summer."

"Have you discussed marriage?"

"No. We haven't had time to talk about much of anything."

Ben chuckled and rubbed his eyes. "I don't doubt it from the way you described your great awakening with the local law-man."

"I don't mean that," I said angrily. "He's been gone almost since then, nursing his daughter and his ex. I've talked to him exactly three times since then, and today was one of them."

"That was one stilted conversation," Ben said. "I wasn't sure who you were talking to. It could've been our great-aunt Lulu in Humptulips, judging from your prissy expression."

"Aunt Lulu's been dead for thirty years."

"I didn't know she was sick." He grew more serious. "At least you finally buried Cavanaugh's ghost. Oh, Tom was okay, just messed up — and married. How's Adam going to react?"

"Good question," I said. "For now, he doesn't need to know."

Ben lifted his hands helplessly. "Why rush after fifteen years? I, a celibate priest, knew Dodge was nuts about you from way back."

"I knew that, too. He mentioned marriage years ago, but I didn't reciprocate. May I remind you, Stench, you weren't always celibate? Do the names Rosemary and Colleen and Terry Lynn ring any bells?"

"Not so much anymore." He sighed. "Oh, hell, it was fun while it lasted." He stood up. "Feast of the Holy Family Mass at ten."

"Right," I said, wishing Ben wouldn't go. Having unloaded my burden, I wanted to talk more about it. But men aren't like women, and I knew better than to press him. My brother always needed to think things through. Maybe he didn't take me seriously and my apprehension had been wasted.

"Tomorrow's dinner with Adam and leftovers," I told him.

He put on his jacket before kissing my cheek and going out into the wet Alpine night.

As soon as he pulled onto Fir Street, narrowly missing my mailbox, I turned out the lights on the tree. The fire still burned in the grate. I emptied the dishwasher, reloaded it, and finished tidying up. When I was done, I stood at the sink, staring out into the carport.

Marriage. Milo and I hadn't discussed it. When he'd left my house the morning after his return to Alpine from his Bellevue ordeal, we hadn't talked much. He'd spent most of that Sunday at the office organizing everything for his subordinates before driving back to Bellevue. He'd been there ever since.

Marriage. I'd been engaged twice, a mother

once, but never a wife. Ben had never married and Adam wouldn't, either. Maybe we Lords weren't the marrying kind. I'd dumped my first fiancé after I met Tom. Our affair had resulted in Adam's birth, but Tom had dutifully returned to his unbalanced wife while I fled to the Mississippi Delta to have my baby on Ben's watch. Twenty years passed before I saw Tom again, and almost another decade went by before he was free to marry me. Sandra Cavanaugh had taken too many of her funny-bunny tranquilizers and dropped dead. But when Tom proposed, I'd dithered. It wasn't just my natural perversity, but the possibility of giving up the *Advocate* and moving to San Francisco. It was Milo who told me to give Tom a choice and ask if he was willing to move to Alpine. For one fateful moment, I'd considered dumping Tom and falling into the safe, sure arms of the sheriff instead. But that would have dashed my precious dream. And Adam wanted his parents to live out their lives together. Tom had agreed to move to Alpine. San Francisco had too many sad memories for him. I said yes to his proposal.

Marriage? It never happened. Tom had been killed, and I was bereft. Again, I turned to Ben, who dragged me off to Rome. I'd found solace in the colorful, crowded streets and alleys, the glorious churches with their fabulous yet soothingly familiar art, and the sound of an ebullient people who seemed to sing even when speaking in whispers. Ben had been a source of hope and faith — his, not mine. For a while, I felt I'd lost everything when I lost Tom.

My head hurt. I turned off the kitchen light and went into the living room. I was tired. I was happy Adam was coming. I felt sorry for Mitch and Brenda Laskey. Most of all, I missed Milo. I went to bed early. And alone.

THREE

My brother's homily surprised me the next morning. instead of his usual dry dissection of the Gospel, he took the Holy Family theme and talked about ours. He spun a couple of amusing anecdotes about growing up in Seattle, but spared me embarrassment by not including any of the dopey things Sluggly had done to annoy him. The parishioners laughed and chuckled, but best of all, they stayed awake.

After Mass, there was a lineup of admirers in the vestibule. At least two dozen parishioners were delighted at his return to sub for Father Den, who, Patsy Shaw asserted, ". . . is sorely missed, but you're a superb replacement."

"If I stayed around, you'd get sick of me," Ben said, looking beyond Patsy and her husband, Bernie Shaw, to where I waited by the bulletin board. "Emma needs rescuing now and then. I neglected to mention that in my sermon."

I smiled indulgently as the Shaws and a couple of the other parishioners turned to look in my direction. After a few more greetings, Ben was set free by his parish fans. I traipsed after him into the vestry.

"You're a big hit around here, even going up against stiff competition like Den," I said. "You brought your 'A' game today."

"If I stay awake, folks in the seats should, too," he said, shedding the chasuble that had been made for him by Navajo women during his Tuba City tenure. "Didn't Bernie used to be called Brendan?"

I nodded. "He changed to Bernie a few years ago because he got tired of being called Brenda Shaw. It didn't suit his image as the local insurance guru. Bernie's a good guy, though. It was when Edna Mae Dalrymple called him Brenda *Starr* that he really got ticked off. Of course, Edna Mae sometimes gets confused about —"

My cell's ring startled me. I fumbled in my purse, but couldn't find the blasted thing until it switched over to voicemail. While I waited for the message to finish recording, I saw the call had originated from the sheriff's office. I wondered if Milo had returned.

It was, however, Dwight Gould's dry bass

voice that filled my ear. "Maybe you're not working today, but I am, damn it. Somebody has to mind the store while the boss is in godforsaken Bellevue. A couple of geocachers or whatever just showed up. They found a decomposed body near a logging road on Mount Sawyer at the twenty-five-hundred-foot level. I'm headed up there now. I'll keep you posted. Don't those damned fools know it's a holiday weekend?"

Having removed his vestments to reveal a Marquette University sweatshirt and old blue jeans, Ben eyed me curiously. "Bad news?"

"Only for the dead body some geocachers found this morning. That was Dwight Gould, the senior deputy in charge while Milo's away."

"Not Catholic, right?" Ben saw me nod. "Jack and Nina Mullins were here. I didn't see Jack being called away to duty."

"He's not motivated unless his real boss is in charge," I said. "Besides, whoever it is has been dead for a long time."

"What is this geocaching thing?" Ben asked, putting on his jacket.

"It's been around for a while. My former reporter Scott Chamoud did a piece on it last spring. It's a high-tech treasure hunt, using GPS devices to find hidden items.

Whoever finds the cache is supposed to replace it with something else for the next searchers. Scott said there were a couple of dozen locals already into it."

"Sounds like it might be fun," Ben said, grabbing my sleeve. "You're taking me to breakfast. I took a vow of poverty, remember? I've got that fifties diner the Bourgette family owns in mind. Every time I looked at Dick and Mary Jane in the third row, my stomach growled."

I'd eaten only a piece of toast before going to church, so I didn't argue.

Predictably, on the Sunday after a holiday, the diner's parking lot was almost full. Alpine's cooks must have been tired of kitchen duty.

When we got inside, there was a line about fifteen deep. "Huh," Ben muttered. "I wonder if I should pull clerical rank."

"Doubtful," I said. "You look like an aging grad student."

The hostess, Terri Bourgette, had spotted us. She waved a sheaf of menus in our direction. "This way, Father. I held a table, just in case."

My brother shoved me ahead of him past several scowling Alpiners I knew only by sight, not by name. "RCs twenty-one, Prots zero," he murmured as we followed Terri down the aisle to a booth near the back.

"Since our family has the only Catholic-owned restaurant in town, I had a feeling you'd come here," she said, ushering us into a booth with glossy photos showing Ed Sullivan in the company of his famous guests and posters for movies shot in Cinema-Scope's early era. Terri made a face. "I couldn't get to Mass this morning. I had to work."

"God and I understand," Ben said. "Your parents and a sibling or two subbed for you. Go with God, my child, and bring on the coffeepot."

Terri giggled in her charming way and hurried off.

"Cute girl," Ben commented. "How come she's not married?"

"She's been going with Chili MacDuff's brother for a year." I saw Ben's puzzled look. "Chili is Kip's wife. Her real name is Charlotte. The MacDuffs are Presbyterian, Vida's fellow worshippers."

Ben grinned. "I'm anxious to see Vida. Tell me what she's been doing since discovering that Roger's halo has slipped down over his double chin."

I told him, concluding by relating my uncertainty over whether or not the Hibberts had kept the child. "You know how

Vida is," I said. "She might be the only person who could get you to break the confessional seal, but when it comes to her private life, she's a clam. I'm not sure she confides in Buck, let alone . . ." I stopped as Terri returned with our coffee.

"Here you go," she said, filling our mugs. "Guess what?" She leaned closer and lowered her voice. "Some people who just came in found a body on Mount Sawyer this morning. Isn't that weird?"

"Dwight Gould called me about that," I said. "Father Milk of Human Kindness proved indifferent to the news."

"I hadn't had any coffee," Ben protested. "I was on autopriest."

Terri seemed puzzled. Maybe she thought I should apologize. "Sorry. Father Lord was a brother before he became a father." Seeing that Terri still seemed mystified, I tried to clear up any misconceptions. "I mean, he was *my* brother. But a Father, as in his final vows. Not —"

"Stop," Ben broke in. "My sister's not herself this early. In fact, sometimes even I don't know her," he added with a sharp glance at me.

Terri finally laughed. "I keep forgetting you're related. I don't know why. There's a resemblance, but . . ." She shrugged. "Grow-

65

ing up Catholic, you tend to think of priests as being only priests. Some never even talk about their families. It's like they were born in the seminary."

"Yes," Ben said with mock seriousness. "I can see why certain priests avoid mentioning their relatives." He gave me an even more severe gaze, the same one I used to give Ed Bronsky when he explained how he hadn't sold any advertising and why that was a *good* thing.

Terri was still smiling. "I'd better get busy. I'll send a server."

"No need," Ben said, giving his menu to Terri. "Pancakes, two eggs over easy, link sausages, large tomato juice. Thanks."

I hadn't looked at the menu, but I also handed mine to Terri. "The same, except just one egg and a small apple juice."

"How," Ben asked, after Terri left us, "have you run a newspaper for so long, Sluggly? Does Dodge realize what you're like?"

"Yes," I said haughtily, "and he's often vexed by my many flaws."

"Serves him right." Ben drank some coffee. "Okay, do you know anything more about the body other than that it was found by people doing something I'd never heard of until now?"

"No. Dwight had no details. He had to go up to Mount Sawyer to see for himself. Are you thinking of giving the Last Rites to the corpse?"

"You do recall it's been renamed the Sacrament of the Sick?"

"The body has started to decompose. I doubt any sacrament could revive him. Or her." It occurred to me that I should talk to the body finders, since they were right here in the diner. This was a story, and Mitch might not be able to cover it. "Okay," I said, sliding out of the booth, "despite my personal and professional inadequacies, I'm off to investigate. You can stay put and show off the unholy holes in your Marquette sweatshirt. Good luck with that."

Ben didn't say a word. He just sat there looking superior.

Terri pointed out the couple who'd made the discovery. "I don't know them but they're from around here. They know the area."

The middle-aged man and woman were studying their menus. Unlike Vida, who would've come on like their long-lost best friend, I used a less aggressive tactic. "Excuse me," I said, stopping at the barrier between their booth and the adjoining one, "I'm Emma Lord, the editor and publisher of the local newspaper." I paused for their reaction.

Both husband and wife — they wore matching wedding rings — eyed me curiously. "Is this about the body?" the man asked politely.

"Yes," I said. "Are you familiar with the *Advocate*?"

The woman, a pretty, plump brunette, twisted around to get a better look at me. "I've seen it. I grew up outside of Snohomish on a farm. Jim and I live in Maltby now. Would you like to sit down?"

I feigned hesitation before accepting the offer. Jim's wife moved over in the booth. I sat down beside her. She held out her hand. "I'm Melody McKay. That's my husband, Jim." I shook hands with both McKays. Before I could say anything, a young waitress with a magenta streak in her short, fair hair came to take their order. Melody requested an omelet with ham, Swiss cheese, and mushrooms, no coffee, just orange juice. Jim went for the waffles with bacon and eggs.

"You must think we're ghouls," Melody said, "having such appetites after finding that poor dead person. Jim and I are adventurers at heart. So are our boys. We've done so many crazy things that discovering a

68

corpse doesn't seem so weird. Our friends were upset, though. They headed straight home."

"I only know what came from the sheriff's office," I said, hoping to give myself credibility. "Could you tell if it was a man or a woman?"

Melody and Jim exchanged glances. "I'd guess a man," he said. "There wasn't much left, fairly skeletal. Clothes just about gone, too. But judging from the bone structure, a male is my call."

"I won't argue," Melody said. "The body was sort of scrunched up and we didn't want to touch anything."

I nodded. "Right. This was where on Mount Sawyer?"

Jim and Melody both grinned as he took something out from the pocket of his flannel shirt. At first I thought it was a cell phone, but I was wrong. "I can tell you exactly where we found that body. Ever use one of these?" He held out the small black device in his palm.

"No," I said. "What is it?"

"It's a handheld GPS tracking system," he replied. "You may have seen them installed in some of the newer Cadillac Escalades and other high-end vehicles. But this baby packs light. I got it for Christmas from Santa

Claus." He winked at Melody. "I couldn't wait to try it out. We followed a forest service road to about the twenty-five-hundred-foot level of Mount Sawyer and then hit the trail that's kept open for winter recreation. Not much snow this year, though," he continued, slipping the new toy back into his pocket. "We were supposed to find the treasure cache near the trail's end. But when we got there, Don and Dee — the couple from Index who went with us — noticed there'd been a recent rockslide about fifty yards from the end of the trail. Don's a geologist for the state, so he wanted a look. Until we got up close, we couldn't see that there was a hole no bigger than this booth in the mountainside. Don knows how to deal with that sort of situation without having the whole blasted thing fall in on him, so he went first. He got more than he bargained for."

Melody rolled her eyes. "He let out the biggest yip. Dee was afraid something had happened to him, so she ran inside. We were right behind her. There was the corpse, with poor Don looking thunderstruck. And then," she added, unable to keep from laughing, "Dee threw up. Jim and I got them out of there and took another look. We knew we'd have to notify the local au-

70

thorities."

"So we did," Jim said. "The Krogstads didn't want to stick around. We went to the sheriff's office and told the guy on duty about it." He shrugged. "After I gave him the GPS coordinates, we left our contact number in case they want to talk to us again."

The waitress delivered Melody's juice and poured Jim more coffee. "Are your friends related to the Krogstad who used to be the superior court judge here?" I asked after the magenta-striped server went away.

"Yes," Melody said. "Don's the judge's youngest son. The old guy is in a nursing home in Everett now. Very sad. Dementia, I think."

I recalled that Judge Krogstad's condition had become apparent in the last few years he'd sat on the bench. I'd had trouble keeping Carla from writing a story about him hitting an out-of-town attorney on the head with his gavel and insisting he was playing Whack-a-Mole with his grandkids at the Evergreen State Fair in Monroe.

"I'd like to have your contact number, too," I said. "Just in case."

"Here," Jim said, reaching into his other shirt pocket and pulling out a card. "That's my business information. I'm a private pilot.

71

I run my own operation."

"I'm a mechanical designer," Melody said. "I take calls on Jim's phone when he's away."

I scooted out of the booth and thanked the McKays. By the time I got back to Ben, he was halfway through his pancakes. There was no food on my placemat. "Did you eat mine, too?" I asked.

"I sent it back. You hate cold food." He wiped his mouth with a napkin. "Pry anything out of your witnesses?"

"Not much more than I already knew. It's weird, though."

"How so?"

I told Ben about Roy Everson showing us the bones the little boys had dug up. "Their parents were geocachers, too, but not locals."

"Sounds like you're on the case," Ben said before stuffing more pancakes into his mouth.

"I don't know if it's a case," I said as Terri arrived with my order.

She nimbly set everything down, including my apple juice. "I had them start a new order." She turned to my brother. "I think you're going to clean your plate, Father."

"I have to," he said. "Emma won't feed me. She thinks I took a vow of starvation."

72

Terri giggled as if she thought Ben was a real wit. I thought he was a real twit.

"Stop looking like Mrs. Diffelhoffer in third grade at Latona Grade School," Ben said after Terri had gone.

"I didn't have Mrs. Diffelhoffer," I said. "They only sent the bad kids to her third-grade class. I had Miss Swift."

"Miss Swift was a dish," he declared.

"She was nice. It's now John Stanford International School and only bright kids can go there. You wouldn't get through the front door."

"Neither would you. You've got egg yolk on your sweater."

"Oh!" I dabbed my napkin in my water glass and rubbed at the spillage. We reminisced about school days for the rest of the meal. When we got to my car, Ben said he'd been invited by the Shaws, the Bartons, and the Daleys for drinks and would see me at dinnertime.

"Swell," I said, turning onto Alpine Way. "You'll be trashed by the time you get to my house. Some example for your nephew."

"I have to keep the folks happy in Den's absence. In a couple of days you'll be tired of having me around."

"Not likely, but," I said, turning onto Cedar, "I'm not sure how long Adam's staying. He never plans his personal life more than an hour ahead. I'm still waiting for him to change his mind and join the circus."

"If he sticks around, maybe we can team up and go searching for more bodies. Or at least more body parts. Is this a big story?"

I pulled into the church parking lot. "I doubt there's much to Roy's bones. They may not be human. The Eversons have tried to foist off everything from a barn owl to a mountain goat as Mama's spare parts. They've got a serious fixation. The cave thing is different." I stopped by the rectory entrance. "I hope Dwight's going by the book with that body. Maybe I'll drive down to the sheriff's office to see what he's doing."

Ben laughed. "What will you do there? Sit in Dodge's chair and pretend you're in his lap? You really are still fifteen years old."

"Get out," I said. "I mean it. Now you are fraying my nerves."

Ben sobered immediately. "If I don't laugh, I'll cry. Being with you brings out my brotherly instincts. It's as if we both forget I'm a priest. But I answer to God, not anyone else. And I have to tell you, I believe you're about to go off the rails. You've got some deep thinking to do. You may have figured out what you want to do with your body, but you've got a soul to save. If you lose that, you won't find it in the sheriff's bed or the *Advocate*'s lost-and-found ads."

Ben got out of the car and slammed the door. I watched him stride up the rectory steps. The drizzle was turning into heavy rain, but Ben hadn't bothered putting up his jacket hood. It wasn't his wrath that upset me as much as it was that little voice inside asking if he was right. It took me a while to realize that it was my conscience.

Dwight Gould hadn't returned from Mount Sawyer. A glum Sam Heppner was behind the curved counter in the sheriff's office. He didn't seem very glad to see me. Sam was a confirmed bachelor who never seemed glad to see any woman invade his domain.

"Don't ask and I won't tell," Sam said, looking down his buzzard beak of a nose at me. "If I didn't hate being around my sister and her family so much, I'd have told Dwight to go screw himself and stayed in Sultan. If that stiff's decomposed already, what's the rush?"

"Dwight's in charge," I reminded him. "Besides, he could hardly leave a corpse for other people to find. When do you expect him back?"

San shrugged. "It'll take time. That trail

75

zigzags all over. It'll be a bitch getting the corpse out. An ambulance can't go far, so they'll have to carry it to the road. The only option is a chopper to airlift it. You ever hiked up there? It's not far from your place, being part of Tonga Ridge."

"I haven't done much hiking since I was a kid," I admitted.

"City girl," Sam muttered. He thought even less of cities than he did of women. "At least you're not fat, so you don't need the exercise."

That was probably as close to a compliment as I'd ever get from Sam. I obviously wasn't going to get any news out of him, either. I asked if he'd have Dwight call me and then I went home.

Adam arrived a little before five o'clock. He looked tired, unshaven, and so much like Tom that it still startled me. My genetic contributions were the brown eyes and his hair — not as dark as his father's. For the first time since he'd become an adult, I saw him without having my heart ache for Tom.

"Mom," Adam said after we hugged, "you look beat. How come?"

I couldn't admit the reason, so I waffled. "It's the busiest time of year." I tried to smile. "I'm so happy to see you."

"You might try a little harder to look like

76

it," he said, grinning. "Hey — where's that disgrace to the clergy, Uncle Ben?"

"He's visiting parishioners." I stared at the backpack he'd slung down on the floor. "Is that your only luggage?"

"I travel light," he said, echoing Ben. "What time do we eat?"

"I was waiting for you."

Adam shed the two-hundred-dollar parka I'd bought him at REI a couple of years earlier. "Didn't Uncle Ben let you know when I was coming? I texted him as soon as I got off the plane around two."

I kept my voice light. "He's glad-handing St. Mildred's donors."

"Guess I'd better text him again," Adam said, taking out his cell. "You should get one of these, Mom. It'd make life easier for us both."

"I have one," I admitted, relating how I'd left Ben's birthday present at the office. "I will learn how to use it. Kip MacDuff's a good teacher, as long as he takes it slow. Do you want something to eat now?"

"No. I need a shower. No shave. It's warmer with a beard." He fingered what looked like a two-day growth. "What do you think?"

To my horror, I turned away and burst into tears.

"Mom!" Adam put his arms around me as I bent over by the sofa. "What's the matter? Did Dad have a beard I never saw?"

I couldn't tell my son the truth. When Milo decked Fleetwood *and* Mullins for tasteless comments about the two of us, Sheriff Go-by-the-Book Dodge suspended his deputy — and himself. During those two days, he hadn't bothered to shave. After the standoff in Bellevue and his brief return to Alpine, he still hadn't shaved, toying with the idea of growing a beard — unless I didn't like the idea. At that point, I wouldn't have cared if Milo had grown tusks. Since I hadn't seen him for almost three weeks, I didn't know if he still had the beard. I was furious with my brother for lecturing me, hating myself for feeling guilty, knowing I was ruining everything, even Christmas.

As my son stared in bewilderment, I got myself under control. "The last month has been rugged," I said. "I caused a death."

Adam was startled. Maybe he thought I was crazy. But his next words reassured me. "Did you lose your driver's license afterwards?"

I managed a faint smile. "No. It was accidental, not involving a vehicle. It was also self-defense. I'll tell you about it later. In fact, I only glossed over it yesterday with

Ben. It's complicated. Can you get me some Kleenex from the bathroom?"

Adam started for the hall. "Life in Alpine is more exciting than small-town stereotypes. Maybe your crusading journalism stirs the pot."

When he returned, I was sitting up, focused on dinner. "I sure hope you can wait until everything's hot."

"I'm okay," Adam said, though he seemed thinner than when I'd last seen him in the summer. At six-two, he was as tall as Tom, but at least twenty pounds lighter. "I'll pick at the turkey while you cook."

I stood up. "Let's. You can tell me about life in the frozen North."

When I took the turkey out of the fridge, Adam helped himself to a beer. "It's routine, but 'routine' is different," he said, leaning on the back of a kitchen chair. "At best, the road to the village is accessible six months of the year. Otherwise, I have to fly, but I can't do that when there's no ice runway available. There are times like the day before yesterday when that's not doable. Did I leave out fog? It's a problem, too."

I stepped aside so Adam could pluck off a chunk of white meat. "I honestly can't imagine what it must be like. That's why I keep putting off visiting you. If I see how you live firsthand, I'll worry even more."

"Let's talk the upside," Adam said, after eating the turkey in one bite. "The people are amazing. Not to mention the stark beauty of the surroundings. That's a spiritual experience all by itself."

I shook my head. "I can't believe this is you — who spent a year at the U. of Hawaii worrying about your tan and forgetting to attend class."

"Hey," Adam said, yanking off a crisp piece of drumstick skin, "I still wouldn't mind doing that beach thing. Maybe I'll get sent to Tahiti."

"How long do you think you'll stay in St. Mary's Igloo?" I asked, seeing lights glow just beyond the carport. "I think Uncle Ben is here. Why don't you open the front door for him?"

Adam frowned at me. "He can't find the back door?"

"Probably not," I said. "He's getting senile."

As my son headed out of the kitchen, I finished putting the cut-up turkey parts into the oven while girding myself for what might be an uneasy confrontation with Ben. I was about to slide the dressing into the oven when I realized that whoever was at the door wasn't Ben.

"Mom," Adam called. "The sheriff's here."

I almost dropped the stuffing. "Okay," I croaked. "Hold on."

I knew I looked like a wreck. I felt like one, too. I dithered, at a loss for how to handle the situation. I heard Milo say something — about the weather? Alaska? Fishing? My ears seemed plugged. Finally, I went into the living room.

Milo was still by the door. He looked a bit discomfited, too, but hid it better than I did. He'd shaved off the beard. I was glad, lest my son connect the dots. Adam was by the sofa, seemingly at ease. He spoke first. "I was going to ask the sheriff if he wanted to have dinner with us."

"Oh . . . ," I started to say before Milo interrupted.

"I can't," he said, moving closer. At six-five, he loomed over me by more than a foot. "We've got a body up on Sawyer. Dwight's bringing it down," Milo went on, near enough for me to see the longing in his hazel eyes. "Sam said you stopped by. He filled me in on the Laskey kid's escape. I figure Mitch can't cover the story. Are you doing it?"

"I'll have to," I said, wishing he wouldn't stand so close that I could hear his heart beating. Or maybe it was mine. "No word

81

on Troy?"

"No. If he's smart, he headed to Seattle." Milo sucked in his breath. "I better go. The body's due at the hospital morgue."

I nodded dumbly. Milo started for the door. "Wait," I called after him. "Adam — can you put the stuffing in the oven on the upper rack? I have to ask the sheriff a couple of questions."

"Sure," my son said, and headed to the kitchen.

I practically shoved Milo through the door. "Oh, God," I said as soon as we were out of the house, "I'm a mess!"

He looked over his shoulder before putting his arm around me. "You look frazzled as hell. Did you set fire to the turkey?"

"No. Do you really have to work? Are you back for good? Is everything all right?"

"Hey!" He chuckled and pulled me closer. "Yes, I have to work. I hope I'm back for good, but who knows with those idiots in Bellevue. As for being all right, I was until I saw Adam. I didn't notice a strange car in your driveway, so I thought you were alone. Where's the other priest?"

"Not here yet. Adam parked on the verge. Oh, Milo, I'm so . . ." I felt on the edge of more tears, but controlled myself. I pressed my face against his chest and soaked up the warmth of his body next to mine.

"You feel like you've shrunk," he said. "Have you been sick?"

"Just upset." I looked up at him. "Adam doesn't know about us."

He touched my cheek. "I wondered. What about Ben?"

"He gave me a bad time. We have to talk. Oh, I'm so glad you're here." I raised my face for his kiss, but saw headlights approaching my house. "Damn! Here's Ben!"

Milo swore under his breath and let me go. "I have to move the Cherokee." He swore some more as he strode away to his vehicle.

I went back to the front porch. Apparently Ben had seen the Cherokee's lights before he made the full turn into the driveway. He backed up just enough to get out of the way. I waited in the doorway, realizing that I was cold. And wet. From behind, I heard Adam's voice.

"You okay, Mom?"

"Yes. Ben's here," I said, surprised that I sounded normal.

"Great!" Adam had come up behind me. "I haven't seen him for . . . I can't remember when."

Instead of watching my brother pull in, I kept my eyes glued to Milo's car as it disappeared down Fir. It was dark, of course, and I could see no farther than past the Marsdens' house next door. Moments later Ben got out of his rental car and walked over to greet us.

The two men wrapped each other in a bear hug. Ben had changed into respectable clothes — a dark blazer, navy turtleneck sweater, and dark slacks. After we went inside, he seemed to avoid my gaze. Deciding that a woman's place was in the kitchen, I finished readying dinner. I felt as if I were seeking a safe haven from the men in my family. After Adam and Ben had finished their greetings, my son came to the doorway. "Can you get Uncle Ben a Scotch-rocks and grab me another beer?"

"Is he still sober?" I inquired disdainfully.

"Pretty much," Adam said. "You should make yourself a drink."

I set a kettle of gravy on the stove. "Good idea. The serving wench will join you as soon as she puts the green beans on the burner."

Unfazed by my sarcasm, Adam returned to the living room. When I arrived with the beverages, Ben seemed in a jovial mood. He was in the easy chair; Adam was on the sofa. I sat next to my son, by the phone. Uncle and nephew were talking about their priestly experiences, some funny, some sad. Not having any of my own, I kept my mouth shut, offering an occasional shake of my head or a tight little smile. I felt as if I might as well not be there.

Dinner was ready at six-thirty. Ben deferred to Adam to say grace. He made short work of it. We'd barely said "Amen" when the phone rang.

I stood up. "Sorry. I better take that. The corpse, you know."

Ben seemed indifferent. Adam, having been raised by a mother who frequently interrupted meals, helping with homework, and even stern maternal lectures to keep up with her own vocation, kept on eating.

"The dead guy — think it's a guy — is here at the morgue," Milo said. "Doc Dewey's on his way. Do you want to escape the holy terrors?"

My conscience won. "We're eating. Later, after Doc's done, okay? I gather it can't be Myrtle Everson."

"What?"

The sheriff sounded puzzled and I realized he didn't know about Roy's latest find. "Roy has some new relics. They're awaiting your okay to send them to Everett."

"Oh, shit! Why don't they give it up? It's been twenty years."

85

"Sixteen, according to Vida."

"Fine. She's probably right. The old girl's disappearance has haunted me since I've been sheriff. Want me to call with Doc's results?"

"Yes, please."

"Will do." Milo rang off.

Ben looked up from dishing up more beans. "Breaking news?"

"The body on Mount Sawyer has come to town," I said.

"What body?" Adam asked.

I summed up the story in brief, breaking-news style. "I may have to go to the hospital after dinner. I don't want to call Mitch unless I have to and Vida won't be back at work until the day after tomorrow."

Ben eyed me suspiciously. "Isn't your deadline Tuesday?"

"We have an online edition," I informed him. "I'm not completely in the dark ages of technology."

"You should've told me," Ben said. "I might check it out."

Adam chimed in. "I didn't know, either. When did you start that?"

I glared at them. "I told both of you when we did it a couple of months ago. Kip manages the site."

"Hunh," said Adam.

"Hmm," said Ben.

They returned to their more congenial tales of tending their flocks. I retreated into my own little world, just to make sure I still existed. After dinner, we opened presents. I had been fairly lavish, especially with Adam. Somehow I'd managed to come up with enough money to fulfill almost all of his requests, including three sets of dual-layer underwear, waterproof boots, an insulated bomber hat, and a new hooded jacket for above-freezing temperatures. I gave Ben a forest green pullover and a brown cardigan as well as some books, one of which was *On the Banks of Monks Pond,* containing the correspondence between Trappist monk Thomas Merton and poet Jonathan Greene. His present to me was the usual hundred-dollar Nordstrom gift card.

I saved Adam's present for last. He looked very pleased with himself as I unwrapped the small package. Inside were a white bracelet and a pair of earrings carved in the image of polar bears.

"A parishioner made those from walrus tusks," he said. "I thought of bringing you some frozen seal steaks, but decided not to."

"They're lovely," I said, not wanting to tell my son that the earrings were for pierced ears, a vanity I'd avoided. I slipped on the bracelet. "Elegant," I declared, leaning over to kiss Adam's cheek.

Ben had gotten a keychain made from the same material — maybe the same walrus, for all I knew. In fact, the small figure that was attached to the links was a comical walrus. Adam waxed eloquent about his villagers' accomplishments, which included basket- and doll-making. For a few minutes we seemed like real family. There was a relaxed give-and-take, no censure or hostility lingering in the air. Then it dawned on me that Adam was talking about his other family, a subject Ben could warm to from his experiences on the Delta and the reservation. I realized that the *Advocate* staff had become the surrogate family for me: Vida, Leo, Kip, even the newcomer, Mitch, and the truant, Ginny.

I was still dwelling on this when the phone rang again.

"Doc's done his thing," Milo said. "You want to come over to the hospital or down to the office?"

"Where is Doc?"

"He went home. Come to my office. I'll be there in ten minutes."

"Okay," I said. "I'll get Ben to move his car."

"I'll pick you up," Milo said. "Or would that be a bad idea?"

"Probably," I said, having visions of the sheriff decking my brother and maybe my son, just for the hell of it. "It's no big deal."

I interrupted a discussion about Southwest and Alaskan native tribes. "I have work to do. Ben, can you move your car so I can get out?"

Adam got up. "I'll take you, Mom. I'm parked by your mailbox."

I shook my head. "No. You two are having a good time. You yak it up while you clean the kitchen, okay? I have to earn my keep, even on a Sunday. But then, you both do that all the time, don't you?"

If Adam heard the spiteful note in my voice, he didn't show it. Ben's brown eyes sparked, however. To his credit, he made no direct comment, but dug out his car keys before he spoke. "I can use that new key ring," he said to Adam. "This one's been around since I started in Tuba City. It's got desert crust and rust on it."

Ben went out the front door, not bothering to put on his blazer.

"It's great to see Uncle Ben," Adam said. "He's one cool dude." My son frowned. "Do you feel like going out? You still look pale."

"I won't be long," I assured him. "I have to decide if we should put this on our site. Spencer Fleetwood is away, so his subs at the radio station might not know about it. They're college kids and their main job is to fill up airtime."

When Ben came inside, he spoke only to Adam. "Let's mop up."

I left them to it. It was still raining, a factor that natives like me rarely notice. Less than five minutes later, I arrived at the sheriff's headquarters. Milo had just pulled in. He waited on the sidewalk, hatless, out of uniform, and as impervious to the rain as I was.

"I've got Dwight doing the paperwork, so I'll send Sam home," he said, opening the door. He paused inside, taking in his domain. "God, it's good to be back. Take a hike, Heppner. You're off duty."

"Thanks, boss," Sam said without enthusiasm. "Glad you're here. This place really stinks without you." He shot Dwight a dirty look.

Milo opened the half door in the counter, ushering me in the direction of his office. "I'll go first," he said. "Mullins may have booby-trapped it after I left town. I wonder if he's still pissed."

"Do you care?" I asked as Milo switched

90

on the lights.

"Nope. He deserved it. So did Fleetwood. Did his nose ever heal?"

I shrugged. "I haven't seen him since he kept the TV watch with me during your crisis."

Milo made a face. "It wasn't pretty. Ahhh." He'd lowered his big frame into the leather swivel chair and was grinning. "There were times when I thought I'd never do this again."

I'd settled into a chair on the other side of the desk. The sheriff had left the door open. He was definitely back on the job. I felt a stab of disappointment, but knew it could never be any other way with Milo. I got down to business, too. "How long for Dwight to do the paperwork?"

Milo had taken a pack of Marlboro Lights out of his denim shirt pocket. "As long as it takes him to look up all the words in the dictionary." He held out the cigarettes. "Want one?"

"Yes," I said, still feeling rebellious. "Thanks."

He lighted both at the same time, and handed mine across the desk. "Just to give you the main points — are you taking notes?"

"Uh . . . yes." I got the ubiquitous notebook out of my handbag.

Milo pushed the NRA ashtray toward me so we could both use it. He looked worried and dropped his voice. "You sure you feel all right?"

"How do you think I feel?" I said in a virtual whisper. "I haven't had a decent night's sleep since you left."

He nodded. "Neither have I. In fact, I was lucky to get in three or four hours in a row, between Tanya and Mulehide. Nightmares, hysteria, the whole nine yards. I haven't had a decent meal, either." He patted his midsection. "I figure I lost at least ten pounds. I almost took Adam up on his offer of staying for dinner. Then I decided it was a bad idea."

For the first time, I realized his face was thinner, too. "Bad idea is right." But I couldn't resist smiling. "You can spare that much, big guy."

We sat there just looking at each other for a long time. Finally Milo took a deep drag on his cigarette, exhaled, and sat back in the chair. "Okay. The deceased is a male, probably between thirty and fifty — that's as close as Doc can come. We'll have to ship the damned stiff to Everett for the full autopsy. Might as well send Roy's bones, too. Maybe SnoCo can give us a discount.

Probably been dead for six months or even more. Hard to judge, because Dwight couldn't tell if the entrance to that cave was sealed before the rockslide came down off the ridge."

I frowned. "You mean the body could've been there for a year?"

Milo shook his head. "I don't know, but that's doubtful. Doc said he thought animals or birds may have gotten at what was left of the clothes. There wasn't much, though, which made me wonder if the guy was wearing shorts or some other kind of summer rig. He wasn't a serious hiker — no boots, just the remnants of sneakers."

I'd gotten over feeling light-headed after the first two cigarette puffs, not having smoked in some time. "Any way to tell how he died?"

"No. Not a blow to the head, Doc said. Dwight looked for shell casings, but no luck. The guy could've been shot somewhere else. Or it could've been an accident. He's alone, goes in the cave, gets hurt, dies of starvation and dehydration. It happens."

I shivered. "Horrible. No cell or other way to call for help?"

"Not even ashes from a fire to send smoke signals." Milo looked faintly peeved. "Wouldn't I mention it if there was?"

"Sorry. I won't ask about ID, though it's *possible* an adult would've had some. He didn't walk from his house to the end of that trail."

"He might, in good weather. It's not too far from Deception Falls."

"A good three miles on foot. No abandoned vehicles in the log?"

"Dwight already checked. No such report in the past year and none that either of us remembers ever in that area."

I grew thoughtful. "Why do I sense you're thinking foul play?"

Milo stubbed out his cigarette. "Because that's what I'm thinking."

"Can I say that in print?" I asked the sheriff.

"Nope," he replied. Putting his feet up on the desk, he folded his hands behind his head. "I doubt the autopsy will show anything that leads to that conclusion. All we can hope is that a missing-person report was filed. The problem's obvious. We don't know where he came from, and we'll get a boatload of reports even if we only go statewide."

"You're sure there was nothing even vaguely personal?"

"Dwight says no." Milo lowered his voice again. "If nothing else, he's thorough."

"True." I turned to look into the deputies' area. Dwight was still hunched over in his chair. "Slow, too," I murmured. "How long does it take him to fill out paperwork?"

Milo looked at his watch, which was new. "Want to spend New Year's Eve here with me?"

"Not if Dwight's here." I pointed to the watch. "Is that a present?"

"Are you nuts? I bought it at a drugstore on Pill Hill in Seattle," he said, referring to the area where many of the city's hospitals were located. "You may recall how my old one exploded when I was rolling around on the carpet with a certain female predator."

"Hush!" I whispered. "*I* was not the predator. You started it."

He scratched at the graying sandy hair behind his ear. "I suppose so — in a way. But I didn't toss the old watch out."

"Oh, Milo," I said under my breath, "what's to become of us?"

He grew serious. "I won't know until I hear about your brother."

"I can't tell you here." I put out my cigarette and stared into my lap. "Let's stick to less ghastly subjects, like dead people."

"Sure." He moved his legs off of the desk and swiveled around in his chair. "Hey,

95

Gould," he called. "You finished that novel yet?"

Dwight didn't turn around. "Almost. What's the rush?"

"Ms. Lord has company," Milo replied.

Dwight grunted. I suspected there was more he wanted to say, but didn't care to end up like Fleetwood and Mullins.

"Oh," I said suddenly, "how big was the dead man?"

"Doc put him at five-ten, five-eleven, with a frame that could carry anywhere from a hundred and thirty on up. The SnoCo crew will be more accurate. We aren't sure of his race, but Doc says not Asian."

"Hair?"

"Enough to tell it was dark brown. No gray in it."

I closed my notebook. "Still nothing on Troy Laskey?"

Milo shook his head. "No SkyCo sightings. I haven't had a chance to check the other counties."

"Did Mitch come here to make inquiries?"

"I don't know." Milo stood up and went to the door. "Hey, Dwight, has anybody seen Laskey since his kid busted out of Monroe?"

Dwight turned around in his chair, looking toadlike with his squat physique. "Why would he? We're not hiding the S.O.B. in the break room. I've been juggling all the crap I can handle since you took off."

"That's your job, *Deputy*," Milo said.

"Awrrr . . ." Dwight hunkered down again over his paperwork.

Milo sighed and gazed at the ceiling. "Don't take all night. I'd like to finally get some kip."

"I'll bet you would," Dwight muttered, but hastily added, "sir."

The sheriff made a choking gesture with his hands and mouthed the word "asshole" at me. "You want to stick around or do you have enough?"

"I do. By the way, is there a description or a photo of Troy?"

"There must be. Ask . . ." He peered at Dwight. "Skip it. I'll look."

We went out to the wire basket by Lori's desk, where the sheriff kept bulletins. "Oh," I said, "did you know Alfred Cobb dropped dead?"

"Yeah," Milo replied, flipping through a stack of printouts. "Dustin Fong told me when I checked in on Friday. Cobb was way past his pull date . . . Here. No photo of the Laskey kid, though. Lori was probably gone when this came in, so maybe some of it got

97

mislaid." He glanced again at Dwight.

I read the APB information: "Twenty-three-year-old Caucasian male, six foot, a hundred and forty-five pounds, light close-cropped brown hair, green eyes, tattoo of wolf on left forearm, tattoo of Star of David on right bicep, small mole just under right jawline." My sympathy for his parents rose up. "Damn," I said, "why couldn't he stay put?"

"Busted for dealing or using or both?"

"I'm not sure. It wasn't Mitch's favorite topic of conversation."

"He's in a real world of hurt now," Milo said. "Damn kids."

"Right." I felt guilty for my irritation with Adam. It was so petty.

"What's wrong?" Milo asked.

"I'm an idiot," I said, biting my lip.

"Hey," he said quietly, steering me away from Dwight, "do you want to say something? I *can* close my office door."

"Not now. Really." I fought my urge to cry. "I have to go."

"I'll walk you to your car. You're not going to the office, are you?"

"I thought about it, but I'll call Kip when I get home."

"Good. Even if Laskey hasn't been sighted, be careful. It's surprising he hasn't contacted his folks. Hell, maybe he has and we didn't hear about it. Aside from their house, what other place in Alpine does he know but the newspaper?"

"True." We were outside. "I'll see if Troy's hiding in the backseat."

"No — I'll check it for you. Give me your keys."

I handed them to him. Milo went to my Honda, opened the doors, and peered around. "All clear."

"Thanks." I looked around Front Street, which had been quiet when I arrived. The Whistling Marmot Movie Theatre had just let out. There were at least three dozen people milling around between the Venison Inn and the Burger Barn. To stamp a more emphatic *finis* to any intimacy between us, Dwight opened the front door.

"I'm done," he announced, with uncharacteristic glee.

"Yes, Dwight, you are," Milo said, turning away. " 'Night, Emma."

" 'Night, Sheriff," I said, getting into the car.

Milo went inside with Dwight. I drove home to the priests.

FOUR

Adam opened the back door for me. He and Ben had gravitated from the living room to the kitchen table, both now drinking beer. The kitchen was still a mess. The only thing they'd done was remove our dirty dishes from the table and pile them on the counter and in the sink.

"Got a headline?" Adam inquired.

"I'll have a couple of heads," I said, "if you two don't get off your lazy butts. Who keeps house for you, Adam?"

"A couple of local women," he replied, looking puzzled. "Why?"

Ben raised a hand. "Mrs. Kupchik. Absentminded but well intentioned. Attends daily Mass."

"Goody," I said, yanking off my jacket. "Give her my address."

Ben chuckled and drank some more beer.

Adam was studying the dishwasher as if it were a UFO left by our resident space case,

Averill Fairbanks. "How do I tell if it's finished?"

"The green light, Idiot Boy," I said, and stomped out of the kitchen.

In the bathroom, I stared in the mirror. Before I left to see the sheriff, I'd put on lipstick and brushed my untamable hair. But there were circles under my eyes and I was pale. Milo had often seen me look this awful. We'd never lived together, but we'd grown older together — and that wasn't a bad thing.

The rest of the evening passed pleasantly. Ben had drunk enough to grow fairly mellow. Adam basked in his attention — and mine. By the time my brother left, he deigned to kiss my cheek, thanking me for dinner and the gifts. By then, I'd already called Kip, asking him to put the corpse recovery on our site. He could do that from home, so I didn't feel guilty about disturbing his Sunday.

My son finally succumbed to fatigue. During the evening, I'd learned he hadn't reached Fairbanks until morning. He'd concelebrated Mass at Nome's St. Joseph Church after spending the night at the rectory. Adam headed for bed in his old room just before eleven.

I slept better that night. The next morning, I was eating cornflakes and drinking coffee when I heard my son go into the bathroom. It was a quarter to eight. I could wait for him to come out. Kip had the bakery run. Alison would be on the job, but Mitch was questionable. He hadn't called, no doubt occupied with his family drama.

Ten minutes later, Adam emerged from the bathroom, wrapped in a big blue towel. "You don't have a bathrobe?" I said.

He shook his wet head. "Don't need one. I just throw on a couple of bearskins back home. Of course, I have to shoot the bears first."

I shook my head. "I'm a bit late for work. Do you want to meet for lunch?"

Adam thought for a moment. "Can you bring a lawyer?"

He didn't seem to be joking. Naturally, I was alarmed. "Why?"

"It's time to figure out the best way of handling my income from Dad's newspapers," he said. "I need a lawyer. The only time I touch the money is for my people. Even then I'm afraid I'll spoil them. They don't know I'm technically rich."

"Yes," I said. "It's hard for your mother to realize that, too."

He looked put off by my remark. "I didn't think Dad would leave the newspapers to me instead of you. I guess he felt he had plenty of money to keep you in a style to which you weren't accustomed. It's not his fault he got killed." He lowered his head. "Well, maybe it was, but . . ."

"Skip that part," I said. "I hate the replay." Having Tom die at my feet was only now fading to black. "I was ambivalent when his other kids, Graham and Kelsey, made good on the later will that had disappeared. I didn't care when the original version was filed for probate. Then your half-siblings wanted out. I had to accept their signing the newspapers over to you, if only to honor your dad's intentions to make up for being AWOL while I raised you alone. Luckily, he had a capable man to run them."

Adam looked up again. "I only met Phil Corrigan once, but he seemed like a solid guy. He and Dad went way back. But I can't act like I'm rich. I might start thinking that way. That'd be a bad idea."

I understood. "You don't know Marisa Foxx, but she's a lawyer and a parishioner. I'll call her. Check with me after ten. You need anything?"

Adam grinned. "Mom, I'm used to living on my own. I'll manage."

"Right." I blew him a kiss and headed out the door.

When I got to work, Alison was at her post, taking a classified ad over the phone. We exchanged waves as I entered the newsroom. Mitch was at his desk, eating a sugar doughnut.

"Mitch!" I exclaimed, surprised. "How are you?"

He flicked sugar off his chin. "Waiting for the other shoe to drop."

I placed a hand on his visitor's chair. "As in . . . how?"

"Troy will get caught or he won't. There's a third scenario, but I won't think about it."

"Do you feel like talking?"

He shrugged again. "What's to say? He hasn't contacted Brenda or me. We're wrecks, especially Brenda. She couldn't sleep last night."

"Look," I said. "If you want time off, take it. If you want to talk, I'm here. I've got a story for you, if that'll help."

Mitch's expression was ironic. "A first-person piece on 'My Son the Escaped Con'?"

"We can do that," I said, straight-faced. "Why not have Brenda write to ask for Vida's advice and have her sign it 'Ma Barker'?"

Mitch laughed, as I'd hoped he would. "That's what I like about you, Emma," he said. "No bullshit. You meet things head-on." He paused. "Vida's lucky her grandson didn't end up in jail. I hope she thanked Dodge for temporarily going blind."

"Roger cooperated," I pointed out. "He gave up the perps involved with the drug trafficking and the truckers. If the kid so much as jaywalks, Milo will bust him and toss the key into the Skykomish River."

"Vida," Mitch said thoughtfully. "It took me a while to get used to her." He paused before looking me in the eye. "Okay, what's the story?"

"Let me get some coffee and a doughnut first, then meet me in my office," I said. "I take it you haven't checked the sheriff's log yet?"

"No. I'm not eager to face the local law enforcers."

I considered my next words carefully. Milo's name had been kept out of the Seattle media in the Bellevue standoff coverage, a professional courtesy by the King County sheriff's office. I hadn't run anything about the tragedy in the *Advocate,* despite the involvement of former Alpiners. Spence had also gone silent, if only for fear that he'd end up with no nose at all. But the locals recognized the names of Tricia and her ex, former Alpine High teacher Jake

Sellers. Of course tongues had wagged all over town for a few days until Toyota dealership owner Gus Swanson ran off to Vegas with the local florist, Delphine Corson.

I stood up. "Don't be embarrassed. The sheriff and his deputies have seen it all. The ugly side of life is no stranger here. And yes, I saw the bulletin about Troy last night."

He ruffled his graying hair. "I need to stay busy. I told Brenda to keep weaving." He sighed and turned away.

I went behind his desk to get coffee and a French doughnut. Five minutes later, I called Marisa Foxx, whose secretary, Judi, was another of Vida's nieces. Judi said her boss was busy, but would get back to me soon. I'd just hung up when Mitch came into my office. After I briefed him on the body in the cave, he headed off on his beat. Alison came into my cubbyhole just as I finished my doughnut.

"Pete Patricelli is here to see Leo about a change in the coupon he's running in the paper. Should he talk to you or to Kip?"

"What's the change?"

Alison smiled. "He forgot to mention that the two-for-one is only for the regular pizza, not the deep-dish kind."

"Send him to Kip," I said. "I wouldn't have a clue."

She nodded and went on her way.

Pete, however, did not go on his way. To my surprise, he came into my office five minutes later via the back shop.

"Hi, Emma," he said, his round face looking worried. Even his mustache seemed to droop more than usual. "Got a minute?"

"Sure. Have a seat. What's wrong?"

A rotund man in his late forties, he squatted in the chair and gave me a feeble, gaptoothed smile. "Kind of empty around here, isn't it?"

"I do give my staff some time off. Leo and Vida return tomorrow."

He nodded absently. "Um . . . I looked at your site this morning. I wanted to make sure the ad I'm running on it didn't have anything about this coupon deal yet." He paused, licking his lips. "I saw the notice about the body on Mount Sawyer. You got more news on that?"

"No. It'll take some time. The sheriff has to send the remains to SnoCo for a full autopsy."

He nodded again. "That's what I thought. I . . . well, I don't know how to put this . . . you didn't see the body, did you?"

"No. Why?"

He lowered his gaze. "Do you remember my kid brother, Gus?"

107

Pete came from a family of eleven children. "Gus? No."

"So you weren't here when Gus got in trouble." Pete's dark eyes strayed to my SkyCo map. "It was just before Marius sold the paper."

"Over fifteen years ago," I said, wishing he'd get on with his story.

He nodded. "Gus was working for an escrow company in Everett, saving money for college. He was the youngest. You knew Mamma Mia."

It wasn't a question. I remembered Appollonia — known as Polly — for her extreme piety, lighting so many votive candles after Mass that I thought she'd burn down the old wood-frame building.

"Gus was fourteen when Papa died," Pete went on. "Mamma Mia really spoiled him after that. Anyway, he stole money from the escrow company, got caught, and went to prison. He served five years, then got released, but he couldn't keep out of trouble and was caught stealing from a Lynnwood convenience store nine years ago. Thank God it didn't make the news here, being in Snohomish County."

"He held up the convenience store?"

"No. He worked there. Gus would never hold up anybody. The only thing he ever shot was a camera. He loved taking pictures. I bought him a nice one when he was paroled from Monroe last spring, on the first anniversary of Mamma Mia's passing." Pete paused to clear his throat. "Gus stayed with Shari and me while he looked for work. I had him help out at the pizza parlor, but I didn't need him full-time, and I couldn't pay what he might make somewhere else. He had some pride, too. He wouldn't take money, saying he was trading his work for room and board." A faint smile was on Pete's lips. "To be honest, he wasn't very good in the kitchen. He was kind of clumsy. Once he dropped a quarter or something in the topping and Davin Rhodes broke off part of a tooth. I was afraid his parents, Oren and Sunny, might sue me, but they were nice about it. Then, not long after that, Gus went on one of his long walks. He never came back."

I could guess where Pete was going with his account. Given his long pause, I decided to help him out. "You think the body may be Gus?"

Pete couldn't seem to give voice to a simple "yes." But looking into his dark eyes, I knew the answer. The only advice I could offer Pete was to get in touch with the sheriff. "That'd be a big help," I told him, "not just to you, but to the law enforcement people. Otherwise, they're looking for a needle in a haystack."

Pete had composed himself. "I don't care about that. I want Gus to have a church burial if Father Den will do it. Mamma Mia will rest easier."

I kept from saying Polly was resting as well as she could. "That shouldn't be a problem. Do you have anything with Gus's DNA?"

Pete frowned. "Like what?"

"He must've left clothes behind. Or a brush with hair in it."

"We've got his clothes," Pete said. "I don't think he had a hairbrush. Gus was going bald faster than I am." He put a hand to his receding hairline. "Should I take the stuff to the sheriff?"

"Yes. Bag all of it carefully to avoid disturbing the DNA sample."

Pete nodded. "I will. Gus didn't own much."

"What was he wearing the last time you saw him?"

"My bathrobe," Pete said. "He'd just gotten up. But Shari may know what he wore when he left." He stood up. "Thanks, Emma. I'm really glad I asked. I'll make sure that stuff gets to Dodge today."

"Do you want me to call and let him know

you're coming? He may've already shipped the body the geocachers found."

Pete frowned. "The who?"

"It's like a treasure hunt," I said, avoiding details. Maybe Pete hadn't read Scott Chamoud's story about the sophisticated hobby. "Don — Judge Krogstad's son — and his wife, Dee, found the body. They were with a couple from Maltby."

Pete shrugged. "Oh. I know Don from high school. Thanks."

As soon as Pete left, I called Milo. Jack Mullins answered the phone. "Sorry, Emma. The boss is chasing reindeer."

"No kidding," I said. "He can't find a rainbow in this weather."

"I thought he already . . . hang on." I heard muffled voices in the background. "Got a stalled semi on Highway 2 blocking traffic," the deputy said. "Can you make it quick? I've got to go."

"Then go," I said. "Is somebody else in the office?"

"Yeah — I'll pass you off to the Dust-man."

Dustin Fong's pleasant voice came on the line. "Hi, Ms. Lord. How was your holiday?"

"Fine," I said to the only male deputy besides Vida's nephew, Bill Blatt, who didn't annoy me. "Can you translate Jack's reindeer remark?"

"Rudolph," Dustin replied. "One of the Overholts found him in their barn. You know — the plastic reindeer that got swiped from Old Mill Park. This isn't official," he went on, lowering his voice, "but Dodge knows who did it. He went in person to nail the kids."

"Dare I ask who?" I inquired, hoping it was Roger.

"Aaron and Tyler MacDuff, Kent and Jennifer's kids and Kip's nephews," Dustin said. "Your back shop man will be mad about that."

"Yes, he will," I said. "How old are those kids? I seem to recall that they were toddlers the last time I heard anything about them."

"Aaron must be fourteen, Tyler's a bit younger," Dustin replied. "Being underage, their names won't go in the log."

"Just as well," I said, recalling that Milo and Kent MacDuff had a history dating back to the first murder investigation I'd covered in Alpine. Hopefully, Kent wouldn't get arrested for assaulting a law officer after the sheriff chewed out the boys and their parents. I let the subject drop and relayed Pete's speculation about the body in the cave.

"The body's still at the hospital," Dustin said, "but as soon as the highway's cleared, it'll be sent to Everett. We're shorthanded with Doe and Bill taking time off. Dwight's coming in late after pulling weekend duty and filling in for Dodge as the senior deputy."

"Keep an eye out for Pete when he brings his brother's belongings."

Dustin said he would. I went to the back shop to tell Kip about his nephews. He wasn't surprised.

"I love my brother," he said, "but Kent's always been full of himself. He sees his kids as copies of what he was like. Being the oldest, you'd think he'd be more disciplined, but that's not how it went down. You're lucky. You seem tight with your brother, even if he doesn't live here."

I smiled wryly. "Maybe that's why." I changed the subject to the stalled truck so Kip could alert our readers on the website.

Marisa called back before nine. Lunch was out because she had a court appearance at two and needed to talk to her client first. She suggested dinner at King Olav's. I agreed. Adam and I would meet her at six. She asked if Ben might join us. I told her I'd find out.

I called Adam, who okayed the plan. Ben

had asked if he wanted to help take communion to the nursing home. "Then we'll catch lunch and call on some shut-ins to show the priesthood still gets younger dudes."

"Go for it," I said. "I'll see you at home."

Mitch returned just after eleven. He'd heard about Rudolph and had gone up to the Overholt farm to take photos.

"I got some of Rudolph in a horse stall," he told me when I came out to refill my coffee mug. "Dodge wouldn't let me take his picture with the reindeer. For such an imposing guy, he keeps a low profile."

I shrugged. "He doesn't like the spotlight. Even when his job was elective, Dodge shied away from grandstanding."

"He seems like a solid guy," Mitch said. "I was surprised he didn't ask about Troy."

"He wouldn't," I said. "As you may recall, he, too, has children."

Mitch looked sheepish. "I forgot he's been out of town because of that trouble with his daughter and her fiancé. The deputies must've closed ranks on that. Did the girl survive?"

"Yes," I said. "She's been recovering at home for the past couple of weeks." His lack of interest puzzled me. Did he and Brenda lead such exclusive lives that they hadn't heard any of the gossip about the Bellevue tragedy? Maybe Vida was right about Brenda being distant. Apparently, Mitch was, too.

I was still musing on this conundrum when I realized he was talking to me. ". . . Or do you think that's too subtle?"

"Well . . . ," I said, wondering what he meant. "What do you think?"

"It's better than what I came up with last week. Rudolph's tired, like everybody after the holidays. He hits the hay, hoping the new year's better. Sure, it's corny, but I'll try to write some clever copy."

"I think it'll work," I said. "How big?"

"Four by five above the fold to allow for copy alongside?"

"Okay. The big story will be the body discovery, but since we may not have any ID, it can go below." I started back to my office.

"Emma?" Mitch called.

I turned around. "Yes?"

"Are you busy for lunch?"

I shook my head. Mitch and I had only gone to lunch twice since he arrived in Alpine. "Where?"

"How about the ski lodge?"

"Sure. The coffee shop?"

Mitch thought for a moment. "No. Let me treat. We'll eat in the main restaurant,

King Oily or whatever it's called."

"King Olav," I said, realizing I'd end up having two meals there in one day. "Don't forget the local Scandinavian influence."

"Guess I haven't assimilated yet. Not sure how long it'll take . . ." He uttered an abrupt little laugh. "I'm not sure of anything right now."

I knew the feeling.

We took my Honda to the ski lodge. The first thing he asked me after we started up Alpine Way was if it ever stopped raining. I told him it didn't — unless it snowed. My answer evoked only a slight shake of Mitch's head.

"Have a drink if you want," I told Mitch after we were seated at a table under a sculpture of Frigg, the Norse goddess who may or may not have been Odin's wife. "It's still the holiday season in my world."

"Are you going to?" he asked.

"Why not? Vida isn't around to give us a sniff check."

Mitch chuckled. "I haven't had a drink at lunch in a long time. I try to avoid being the stereotype of the journalist with a fifth in the drawer at work. When I broke into the newspaper business, it wasn't just a stereotype. There were still a lot of guys — and gals — who did that."

116

I nodded. "I recall that from *The Oregonian.* Now everybody's so damned earnest. I'm not sure it's an improvement. But maybe it doesn't matter, with newspapers heading for the dust heap. There's nothing colorful about reading news on a monitor."

Yet another pretty blond waitress came to take our order. Her nametag said Gala, but I didn't recognize her and she returned the blank stare. I asked for a screwdriver; Mitch ordered a stinger. Gala slithered off as if she were part of an exiting chorus line.

Mitch was studying the menu. "What's this lutefisk special?" he asked. My look of horror made him laugh. "Not so good?"

"It's soaked in lye and smells ghastly," I said quietly, lest I offend any Scandinavian within earshot. "I've never tasted it, but the smell's enough to put me off."

"I'll skip it then," he said, putting the menu aside.

We sat in silence until our drinks arrived. Mitch lifted his glass before he drank. "To you, Emma, for being a good boss and the best-looking one I've ever had."

We clinked glasses and took a first sip. "Thanks. No women bosses on the *Free Press*?"

"Not on my beat," he said as his gaze took in the etched glass wall behind the bar, depicting tall trees and waterfalls. "Maybe Brenda and I are crazy for moving here to visit a kid who escapes from jail, thus making our efforts seem futile."

I shook my head. "I'm afraid to visit my son in Alaska because I know how he lives. That, too, is crazy."

"It beats being locked up," Mitch pointed out.

"Not in the winter," I said. "He might as well be. It's just a different kind of isolation from the rest of civilization."

"But Adam's doing good things. That's a big consolation."

"Oh . . . yes," I said. "Do you have any idea where Troy might be?"

His gaze was wary. "Are you being my editor or my friend?"

I waved an impatient hand. "You know which one it is."

He nodded. "I have no idea where Troy is. He was arrested in Yakima. It's not within walking distance."

"Did he have a job there?"

"Yes. He was a Good Humor man. That's how he dealt."

I couldn't help it. I laughed. "You're serious."

"Of course."

"Makes sense," I said. "One way or the

other, he was putting customers in a better mood, at least temporarily."

"You could look at it like that. The law has a different view."

The first sips of my screwdriver had given me the courage to chip away at Mitch's stone wall. "How'd he get out here in the first place?"

"He'd enrolled at Wayne State, undeclared major. Troy's grades were okay, but he had no focus. We finally told him to figure out what he wanted out of life." Mitch frowned. "You're smirking. Why?"

"Adam campus-hopped. While he was at ASU in Tempe, he hung out with my brother at his Tuba City mission. Then out of the blue, he decided to become a priest. I was stunned. Sometimes I feel as if Adam is Ben's son, not mine." I made a face. "Sorry. I wasn't going to dump on you. Please, go on."

It took a deep sip of stinger to get Mitch back on track. "Troy decided what he wanted was a girl named Libby. Smart, pretty, but kind of wild. Her parents yanked her out of Wayne State and sent her off to Gonzaga in Spokane. They were Jewish, but thought a Jesuit school might straighten her out." He stopped as Gala came to take our orders.

119

Mitch went for the meatballs with egg noodles. I requested a seafood salad. Gala nodded curtly and sidled away.

"Troy followed Libby a couple of weeks after she took off for Gonzaga. He left during the night, hitchhiking across the country. We had no idea what'd happened to him until he called from a rest stop in Montana. We didn't hear anything more until several weeks later. He'd been picking apples in Wenatchee. Libby had met someone else."

"Fast worker," I remarked.

Mitch looked pained. "I don't think Libby ever cared that much for Troy. Brenda contacted her mother at some point. Mrs. Weinberg said Libby was happy in Spokane, looking forward to doing all kinds of new things that didn't necessarily include hitting the books. Libby was a water-skier, but she wanted to try snow-skiing and horseback riding and be close to a year-round recreational area. The fact that Libby told Troy to get lost didn't mean much to the Weinbergs."

"I suppose he was ashamed to come home?"

"You got it. But like Libby, he liked the freedom, liked the West, liked the weather, liked picking those freaking apples." His green eyes were a bit misty. "Brenda had a breakdown. Troy was her baby."

"The season's short," I noted. "Is that when he moved to Yakima?"

"I'm not sure. We didn't hear from him for six months. He was in Yakima, very upbeat." Mitch grimaced. "I should've figured out why. Troy was using, too. He said he had a truck-driving job — if you can describe a Good Humor wagon that way."

"Yes," I agreed. "How long did his Good Humor gig last?"

"Until a year ago around Labor Day, when he got arrested. Ironically, he was busted for a DUI." Mitch's face turned grim. "He hit a ten-year-old boy who'd run out into the street between parked cars. The boy survived, but was seriously injured. Legally, it was the kid's fault, but the cops who showed up took one look at Troy and knew he was high."

"Is that how they found out he was dealing?"

Mitch, who had taken another big swallow of his drink, nodded. "They found the stuff in the wagon. I came out to Yakima during the preliminary hearing and what turned out to be a plea bargain. The court-appointed defense attorney thought there was no probable cause for the cops to search the wagon, but it turned out Troy had been ticketed a couple of times earlier. Brenda was still in bad shape, so she stayed home. After Troy was sent to Monroe — that must've been late October — I went back to Royal Oak. Brenda was beating herself up because she hadn't come with me. The next thing we knew, he'd escaped."

I was puzzled. "I thought you visited him after you moved here."

Mitch's expression was ironic. "I'm talking about the *first* time he escaped, in the spring. They caught him two days later in a deserted shed near Sultan."

"Did you come here when you learned he'd escaped the first time?"

"No." He paused to sip from his drink. "By the time we were notified, a few hours later Troy was back in custody. Brenda felt we should be closer to him. I didn't argue, if it would help her frame of mind. The *Free Press* was downsizing. Sooner or later, they'd offer a paper parachute and show me the door. It took a while to find a job not too far from the prison. I couldn't believe my luck when I saw your opening last summer."

"The job was open because I was desperate after hiring the nitwit who replaced Scott Chamoud." I smiled. "If I'd found someone more competent back then, I wouldn't have hired you. I'm glad I did."

Mitch smiled. "You're a nice person, Emma. Really. How have you adjusted to a small town?"

"One day at a time?" I said lightly.

He tipped his head to one side. "I know about Tom Cavanaugh. Even in Detroit, his death made news. I won't ask anything personal."

"Time does heal," I said a bit stiffly. "I'm fine. Is there any chance Troy would try to find Libby?"

Mitch leaned back in his chair. "I don't think he's been in touch with her since he left Spokane. For all I know, she's not there, either."

"Is there anyone else he made friends with before his arrest?"

"Troy mentioned some guys at the prison. He pointed out one to Brenda and me, a black kid about his own age. Nice-looking, smart, according to Troy. He talked about an older guy, a big brother type. I never saw him." He shrugged. "There was a guard he liked, too. I only saw him from the back — a big Samoan, the kind nobody sane would mess with. But Troy said if you behaved, he was a pussycat."

Our food arrived. Gala's service seemed

begrudging. As we began eating, the conversation shifted away from personal dilemmas. Evidently Mitch had unloaded everything he was willing to reveal. And I preferred sticking to neutral topics.

We were back in the office by one-twenty. Kip was holding down the fort with Alison in the front office.

"Ginny called," he said. "She wants a trial run to test her sister-in-law's day-care patience. Donna isn't keen on taking all three kids."

"I don't blame her," I said. Donna Wickstrom also had an art gallery to run. I was about to add that Ginny should skip coming back at all when Alison answered a call for me.

"It's a Mrs. McKay," she said. "Shall I tell her to call back?"

It took a moment for the name to register. "No, I'll talk to her in my office." Hurrying into my cubbyhole, I picked up the receiver. "Hi," I said, awkwardly sitting down. "Have you found another body?"

"No," Melody replied in a cheerful voice, given the subject matter. "Jim and I were curious about whether the remains have been identified. I called the sheriff's office, but someone named Heppner was sort of curt."

"He can be, but he's following orders. It takes time to get an ID."

"I should know better than to ask," Melody said, still cheerful. "We had a similar problem when some idiot tried to steal Jim's plane last June. Everything has to go through the FAA these days since 9/11."

"How," I asked, "could anyone but a hijacker steal a plane?"

"The same way cars are stolen," Melody replied. "We keep the Cessna at Harvey Field in Snohomish. They're very tight about security, but a young man with a pilot's license talked his way in, saying he was doing a favor for a friend. Luckily, he couldn't get the Cessna to taxi onto the field. Rupert — a skydiving instructor — saw the kid and realized he wasn't anyone who'd ever been with us. Rupe got security and they dragged him out of the cockpit. Then they notified the FAA. The kid's friend was never found. It took us two days to learn the details."

"Too bad it didn't happen in SkyCo," I said. "It would've made a good story." I heard a raised voice in the front office, so I had to cut the call short. "Thanks, Melody, for an entertaining anecdote."

We rang off. I hurried into the newsroom, where I found Alison, Kip, and Mitch being badgered by an agitated Roy Everson.

"I need help," he cried, thrashing his arms and stomping his feet like a maniacal rooster. "How do I get a lawyer real fast?"

I spoke first, having been asked a similar question earlier in the day. "Why do you need one, Roy?"

He batted at his USPO rain slicker. "The body on Sawyer might be Mama. It's where she went berry-picking. I need a court order."

"Do you want the sheriff to hold the body here?" I inquired calmly.

"I want to *see* it," Roy stated. "Mullins fobbed me off, says it's county property. I'm a *federal* employee, so I outrank him, right?"

Mitch sidled up to Roy. "You're a federal employee, but your request's personal. Dewey says the corpse is male. Do you trust Doc?"

Roy looked uncertain. Behind me, I heard Alison rustling papers and Kip tapping his foot. "Doc's in on the conspiracy. Mama's disappearance is a cover-up for bigger things, so the local powers unite. I know. I work for the post office!"

"Why," Mitch asked calmly, "would anyone do such a thing?"

Roy threw up his hands. "Don't ask me!"

He grabbed Mitch by his raincoat. "Can you help? An exposé, like Watergate. You're from D.C."

"No, I'm from D.T., as in Detroit," Mitch said, gently freeing himself from Roy's clutches.

Roy backed off, rubbing his balding head. "I knew it had a 'D' in it," he murmured. "I've seen the postmark."

"Hey," Mitch said, "why don't we go have coffee and talk this over?"

Roy looked dubious. "Well . . . I don't know . . . I should get back to . . ." He turned, staring at Alison. "Where's Amanda?"

Alison darted a glance at me. "Amanda Hanson?"

"Yes," Roy replied fretfully. "She can take over. I won't be long."

Alison did her best imitation of a smile. "Of course."

Mitch looked at me. "I'll take good care of Roy," he said, taking the other man's arm and ushering him out the door.

"Whew!" Kip exclaimed. "Roy's really gone postal!"

"I don't get it," Alison said. "Is it Mama or the holiday rush?"

"A combination?" I suggested. "Christmas does odd things to people."

"I guess," Kip murmured. "What's Mitch going to do?"

"I don't know," I said, "but he can't do much harm."

As it turned out, I was mistaken.

FIVE

Back in my cubbyhole, I called Amanda Hanson at the post office. "Are you busy?" I asked.

"Not now," Amanda replied. "The lunch hour was hectic with gift returns. Are you going to ask me to come back to work for you?"

"Not yet, but I may. Ginny's status is shaky. My priority is your boss, Roy. He was here a few minutes ago, acting strange."

"Ohh . . . the Mama bit?" she inquired, lowering her voice.

"Yes. I hate to be blunt, but he seems to have gone off the deep end. Mitch had to hustle him out of here and I don't know what's going to happen next. It sounds as if you're not surprised."

"I'm not," Amanda said. "The last few days have been worse than usual because Roy hasn't been himself. He's fixated on Mama."

"Who's in charge when Roy's not around?"

"Duane Swanson, the Toyota guy's younger brother. He went to lunch a few minutes ago." She paused. "It's going on two. Roy was supposed to be back by now. When did you last see him?"

"Five minutes ago? He left with Mitch."

"Roy went to run an errand just after one, saying he'd take lunch after Duane got back. I didn't know he was coming to see you."

"He wasn't. He went to the sheriff's office about the body on Sawyer, but Mullins fobbed him off and Roy had a tizzy."

"Oh, damn!" Amanda exclaimed. "I should've guessed. Roy was talking about it all morning to anybody who would listen. Grace Grundle was so upset hearing about corpses that I had to get her some water. Got to go. There's a lineup at the counter. Keep us posted, okay?"

I told her I would. After hanging up, I realized the office was unusually quiet, especially for a Monday, when we always were scurrying around for the Tuesday deadline. At least the paper was almost ready to roll once Mitch finished his lead story on the unidentified body.

I felt at loose ends. Just weeks ago, I'd

have walked the block and a half to the sheriff's office to find out what happened with Kent MacDuff or how Roy acted when he asked to see the corpse. Now I was self-conscious about facing the deputies. I didn't want to see Jack smirk or Sam glare or Dwight try to decide whether I was the sheriff's salvation or his ruination. Bill Blatt would let his aunt Vida's perception prevail, and Dustin Fong wouldn't pass judgment.

"To hell with it," I said aloud. I couldn't just sit and brood. I put on my jacket and my professional air before heading out to Front Street.

Milo and Sam were behind the counter, going over a map of Highway 2. They looked up when I came through the swinging door. Sam's face turned to stone. Actually, he always looked like that. The sheriff registered only the faintest hint of surprise. "If," he said, "you're asking about the highway, it's open. Does it matter?"

"Only to people who want to drive on it," I retorted. "I assume nobody called Kip while I was out?"

Milo looked at Sam. Sam shrugged. "Drivers who want to use the highway will find out when they get there."

"It's called a public service announcement," I said.

"Then that's not news," Sam said.

I'd long ago stopped trying to convince law enforcement and anybody else in state, county, or city government what was news. "Skip it," I said. "That's not why I'm here. I want to ask about Roy Everson."

Milo looked again at Sam. "You're on. I wasn't here." He turned his back on me and headed to his office.

"Well?" I said when Sam seemed to have become a clam. "I know Roy's off his rocker. Mitch has him in reporter's custody."

Sam was startled, an unusual expression for the deputy. But any expression except dour was unusual for him. "What do you mean?"

"He lost it in the *Advocate* front office. Roy thought he was still at the post office. Mitch hauled him away."

"Away where?"

I shrugged. "I don't know. That's why I'm here. I wanted to find out if he acted peculiar when he called on you guys."

"I didn't talk to him," Sam said. "Mullins did."

"Where's Jack?" I asked, hearing the phone ring.

"Lunch," Sam replied, glancing at the console that was usually manned by Lori.

The ringing stopped. I could hear Milo's voice in the background. "Even deputies have to eat. Mullins didn't get back from Highway 2 until almost one o'clock."

"Okay. No news here." I turned to go, but Milo yelled my name.

"What?" I shouted back, seeing him with the phone still at his ear.

The sheriff waved an impatient hand at me while speaking into the receiver before hanging up. A moment later, he'd grabbed his regulation jacket and hat before striding out of his office. "Your reporter took Roy to see Dr. Sung at the clinic," he said, pushing through the counter's half door. "Roy's not a patient patient. He's tearing up the waiting room."

"Oh, no!" I cried. "Is he okay?"

"Who gives a damn? He threw Marje Blatt on her ass." Milo was out the door, with me trying to catch up.

"Hey!" I yelled as he went straight to the Cherokee. "You can't go without me! What about Mitch?"

"What about him?"

I was by the passenger side's locked door. "Let me in."

"Are you nuts, too? This is police business. Go away, Emma."

He ducked down to get into the driver's

seat. I had no choice but to step back as he turned on the engine and reversed onto Front Street. I wanted to kill him. I decided to walk to the clinic on Pine, even if it was uphill with the wind and rain coming right at me from the south. Pulling my hood up more securely, I crossed Third, waiting for a handful of cars and trucks to go by. The sheriff had already passed me by. He hadn't turned on the siren, so I assumed no one was dead. The chilling rain mixed with snow blew into my face. I cursed Milo with every step up the hill.

The Cherokee was parked in the clinic's loading zone. When I reached the main entrance, the blinds were shut and a Closed sign hung on the door. Momentarily thwarted, I swore under my breath. But I wasn't running up the white flag. I got out my cell and dialed Mitch's number. He answered on the third ring. "Are you all right?" I asked, hearing voices that included Milo's in the background.

"I think so," he said. "I may not be back to the office until —"

"Stop," I interrupted. "Open the door and let me in. I'm standing in freezing rain."

Mitch didn't speak for a moment. Instead, I heard Marje Blatt's voice, unusually shrill. "I can't," my reporter finally said.

Damn! Now Milo and I were even. This was *my* business, too. "Yes, you can. Go down the hall and turn right. There's a private entrance. Open it for me." I clicked off before Mitch could argue.

When I got to the other part of the clinic, the door was still closed. As I wondered if Milo had strong-armed Mitch, the knob turned.

"I think," he said, moving aside to let me in, "I screwed up."

"How so?" I asked, pulling off my hood and wiping rain from my face.

"I used a trick that often worked on reluctant interview subjects in Detroit. I told Roy I thought he had skin cancer on his neck and that he better have it checked ASAP. Instead of sitting with me and meekly waiting for the doctor — which usually gives me enough time to get answers from a witness — Roy jumped from the chair and attacked Marje Blatt. After she went down, he started smashing up the place. Dr. Sung came out and subdued him. That guy's ripped, and he knows martial arts. After Sung got Roy on the floor, he had Marje give him a shot. Now he's out like a light. I feel like a fool."

I patted Mitch's arm. "You did fine. Roy's in the right hands."

Mitch didn't act convinced. "Maybe."

We reached the waiting room. Dr. Sung was talking to Milo, who had his back to me. Roy was lying unconscious by the fish tank with a blanket over him and a pillow under his head. Marje, disheveled and upset, was huddled in a chair next to Amer Wasco, the local cobbler. A broken lamp was on the floor near an upended century plant. Two chairs lay on their sides and magazines were scattered everywhere. I gingerly stepped around the dirt scattered by the fallen planter and went over to ask Marje if there was anything I could do for her.

Before I could open my mouth, Carla Steinmetz Talliaferro came out of the exam room area holding her five-year-old son, Omar, by the hand. "Emma," she said, "are you sick or is this a story?"

"Carla," I said to my former reporter, "you decide. Aren't you still advising the student newspaper at the college?"

Carla started to answer, but Milo had turned around. He took one look at me, started to say something I figured wasn't fit for Omar's ears, and turned away again. If exasperation had feet, I would have felt it walking right up from my toes to my nose.

"I'm on winter break," Carla said, surveying the damage. "What happened? I heard a ruckus, but Omar wouldn't put his clothes on, so I had to wait. He's got a sore throat, but not strep. This place is a mess." She lost her hold on Omar, who scurried over to where Roy was lying.

"Is he dead?" Omar asked hopefully.

Carla studied Roy's inert form. "I think he's napping, sweetheart. Which is what you'll do when we get home." She turned back to me. "That's Mr. Everson from the post office. What's wrong with him?"

"He's . . . sick," I said. "Have you met . . ." I turned around to introduce Mitch, but he wasn't in sight. "Where he'd go?"

"The man you were with?" Carla asked, tossing her long black hair. "He must've gone back down the hall. Isn't he my replacement?"

"Thrice removed," I said. "He's good." *He hasn't yet made a single horrendous typo like some of yours. If you wrote a story about the people in this waiting room, they'd turn out to be Amer Wacko, Marje Blott, and Dr. Dung.* "Watch out, Carla. Omar's getting under the blanket with Roy."

"Oh." She went over to take her son's hand. "Come on, sweetheart. We're going home. Nice to see you, Emma."

Mother and child got to the door. "It's

137

locked," Carla said.

"Use the back way," I urged her. "That's how I came in."

"Okay." Taking Omar's hand, Carla maneuvered through the wreckage and carnage with the same lack of awareness she'd often shown to any newsworthy action going on right before her eyes.

She had no sooner trailed off down the hall than a buzzer sounded. "Ambulance," Dr. Sung said. "I'll get the door. Hi, Emma." He left Roy to let the medics in.

The sheriff was leaning against the pillar by the office area. His regulation high-crowned hat made him close to six-ten. The foot and half difference in height between us might have intimidated me if I didn't know him so well. I noticed the glint in his eyes had changed to amusement. And I'd never been able to stay mad at him for long.

We both had to get out of the way for the gurney that Del Amundson and Tony Lynch were bringing through the door. The sheriff backed into the office area. I sat down in the only remaining waiting room chair that hadn't been turned upside down.

"How are you doing, Marje?" I asked.

"My back," she said. "I wrenched it when Roy shoved me. He's crazy! That's not like him."

"I know," I said. "It's a shock."

"Nice man," Amer said. "Good man." The cobbler was Finnish, having come to this country after World War II with his wife, DeeDee. They'd met in a DP camp and married before emigrating. Amer retained a faint accent. "One time, not long ago, Mr. Roy found boots he thought belonged to his mama. He brought them to me, asking how old they were. I say a year, no more. He asked was I sure. I told him, yes, very little sign of wear, though scuffed. He was not happy about that. They were *men's* boots. What was he thinking?"

"How long ago was that?" I inquired.

"Oh — in the summer. Late June, early July."

"Did he keep them?"

Amer shrugged his rounded shoulders. "He took the boots with him. Maybe he hoped I was wrong. But I was not."

I nodded. The medics were rolling Roy out the door. As soon as they disappeared, Mitch entered carrying a camera.

"Hey," Milo barked, "what are you doing, Laskey?"

"My job, Sheriff," Mitch replied. "Just like you."

"No pictures," Milo said, looming over my reporter. "I don't think Doc Dewey and

139

Dr. Sung would like that."

"They would for insurance purposes," Mitch said. "Ask Dr. Sung."

"Screw that," Milo said. "Will you use the pictures in the paper?"

Mitch glanced at me. "Ask the boss. I just work for her."

I got out of the chair. "Maybe the sheriff's right. I mean . . ." Wavering, I wasn't sure whose side I was on. "Somebody should take pictures for the insurance. Where's Dr. Sung?"

"He went with the patient," Mitch said irritably.

I turned to Marje. "What do you think?"

"I don't know," Marje said miserably. "I need a pain pill."

Mitch shot Milo an irate look before stalking out of the clinic.

Milo glared at me. "Didn't I tell you to stay put?"

"No, you wouldn't give me a ride, so I had to walk in rain and snow and wind and . . ." I winced, aware that I'd raised my voice.

"Great," Milo muttered. "If you get pneumonia, I'll have to . . ." He turned away. "Skip it."

I took two quick steps closer to the sheriff — and tripped over the century plant. I fell, hitting my knee on the ceramic pot and grazing my arm on an overturned chair.

"Oh, good God!" Milo cried. "You are the clumsiest . . ." He knelt down beside me. "Are you hurt?"

I did hurt, but I was mostly stunned. And even more humiliated. "No," I said in a ragged voice.

"I think your eyes are crossed," the sheriff said. "Do you want me to lift you up or did you break something?"

"No! I mean, I didn't break anything." I made a feeble attempt to pull myself into a sitting position, but failed. My feet were entangled in something I couldn't see but guessed was the lamp cord.

"Amer," Milo said, "can you free Ms. Lord at your end? I'll get the rest of her."

Amer grunted as he bent over. The only thing I was thankful for was that Mitch hadn't been here for my latest disaster. Once Amer unwound the cord from my feet and ankles, Milo picked me up with his usual almost effortless ease. He'd had enough practice.

"Come on," he said, "I'll take you out to the loading dock."

"That sounds right," I mumbled. "Where are you sending me?"

"Good question," he said. "Anybody at

141

your house?"

"I don't know," I said, realizing we were on the sidewalk. Sky Thai and Cascades Health Store were across the street. "Can you put me in your car so we don't look like Superman rescuing Lois Lane?"

"That's what it feels like. Oh, hell. I don't give a rat's ass what people think." To prove it, he bent down to kiss me. Hard. And long.

"Oh, Milo." I pressed my face against his chest. "I do love you."

"Took you long enough to figure it out. Hang on while I load you."

Moments later I was in the passenger seat and he was behind the wheel. "You didn't say if anybody was at your house," he said. "Well?"

"I don't know," I repeated. "Adam's visiting shut-ins with Ben."

Milo tried not to laugh. "That's . . . nice. Then we'll go to my place."

"Don't you have to work?"

He pulled out onto Pine. "I am working. I'm helping an injured citizen who can't stand on her own two feet. Honest to God, Emma, you're the klutziest human being I've ever met."

I hung my head. "I know."

"I'm not complaining," he insisted. "I just don't see how you've survived without killing yourself. Have you ever broken any-thing?"

"Um . . . I fell in the gutter by the *Oregonian* and broke a bone in my foot and broke my thumb tripping over Adam's *Star Wars* spaceship."

"You're damned lucky."

We were going past Vida's Presbyterian church on one side of the street and the Tall Timber Motel on the other. "Why were you so abrupt when I was in your office earlier?"

Milo shot me a wry glance. "God, you're dim. I've hardly seen you in weeks, and now I can barely keep from jumping you in the middle of headquarters. Why do you think I offered to close my door last night? A good thing you nixed it. I need my employees to respect me."

"Oh," I said meekly. "I guess . . . um . . . after so many years of being able to . . . to spend time together without . . . I mean, *most* of the time . . . ."

"Stop. You left your brain in the potted plant." He took a right onto the Icicle Creek Road. "I warn you, I haven't been home enough lately to clean the place."

"You don't do much of that even when you are home," I said.

"Maybe that's because it hasn't felt like home for a long time." He took a quick left into the Icicle Creek development where he lived in the split-level house he'd shared with Mulehide and their three children. "I always feel more at home at your place."

I squeezed his arm. "You always look more at home, too."

He brushed my lips with his forefinger. "Come on, let's go inside before I do you right here. Can you walk or should I carry you?"

"No. I can walk. I think."

"Just to make sure, wait for me to get around to your side."

I was wobbly when I stepped onto the driveway, but remained upright. "I should be at work," I murmured, suddenly remembering I owned a newspaper.

Milo opened the front door. "Why?"

I went inside, focused on the split-level entranceway. It'd been years since I'd been at his house. "What?" I forgot what I'd said.

"Never mind." The sheriff kicked the door shut and gathered me up in his arms. We didn't speak again — at least not in coherent words — for a long, long time.

It was almost dark when I rolled over to put my chin on Milo's bare chest. "What time is it? You're the one with the new watch."

He lifted his arm to peer at the Timex with

its leather strap. "I can't read the damned thing. Check the clock, or did we bust that, too?"

I propped myself up on one elbow, aware that I was stiff, though unsure whether it was from falling down in the clinic or falling into bed with Milo. "Oh, no! It's five to four!"

"No shit. You got a date?"

"No. Yes, I'm having dinner with Adam and Marisa Foxx — and Ben, except I forgot to ask him."

He pulled me back down on the bed. "Cancel," he said.

"I can't. You know that."

Milo sighed. "Right. When are we having that talk about your brother? It's not one of those dumb 'share your feelings' things, is it?"

"No. Ben doesn't do that. But it can wait."

"So can he." Milo rolled over, half covering me with his body.

"Milo . . . you haven't said you loved me, except once, years ago."

He traced my profile with his finger. "Wasn't once enough? I never stopped. If I ever do, I'll let you know."

I wrapped my arms around him and forgot all about Ben.

Six

Milo drove me back to the *Advocate* at ten to five. He was going to check in at his office, too. As I was about to get out of the car, I said I couldn't believe that neither of us had gotten a phone call while we were in bed. "That seems odd," I said.

"Does it?"

I caught that amused glint in his eyes again. "What did you do?"

"I shoved both our cell phones in the freezer. Don't worry, I put yours in your purse. It'll thaw. Be careful — look where you're going."

Alison gasped when I came through the door. For an awful moment, I wondered if I'd put my crew-neck sweater on backward.

"Emma! Where've you been? Kip and I've been trying to reach you. Your car's still parked outside, so we knew you were around . . ."

I held up my hand as Kip came down the

hall from the back shop. "I've been tending to a few things. I've got company, you know."

Alison nodded. "Your brother called twice, and Adam's worried."

"My God," I said, "what could happen to me in the middle of town?"

Kip also looked relieved. "We were about to call the sheriff."

Great. I suddenly felt panicky, wondering if Ben or Adam had done just that. "You're all crazy," I said, attempting a quick exit.

It was Kip who stopped me. "Emma, wait. Mitch's son was found."

I gaped at him. "Where?"

"By the library in Skykomish," Kip said. "He'd hitchhiked that far. Maybe Troy was trying to come see his folks."

The news snapped me back into the real world. "Who found him?"

"The librarian," Alison replied. "Troy had passed out by the book drop. He's really sick."

"Oh, no!" I exclaimed, leaning against the doorjamb. "Poor Mitch. Poor Brenda. Is he in custody?"

"Gould and Mullins brought him back here less than an hour ago," Kip said. "Mitch took off like a shot. We haven't heard anything since."

I tried to collect my thoughts. "I have to cover this," I said. "Damn. I wish Vida were here. She could do some of the digging. I wonder when she left Bellingham."

"Should I try to call her?" Alison asked.

"Call her home number. If she's driving, she won't pick up the cell."

"What can I do?" Kip inquired.

"You could offer the Laskeys moral support. I'd do it, but I have to stick to the official line. This is damned tricky. Do you mind?"

Kip looked dubious. "Would Mitch feel I was stomping all over his private life?"

"This isn't only his private life," I declared, "it's news. It'd be unethical to cover it up. That's why it's better for you to handle the personal part. I should stay neutral. Have you listened to KSKY since it happened?"

"No," Kip said, "but we can just make the hour turn. Flip the switch behind you, Alison."

I moved all the way into the front office. Sure enough, Spencer announced the news break. Before he could say more, my cell phone rang. Swearing under my breath, I retreated to the newsroom.

"Where the hell have you been, Sluggly?" Ben demanded loudly.

"In crisis mode," I said, figuring that the best defense was a good offense. "Have you heard about Troy Laskey?"

"What about him?" Ben asked, easing up on the volume.

"He's been found, but he's very ill," I said. "Look — I can't talk long. Did Adam tell you about his dinner with Marisa tonight?"

"He mentioned it. Why?"

"Marisa invited you, too," I said, "but you were busy and then this mess happened, so I didn't have a chance to tell you." Not exactly a lie, just an omission of two hours. "Are you free?"

"Is this about Adam's money?"

"Yes. You'd be better at that than I would, so if —"

"Hold it," Ben broke in. "You can't make it?"

"I don't know yet," I said. "I'm stuck with Troy's story. It's not just a heartbreak for Mitch, it's a conflict of interest. And Vida's still gone."

"Okay," Ben said after a pause. "I'll come off the bench for you. Why didn't you answer your phone?"

"I didn't hear it ring," I said. That was the truth.

"Have you juiced it recently?"

"Yes. Maybe it was a technical problem.

We're in the mountains, remember? It happens." Semi-truth. Why couldn't Ben shut up? "Can you let Adam know? I'm in a bind." I glanced into the front office. Alison and Kip were talking to each other, so Spence apparently had finished the breaking news on Troy.

"Do you think you might show up later?" Ben asked.

"I'll try. I honestly don't know, and yakking at me doesn't help."

"Sorry. Later, Sluggly." Ben clicked off.

I went back to the front office. "What did Spence say?"

"Not much," Kip said. "He wants to do a remote at the house. He told listeners to stay tuned for breaking news."

"That jerk!" I tried to calm down. "But I understand. It *is* news."

"You already said that," Kip reminded me.

"Yes, go to the Laskeys' house. We have to be a presence there. Vida can take over." I turned to Alison. "Did you get hold of her?"

"No answer. Can I help?" she asked. "I'm a fancy-free single girl."

"Sure," I said. "You stay here while I go to the sheriff's office."

"Got it," Alison said, saluting. She was obviously enjoying the excitement, which, I supposed, was a change from teaching how to apply blush and outline lips with a pencil. "Shall I keep trying to get Vida?"

"Yes, but wait until closer to six," I said, halfway to the door. "I don't know who's taking care of her canary, Cupcake, but Vida may go home first to make sure he's covered for the night."

My feet felt heavy as I trudged down to the sheriff's office. I wondered what kind of reception Milo had gotten after he was confronted with the news of Troy's recapture. If only the SnoCo or KingCo sheriff's deputies had been called in — but despite jurisdictional differences, SkyCo's headquarters was mere minutes from Skykomish.

The first thing I noticed was Milo's Grand Cherokee — with Milo behind the wheel. My feet suddenly took wing. I yelled, I waved, and miraculously, he stopped halfway out onto Front Street. I went to the passenger side. He rolled down the window.

"What's happening?" I asked, breathless.

"I'm going to the hospital. That's where the Laskey kid is." He paused, frowning. "Oh, get in. I don't have time to argue."

"He *is* my employee's son," I said, flopping gracelessly into the passenger seat. "How sick is he?"

"Sounds like pneumonia," Milo said, waiting for passing cars. He rolled down his window, reached out to put the flasher on the roof, and turned on the siren. "Freaking traffic," he muttered, rolling the window back up before cutting off an oil truck. "Dwight and Jack are still with him. So, I suppose, are Mitch and his wife, Belinda."

"Brenda," I said. "How were things otherwise at the office?"

He lifted one broad shoulder. "Fine. Sam was alone. He knows better than to ask dumb questions."

It was a short trip, the hospital being situated even closer to the sheriff's headquarters than the clinic, one block east. "Everything okay at your end?" he asked, pulling into a No Parking zone by the main entrance.

"Yes. I told Ben I might not make it to dinner with Marisa tonight."

"Oh?" Milo shot me a speculative look before opening his door. "Can you get out without killing yourself?"

"I'll try."

I managed without assistance or mishap. We went up to the main desk, where Jenny Bjornson regarded us with mild curiosity.

"I'll bet you want to see that Monroe prisoner," she said to Milo. "Is he dangerous?" The thought seemed to make her blue eyes sparkle.

The sheriff ignored the question. "Where is he?"

"Um . . ." Jenny frowned. "They took him to the ER about an hour ago. Omigod!" she cried. "It's after five! I'm supposed to be off duty. Stacey's late."

"Not my problem," Milo said, barely controlling his impatience. "Where's Troy Laskey?"

Jenny blushed, but kept her eyes riveted on the sheriff. No doubt she wasn't pleased to see me. We'd clashed over another patient a few weeks earlier. "Probably on the second floor now. Should I call?"

"No," Milo said, heading for the elevator. "I can find the '2' on the damned button. Come on, Emma." The elevator was waiting. "Dumbshit," he muttered before the doors had even closed. "She should stick to business when I ask a question. Hell, her old man works for me."

"Ron's a good handyman, isn't he?"

"He's okay. At least the price is right."

The door slid open. Milo practically shoved me into the hall, but his long strides beat me to the nurses' station. Luckily, none of the RNs or LPNs I'd alienated in recent weeks was in sight. Instead, Julie Canby was at the desk. "Sheriff," she said pleasantly. "Hi, Emma," she added, leaning to see me behind Milo's back. "You're here for Troy Laskey?"

"Right," the sheriff said. "Where is he?"

Julie pointed down the hall. "Third door on the right. Oh — there's Jack Mullins now."

Jack had just come out of the room. Milo started toward him, but paused, turning back to me. "Stay put, Emma. I go first."

"Sure," I said, turning to Julie. "Are Mitch and Brenda here?"

"They went down to the cafeteria," she said. "Mrs. Laskey is a wreck. She should be in the hospital, too. Poor people. We're almost at capacity. Bebe Everson is across the hall with poor Roy."

"What's going to happen with Roy? I assume he's okay physically."

"Yes, according to Dr. Sung. I heard that he started acting really crazy at your office. He's still sedated."

"It's his Mama fixation," I said. "After all these years, Roy and the rest of the family should give up."

Julie shook her head. "I wasn't in Alpine then. In fact, I didn't know anything about it until today when I came on duty at four."

"Are you full-time now?" I inquired.

"No, I'm still holiday relief," Julie said. "Spike hasn't found anybody to take over the kitchen at the Icicle Creek Tavern. Having a patron drop dead has really shaken my husband." She adjusted her plain white cap. Doc Dewey's nurses had to dress up to their profession, not down to looking like the cleaning crew. "I hope Spike recovers faster from that episode than it's taken Roy to give up on his poor mother."

I smiled. "You won't let him get too morose."

"I hope not," Julie said. "But I'd rather be here instead of slinging onion rings at the tavern. That's hard for Spike to accept. When he bought that dump, it was a relic of the old drunken logger brawls." She shook her head. "He was making progress before Al De Muth died on the tavern floor. Business has slowed since, but I can't tell him we'd have more money if I worked full-time here. That'd hurt his pride."

"Understandable," I said. "Speaking of husbands with emotional fixations, how's Bebe Everson coping?"

Julie leaned closer. "She's distraught, but Bebe . . . how should I put it? Not grounded, I guess. She insists Roy hasn't been himself since the Pikes' murder-suicide last winter next to their house by the dump site."

I winced at the memory of the elderly

155

couple's tragedy. "I was there when the sheriff found them. It was pretty horrendous."

Julie nodded. "Bebe told me Roy liked Pike. He kept some of the junk Pike used to sell."

My gaze had fixed on Troy's closed door. "Who's in there besides Troy, Jack, and the sheriff?"

"That's it. Gould went with the Laskeys. The poor kid doesn't need a guard. I could stop him by putting my foot out."

"It is pneumonia?"

She nodded. "He wasn't dressed for this weather. Just his prison uniform with a light jacket. At least he had decent footwear."

"What are they doing in there? Can Troy talk?"

"A little," Julie said. "But he should rest." She stood up. "I have to make rounds, Emma. Are you going to see him?"

Julie's description of Troy discouraged me. "I don't want to bother Troy or his parents."

"Good thinking," she said, coming out into the hall. "Take care."

Julie had just gone into the first room on the left when Milo reappeared. "Well?" I said.

"Dumb kid," Milo murmured. "He's lucky he was found before he died of exposure. You aren't interviewing him, are you?"

I shook my head. "Julie convinced me it was a bad idea."

"She's right. I don't need Jack here, but I have to follow procedure until Monroe touches base with me. They may move Troy to their infirmary." He held out something in his hand. "This is your bailiwick. What is it?"

I stared at the tarnished medal and chain. "It's a saint's medal. Let me see it under the light. I can't read the name."

Moving to the nurses' station, I saw a figure wearing a miter and holding a staff. I peered at the tarnished letters on the rim. "It's Saint Augustine."

Milo lifted his shoulders. "Which means . . . ?"

"Saint Augustine was probably the owner's patron saint."

"And . . . ?"

I sighed impatiently. "Catholics have favorite saints. We pray to them to intercede for us with God. It's like a spokesperson in heaven."

Milo shoved his hat back on his head. "That's one of the dumbest things I've ever heard. What's next? Emailing angels? How about that Facebook thing? Why can't you just 'friend' God and get it over with?"

"Skip it," I snapped, thrusting the medal at him. "Where was it?"

"Troy had it," he replied, pocketing the item inside his jacket. "Isn't Laskey Jewish?"

"Yes," I said, simmering down. "Did you ask Troy about it?"

"Yeah, but he either couldn't or wouldn't say. Are you done here?"

"I ought to see Mitch and Brenda," I said. "What about you?"

Milo sighed. "I should, too. Gould's a lousy conversationalist."

"What about Roy? He's right across the hall."

"Not my problem," Milo said, nudging me toward the elevator. "There's no crime in being nuts."

"True," I allowed. "Poor Roy."

The elevator arrived. We got in and the door closed, but Milo didn't hit the button for the main floor. "Ever make love in an elevator?"

"Milo!" I giggled. "Don't even think about it."

"Can't think about much else." He looked around. "This thing's kind of small. We'd probably kill ourselves." He punched the button. "Maybe we could find a bigger elevator."

158

"Not in Alpine," I said, his hand at the back of my neck. "Don't."

Milo hit the Stop button. The car rocked, making me fall back against him. He turned me around, shook off his hat, and kissed me. An alarm went off.

"Shit!" he bellowed, straightening up, but still holding on to me. "Grab my damned hat, will you? I can't reach it."

"Then let go of me," I said, afraid the door would open any second.

Milo complied. The car stopped. I handed him his hat as the door opened onto the main floor. A plump brunette was sitting in Jenny's place. She looked at us with concern.

"What happened?" she asked. "Is the elevator broken? Are you okay? Should I call maintenance? Aren't you the sheriff?"

"Unfortunately," Milo said, "I am. It might be a good idea to have that thing checked out. You wouldn't want somebody getting hurt and suing the hospital." He'd leaned a bit closer to me — and grabbed my rear. "Besides, you're running out of beds."

I gave a start. The receptionist, whose nametag identified her as the tardy Stacey, blinked a couple of times before nodding. "Um . . . you're right, sir. I'll do it now."

"Good." The sheriff seized my arm and hauled me down the corridor to the cafeteria.

"Are you nuts?" I demanded. "Are you trying to lose your job? Are you trying to ruin my reputation?"

"She couldn't see what I was doing." He stopped just short of the cafeteria's double doors. "Listen up," he said, backing me against the wall. His hazel eyes bored into my face with unfamiliar ferocity. "I've waited a hell of a long time for you to come around. I've had lousy luck with women, you included, but you were the only one worth the trouble. I'm fifty-five years old. I've spent my whole adult life trying to keep law and order in this county. For the past three weeks, I've been in crisis mode, wondering if maybe I wasn't only a lousy husband, but a crappy father. I blamed myself for Tanya getting mixed up with a screwball who almost killed her. The only thing that kept me from going nuts was knowing you were waiting for me. If I can't let loose now before I keel over with a heart attack, then the job's not worth it. As for your reputation, that got ruined the day you came to town with your bastard kid. Maybe you didn't hear the gossip, but I did. You sounded like Jezebel on the local grapevine.

Then I met you and I thought, 'That's no Jezebel, that's just another poor soul who's been battered and bruised along the way — like me.' You're mine now and I don't care who knows it." He grabbed my chin in a tight grip. "Got that straight?"

I tried to nod, but couldn't. "Uh-huh," I said in a sort of squeak.

He let go. "Good. Let's make nice with the Laskeys."

I was rattled, traipsing after Milo to the table where Mitch and Brenda were sitting with Dwight. The sheriff started speaking, his voice low and sympathetic. Dwight was eating something — chocolate cake, maybe. I fumbled with a chair and sat down opposite Brenda. She was pale and red-eyed, apparently unable to focus. In less harrowing times, she was attractive, with tastefully tinted fair hair and fine features. Mitch looked gaunt and haggard, his face almost matching his gray hair.

The cafeteria was less than half-full, but all eyes seemed to shift in our direction. I didn't recognize any of the diners. Several looked like visitors who might've been out-of-towners calling on relatives or friends.

Milo finally sat down at the head of the table as if he were calling a meeting, which, in a sense, he was. But first he told Dwight to go home. "You've already put in plenty of overtime. Take a hike, Gould."

"Is that an order?" the deputy responded.

"You bet." Milo's face softened. "You've been on double time for three weeks. SkyCo can't pad your paycheck any more this month."

Dwight brushed crumbs off his shirt. "It figures," he growled, before looking at the Laskeys. "Good luck, folks." He went by me without so much as a nod.

"Okay," the sheriff said. "We're not playing by my rules. It's a state matter, so I'm waiting on them to tell us what to do with Troy. I don't like to speculate, so I won't. This is the second time your son broke out. Do you know where he intended to go the first time?"

Brenda looked vague. Mitch shook his head.

Milo persevered. "He was found near Sultan the first time, right?"

Brenda still sat motionless. Mitch nodded.

"Do you know where he was going before he was reapprehended?"

Brenda turned her head, but didn't speak. Mitch stared at his uneaten salad, but finally replied. "He wasn't sure. Troy was . . . lost."

Milo inclined his head. "What about this time?"

"I don't know," Mitch said helplessly.

"Was he coming to see you?"

Mitch turned to Brenda. She didn't meet his gaze. "I assume so," my reporter finally said.

"Okay." Milo paused, as if his silence might prompt a response from the Laskeys. It didn't. "Troy escaped Thursday afternoon," he continued. "That's five full days. It's some thirty-five miles from Monroe to Skykomish. He could walk it in a day. Have you any idea why it took him so long to cover that distance?"

"No," Mitch said abruptly. "He hasn't told us, either. Sorry, Sheriff, we can't help you."

"That's too bad," Milo said. "That doesn't help anybody."

Mitch again gazed at his salad. The sheriff rubbed his chin. Just hours ago, the two men hadn't parted on good terms. No wonder the tension hung in the air like sheet lightning. Troy might be the obvious cause, but it dawned on me I might be watching a turf war.

Milo reached inside his jacket and took out the medal. He slid it at Mitch. "Do you recognize this?"

Brenda deigned to glance at the tarnished

trinket. Mitch frowned. "No," he said. "It's some kind of religious thing, isn't it?"

The sheriff gestured at me. "Ask your boss. She's the resident expert on this stuff."

"It's a Saint Augustine medal," I said, surprised I could still talk. My chin felt sore. Maybe by the end of the day I'd be a mass of black and blue. "He's one of the great doctors of the Catholic Church."

Milo scowled at me. "You told me he was a bishop, not a doctor."

"It's a term for a theologian. If you want to know more, ask Ben."

Milo's eyes snapped. "No thanks." He turned back to Mitch. "You're Jewish. Why would your son have one of these things?"

"I've no idea," Mitch said stiffly. He looked at Brenda. "Do you?"

Brenda shook her head.

Milo stood up. "That's it. I'm going to check in with Monroe."

"Wait." Mitch had also stood up. Heads swiveled in our direction. The cafeteria had grown ominously quiet. "You can't let them take Troy away from here. He's very sick."

Milo made a helpless gesture. "It's not my call. You cover our office, Laskey. You know jurisdictional differences. I'm outranked."

My reporter turned pleading eyes on me. "Can't you do anything?"

I was puzzled. "Like what?"

"Whatever! Brenda's falling apart. Can't you intercede?"

I didn't dare look at Milo. "Come on, Mitch. You know better. You and Brenda have more clout as Troy's parents than anybody."

"Troy's not a minor," Mitch snapped. He grabbed Brenda by the arms, pulling her out of the chair. "Let's find Dr. Sung."

Wordlessly, Brenda clung to Mitch as they made their exit. Milo scooped up the medal. "Why would the Laskey kid have this thing?"

I struggled out of the chair. "Did Jack ask Troy about it?"

Milo put the medal inside his jacket before we walked to the exit. "No. I told you, the kid's pretty much out of it. Why? Do you think it's not Troy's?" He opened one of the double doors for us.

I grimaced. "I don't know. It just feels *wrong*."

"Okay. If you figure out why, let me know."

We couldn't guess that what was right was wrong — dead wrong.

SEVEN

"Hold it," Milo said before we reached the hospital exit. "I have to call those dawdlers in Monroe."

Stacey was at her post. She smiled faintly. "Is everything okay?"

The sheriff had gone to the far side of the lobby and turned away to use his phone. I walked over to the desk. "You mean with the Laskeys?"

She nodded. "Jenny told me about their son. That's sad. I don't know Mr. Laskey, but my folks live next door to them."

I scrutinized her nametag. "You're Dutch and Tina Bamberg's daughter," I said. "How's your father's video store doing since the advent of Netflix? Leo Walsh tells me it's been hard on him."

Stacey looked blank. I realized she didn't recognize me. "I'm sorry," I said, putting out my hand, "I'm Emma Lord from the *Advocate*."

Stacey blushed as we shook hands. "I recognized you. I mean, you looked familiar, but I thought you were Mrs. Dodge." She faltered. "Couples who come together usually are . . . couples."

"There is no Mrs. Dodge," I said stiffly. "The sheriff and I both have an interest in the Laskey case. Tomorrow is my deadline for the paper."

"Oh — sure," Stacey gulped. "What did you ask me?"

"About the video store." To make amends for causing the poor girl embarrassment, I smiled. "Leo's my ad manager. He knows your dad."

"It's been hit pretty hard," Stacey replied, her color returning to normal. "Christmas helps because people buy gifts from us. Mom says we should switch to selling cameras and photography equipment. Dad's always liked taking pictures. He could still sell DVDs and CDs, too."

"That might be smart," I said, noticing that Milo had finished his call and turned back to face us.

"Get your butt over here, Emma," he said. "You know how much I hate hanging out in hospitals."

With a bleak glance at Stacey, I trudged across the entry area. "Asshole," I said to

Milo under my breath as he opened the door.

"What?"

"Poor Stacey thought I was your wife. I told her I wasn't. Now she probably thinks I was lying, because you sounded just like a husband."

"Hey," he said, putting his arm around me, "I like that idea. Besides, you know I hate hospitals."

"You're impossible. What did Monroe have to say?"

"Wait till we're in the car. Can you make it —"

"Yes! Get away from me!" Luckily, I got into the car on my own.

Milo put the key in the ignition. "Are you mad?"

"No." I gave him a flinty look anyway. "But tell me about Monroe before I change my mind."

"They'll be here in ten minutes," he said, waiting for a motorcycle to pass before pulling out onto the street. "I can't get caught in the middle. I'd be overstepping my bounds if I did."

"You mean if you took the Laskeys' side."

"There are no sides. It's a cut-and-dried situation. The state's in charge. SkyCo just got caught in the middle."

I nodded. "I wish the Laskeys could keep Troy in the hospital here. I'm sure he'd have much better care and they could be with him."

Milo didn't say anything, rarely allowing sympathy to interfere with holding the line and going by the book.

"Hey," I said, realizing that after turning onto Front he was slowing down by his headquarters. "Aren't you going to let me off at the paper?"

"Oh." He kept going and pulled into Vida's vacant parking spot. "How long are you going to be there?"

"I don't know," I said. The dashboard clock registered five after six. "If everything's okay, I can still make the dinner with Adam and Ben."

"They're adults. They can't get along without you?"

"Milo . . ." I hated it when he looked at me with obvious longing. No, I didn't hate it, but there *were* limits. "Damn, aren't you *tired?*"

"Not particularly. Are you?"

"Yes. And I hurt. You really *are* a bear, big guy. Don't lean so close. I, too, have family duties."

He backed off. "I know. How long will they be in town?"

"*Too* long," I said — and could've bitten my tongue. "That's awful. I hardly ever see them and I was mad at Thanksgiving when they canceled and now . . ." Feeling stupid, I looked at Milo. "Am I selfish?"

He stared through the windshield and shook his head. "No. More like you're turning into me. You want something you've never had."

I didn't respond right away. "I had Tom."

"Not for long."

"I thought it was going to be forever."

"You were wrong."

"Did you give up on me when I was on the verge of marrying him?"

"Almost." He finally looked at me again. "Don't get mad or upset, but I never thought it would happen."

I was shocked. "Why?"

He shrugged. "The S.O.B. never lived up to any of his promises. I figured there'd be another crisis with his screwy kids or one of his newspapers would get blown up or . . ." He shrugged again. "He was a . . . what's the word? A chimera?"

I couldn't help but smile. Milo had a good vocabulary, but it wasn't exotic. I nodded. "I could never depend on him. When I told you Tom and I were engaged, you said if things didn't work out, you'd be there for me. I was so touched — I thought you meant as a friend."

"Well . . ." His expression was wry. "Maybe I did, maybe I thought it was all I could ever be to you. But I figured you marrying the guy was damned iffy." He sighed. "Remember the big snow when I walked in on the two of you? I didn't know Tom was in town. I wanted to . . . not kill him, but he'd taken you away from me, he was where I felt at home. I gave you both a bad time. That was a rotten thing to do."

I thought back to that December six years earlier. "That's strange. All I could think about was how *you* felt. I felt guilty for hurting you. I never gave Tom a thought. And he knew about us, even before you made a point of . . . what we'd had."

"Damn." Milo looked surprised. "I wish I'd known that then."

"You do now," I said softly. "I wish I'd figured out *why* I reacted that way. But Tom had another domestic crisis, taking off without a word two days later. He always needed to be needed — except by me. He never realized *I* might need him."

Milo picked up my hand — gently. "I'm not like that, Emma."

I lifted his hand to my cheek. "I know you aren't. You never were."

We looked at each other for a long time. A dozen, two dozen people could have passed by on the sidewalk. A circus parade could have gone down Front Street. The *Advocate* could have caught fire, raging on for a block and a half to envelope the sheriff's headquarters. There was nothing, nobody in the whole world except us.

He slowly removed his hand. "Go on, do what you have to. I'll see you tomorrow."

"Yes," I said, opening the car door. "You will."

I got out and walked across the sidewalk to the *Advocate*'s entrance. The sheriff didn't pull away until I was safely inside.

"Vida's on her way," Alison announced when she saw me.

"Great!" I exclaimed. "Did she just get back from Bellingham?"

"She got home before five, but went grocery shopping. She's going to invite you and your brother and your son to dinner later this week."

First the good news, then the bad news. I wondered what inedible concoction Vida would devise for the Lords. We couldn't all claim illness as an excuse for turning her down. "Do you want to leave now?"

Alison seemed uncertain. "I haven't been back to the apartment since Christmas Eve morning," she said, referring to the two-bedroom unit she shared with Lori Cobb at Pines Villa. "Lori called earlier. Her grand-father's funeral is Friday. Kip posted it on our site. I'll find out if she's with her folks. If she isn't, I'd be a bad friend to abandon her."

"Go ahead. Oh — how are your folks? I haven't had time to ask."

She smiled. "They're fine. They were upset when my birth mother's death came back to haunt us, but once that was over, they were relieved. Dad worried he'd become the prime suspect again."

"I wondered," I said. "It all happened so fast after you started working here." I sup-pressed a shudder at the memory of how the tragedy had ended that fateful night in early December. "By Monday, I was still so wrung out that I could barely help Mitch put the story together."

Alison sighed. "In the long run, it was all for the best."

The door burst open and Vida appeared. "Well now!" she cried. "A fine kettle of fish! I should never leave Alpine. Look what hap-pens!"

I hugged her. "How was Christmas?"

"Ohh . . ." She re-pinned her red velvet beret. "Having everyone together was pleasant. Roger toured the campus, but hardly anyone was around. He didn't seem enthused about transferring there, though it's certainly better than the Marines."

"My uncle was in the Marines," Alison said. "They have really great uniforms. Uncle Abe looked like a movie star."

In my mind's eye, a vision of the tubby Roger stuffed into a Marine uniform looked more like a moving van.

"Yes," Vida said fretfully, pulling off her gloves, "but now I must focus on the matter at hand. Can you summarize for me, Emma?"

"Sure, but let's go into the newsroom," I said.

"Can I come?" Alison asked. "I should get caught up before I go."

"Of course," I told her. "You're staff. Where's Kip?"

"He's on his way back," Alison replied. "The Laskeys aren't home. Kip said Fleetwood was leaving, too, heading for the sheriff's office."

"A good place for him," I said, sitting down at Leo's desk. "Milo can handle him." I winced inwardly. The last time the sheriff had "handled" Spence, he'd broken Mr. Radio's nose. "No remote?"

Alison shrugged. "If he did one, he had to

talk to himself. I didn't realize the Laskeys had an Escalade. It must be Mrs. Laskey's car."

"Weaving may be more lucrative than newspapers," I said. "But these days, so is welfare."

Vida sniffed. "Maybe Brenda came from money."

"It's my fault," I said. "We don't know the Laskeys that well. I should socialize more with them. Okay, let me update you." It took ten minutes to do that, even though Vida remained relatively silent. I ended with the latest events at the hospital, the only part of the saga that Alison didn't yet know.

"My, my," Vida murmured, "this is a shame. Mitch won't be able to contribute to his son's story. If he can focus, he might manage to deal with the remains in the cave. What can I do?"

"I'll take up the slack for Mitch," I said, "but anything with Roy is yours. We'll only mention that he's unwell. I assume he'll have to take a leave to glue himself back together."

"Indeed," Vida remarked. "Bebe is no help. She's scatterbrained. Their son, Doug, works for one of the refineries in Anacortes. Brianna, the daughter, recently moved in with her boyfriend in Snohomish." She paused, fiddling with a pencil. "Shall I go to the hospital to offer the Laskeys support? I could see Bebe if she's there."

"You've had a long drive," I said. "Are you sure you feel up to it?"

"Yes," she asserted. "I didn't drive. I rode with Ted and Amy and Roger and . . ." She suddenly coughed. "My! I hope I'm not catching cold. That damp air in Bellingham comes down from Canada, you know."

I knew where the damp air came from, but I suspected Vida had coughed to cover her slip of the tongue. I assumed she'd almost mentioned that Roger's illegitimate child had been with the rest of the family.

"Just don't make yourself sick," I said, playing along with Vida's little game. I checked the time. It was six-thirty. I could still make an appearance at the ski lodge, though I'd have to go home first and change. The rigors of the day had done some serious damage to my work clothes, and I didn't want to embarrass my son or my brother by showing up at King Olav's looking like a bum. My makeup, scant as it had started out, was long gone, and my hair must've looked worse than usual. I stood up, a reminder that I was also sore and stiff.

"What's wrong?" Vida asked. "You flinched."

"I fell down. Roy made a mess of the clinic waiting room. You'd better call your niece Marje. Roy threw her on her rear end."

"Good heavens!" Vida cried. "You left that part out."

"I condensed the day's events," I said. "Marje and I both paid a price for Roy's breakdown." I turned to Alison. "When Kip gets back, tell him there's no need for either of you to stick around. Lock up for the night. I'm off to dinner with my priests and Marisa Foxx."

"Marisa?" Vida echoed. "Why is she dining with them?"

"I'll tell you tomorrow." I was halfway out of the newsroom, aware that Vida despised being in the dark, but I had to hurry if I hoped to arrive before the dessert course. Driving home, I tried to put the day's hectic events aside. I had to refocus on family. Dealing with Adam's inheritance was beyond me, though I had to show him I cared. And I did. But my brain was scrambled by too much happening too fast.

I arrived at King Olav's at seven. Ben, Adam, and Marisa were being served their entrées, all of which looked like halibut. Ben wore the same outfit he'd had on at Christmas, Adam sported a teal sweater I'd given him, and Marisa had on a black wool crepe dress I'd seen at Francine's Fine Apparel. I was surprised. On social occasions, she usually kept to her tailored suits, adding only a more elegant blouse.

"Well, well," Ben said, pulling out a chair for me, "have you saved the day for the news-hungry people of Alpine?"

"That won't get done until we go to press tomorrow night," I said, squeezing Adam's arm. "Has Marisa solved all your legal problems?"

"Ms. Foxx knows her stuff," Adam said. "We'll meet tomorrow morning to review my options."

Marisa nodded approval. "I told Adam — Father Adam — to bring his uncle along. I knew you'd be busy getting out the paper, Emma."

The glum Gala who'd served Mitch and me at lunch had been replaced by the raven-haired girl named Livna that Vida had mentioned as a tidbit for "Scene." If I hadn't been so frazzled, I'd have asked her how a non-blonde had been hired by Henry Bardeen. But assuming her name indicated Scandinavian descent, she'd probably passed muster. Livna asked if I wanted a drink before ordering dinner to catch up.

"CC double shot, water back," I said. "I'll have the salmon entrée and a salad with honey mustard."

Ben chuckled. "Sounds like Little Sister had a bad day. Why didn't you just tell her to bring a jug?"

"Guess what, Ben," I said, "it *was* a bad day. How would you like to lose your only reporter and have to go it alone?"

My brother's expression was impassive. "I've been going it alone for thirty years. There's a priest shortage, in case you haven't noticed."

I glared at him. "Just be thankful I'm not a mean drunk."

Ben's expression became noncommittal. "You're a lot of things, but not that. I imagine you've found comfort from outside sources."

Adam shifted uncomfortably. Marisa was preoccupied with her string beans. I arranged my napkin on my lap. The sudden silence seemed to echo from one end of the half-empty dining room to the other.

Adam finally spoke. "Uncle Ben and I ran into Pete Patricelli this afternoon. I haven't seen him in fifteen years. He said he'd seen you today. I didn't know he had a brother who'd been in prison."

"Oh," I said casually, "it happened years ago. You were probably away at school. I never met Gus. He wasn't living here when

179

he got arrested the first time."

Marisa frowned. "The only Patricelli I know is Marcella, Paul's wife. She goes to Sunday Mass, but I rarely see Paul with her."

"Paul doesn't like to go anywhere," I said, "especially to work. Marcella supports them with her alterations and tailoring business."

Marisa nodded. "She's very good." She turned to Ben. "Enough about clothes. I want to hear more about your recent assignments."

"Hey, Uncle Ben," Adam said, "tell Ms. Foxx about taking those two eighty-year-old nuns to the Rock and Roll Hall of Fame."

My CC arrived. Ben regaled Marisa with what, under other circumstances, might've been an amusing tale about the elderly sisters who'd been huge Buddy Holly fans and had broken into song with "Peggy Sue" or one of Holly's other big hits from back before I entered my teens. The double took the edge off my more perverse side, but it also made me sleepy. The salmon was dry, perhaps overcooked. When Marisa urged us to order dessert, I just wanted to go home and sleep.

"Please, Emma," she begged, "I already told Ben — Father Ben — this was my treat. I don't often get a chance to do something for the clergy."

"That's kind," I said, "but I have to follow up on Troy Laskey, who may be moved back to Monroe tonight."

Marisa looked puzzled. "Isn't that where he should be?"

"Did I forget to mention the poor kid has pneumonia?"

She put a hand to her short blond hair. "If you did, I missed it."

Ben nodded. "So did I."

"My bad," I muttered, picking up my purse. "Excuse me, I really have to go. I'll see you at home, Adam."

"Sure, Mom," he said vaguely. "I think I'll skip the Eskimo pie. I wonder what that boysenberry cobbler is like?"

The good news was that I wasn't drunk. The bad news was that I wasn't drunk. The last time I'd been drunk was years ago when a clever killer had plied me with liquor. In October, while making drinks for Milo and me, I'd fallen down in my kitchen. I'd already been in a catfight with the town hooker at Safeway's parking lot and I was pretty banged up. The sheriff had called Doc Dewey, who gave me a prescription for Demerol. The result was an extreme case of goofiness. It had not been a night to remember.

As relieved as I was to be home, once I took off my jacket, my log house felt empty. My eyes strayed to the armchair where Milo so often sat. *Stop being a smitten adolescent. Act your age and tend to business.*

I shook myself, sat on the sofa, and called the sheriff. "This is business," I said when he answered.

"Business? Who's there? The priests?"

"No, but they will be. Or at least Adam will. Where are you?"

"In the basement, going through my tackle box. Why?"

"I thought you might still be at work. What happened with Troy?"

"Damned if I know," Milo replied. "The Monroe guys booted Mullins out of the hospital. Jack assumed — you got that? — *assumed* they were taking the kid back to the facility."

"Oh, no," I groaned. "Mitch and Brenda will be even worse than they are already. Can the Laskeys accompany Troy?"

"I don't know," Milo said. "I'm just a lowly county sheriff."

"I wonder if I should try to get hold of them."

"Give yourself a break. Oh — I had time to kill while I waited for Mullins to come back, so I went through Myrtle's file. I knew

I'd forgotten something. I'd had Art Fremstad — Donna Erlandson Wickstrom's first husband — call out the dogs to get a trail on Myrtle after she left the neighbor's house. They picked up a scent leading them along Carroll Creek. By '88 the parcel of third-growth timber had been harvested two years earlier. Hang on. I dropped a lure."

I remembered the area from when I'd seen it for the first time after I moved to Alpine in '89, a great bare swath along the middle of Tonga Ridge and Mount Sawyer, west of my new home.

"Anyway," Milo went on, "they lost the scent after a couple of hundred yards, indicating she crossed the creek — or stopped. But there was no sign of her in the vicinity."

I pictured the scene. "So Myrtle disappeared in the same area that the corpse was found yesterday."

"You got it. Hell of a coincidence, I suppose."

The sheriff didn't like coincidences, so I didn't say anything. But I did ask if the body in the cave had been identified.

"Not yet," Milo answered. "There was no way Pete could make an ID from those remains. The corpse doesn't have a gap between his front teeth like Pete, but neither does Matt or Rita Patricelli. We have to wait for Dr. Starr's old dental records. We'll get them tomorrow. We don't have to send those over to Everett."

"Who's Matt?" I asked.

"The oldest brother, who lives in Yakima," Milo said.

"Oh. I never met him. Did Pete simmer down?"

"He had to. We don't need another local going off his rocker."

I heard a car outside. "Uh-oh. I think Adam's here."

Milo laughed. "Are you afraid your kid will find out you talk to the sheriff on the phone?"

"I'm afraid he'll think I sound like I'm madly in love with said sheriff. Good night." I hung up just as a knock sounded at the door.

My son looked sheepish. "I forgot my key."

"What a shock. Some things never change. Did you lose it?"

Adam kept going, headed for his bedroom. "Hold on," he called.

I closed the door and sat back down on the sofa.

"Got it," he cried in triumph. "I left it under my dirty socks." He came back into the living room and sat down on the floor by the hearth. "Do you want me to build a fire?"

"Sure, but only a small one. I'm tired. It's been a long day."

"It was a long dinner," he said, putting crumpled papers and kindling in the grate.

"You didn't enjoy it?"

He added a log. "Uncle Ben told me Ms. Foxx came on to him."

"What?"

"She was nudging him with her knee," Adam replied, setting off the papers. "He turned down the offer of an after-dinner drink at her place. Uncle Ben practically held me in a viselike grip so I couldn't leave him alone with her. Needless to say, he bagged coming along to my meeting with her tomorrow."

I held my head. "Her making a play for your uncle blows me away."

Adam remained by the hearth. Maybe he was soaking up all the warmth he could get while still in the Lower Forty-eight. "I told Uncle Ben maybe Ms. Foxx thought his leg belonged to the table."

"Those are wooden pedestal tables," I said. "Your uncle does not have legs like a cedar stump."

"He thought it was sort of funny," Adam said. "Maybe it was the booze. We'd had a couple of drinks or so by then."

"Great. You all *seemed* sober enough."

Adam looked at me with a chary expression. "*You* seemed out of it. That's too bad about your reporter's son. Anything I can do?"

I shook my head. "The poor kid's back at Monroe. I should call the Laskeys, but I really don't want to. Maybe Vida already has. She's better at that sort of thing than I am."

"What about calling the sheriff?"

"I already did. He doesn't know anything. It's not his jurisdiction."

"Oh," Adam said. "I never figured out the county boundaries here. We don't have counties in Alaska. We have boroughs, and the vast, uninhabited areas within the borders, those places aren't part of the designation. They're called 'unorganized boroughs.' "

"I didn't know that," I said. "How about 'disorganized boroughs'? If we did that in this state, it'd fit SkyCo, especially the recent history with the county commissioners, one of whom died before Christmas."

"Anybody I know?"

"Dubious. It was Alfred Cobb, whose granddaughter replaced Toni Andreas after her move to Alaska. Have you heard from

Toni lately?"

Adam laughed at the reference to the young woman he'd dated during his college-break days. "Not for . . ." He paused, checking to make sure the fire was catching onto the log. "A year, maybe? She went to Alaska to find a man, and probably did. Men still outnumber women by quite a bit and Toni was good-looking, if dim." He propped himself up on one elbow. "Speaking of old flames, what happened to that AP dude?"

I shrugged. "Rolf retired and moved to France. He sent me a gift package from a fancy Paris shop recently, but I never thanked him. Bad manners, I know, but I didn't want to encourage him. I haven't heard from him since, which is fine with me."

"I thought you liked him."

"I did, but he was an enigma. I never knew whether he was telling me the truth or blowing smoke." I shrugged. "Vida and I ate some of the food he sent and we both got sick."

Adam grimaced. "Unless he was seeing Mrs. Runkel on the side, poisoning both of you is extreme. It sounds as if he felt rejected."

"I kept turning down invitations to visit his Loire Valley hideaway."

"I take it you're not looking for a replacement?"

"I'm not." This was the perfect opening to mention Milo. But I couldn't, not with Ben's disapproval hanging over me. Maybe Adam would side with his uncle. Maybe my son wouldn't want to know I'd finally shoved his father's memory to the back of the linen drawer.

The log burned brightly. Adam had stretched out on his back. I felt drowsy. The silence was pleasant. It had been a long time since I'd had my son all to myself. I should have turned on the Christmas tree, but I didn't want to get off the sofa. I wanted to spend this time with Adam to remind myself that first and foremost, I was a mother. But it wasn't easy. Maybe that was because my son didn't give me many opportunities to practice. Using my credit card to meet his material needs and receiving sporadic emails and rare visits did not fulfill my maternal instincts. Adam no longer needed me. For the first twenty years, Tom had flunked fatherhood. I'd done it all, and not such a bad job at that. Then Ben had taken over. I often felt as if my brother had stolen my son. No wonder I'd had such a void in my life until these last few weeks. Only one person had needed me for the last fifteen years. It had cut both ways, though I'd tried to ignore the fact for too long.

But for now, I was going to savor this time with Adam. To be fair, he'd rallied to my side when I'd been menaced by the wretched, greedy crooks who had posed a threat not only to Tom's legitimate children, but to me as well. I'd misjudged my son at the time, and was sorry for it.

"Mom?"

I gave a start. "What?"

Adam was raised up on one elbow. "Were you sleeping?"

"No," I said. "I was just thinking. About you, mainly."

He grinned. "Not bad thoughts, I hope."

"No." I had to stop. There was a lump in my throat. I swallowed and tried to smile. "I wish you weren't so far away."

He was now sitting cross-legged in front of the fire. "So do I, but there's not much I can do about that. One thing, though — I can't get much farther from here unless they send me to Florida."

"How long do you think you'll be in Alaska?"

"Oh — it's basically Jesuit territory," Adam said. "But they've had those lawsuits over the perv priests, and it's going to take them a while to earn back the respect of the people. I can't believe how that all happened for so long and nobody blew the whistle. The only thing that can even begin to explain it is that until recent years, nobody talked about pedophilia. Not the schools, not the Boy Scouts, not the camp counselors, not the Little League coaches, not the other religious faiths. No excuse, but of course the Catholic Church is always fair game."

I agreed. "The bigger the target, the easier for outsiders to point fingers. And righteous indignation often masks bigotry."

Adam nodded. "Hypocrisy, too. Look at all the politicians and businessmen screwing everybody and getting away with it. You can ruin people without touching them — or knowing who they are except as some poor schmuck way down the food chain. But," he went on, standing up, "until the Jesuits get their act together, a secular priest like me is good to have around. Unless I get caught selling crack or diddling a seal, I'm an icon. Maybe I'll stay on for another three, four years at least."

I made a face. "That's a long time. For you, I mean."

He shrugged. "Guess I skipped the fine print on God's contract."

It was pointless to press Adam. Except for

190

the rigors and dangers of his assignment, he seemed content. "Maybe someday I'll visit you."

"If you do, come in July or early August. If you think Alpine is small and primitive, you'll pitch a five-star fit when you see how I live. Stay ignorant. Do you ever wonder why I don't send videos?"

"Because I wouldn't be able to figure out how to watch them?"

"There is that," Adam said, "but I know you. Besides, I need the break coming here more than you need to come up north. I'll have company when I go back. Uncle Ben is coming with me."

I was only mildly surprised, since my brother had mentioned the idea. "That's great. I thought you had to leave before the weekend."

"Not anymore," Adam replied, going over to the CD player and looking through some Christmas discs. "My sub, Jorge Santos-Medilla, got there late for the same reason I couldn't get out, so he'll stay on a couple of extra days. Nice Jesuit guy from Texas, late vocation after he finished grad school, ordained last June. He'll be fine. Uncle Ben and I'll leave here Sunday after Mass."

"You're not bored in Alpine?"

"After the village, this place is huge. I can

hang with Uncle Ben."

"I should've taken time off this week," I said. "But I couldn't foresee what would happen with Mitch."

Adam selected a CD. "I can amuse myself. You didn't birth a moron, Mom." Mannheim Steamroller burst forth with "Deck the Halls."

"I hope not," I said under my breath.

At least Adam had given me credit for bringing him into the world.

EIGHT

My son had left by the time I got up on Tuesday. A note in the bathroom informed me that he was concelebrating Mass with Ben before the meeting with Marisa. He'd scribbled, "If no deadline crisis, lunch?"

I couldn't predict how the day would spin out. Upon reaching the office, I found Alison one step ahead of me, Vida at her desk, Kip carrying a mug of fresh coffee into the back shop, and Leo taking off his raincoat.

"Leo!" I cried, and hugged him, happy to see my ad manager. "How was your holiday?"

"Really good," he said, with his crooked grin. "I'll tell you later."

Vida waved a pencil at Leo. "I must be included. It's a pity we can't write about staff in the paper, but I can mention in my 'Scene Around Town' that a local ad man enjoyed his California Christmas."

"That'll stump the readers," Leo remarked, "me being the only ad guy in town, unless you count Fleetwood."

"Let's not," I said. "He spent the weekend in Seattle."

He gestured at the vacant desk across from his. "Where's Mitch?"

Vida and I exchanged bleak glances. Naturally, she spoke first.

"Mitch's son escaped from prison not long after you left last Thursday. He was recaptured yesterday, but has pneumonia." She turned to me. "Have you heard anything more?"

"I'll do the sheriff's log. And," I added, seeing the empty tray next to the coffee urn, "the bakery run. It must've been Mitch's turn."

"No," Leo said, chagrined. "It was mine. I forgot. I'll do it now. I've been trying to get the Upper Crust to use color in their ads anyway. Want to come with me, Emma? I'll walk you to the sheriff's office."

"Go ahead," I said. "I need coffee first. I didn't make any at home."

Leo's expression was quizzical. "Your kid doesn't drink coffee?"

"Not this morning," I said. "He's saying Mass with his uncle."

Leo grinned again. "Man, you must be aglow with piety by now. Let me assure you,

194

I went to Christmas *and* Sunday Mass with the family. I kind of liked it."

"Good for you," I said. "You'd better show up this weekend when Adam and Ben put on their final road show."

"I think I will." Leo put his raincoat back on. "Later, ladies." Grabbing his ad portfolio, he left the newsroom.

Vida looked speculative. "Leo's happy. That's a bad sign."

"I know what you mean," I said, "but maybe it won't last. I'd hate to have to replace him."

Vida made a face. "Especially with Ed lurking about." She shuddered, jostling not only her bosom but the small pinecones on her cloche hat. "My, my — it's always something. By the way, Kip says the pass is open for skiing. He put a note on your desk. They must've had more snow up there than we did. Do you have a 'Scene' item? I purposely left room for post-Christmas items."

I reviewed the past few days in my mind's eye, which was a bad idea. "Not a thing, unfortunately."

"That's not like you," she chided. "You're usually aware. Think."

I poured coffee and tried to come up with a memorable sighting. "How long has Stacey Bamberg worked at the hospital as a receptionist?"

"Since last April. Go on."

"Honest, I'm blank."

"You certainly are," she said in disapproval as her phone rang.

I scooted into my cubbyhole. If Mitch wasn't going to show up, I couldn't waste time. I deciphered Kip's note about Stevens Pass being open for winter sports enthusiasts and wrote a two-inch story. I was up against a stone wall on Troy's escape and recapture. I wouldn't mention Mitch and Brenda, but locals would make the connection and the grapevine would be abuzz. My fingers felt like they weighed ten pounds apiece.

"Emma!" Vida shrieked from the newsroom. "I'm shocked!"

I thought she meant literally. Narrowly avoiding a collision with one of my visitor's chairs, I rushed into the newsroom. Alison was already in the doorway, apparently as alarmed as I was.

"What's wrong?" I demanded, not seeing any visible damage.

Vida was looking at Alison. "Don't be upset, dear. I'm fine. Isn't your phone ringing?"

"Uh . . ." Alison glanced over her shoulder.

"I don't hear it, but maybe it will." She returned to her post, obviously having worked with Vida long enough to recognize a semi-tactful dismissal.

I sat on Vida's desk, my back to the front office. "What?" I asked.

"That call was from Mary Lou Blatt, my loathsome sister-in-law," Vida said, lowering her voice. "She's a terrible gossip and sometimes malicious, but I can't dismiss what she told me. Mary Lou is not a liar."

Mary Lou was a lot like Vida — smart, opinionated, and self-righteous. Thus, they were often at crossed swords. "About my priests?"

"Hardly." Vida licked her lips. "Yesterday she was walking from First Presbyterian on Pine across from the clinic, and . . ." She paused. "She saw Milo holding you in his arms and kissing you. Is it true?"

"I fell down, I told you that."

"You fell on the sidewalk? I thought you fell inside the clinic."

"I had trouble getting up."

Vida harrumphed. "Were you or were you not kissing the sheriff?"

"So what? It's not the first time and you know it."

She glowered at me. "I told you that was no way for mature adults to act. Why, back then you weren't even dating! Kissing in public . . . has Milo no sense of the moment? Are you both insane?"

"Yes."

"Oh, no!" Whipping off her glasses, she began rubbing her eyes.

I cringed as her eyeballs squeaked. "Don't. It drives me crazy."

"You already are," Vida snapped, putting her glasses back on. "What happened?"

"I woke up."

"Well, it's about time." She leaned back in her chair, tapping the desk with her pencil. "When? Why? How could I miss it?"

"It . . . it just sort of . . ." I shrugged. "You're not upset?"

Vida sighed. "Years ago, I felt you two were poorly matched. Different backgrounds, little in common. After Tommy died, I was sorry you didn't return Milo's deeper feelings. Then you seemed taken with the AP person, but that fizzled when he went to France. I blame him for making us ill. Flu, indeed. You can't trust foreign food, French or not."

"I don't think Rolf intended to poison us."

Vida waved a hand in dismissal. "Never mind. I'm glad for you and Milo. I had no time for Tricia, though I'm not one to criticize. She wasn't local, but grew up in

198

Sultan. They were married there instead of in one of our nicer churches in Alpine." She made a face. "They met when she worked at the ski lodge gift shop. Tricia never understood how demanding his job was or why he'd go fishing to distance himself from the unpleasant aspects of his work. You've never made that mistake."

"Our jobs are linked," I said. "Sometimes it causes us conflict."

"But you and he don't hold grudges," Vida pointed out. "Tricia was one for that. I suspect her affair with Jake Sellers was to punish Milo for so-called neglect. So silly of her. Tricia preened all over town when he became sheriff. Then she resented the time he spent on the job. She got what she deserved with the teacher. He wasn't from Alpine, either."

For Vida, that was the greatest sin. "I never met Tricia."

Vida shrugged. "Nice-looking when she was younger, but not the sort that ages well. Gone to fat. You, on the other hand, have held up quite well. So has your brother. It must be genetic."

"No doubt," I murmured.

"But," Vida added, wagging a finger, "you and Milo mustn't make public spectacles of yourselves. You both have high profiles in

Alpine. It hardly enhances your professional roles to paw each other on city streets."

"We weren't pawing each other," I asserted. "He kissed me. That's it. He was carrying me because I hurt myself."

"Mmm," she murmured.

"Is the lecture over?"

"It's a warning." Vida smiled. "I'm fond of Milo. He's the only Dodge who isn't an idiot. His brother in Dallas may be a fine biologist, but he openly taunted my Meg in school. Milo's sister left Alpine and later died of cancer."

I knew Milo and his brother weren't close, but he rarely mentioned his sister. "Did his sister die before I moved here?"

Vida reflected briefly. "Yes, in the mid eighties. Emily was thirty-two. Her husband, Earl, was the high school coach at the time. Not long after they were married, Earl took a job at a school south of Seattle. Milo's parents were still alive, but Emily rarely visited them."

"Except for Aunt Thelma and Uncle Elmer, I never think of Milo as having any family other than his children."

Vida sighed. "Michele, marrying right out of high school, divorcing six months later. Tanya and her strange suitors. Brandon had his problems, too, though he's now a veterinarian. I wonder what Tricia will do." She shot me a probing look.

"I don't know," I said, sliding off the desk. "Nor does Milo."

"Young people. Such challenges. So difficult." She looked away.

I knew she was thinking about Roger. Back in my office, I drank coffee and kept Vida's advice about proper public behavior in mind before heading out to see the sheriff.

Snow had fallen during the night, but turned into more bone-chilling rain on this dark, gloomy December morning. Adam lived in the land of the midnight sun — and endless winter nights. I admired him for testing his limits. I was not so self-sacrificing.

At the corner I met Leo, who was carrying a lavender bakery box along with his ad portfolio. "Hungry?" he asked.

"Kind of," I admitted, the cornflakes not having filled my stomach. "I'll wait. Did they go for the color at the Upper Crust?"

"Yeah. I cut a deal on their website ad. Later, babe. I acquired a dislike for gray skies and rain with possible snow while in California."

My ad man moved on, leaving me wondering if Vida was right about Leo considering a lifestyle change. Selfishly, I hoped not.

Lori was back on duty, chatting with Bill Blatt and Doe Jamison.

"No Laskey?" Doe inquired.

"Not yet," I said, "and don't ask. Did Troy go back to Monroe?"

"Yes, last night." Bill grimaced. "I'd better call Aunt Vida now before I get in trouble and end up with a sore butt like my sister, Marje."

I inquired after Lori and her family. She told me they were coping, but the holidays seemed cheerless without Grandpa Cobb.

I scanned the log. Troy's recapture, the traffic tie-up caused by the stalled semi, three minor collisions, one DUI for an out-of-towner, a domestic dispute involving a couple whose names I didn't know, and a mountain-lion sighting near the fish hatchery were duly noted. Nothing, however, about Roy's trashing of the clinic waiting room.

"No charges pressed on Roy?" I asked.

Doe shook her head. "That'd be up to Marje or Dr. Sung."

The sheriff ambled out of his office, coffee mug in hand. "Hi, Emma. You the new cub reporter?"

"So it seems. You the same old bear?"

His hazel eyes sparked. "You bet."

I resumed staring at the log. "I guess I've got everything."

"No, you don't," the sheriff said. "Come into my office."

I glanced at Milo's underlings. Bill was on the phone, presumably with his Aunt Vida. Doe was also on a call, asking for a license plate number. Lori was searching through the files. "Okay," I said warily.

Milo closed the door behind us. I was about to protest when he went to the other side of his desk and sat down. "What's wrong?" he inquired as I settled into my usual spot across from him. "You look like a scared rabbit."

"Vida gave me a lecture. Mary Lou Blatt spotted us outside the clinic yesterday."

"So?"

"Mary Lou probably wants Vida to put it in 'Scene.' "

"So?"

"Milo . . ."

"Vida won't do that. Why do you care? Back before you decided to dump me, you didn't seem to mind if anybody knew we were lovers."

"My bridge club boycotted me for a while," I reminded him.

Milo took a swig of coffee. "That was after you dumped me. Is it the priests?"

I winced. "That might be part of it."

"Is Vida pissed at us?"

"No. She approves, but she thinks we're . . . undignified."

The sheriff burst out laughing. "Oh, God! Hey, we had our clothes on. Relax. Are you scared of being happy?"

"I'm scared of being sappy. So, why did you close the door?"

Milo grew serious. "Nothing personal, but I don't want to start a different rumor. I got a call last night from Don Krogstad. We went to school together. This is more up Vida's alley. You can pass it on to her. Bill Blatt's too young to know about it, so there's no point telling him." He took a pack of Marlboro Lights out of his pocket. "You want one?"

"Why not?"

Once again, Milo lighted mine as well as his. "Don asked if Dwight had found anything else in the cave where he and his wife, Dee, discovered the body. I told him Dwight would've told me if he had. It was a weird question, so I asked Don why he wanted to know. He stalled a bit before saying his dad — our former judge — had a lady friend. They used to picnic by the creek up there. You following this?"

"I guess," I said. "You know my reporters

204

cover the court. I never got to know His Honor. Up until he got goofy, he seemed a model of rectitude. Did the picnics with the girlfriend occur before his wife died?"

Milo exhaled smoke and nodded. "Mrs. Krogstad died eight, nine years ago. The judge has been in the Everett nursing home for about four years. He has his lucid moments, mostly focused on the girlfriend. He keeps asking if she's come home." Milo's eyes held the penetrating look he used to elicit information from suspects. "Guess who."

"Myrtle Everson?"

"You got it." He drank more coffee before continuing. "I don't remember the affair. Or maybe I've forgotten. If anybody knows, it's Vida. Try it out on her. Maybe it'll distract her from bugging you."

I didn't respond right away. "It's odd," I finally said. "As we know, there are few secrets in this town. Wouldn't their affair cause gossip after Myrtle disappeared? Wouldn't the Eversons be suspicious? If Don knew, why were Roy and his kinfolk in the dark?"

"Don didn't find out until after his dad was in the nursing home," Milo said. "He had to go through the old guy's belongings and found a couple of notes from Myrtle.

His dad's nonstop questions about her forced his hand. Don thought if any trace of her was found, it might ease the judge's mind. He'd never told his wife, Dee, about it. Even if he had, he couldn't do much with her puking after they found the body. All she wanted was to get out of there and go home."

"Are you going to search the cave again?"

Milo turned thoughtful. "I doubt it. Dwight may drive me nuts sometimes, but he does his job." He put out his cigarette and stood up. "Mount Sawyer has always been a curse on this job," he said, pointing to it on a section map on the wall. "Between meth labs, lost hikers, forest fires, and all the rest, that area has been a pain in the ass. I've got the scars to prove it." He ran a finger above his right eyebrow, a remnant of a face-off with bikers and druggies. One had cracked Milo with a broken beer bottle before being subdued. "None of us knew what was going on until some of our half-wit teenagers got involved."

"Including Roger and poor Mike O'Toole," I murmured.

"Right," Milo agreed, picking up his mug. "I've wondered if that wasn't what started the trouble those two kids got into later."

I put out my cigarette. "At least Roger

didn't end up dead." Even I wouldn't wish that on the feckless kid. But Buzzy and Laura O'Toole's son, Mike, had been killed in October when his truck went off the road.

"I need a refill," Milo said, standing up. "Any chance you can escape the paper or the priests today?"

I'd also risen. "It doesn't look good. It's deadline day."

"Oh — right. I don't know why I keep forgetting about that."

I refrained from punching him. "That makes two of us, big guy."

Milo hesitated, his hand on the doorknob. "Oh, shit." He sighed. "You better go before I decide you look like you need a refill, too."

"No comment," I said as he opened the door. "See you around."

"Right." Milo went over to the coffee urn. I went through the reception area and out the front entrance.

I paused on the sidewalk, gazing across the street at Amer Wasco's cobbler shop. It was almost nine o'clock and time for him to open his door. After waiting for a Blue Sky Dairy truck to pass, I crossed Front on a whim. Before I could get to the cobbler's, Janet Driggers unlocked the entrance to Sky Travel.

"Emma Lord, my all-time favorite hussy!"

she exclaimed. "Come in, give me every lurid detail of your amoral adventures with our not-so-straight-arrow sheriff! My God, I've been fantasizing ever since I heard about you two! I'm going to buy Al a fake badge and just pretend. I kept wishing our house had been one of the places burglarized in The Pines so Dodge could tie me up and drill . . . I mean, *grill* me. No such luck."

I should've known I couldn't avoid the bawdy wife of Al Driggers, the local funeral director. "I can't," I said. "I've got —"

She grabbed my arm and literally hauled me into the travel agency. "I don't care if you've got diphtheria. Five minutes, that's all I ask. Sit," she commanded, taking off her faux-fur-trimmed winter jacket. "I figured that with no bridge club until the second week of January, I might not have a change to pump you. So to speak. I saw you come out of Dodge's office. Did you two spend the night in a cell?"

I remained standing. "Janet . . ."

"Sit. Please." She pushed me into a chair by her desk. "Sorry I haven't made coffee yet. I cannot believe that you and Milo are . . . doing whatever you're doing in public these days. Is it true he shot Tricia because she flew into a jealous rage over you two?"

"What?"

Janet's eyes were wide with mock innocence. "That's what Dixie Ridley told me last night at dinner."

"Dixie's never liked me," I said. "Of course it's not true."

"Damn. I never could stand Tricia. I was so hoping it *was* true."

"For all I know, Tricia isn't aware I exist," I said.

"Ha! She and Linda Grant were always tight. Linda dislikes you more than Dixie does. She feeds every bit of gossip about you and Dodge into Tricia's pointy little ears. Linda had her gloms on Jake Sellers at the high school before Tricia came along and caught his eye. Then, after Tricia ran off to Bellevue, Linda made a play for Dodge."

I stared at Janet, but said nothing.

"He never told you?" she gasped. "That's why Linda can't stand you. You hadn't been here long before he lost interest in her. Oh, I know he went with that Honoria for a long time, but some of us figured you were the one he was really after." She sighed. "I love that high school. So much goes on in the storage rooms, the boiler room, the library stacks, the basement . . . and that's just the faculty."

I tried to divert Janet. "Isn't Linda seeing Henry Bardeen?"

"Well . . . maybe," Janet said. "He's a bit old for her, but she's desperate. Linda could do better. Being a P.E. teacher, she's in good shape and must have some serious moves, unless you look at her face. But," she said, clasping her hands and leaning toward me, "dish!"

"You know I won't," I said.

Janet glared at me. "No. You won't." She sat up and beamed. "That means it's fantastic. I actually saw Dodge smile yesterday."

I didn't say anything.

"Okay, go away. Leave me to my fantasies." She stood up. "But next time you and the sheriff go at it in public, let me know in advance. I've always wondered what that great big guy was like in the sack. It must be pretty awesome. What you see is what you get?"

I stood up, too. I didn't know what my expression looked like, but it must have revealed something. Janet gave me a big hug.

"Oh, sweetie, I'm so happy for you!" she cried. "You deserve it. You've been through some awful crap. So has Dodge."

"Thanks, Janet," I said as she let me go.

She opened the door for me. "If you two ever want a foursome . . ."

"Goodbye, Janet," I said. "See you at the Cobb funeral."

"Hey — that's a thought! We could do . . ."

I didn't hear the rest of what she said. I'd already turned in to the cobbler shop next door.

Amer was polishing a pair of wing tips when I approached the counter. "Missus Emma," he said with a smile. "You are better now?"

"Just a bruise or two," I replied. "Thanks for untangling me from the light cord."

"Did you hurt your shoes?"

"No," I said, "though I have a pair of flats that need resoling. But I have an odd question for you about those boots Mr. Everson brought in here. You told him they were fairly new and couldn't have belonged to his mother. What kind of condition were they in?"

"Good, not quite new, but very good." His bushy eyebrows came together in puzzlement. "You think they belong to someone you know?"

"No . . ." I grimaced. "This may sound odd, but were they the kind of boots a prisoner might wear?"

"Oh, no!" He smiled faintly. "You think . . . what?"

I didn't want to bruit Troy's name about

or start a rumor about Gus. "I get odd ideas," I said diffidently. "What kind of boots were they?"

"Hiking boots," Amer said. "Good quality, like from . . . that Seattle store . . . with the initials."

"REI?"

His dark eyes lit up. "That's it. Yes, maybe two hundred dollars."

"But Roy found them at the dump site?"

Amer nodded. "He first thought they were Mr. Pike's, from the dump site where he and Mrs. Pike . . . died. Then, I say Mr. Pike never had such fine boots, being a frugal man. I fixed Mr. Pike's boots many times. Maybe, I told Mr. Roy, Mr. Pike found them somewhere. Then Mr. Roy got excited and say Mrs. Pike picked berries where his mama did and maybe she — Mrs. Pike — found them up by Mount Sawyer." Amer sadly shook his head. "I already tell him they were *men's* boots. Sometimes his mama is all he thinks about. Poor man."

"What size were they?"

"Hmm . . . nine?"

"Oh. Thank you," I said. "I'll bring my flats in next week."

"I'm sorry not to help so much."

"Actually, you did help," I said, smiling.

212

The problem was I didn't know exactly how.

There was no chance to tell Vida about the Krogstad-Everson affair. When I returned, she'd left to take photos of the retirement home's New Year's decorations. Leo was in the back shop with Kip. Only Alison was on hand, but she had news of Mitch.

"The Laskeys are in Monroe," she told me. "Troy is improving and his parents are allowed to see him. Isn't this all too sad?"

I nodded faintly. "Did Mitch say when he'd be back at work?"

"No. He didn't talk long." Alison's voice conveyed compassion. "I suppose he can't think of much else except his son."

I felt remiss for not sounding more sympathetic. "If he calls again, can you make sure I talk to him?"

"Of course. Speaking of sons," she said, "Adam called. He and your brother are going to lunch with the Bartons at the diner. He said they'd both see you for dinner tonight at your place."

"Gee," I said in mock surprise, "they have a lull in their social schedule? I'm stunned."

Alison laughed. "Do Catholics have more fun than Protestants?"

"That depends," I said. Back at my desk,

I wrote a succinct front-page piece about Troy's escape and recapture. I started the lead story about the cave remains, but hedged my bets by calling Pete at his pizza parlor to ask if he had a photo of Gus.

"You think it's Gus?" he asked eagerly.

"I've no idea," I admitted. "Dr. Starr or Jeannie Clay won't show up with the dental records until lunchtime." Bob's dental assistant was the nubile blonde who'd consoled Milo after our breakup. Luckily, the sheriff had great teeth and rarely went to the dentist.

"I just feel it's Gus. Are you sure nothing was found in that cave?"

I frowned into the phone. I'd heard that question before, albeit secondhand. What did the locals expect? A treasure trove of Alpine relics on Mount Sawyer? "I understand that Dwight Gould searched the place thoroughly. He's that kind of guy."

"Oh . . . sure, I know Dwight. He's a hard worker. I have a fairly recent picture of Gus, but it's not real clear."

Fuzzy front-page photos were a no-no. "I'll call you back on that. Why do you think it might be him?"

"Gus was still adjusting to being out of prison." Pete sounded disheartened. "He said it's hard to understand what freedom feels like unless you lose it. Gus was thrown for a loop. Shari and I tried to help him. We didn't push socializing. He'd wander off for hours, come back, and we'd ask — casually — where he'd been. He'd shrug, say he'd gone to Old Mill Park or hiked one of the trails and taken some pictures. When he didn't come home, we couldn't imagine he'd just . . . leave."

Pete paused, apparently overcome with emotion. I felt obliged to give him a moment or two, but after what seemed like too long, I spoke up. "So you thought he'd met someone he knew and took off?"

"You mean a woman?" Pete asked in surprise.

"No, just anybody. He grew up here. A high school chum, maybe."

"He wasn't interested in that. Maybe he was embarrassed. You can't blame me for thinking something bad happened to him."

"Like . . . ?"

"Like getting hurt or lost, taking a trail and losing his way. It's a funny thing about him being in that cave. When Mrs. Everson went missing, a bunch of the high school kids went looking for her. Gus had already graduated, but he was fascinated by the whole search thing. He did some looking around the area on his own where she was supposed to have gone berry-picking. That's why I'm almost sure it has to be Gus whose . . ." He couldn't continue.

"You reported him missing to the sheriff?"

"Ah . . ." Another pause. "Not at first. We figured he'd come home. I didn't want Dodge or a deputy showing up to scare Gus. When I finally went to the sheriff's office, I talked to Mullins, being a fellow Catholic. Jack's okay, under his smart-mouth exterior. He said all they could do was put out an APB. That hit me wrong. I don't think Jack ever told the sheriff. I knew Dodge would give me hell for not telling them sooner."

Pete was right. "It might not have made any difference, though," I remarked.

"Well . . . I feel guilty anyway," Pete said. "I better let you go, Emma."

"I probably won't hear anything until early afternoon. By the way, what did you mean about Dwight finding something else in the cave?"

I heard Pete sigh. "A couple of things bother me. Remember I told you I bought him a camera because he liked photography? Shari didn't notice if he had it with him when he took off, but we can't find it. It was real nice, cost a bundle."

"That'd be hard to miss if he took it with

him," I said.

"Maybe he lost it. Another thing . . . well, Gus wasn't too religious, but he always wore a Saint Augustine medal my sister Rita gave him. Augustus is my brother's first name. I wondered if it was in the cave."

I hedged. "No, it wasn't."

"That's a relief," Pete said. "Uh-oh. The early lunch orders are coming in. Got to go. Thanks, Emma." He hung up.

I stared blankly at my monitor. A Saint Augustine medal wasn't common like a Saint Christopher medal. There were two thousand inmates and five hundred staff members at Monroe. An older inmate had been Troy's pal. Could the "big brother" Mitch mentioned be Gus?

It fit — in a disturbing kind of way.

NINE

I was still mulling as I got a coffee refill. Before I could return to my desk, Spencer Fleetwood breezed into the newsroom. "Ah! My cohort and archrival," he said, flashing his almost genuine smile.

"How was your weekend?" I asked, trying not to stare at his nose.

"Enjoyable," he replied, helping himself to the last glazed doughnut. "And yours?"

"Wonderful," I replied, almost convincing myself that it was true. "My son arrived late. He had a whiteout at St. Mary's Igloo."

Spence poured himself a mug of coffee. "Alaska, home of the frozen friars. Aren't you going to invite me into your inner sanctum?"

"Since when did you need an invitation to do what you want?" I led the way. "By the way, Adam isn't a friar, he's a priest."

"As you know," Spence said, "I'm not Catholic. Friar, brother, father, bishop, pawn, whatever — it's all the same to me."

"Why are you here?" I asked after we both had sat down.

His brown eyes danced. "I wanted to see what the sheriff's lady looked like after the great reunion. I've already seen the sheriff."

I locked gazes with Mr. Radio. "Watch it. You only have one nose."

His hand lightly touched the one he still had. "True. Dodge seemed in remarkably good spirits. For Dodge."

I shrugged. "In other words, he didn't heave you out onto Front Street. Darn."

"Emma . . ." Spence adopted a more serious air. "I don't hold a grudge. I, too, have to get along with my sources. I messed up. That was then, this is now. Fill me in on the bones thing. Mullins was some help, but he's prone to hogwash. The Mama quest and Roy's tizzy aren't my kind of news, but I think they'd be good material for *Vida's Cupboard.*"

Spence was referring to the weekly fifteen-minute program my House & Home editor did every Thursday night on KSKY. Vida's show had amazing ratings and had been the main catalyst in a joint endeavor between the *Advocate* and the radio station to pool advertising. While Spence and I might be rivals for news, we tried to maintain a

219

semblance of civility when dealing with our co-op revenue ventures.

His idea about the Eversons didn't strike me as a good one, however. "Ask Vida. I don't know much about it. She should be back any time. Were you thinking about it for this week's show?"

Spence shook his head. "No. She told me she might do a year-end wrap-up, maybe use highlights from previous shows."

I grimaced. "That could be dicey."

"You're thinking of the Petersen brothers almost coming to blows?"

"True," I said, recalling the banking family's nightmare. "And some less dramatic episodes, including Edna Mae Dalrymple getting so nervous about speaking into a microphone that she got Charles Dickens mixed up with Charles Darwin and referred to the Holy Bible as the the Boly Hibble. Not a great radio debut for our local librarian. Edna Mae almost canceled coming to bridge club the next week."

Spence stroked his chin. "Maybe Vida could recount some of the less embarrassing —"

"There she is," I interrupted, rising from my chair. "Vida?"

My House & Home editor turned quickly in my direction. "Oh! Spencer! How nice to see you," she said, walking toward us in her splayfooted manner. "Did you have a very merry Christmas?"

"Indeed I did," he replied, pulling out the other visitor's chair for Vida. "We were just talking about you."

"Well now," she said. "I hope it was positive."

"How could it not be?" Spence responded, helping Vida out of her coat. "We were discussing your plans for Thursday's show."

"I changed my mind," she said, sitting down and adjusting her glasses. "It's redundant. We're running a wrap-up in the paper. Kip and I put it together before I went to the retirement home," she added for my benefit. "I'm inviting Ben and Adam to be on my program. Afterwards they must come to supper. I found a tempting casserole in my file this morning. Shrimp, cheese, mushrooms, and . . . some other things."

"Nice," I said, hiding my horror at the thought of Vida's casseroles.

"You could join us," she offered.

"Ben and Adam would love having you to themselves," I said. *Two hours without anyone at my house, except Milo . . . or Somalian pirates or Taliban terrorists or . . . anything but Vida's casserole . . .*

"Perhaps," she declared, allowing Spence

221

to pull back the chair as she got up. "I must write cutlines for the retirement home photos. Quite ugly, but I can't help that. We won't waste color on them." She gathered up her coat and purse before heading to her desk.

Spence had followed Vida. I busied myself by going through the mail. As usual, there wasn't much of interest. After Spence left, I got up to talk to Vida, but she was headed for the back shop. Instead, I tried to focus on the cave-remains story, but I needed an ID — if there was one. Checking my watch, I saw that it was after eleven-thirty. Maybe Vida and I could take an early lunch. She had returned to her desk, but was on the phone. In fact, she never seemed to get off the phone. Just before noon, there was a lull. I hurried into the newsroom.

"How about lunch?" I inquired.

Vida shook herself, always an awesome sight. "Is it that time?" she said, glancing at her watch. "The morning has flown. I still need 'Scene' filler. Do tell me you noticed a usable item this morning. I have two iffy ones, it not being unusual for Darla Puckett to drop her purse all over the sidewalk or for Crazy Eights Neffel to talk to a lamppost."

"Did the lamppost talk back?"

Vida gave me her gimlet eye — just as her phone rang again. "Don't move," she said before picking up the receiver.

I disobeyed, but only went as far as Leo's desk. Watching my House & Home editor purse her lips and run an agitated hand through her unruly gray curls kept me occupied, though listening to her end of the conversation piqued my curiosity.

"No, no," she was saying after a lull on her part, "I won't use that, Ione. Second-hand sightings are unacceptable. But I will pick up those sale items by tomorrow. We have a deadline here, you know."

Vida hung up. For one fearsome moment, I was afraid she was going to attack her eyeballs. "Ohh! People are ninnies!" She practically bolted out of her chair. "Let's leave now. The Venison Inn?"

"Sure," I agreed, heading back to get my jacket and purse.

By the time I reached the front office, Vida was waiting for me outside. Alison was still on duty, taking a call and rolling her eyes. I didn't want to know what the caller was saying, so I made my exit.

Once I joined my House & Home editor, I put her on the spot as we walked the half block to the VI. "What kind of sale items did you buy at kIds cOrNEr?" I asked, referring to the store with a logo that spelled owner Ione Erdahl's first name in caps.

"Clothing," Vida said — and suddenly became tight-lipped.

"He must be growing fast," I remarked.

"Emma," she said so low that I barely heard her, "please don't vex me with questions about Diddy. The subject distresses me to no end."

I assumed "Diddy" was the nickname for the child that Roger had fathered with the town hooker. I'd heard Vida mention the name before. We'd arrived at the restaurant, so I had to drop the subject.

Vida was dismayed when we went inside. "No window tables? We should have started earlier." She stalked off to a vacant booth halfway down the aisle, slowing her pace only to acknowledge some of the locals. I was conscious of stares, whispers, and a few snickers.

"What is it?" I demanded in an irritated voice.

Vida was unmoved. "I warned you. What do you expect?" She opened the menu, seemingly engrossed in studying the Tuesday specials.

I glanced across the aisle, where Lloyd Campbell, owner of Alpine Appliance, was with a man who looked like a sales rep. They were the only other diners I could see from my vantage point. "What," I asked, "is it about Milo and me being a couple that's odd? A long time ago, we were together for a year and a half. I don't recall any big fuss then."

At first, Vida didn't seem inclined to respond, but she finally put the menu aside. "Long before you two became intimate, there was buzz about you despite Milo having a girlfriend in Startup."

I kept a straight face. Honoria Whitman and the sheriff had been an item for several years, but perhaps no one in town believed it could be serious because she didn't live in Alpine.

"You and Milo spent a great deal of time together," Vida went on. "After Honoria moved away, you became romantically involved. Everyone thought you were going to marry him. People kept asking me why there wasn't an announcement in the paper. What could I say? For all I knew, that was imminent. I never pry."

This time, it was hard to keep from laughing. Before I could do or say anything, a dark-haired waitress named Nicole came to our booth. "Hi, Aunt Vida," she said in a chipper voice. "Skip the specials," she continued in a whisper. "They're leftovers

225

from the weekend."

"I wondered," Vida murmured. "I'm back on my diet. Christmas — so fat-making. I'll have the chicken salad with a dab of honey mustard dressing. The roll comes with it, correct?" Nicole nodded. "A bit of extra butter, though, as the rolls are often dry. Oh! I noticed something about crinkle fries. Are they new?"

Nicole shook her head. "The kitchen crew didn't know how to use up the leftover potatoes from the holiday. They're not bad. Very crisp."

"Hmm." Vida mulled briefly. "Oh, why not? If they're crisp, they can't be fattening. And hot tea, of course, dear."

I asked for fish and chips, a side salad with Roquefort dressing, and a vanilla malt. "Nicole is . . . ?" I said after our waitress left us.

"A Gustavson," Vida replied. "She started work in early December. A relation by marriage, but she's always called me 'Aunt.' Goodness, I can hardly keep track of all my relatives sometimes."

"I sure can't," I admitted. "As you were saying . . ."

"Where was I?

"Not prying."

"Oh, of course." Vida adjusted her hat

226

with its pinecones. "It's not difficult to understand. After you broke up with Milo, Tommy came to town. An engagement was imminent — but not to the sheriff. Naturally, people in Alpine found that . . . strange." Apparently expecting me to explode, she held up a hand. "No one knew Tommy. He embodied so much that's foreign to Alpiners. A big-city, big-business type. How could he have fit in? Many felt he wouldn't try. He'd buy the paper and whisk you off to San Francisco, putting a California sharpie in charge of our *Advocate*." She paused while Nicole brought our beverages.

I waited for Vida's shirttail relation to leave. "As you may recall," I said, "where we'd live was almost a deal-breaker for me. But Milo felt it was unfair that I got stuck with that decision and told me to dump it in Tom's lap."

Vida was startled. "Milo did that? I didn't know. Had he gone insane? Did he know how crucial it was for you?"

Milo had been sane — and sensible. I'd taken his advice. "Maybe he was being noble."

Vida sniffed. "More likely he felt Tommy would run like a deer."

"I don't think —"

227

She waved an impatient hand. "Never mind. I'm just surprised. Let me finish what I'm saying about now, not then. Oh — here's our food."

Nicole set our orders on the table. "Anything else?" she asked.

Vida studied the dab of dressing. "Oh, dear. I forgot how much lettuce came with this. Could you bring a bit more honey mustard? Not one of those little cups — the small boat should be about right."

"Sure, Aunt Vida," Nicole said, and went on her way.

"So skimpy," Vida murmured. "Oh, well." She shook salt and pepper onto the salad before tasting a crinkle fry. "Mmm. Rather tasty." She added salt to the fries as well. "Anyway, what upset everyone was Tommy getting himself killed during the Summer Solstice parade."

I gaped at Vida. "That didn't upset *me?* I almost lost my mind!"

She put a finger to her lips. "Lloyd can hear you."

"So what?" I muttered.

"You must admit," Vida went on, "it ruined the town's big event that summer. But that's not why people are making a fuss now. They consider you fickle. You're still an outsider. Milo belongs to us. As our sheriff, he symbolizes the law and all its virtues. He can be pigheaded, even obtuse — or pretend to be — on occasion. But except for a few critics, Milo is admired and respected. We don't want him making a fool of himself over a woman who may discard him on a whim."

" 'We'?" I said bleakly.

"Yes. *We*." Vida's gray eyes were hard as granite.

Nicole brought the boatload of honey mustard dressing. Neither her aunt nor I spoke until she was gone.

"Vida . . . ," I finally said weakly. "Do you think I'd do that?"

"You already did it once."

"I was . . . stupid."

"That's the thing about stupidity," she said. "People don't realize they're being stupid when they're being stupid."

I'd eaten only some of my fish and chips and almost none of my salad. I'd lost my appetite. "I won't be stupid again."

"I hope not." She slathered more dressing onto her lettuce. "For now, you and Milo must behave properly. I've heard everything from a mere kiss to shocking activities in the sheriff's locked office."

"That is not true!"

"I thought not." She frowned. "I hope Ben

and Adam don't hear the gossip. It could be harmful. You Catholics are a minority."

"They're grown-ups," I said. "And they don't have to live here."

"A good thing," Vida remarked, and made a face. "That is, for *them*. I truly feel sorry for people who don't live in Alpine."

I felt sorry for Milo and me. "Is this lecture over?" I asked bleakly.

"You wanted to hear what's being said. After all these years, you know the grapevine is active and sometimes hurtful."

"Right. Let's move on. We have a paper to put out." I told Vida more about the body in the cave. I did not, however, mention the Saint Augustine medal. I also brought up Don Krogstad's call about his father and Mrs. Everson. For once, Vida didn't pounce on gossip.

"Harold Krogstad was an unlikely man for an affair," she asserted. "I recall some tongue-wagging, but Myrtle had a property dispute going on after her husband died. Perhaps Harold thought a picnic would be a pleasant way to discuss his ruling."

"For or against her?"

"Against her," Vida replied. "That's why he may have wanted to soften the blow with an outing. He ruled in favor of the county. It's that property by the dump site. Myrtle thought it belonged to her, but it had been abandoned by previous owners and reverted to SkyCo."

It was pointless to argue. At a quarter to one, we left the VI. A few more snickers and stares followed in our wake. It occurred to me that maybe some of them had been directed at Vida. Trying to hide an illegitimate grandchild in plain sight was harder to do than putting up with gossip about a middle-aged couple playing kissy-face in public.

The sheriff called around two. "According to Bob Starr," Milo said, "the dental records match Gus. I called Pete first. The poor bastard lost it. A full autopsy won't be ready until Friday, if then. Too many people hang on through Christmas before they croak. SnoCo's backed up."

"You can't pinpoint time of death?"

"We can come close, because Pete knows when Gus disappeared. Although the fact that he didn't notify us at the time really pisses me off."

It was pointless to bring up the medal yet. My worst fears about Troy depended on the timing of his previous escape. "He did tell Jack."

"Damn!" the sheriff exploded. "Mullins

231

never told me. Do I have to kick his ass again?"

"Why not? I hear you've been in a good mood lately. If you stay that way, nobody will recognize you."

"If you don't lose those priests, I won't need Mullins to kick around. Hang up before I go down the street and cart you off over my shoulder."

"Can't do that. I have a deadline. Bye, Sheriff." I clicked off.

"Well?" Vida was standing in the doorway.

I relayed what Milo had told me about Gus.

She shook her head. "He was the baby. Spoiled and not very bright. Polly was a doting mother, especially after she was widowed."

Vida's imposing form almost filled the doorway, but I saw Leo and Ed Bronsky enter the newsroom. "Oh, no," I murmured, "here's Ed!"

Vida turned grim as Ed kept coming toward us after Leo went to his desk. "Well?" she said, not budging, "why are you so overwrought?"

"Gotta sit," Ed gasped, trying to figure out how to circumvent his former co-worker. "Come on, Vida, move. I'm weak at the knees."

"And the head," she snapped. "Why are you panting?"

"I'm hyperventilating," Ed said, clutching at his throat. "Please."

"Oh, very well," Vida said, heading back into the newsroom.

Ed collapsed in a visitor's chair, which creaked in protest. "Written your editorial already?" he asked, still red-faced and short of breath.

"Yes," I said. "Why?"

It took Ed a few moments to compose himself. "Alfred Cobb isn't in his grave yet and his county commissioner job has already been filled. How unfair is that? It's not Lori, it's her dad, Myron. He's retired, he's at least seventy. We need fresh blood, someone younger and rarin' to go, like me. I got ideas!"

A few stinging retorts came to me, but I stifled them. "It's official?"

Ed frowned. "It can't be, not until the next meeting." He glanced at my Sky Dairy calendar on the wall. "You still got this year's up there. When will they meet?"

"The same night they always do," I said calmly.

Ed scratched at his bald spot. "Yeah . . . well, they keep changing it . . . Last month,

I mean this month, it was the first Monday, right?"

"Tuesday," I said.

"So it's the . . . ?"

I gave Ed a chance to redeem himself. He couldn't. "Tuesday, fourth of January," I finally revealed.

"A whole week," he murmured. His high color had subsided and his breathing had become more regular. "Then you can do it. Twice."

"Do what, Ed?"

He scooted closer to the desk. I winced as the wooden chair legs squeaked again. "A one-two punch. Back-to-back editorials about why Myron Cobb isn't as qualified as me."

"I don't know that. Given Alf's inability to focus in recent years, Myron probably helped keep his dad on track with the county agenda." Seeing Ed about to argue, I went on. "A second editorial would come out *after* the meeting. Did you forget, Wednesday is our pub day?"

"Oh." Ed fell back in the chair. "Well. You know me — always thinking deadline. Always have. And that's Tuesday."

"There's nothing official about this," I said. "Until Myron tells me he's taking his father's place, I can't print it. It makes sense for him to fill the vacancy until the election a year from this coming fall."

"They could call a special election."

"They could, but that costs money, and the county is strapped."

Ed grew thoughtful. "Maybe if I talk to the other commissioners, Hollenberg and Engebretsen, they'll realize Myron isn't the right pick."

"Go ahead," I said.

Ed's eyes widened so I could see them instead of the usual squint in his pudgy face. "You agree to me being the better choice?"

"I keep an open mind."

He bounced in the chair. "How can you —" The chair collapsed. Ed disappeared except for his feet. He let out a series of howls that brought Vida and Leo rushing to my office. I tried not to laugh.

Arms folded across her jutting bosom, Vida studied Ed's writhing body. "Oh, settle down!" she admonished. "Do we need an ambulance?"

Ed moaned something that sounded like "Sure." Leo sighed and got out his cell, mouthing what looked like "forklift" to me. My current ad manager then turned his back to summon help.

Vida shook her head. "Oh, stop making so much noise! You broke Emma's chair." She reached over him to grasp the back and seat. All four legs must have been under Ed, who was still moaning, "Sure, sure, sure."

"At least," Vida said, "I have another item for 'Scene.' "

Leo had finished his phone call. Ed had gotten a grip on the desk and was pulling himself up. He'd stopped yelling, but was still gasping. "Don't . . . need . . . ambulance," he huffed, his chins resting on the top of my desk. "Want . . . Shirl . . . *Shirley* . . ."

"Too late to call your wife," Leo said. "The medics are on their way. We'll get hold of her once you're safely out of here."

Vida had gone into the newsroom, where she placed the chair pieces by the door to the back shop. Alison was halfway to my cubbyhole, eyes wide. "What happened?" she asked.

"Ed had an accident," Leo said. "The ambulance is coming."

"Oh!" Alison exclaimed. "I'll open the door."

Ed got to his knees. "I'm fine. Just kind of banged up."

"Stay put," I said. "Let the medics check you over. I'll get out of the way in case they have to move my desk." I didn't want Ed to sue me. Grabbing my purse and jacket, I hoped to avoid the dismal sight of the medics trying to deal with my ex–ad manager.

"Fool," Vida said, standing by Mitch's desk. "What did he want?"

"Alfred Cobb's job," I said under my breath.

She shook her head. "Heaven help us."

I heard the medics arrive. Feeling confident that Vida, Leo, and Alison could handle Ed's removal, I decided to sneak out the back way. Before I could reach the door, I almost ran into Kip.

"Where'd those sirens go?" he asked. "They sound really close."

"See for yourself. It's not one of us, it's Ed." I kept going.

Once outside, I contemplated what to do. A replacement chair was necessary, not new but secondhand. The broken one — along with its mate, which was also rickety — was from the Marius Vandeventer era. My first thought was Goodwill, but a freight train had stopped, cutting me off from the store on River Road. My next choice was the antique shop in the Clemans Building. I rarely went there, but I'd seen some chairs in the window recently. I headed along Fourth to Front Street and was at the corner when I saw Milo hurrying toward me.

"Emma!" he shouted. "Wait up!"

I stopped. Maybe he had something news-worthy to tell me.

"Jesus," he said, grabbing my arm. "What the hell's going on at your place? I thought maybe you finally had broken your neck."

I laughed. "I'm fine. Ed broke my chair and fell on his butt."

The sheriff laughed, too. "So you ran away?"

I shrugged. "I can't work while they try to wedge him onto a gurney. Besides, I have to buy a new chair. Or two."

"I've got a couple of old ones in my base-ment that Mulehide never liked. Want to check them out?"

"Milo . . ."

"Not now," he said, "but before you throw your money around." He put his arm around me. "Let's see if Ed's still alive. This could be fun."

"Aren't you supposed to be solving cases and arresting perps?"

"I just did," he said as we neared the *Advocate* office. "Remember the three houses in The Pines that had their Christ-mas presents stolen from under their trees? When I left Overholts' farm after taking Rudolph into custody, I saw some pieces of gift paper on the side of the road on Fir, and then more and more of them, leading from the high school in a straight line to The Pines. The wraps stopped just past your house. Guess who?"

"My rotten Nelson neighbor kids?"

"The younger two. You hoped they'd get busted. So I busted them." He paused as medic Vic Thorstensen appeared on the sidewalk.

"Hey, guys, I'm good!" Ed yelled. Only his lower half could be seen as the gurney came through the door. "I'm one tough customer," he insisted as his head appeared with medic Tony Lynch at the other end.

"Easy, Ed," Vic said. "It never hurts to get checked out."

Ed turned enough to see Milo and me. "Emma! Where'd you go?"

"To buy another chair," I said.

"Hey, hey," Ed said as the medics took deep breaths before loading him into the ambulance, "I've got some great stuff from the villa in storage. I'll give you a real deal on some chairs . . . and a bed. Oof! Careful, fellas," he said to the medics. "That jarred me."

"I'd like to jar Ed," Milo grumbled. "Why can't people shut up?"

"Ed isn't people," I murmured. "He's Ed. Ignore him."

"Let's get out of here," Milo said, making a quick surveillance of Front Street. "Damn! There's about forty people gawking."

"You want to call for crowd control?"

Milo's eyes narrowed at the onlookers. "Hell, no," he said as Ed was loaded into the ambulance. "Let's give them something to talk about." He picked me up and carried me into the *Advocate*. "Hi, Alison. I found this baggage on the street. Where shall I put her?"

"Uh . . ." Alison seemed torn between titillation and shock.

"Never mind," Milo said. "I'll put her in her place — her office." He strode into the newsroom, where Vida, Leo, and Kip were goggle-eyed. The sheriff ignored them and kept going until we reached my cubbyhole. "Dare me to close the door," he said, his face almost touching mine.

"No. Please?"

I felt him shrug before he set me on my feet. "See you later, Emma." He left the building without another word.

TEN

Vida couldn't have moved faster if she'd been wearing a jet pack. "That," she shrieked, "is what I warned you about! How could you? How could Milo? Oooh . . ." Collapsing in the remaining visitor's chair, she yanked off her glasses and rubbed her eyes with unbridled fury.

I took off my jacket and assumed my place behind the desk. "What am I supposed to do? I can't stop him. Milo is . . . I mean . . ." I didn't know what I meant. I cringed at the noise she was making. "Stop!" I yelled.

I endured four more squeaks before Vida dropped her hands and gazed at me with bleary eyes. "What would you say if Buck and I acted like that in the middle of Front Street?"

Did Vida and Buck act like that when they *weren't* in the middle of Front Street? "Uh . . . well . . . your hat might fall off."

"Emma!" Vida seemed to be having

trouble putting her glasses back on. Maybe she was thinking about the same thing.

"Let's get back to business," I said. "Milo arrested my neighbor's kids for those burglaries before Christmas. Damn — I mean, *darn.* We can't use their names because they're juveniles."

"*They're* juveniles?" Vida said with more than a touch of asperity.

"Okay," I said, "why don't you call the sheriff and get the details? He picked them up this morning. Or this afternoon. Or sometime . . ."

She wagged her finger. "You see? Neither of you is focused."

"I just found out. It won't be logged yet, but we can still use it."

"Oh . . . I'll call Billy. My nephew's not a disgrace to his uniform." She rose from her seat with great dignity. "You must get a replacement. These chairs go back to the Depression. They were old long before I went to work for the *Advocate.*" She made her exit.

My phone rang. I managed to pick up the receiver without dropping it on the floor.

"Mom!" Adam cried. "You're okay?"

"Of course," I replied. "Dare I ask why you're asking?"

"Uncle Ben and I just got back from

lunch. Mimi Barton came along with the rest of her family, so we drove her to and from the rectory," he continued, referring to the parish secretary. "Betsy O'Toole called to say she'd come out of the bank and there was an ambulance in front of the *Advocate*. Uncle Ben and I are worried. What happened?"

I briefly explained Ed's mini-disaster. "I doubt much is wrong with him since he's so well padded, but he did seem short of breath and not himself when he came to see me."

"Oh," Adam said. "Ed. So did he fall on top of you?"

"No," I replied, puzzled. "I was safely ensconced behind my desk."

"Then how come Dodge was carrying you into your office?"

Oh, double damn! How could I not see this coming? "I felt faint," I lied. "Ed was outrageous. I got upset and then felt guilty when he broke my chair and I went outside and I got light-headed and . . . what can I say?"

"Gosh, Mom, aren't you used to Ed by now?"

"I should be," I admitted. "I think Vida hoped he'd broken his neck. What would you and your uncle like the cook to make for dinner?"

"Lasagna," Adam replied promptly. "I haven't had yours since I was in college."

I hadn't made lasagna since. "Red or white sauce?"

"The red. Uncle Ben likes it, too. Can you put some Italian sausage in it along with the hamburger?"

"Well . . . sure, why not?" I had to stop at the Grocery Basket to get some of the other ingredients anyway. "This is deadline day, so don't plan on eating until closer to seven than to six, okay?"

"Will do. We had a big lunch. Can you pick up more dark ale?"

Alison was at my door, pointing to my phone and mouthing a single word that I realized was "Mitch."

"Yes. Got to dash." I hung up. "Line two?" I asked Alison.

"Right," she replied. "I've got Rita Patricelli holding on line three." She practically ran off through the newsroom.

Rita, I thought, Pete and Gus's prickly sister, who managed the Chamber of Commerce office. Just what I didn't need right now. I pressed line two. "Mitch? How are you?"

"Still alive," he said in a heavy, weary voice. "Troy's improving. The antibiotics must be kicking in."

244

"That's good news," I said. "It's not viral, then."

"No. Hey, I'm sorry I ran out on you. I couldn't do much else."

"No need to apologize. We're fine." I didn't want to press him about how long he'd be away. "Are you staying at a motel in Monroe?"

"We did last night," he said. "I'm not sure what to do now. Brenda's still in shock. I wonder if she shouldn't be in the hospital, too."

"Valley General is right across from Sky River Medical Center. They're both off the Highway 2 exchange by the fairgrounds."

Mitch didn't respond at once. "I'm not sure they have the kind of help Brenda needs. But thanks. I appreciate your understanding."

"No problem," I said quickly, if untruthfully. "By the way, when did Troy escape the first time?"

"Why do you need to know?" my reporter shot back.

"I just wondered," I said.

"Are you doing a big story on this mess?" He sounded angry.

"No." I was indignant. "We're running under two inches."

"Why run it at all?"

"Because SkyCo's deputies found him," I retorted. "Did you lose your professional ethics between Alpine and Monroe?"

"Sorry," he said after another pause, though hostility lingered in his voice. "But this isn't local news. It's out of SkyCo's jurisdiction."

"Oh, right. Why don't we just pretend our deputies never found Troy and he died of exposure on the banks of the Sky or got hit by a train? It's not their fault he escaped in the first place — or the second place, given his history."

Vida had heard me raise my voice and had tromped into my office. Leo was close behind her. I clutched the receiver and waited for Mitch's response. There wasn't any. It took a few seconds for me to realize that the line had gone dead. "He hung up on me," I said.

Vida gave me a reproachful look. "I can hardly blame him."

"He wanted me to ditch the story. What would you have done?"

"Not shrieked like a fishwife."

I appealed to Leo, who was shaking his head. "Mitch was violating ethics. If he'd do that now, what else might he do?"

My ad manager was standing beside Vida. "Relax, Duchess," he said in a soothing

246

tone. Then he turned to me. "Both my favorite Alpine ladies are a little strung out. At least Mitch isn't like his callow and irresponsible predecessor. Did Curtis really confess to shooting *me?*"

"He confessed to shooting everybody except Abraham Lincoln," I said in disgust. "Milo wanted to strangle the little twerp."

"Such a disaster," Vida murmured, looking vaguely contrite after her outburst. "Too many big ideas, so little brain."

"A head case," I said, "as is Brenda. Mitch is having her checked."

Vida pursed her lips. "What's wrong with her?"

"Shock?" I hedged. "Last night at the hospital she was out of it."

Vida bridled. "Didn't I say she wasn't all there? No powers of recovery. If you raise a criminal, you reap the rewards. Look at Gus, no doubt because Polly made such a fool of him when he . . ."

To my astonishment, Vida erupted into tears.

Leo put his arm around her. "Hey," he said softly, "easy, now. Want me to take you home and make a pot of tea?"

"Oh, Leo!" Vida wailed, but she didn't rebuff his embrace even as she tried to get control of herself.

He gave me a helpless look. "What do you think? It's after three. Why not give us the rest of the day off? I've finished my workload."

I threw up my hands. "Go ahead. I should leave early, too, with Ben and Adam coming to dinner. In fact, why don't you two join us? I'm making lasagna and I always have enough for a small regiment."

He gave Vida a little hug. "What do you say about that, Duchess? We've never gone on a date before. Isn't it about time?"

Vida was now down to sniffles. "I'm an old fool," she muttered, moving out of Leo's arms. "You're right. It *is* a difficult time of year."

Leo nodded. "We're supposed to be merry even if we aren't. That's rough." He put a hand on Vida's back, steering her into the newsroom. "I'll drive your Buick, then we'll go to Emma's . . ."

I didn't hear the rest. Alison buzzed me on the intercom. "Rita wants you to call her ASAP." She dropped her voice. "Is everything okay or is this just a bad dream?"

"Yes. No. Don't worry. I'll call Rita."

I was still rattled and couldn't remember the chamber's number, so I had to look it up. Rita answered on the first ring. "Finally!" she exclaimed in her usual hostile manner toward me. "You're lucky I don't pull the chamber's ad wishing every S.O.B. in Alpine Happy New Year!"

Leaning back in my chair, I wondered how much more abuse I could take in one day. "The same to you, Rita," I said. "How can I help?"

"By getting my brother's medal back to me," she snapped. "Jack won't give it up. When did he get so pious?"

"Hold it," I said. "Who told you about the medal?"

"Who do you think? It wouldn't be that brute of a sheriff you're banging. It was Jack."

I gritted my teeth. *Do not react to any remarks about Milo, no matter how vile.* "Why did Jack do that?"

Rita heaved a big sigh. "Long before I married my loser ex and Jack married Nina, we were a couple. We were together when I gave Gus the medal for his confirmation back in '84. Jack told me some BS about not finding it with Gus's body. He wouldn't show it to me, insisting it was part of another investigation. Jack's showing off. It had to be in the cave where the Krogstads found Gus. He never took it off."

I considered my response carefully. "I hate to say so, Rita, but you're mistaken. Jack found that medal in someone else's possession. I know, because I was there when he handed it over to the sheriff."

"Wow," Rita said, "Dodge lets Jack in when he's doing you? The sheriff acts like he's all business, but isn't that pushing it? So to speak?"

Do not threaten to kill Rita even if you have to put your fist in your mouth. "I can't comment further," I said stiltedly, "but it was in public."

"So? That doesn't seem to stop you and the sheriff."

Count to ten. Count to a hundred. Count yourself out. "Rita," I said, "this conversation has deteriorated. If Jack says he can't give you the medal, he can't. It has nothing to do with me. Unless," I added, going for the jugular, "you were going to ask if I'd intercede with the sheriff to get it for you. If so, forget it." I hung up.

But the call from Rita bothered me. Not because of the crude references, but because she'd raised a point about the medal I hadn't considered. Why had Jack kept the medal? What other investigation was he alluding to besides how Gus had died? Was the sheriff's office a step ahead of me in wondering why Troy had such a thing in his possession? For all his flippancy, Mullins

250

was a practicing Catholic. Unlike Milo, Jack would understand the medal's significance. He'd also be sympathetic to Rita's request — he would have honored it if he felt he could.

I was angry with myself for getting into a row with Mitch on the phone. I'd botched finding out when Troy made his first escape. Maybe Vida was right — I wasn't focused. But Mitch shouldn't have asked me to omit the story about his son's recapture. I wondered if he'd suppressed news on the *Detroit Free Press*. Nothing personal, maybe, but at the request of higher-ups or influential outsiders. I had a right to be mad at him. This was small-town Alpine, not the Motor City.

I wasn't sure where my thoughts were leading. I remembered nothing about Troy's earlier escape. Had it been in the log while Scott was still my reporter? Or had it happened after I'd hired the hapless Curtis Mayne? Curtis had been careless to the extreme. I wouldn't put it past him to have omitted an item in the log, especially during his first weeks on the job in early June.

Leo broke my musings. "Vida and I are off. What time is dinner?"

"Sevenish." I looked beyond him into the newsroom, where my House & Home editor was putting on her coat. "She's okay?"

"She's tough," Leo replied, lowering his voice. "In fact, we're each going to drive our own cars. It's Roger, isn't it?"

"Who else?" I said glumly. "She's having trouble coping with the realization that she had a hand in how he's turned out."

"Understandable," Leo said. "Hell, any scrapes my kids got into were probably my fault. See you this evening. Can I bring anything?"

"Just your newly found piety," I said. "The priests will love you."

Leo made a face. "Let's not get carried away." He made another face. "Sorry, Emma, I didn't mean . . ."

"Skip it or I'll start rumors about you and Vida."

"That might be fun," Leo said before leaving my office. He called to Vida, "Hey, Duchess, want to stop at Mugs Ahoy for a couple of tall cool ones?"

"Really, Leo, you are a wretched person. Why am I letting you come home with me?"

"Because I've never met your canary," Leo replied. "What's the bird's name? Beefcake?"

"Leo! Of course not. It's Cupcake, as you know perfectly . . ."

Their voices followed them out of the

newsroom. I stared at my monitor. The same two paragraphs about Gus stared back. I had to finish the story. I called the sheriff's office. Bill Blatt answered.

"The boss man's not here," he informed me. "We got a pair of belligerent out-of-towners at the ski lodge who got into a fight over a fender bender. Dodge and Mullins went up there to straighten them out. Is there anything I can do?"

I asked if he'd talked to his aunt recently about the Patricelli story.

"I did," he replied, "but I couldn't tell her when the funeral would be since we don't know when the remains will be released by SnoCo."

"I mean the case itself," I said. "I have to finish the story for the paper and I'm stuck. Can I say foul play hasn't been ruled out?"

"Gosh," Bill said, "I can't be quoted on that. Ask the boss. He should be back here by four, four-fifteen."

"Did you find out from Pete or anybody else in the family exactly when Gus disappeared?"

"Not yet. I guess his disappearance was never reported. Do you want me to check the log?"

I started to say no, since Jack had kept that bit of vital information to himself. But

I switched gears. "Don't bother doing that, but could you take a look back into May or early June to see if there's anything on Troy Laskey's first escape?"

"Troy . . . oh, you mean Mitch's son? I can check for you. Wouldn't you have had it in the paper?"

"Do you remember Curtis Mayne?"

"Who?" Bill seemed to be having a case of the dumbs, not that I could blame him. Curtis's tenure with the *Advocate* had been brief. I preferred forgetting him, too.

"That reporter I hired last June," I said.

"Oh, *that* guy," Bill said, and chuckled. "Man, he was a piece of work. Hold on. In fact, can I call you back? It may take me a while."

"Sure. Just try to get back to me before four-thirty, okay?"

"Will do," Bill promised, and hung up.

The phone rang just as I'd put it back in place. "Oh, Emma," Shirley Bronsky exclaimed, "what did you do to Ed? He's a mess!"

This was not news. "Did he break something besides my chair?"

"Ed almost had a stroke," Shirley replied, her voice quivering. "His blood pressure is out of sight. What did you say that set him off?"

"Nothing," I asserted. "He was red in the face and breathing hard when he came to my office. That's one of the reasons Leo called for help. Do you know where he'd gone before he arrived here?"

"Leo!" Shirley cried. "He's not half the man Ed is!"

That was unarguable. Not even a third, given Ed's girth. "Please calm down," I said sharply. "Ed was upset after he heard that Myron Cobb is taking his father's place. It set him off before he got here."

"How dare Myron!" Shirley cried. "He has no qualifications!"

I didn't want to argue with Shirley. "Never mind. How is Ed?"

"He has to stay overnight so Doc Dewey can make sure he hasn't had a stroke," Shirley replied glumly. "It's a good thing we've got medical coverage through the schools since I began substitute teaching."

I glanced at my watch. It was after three-thirty. "Ed didn't seem in any serious distress when he left here. You've seen him, right?"

"Of course not," she snapped. "We only have one car now. He took it with him. I'm stuck here on the river by the fish hatchery." She paused, and when she spoke again, her tone morphed into a whine. "Do you have time to come get me so I can pick up the only Mercedes we have left and go see Ed? He parked by the courthouse."

"We're up against deadline. You remember what that's like."

"Oh . . . yes, Ed was so keen on getting his ads in on time. All those years of dealing with advertisers took its toll."

The bells had tolled for me during Ed's tenure, wondering if I could make payroll. An evil brainstorm struck me. "I'll call the rectory. Ben and Adam rented cars. Maybe one of them can get you. How's that?"

"Oh, you're a darling! Ed always said you had a heart of gold."

My heart might have been gold, but the *Advocate* account was dross while Ed was aboard. I told Shirley I'd do my best and rang off.

Mimi Barton answered the phone at St. Mildred's. "Hi," I said, "this is Emma. Is one of your temporary priests available or are they both shooting pool at the Icicle Creek Tavern?"

"Father Ben is with the Patricellis," Mimi replied, in hushed tones befitting a devout spinster speaking about a bereaved family. "I believe Father Adam is with them, too. This is not a good time, Ms. Lord."

Feeling chastised, I agreed. "Okay. I was

inquiring on behalf of another parishioner who's in the hospital. Never mind."

"Wait," Mimi said, a bit more life in her voice. "Who is it?"

"Ed Bronsky," I replied. "I thought Adam might've told you."

"No. They've been busy. It's wonderful to have two priests here."

"I'm sure it is," I said. "Ed will be hospitalized overnight, in case one of your gypsy priests would like to see him. The doctors thought it might be a stroke. Shirley has no car. Thanks, Mimi. Bye-bye."

I felt a tinge of guilt after hanging up, but knew she'd relay the message. If the Bronskys hadn't been so foolish spending their money on monstrosities like Casa de Bronska and matching fur coats and faux-antique furniture, they wouldn't be in such a mess.

Kip was in my doorway. "How much is still coming?" he asked.

"The Gus story," I said. "I'm waiting on Bill Blatt."

"How many inches?"

"Four, five. Pete didn't give me Gus's photo. Do we have one?"

Kip made a face. "Not unless it was on a Wanted poster. Gus never married or got engaged. How old is he? We might have a high school photo in the Bucker annuals."

"Mid-thirties," I said, "so figure circa 1986?"

"I'll check. I could scan it. Anything else?"

"Oh, damn! Did Vida turn in something about the Nelson kids who stole the Christmas presents last week from the houses in The Pines?"

Kip nodded. "She zapped it to me before she left with Leo. What was up with that?"

"Vida had a minor meltdown. Leo played Good Samaritan."

Kip grimaced. "Roger?"

"Who else?"

"That kid's a train wreck," Kip said. "Any word from Ginny?"

"No. Oh — there's a dustup at the ski lodge parking lot between some out-of-towners. Dodge and Mullins were checking it out. I'll ask Bill about that. He's supposed to call me on something else anyway."

"Let me know." Kip went off to perform his assorted tasks.

I added some fluff to Gus's story, hoping he'd done something in high school besides dozing off in class. I omitted his work history, but noted he'd lived outside of Alpine for a while. I felt guilty tiptoeing around the Patricelli family honor, but at least I wasn't deep-sixing the story as Mitch had insisted I should do with his son's misadventures.

Kip reappeared. "Got it," he said, clutching a Bucker annual. "Class of '87, played baseball, sang in the choir, favorite hobby was photography, nickname was Sug."

"Thanks," I said just as the phone rang.

"Hi," Bill said, sounding frazzled. "I found the log, June 10, APB put out for Troy Laskey. No follow-up."

"Damn Curtis! Okay. Troy was recaptured within a couple of days near Sultan. You wouldn't have that, since it didn't happen in SnoCo."

"Right. Got to go. All hell's breaking loose." Bill hung up.

What now? I wondered. I buzzed Kip to tell him I was leaving for possible breaking news. On my way out, I relayed the same message to Alison. I reached the corner before I realized Bill wasn't kidding. Jack was hauling a cuffed man out of his squad car. Milo's Cherokee was parked, so I assumed the sheriff was inside. I cursed myself for not bringing a camera. Not that I could take decent pictures, but something was better than nothing.

"Beat it, Emma," Jack yelled at me, shoving the perp toward the entrance to headquarters.

I stopped some twenty feet away and waited for the deputy to take his prisoner

259

inside. I could only see unruly brown hair, a red shell jacket, and black cargo pants. As Jack disappeared, I got out my cell to call Kip. "Quick, bring a camera to the sheriff's. We might get a perp picture. Duck inside and click. The deputies may be hostile."

"Gotcha," Kip said.

I strolled to the entrance, but stayed outside. There were barred windows in the double doors. I could make out Jack, still grappling with his prey, but he soon moved out of sight. I saw Bill behind the counter and half of somebody else — Doe Jamison, maybe.

Kip came running down the street, coatless, defying the cold, heavy rain, a small-town journalism hero. I opened the door and stepped aside, leaning flat against the wall under the entrance's overhang. A volley of voices erupted inside. I tried to hear Milo's among them, but couldn't. Jack was cussing too loud. Kip dashed back out, grinning.

"Got a good one of Mullins," he said, breathless. "He had the guy by the hair and was pushing him back to the interrogation room."

"You get an extra bonus when I hand them out on Friday," I said. "Go back to the office before you get pneumonia. I'll take it from here."

He didn't need coaxing, though he slowed to a trot as he returned to the *Advocate* office.

When I went inside the sheriff's headquarters, the reception area was fairly quiet. Bill was talking to Doe while Sam listened to somebody on the phone. The action had moved elsewhere. Bill was the first to notice my arrival.

"Emma! Was that Kip?"

"What? I didn't see anybody. What's going on?"

Sam handed the phone to Doe, joining Bill behind the counter. "Why don't you and MacDuff stay where you belong?" he grumbled.

"We belong where there's news," I said calmly. "Who got busted?"

Sam swore under his breath. "Don't ask me. I only work here."

Bill ran a finger under his regulation collar. "No IDs yet."

I leaned an elbow on the counter. "Two arrests?"

Bill and Sam exchanged looks. "Maybe," Bill finally said. "They were both cuffed. The younger guy's got a head injury."

Sam punched Bill's arm. "Shut the hell up, Blatt! This isn't your goddamned

261

mouthy aunt!"

"Hey . . . ," Bill said, but stopped. "Okay. I'll zip it."

"All I want to know is what started the fracas," I said. "Well?"

The deputies exchanged looks.

"No," Bill said.

"Nope," Sam said.

Doe was off the phone. "Oh, can it, you two!" she growled in her husky voice. "Emma's doing her job. Why don't you both do yours?"

Sam started to argue, but Bill grabbed him by the sleeve. "Doe's right. Let's finish our paperwork."

Doe leaned on the counter and rolled her dark eyes. "Men."

"I gather a fender bender started this. I assume it escalated."

"It sure did. The first guy was some city dude who —"

Jack interrupted. "Anybody know where I can find an ice bag?"

Doe barely looked at Jack. "Try the fridge in the break room."

"Oh. I forgot. I've got a headache. Is there more than one? The young perp needs one, too."

"Probably," Doe said. "If not, get ice and a towel — for you."

262

Jack disappeared again.

"Sometimes," she murmured, "I feel like I'm these jerks' mother."

I nodded. Doe was the youngest deputy, but despite a tough exterior, she exuded compassion and a special wisdom I attributed to her Muckleshoot ancestry. Since she was the only woman with a badge, the other deputies often gave her a bad time. But they respected her — as I did.

"Anyway," she went on, "when the city dude left the lodge, the other guy was parking his truck next to him, and scraped the Escalade. They got into it and a fight broke out. Henry Bardeen called us. We don't know what happened next except that they both got busted."

"Dare I ask how the younger guy's head got injured?"

"I'm not sure," she admitted. "In the fight, I suppose."

"Any names?"

"Not yet. Dodge got here just ahead of Jack."

Milo suddenly appeared. "Doe, go —" He saw me and stopped. "Hi, Emma." He turned to Doe. "Go confiscate the damned weapon."

"What weapon?" she asked.

"The freaking snowboard. What else?" He

wheeled around and returned to wherever he'd been.

"How would I know that?" Doe muttered, collecting her jacket and hat. "Sorry, Emma, got to head to the lodge. Is it safe to leave you with those two?" she asked, jerking her thumb at Bill and Sam.

I was pressed for time. "I'm leaving," I said, joining her at the door.

"Emma," she said as we reached the sidewalk, "I want to say something. It's . . . personal."

I put the hood over my head. "Go ahead. You can't annoy me."

She nodded. "You know how much I respect and admire Dodge," she said, looking embarrassed. "I'm glad for you both. I came on board two years ago, so I wasn't here when you broke up. I've heard stories about how miserable he was and how rough it was to work for him back then. It was to his credit that he pulled himself together and nobody quit. I figured you must be a real bitch to do that to him. Then I got to know you and changed my mind. Now you're both happy. Kind of goofy, but happy." She bit her lip. "Sorry. I shouldn't have said that."

I looked up into the glowering gray clouds and the endless rain. "I always thought I was a bit smarter and a lot quicker, but I was wrong. Milo was way ahead of me a long time ago."

Doe smiled. "What matters is that you caught up with him."

I felt my mouth twitch. "Maybe it's that he never let me go."

ELEVEN

"Okay," Milo said on the phone a half hour later. "I've got what you wanted from me."

"Gosh. You read my mind."

"Shut up. I'm tired. Wait — you still stuck with the priests?"

"Yes — and Vida and Leo. They're all coming for dinner."

"Shit. Hey — why can't I come?"

"Uh . . . do you like lasagna? I've never seen you eat it."

"Restaurants don't serve it in a microwavable box. Well?"

"Why not?"

"What time?"

"Seven? Your perps made me late and Ben's taking Shirley Bronsky to see Ed at the hospital."

"He's still alive?"

"Yes. High blood pressure. Big surprise. *Really* big, being Ed."

"Ed." I heard Milo sigh. "Okay. Charles G.

Andrews, forty-six, Seattle attorney, owner of a Cadillac Escalade, in town on business, staying at the ski lodge. Claims to be the innocent victim of having his high-end rear end and side of vehicle damaged by a custom Chevy Ram truck driven by Todd 'Turk' Durgan, twenty-seven, Everett software designer and snowboarder. Both charged with vehicular and bodily assault as well as disorderly conduct, bail set at five grand apiece, plus medical expenses for Andrews's assault on Durgan with Durgan's snowboard and two grand for the snowboard itself after Andrews purposely drove over it with his Escalade. Both set free on their own recognizance after posting bail."

"Wow," I said, scribbling furiously to keep up, "was that as much fun for you as it was for them?"

"They deserve each other," Milo said. "They're a couple of rich, self-centered bastards. I kind of enjoyed subduing the big-city suit. Jack had a little more trouble with the software snowboard dude."

Something niggled at my brain, but I couldn't pinpoint it. "Any idea why this well-heeled attorney was here?"

"Why do you ask?"

"Do I have to tell you?"

"No, I can guess, and I don't know why

he's in town and I don't give a shit. Hang up, Emma, or you won't serve dinner until ten." Milo rang off, leaving me with an unasked question. I called him back.

"What now?" he asked, sounding exasperated.

"Knock it off, big guy. Your browbeaten deputy, Bill, won't let me quote him saying foul play can't be ruled out in Gus's death. Well?"

"I doubt it was suicide."

"Accident?"

"Hell, say what you want. I can't even rule out Gus starving himself to death. He always was kind of pudgy."

"Can I say that?"

Milo hung up on me — again. Madly in love or not, some things never changed. The only difference was that I wasn't infuriated. Thus, I duly wrote that "Sheriff Milo Dodge could not confirm the cause of Patricelli's death until a full autopsy is concluded in Everett. However, Dodge did not rule out foul play or an accident."

I zapped the story to Kip. Then I wrote three inches about the arrests of Mr. Escalade and Mr. Pickup. It was five-ten by the time I finished. Alison had already bid me good night. I found Kip in the back shop, where he showed me the photo he'd taken at the sheriff's office.

"Do you think Mullins will kill me?" he asked.

"It's news," I said.

"Four by four? Maybe two by two. The story's short."

"Hey," Kip protested, "it's my first picture. I risked my life for it."

"Jack won't like you showing him grab the perp by his hair," I pointed out. "He'll worry about police brutality. Look at the copy I sent you. If you think I can add anything, *maybe* we can go four columns."

Kip went to his monitor. "Whoa!" he exclaimed. "Turk Durgan!"

"You know this guy?"

"Who doesn't?" Kip retorted, his expression awestruck.

"How about me — and apparently the sheriff?"

"That's because you and Dodge are old . . . *er.* You aren't into snowboards. Turk's world-class. He's big with gamers, too, awesome snowboarding ones. He's headed for the 2006 Winter Olympics."

"Great. To think I was worried about the big-shot Seattle lawyer."

"What a jackass," Kip said, shaking his head. "He trashed Turk's snowboard? Dodge should've put him in solitary confinement for that."

"There's no such thing in SkyCo," I reminded Kip. "The worst torture is listening to Dwight bitch about women. Have you met Turk?"

"No, but I've seen him at the pass and last year when I went skiing at Schweitzer in Idaho. Awesome." Kip frowned. "I only saw his backside when Mullins was busting him. I wonder why he's here. There hasn't been much good snow until now for a guy like him. Got a cutline?"

"Yes," I replied. "Look below the story. It IDs Jack and the perp. That is, the world-class Olympic snowboarder. But we won't say that."

Kip fingered his chin. "Everybody will know who he is."

"Except us old folks," I remarked.

"Sorry about that, Emma. Really."

"Forget it. I wish we'd known he was here. It'd make a good story. Too late now, unless . . ." I stared at Kip. "Have you ever considered writing a story or doing an interview? Turk may still be in town."

"His snowboard's ruined. But he'll need a new one now that the pass reopened." His face lit up. "Are you serious? I don't know about writing, but I can ask good questions. You could help me."

I considered the pros and cons, given Turk's arrest. "Call Henry Bardeen to see if Durgan's still at the lodge. We'll take it from there."

Kip's face flushed with excitement. "So we go with the bigger pic?"

I grimaced. "No. That's pushing it. Show me the one of Gus."

Kip zeroed in on the typical high school headshot. Augustine Patricelli bore a faint resemblance to Pete. Gus's round face was almost cherubic. What struck me was that the high school senior had no idea he'd never live to see his twentieth Bucker reunion.

"I'm off to grocery-shop," I said, patting Kip's arm. "Call if you need me. I'll be home playing hostess."

"Good luck with that," he murmured.

I didn't admit I'd need it, but at least I got lucky at the Grocery Basket. They were busy with the after-work crowd, so none of the O'Tooles had time to chat. Like me, the other shoppers were operating in a post-holiday fog, absorbed in restocking their larders. I moved along quickly, but it still took twenty minutes before I reached the checkout stand. I barely recognized the elderly couple and the middle-aged woman ahead of me. I had no idea who got in line behind me. I kept my hood up to avoid being recognized and escaped without getting hassled, annoyed, or vilified.

By six-twenty, I had the lasagna in the oven, two loaves of French bread ready for warming up later, and was making a big romaine salad. I was adding the radishes and tomatoes when the doorbell rang.

"Why," the sheriff inquired, kicking the door closed behind him, "don't you get me a key? You're a mess. You've got some kind of slop on your front."

I looked down at my bosom. "It's tomato, I think. You're early."

"I figured you might need some help. And I need a drink." He headed for the kitchen. "You want one?"

"Yes," I said, trailing after him. "Guess what. You don't need a key. You don't live here."

Milo set the liquor bottles on the counter. "Give me time," he said, hooking a long arm around my neck and drawing me closer. "I'd kiss you, but this is a clean shirt. Go clean up while I make the drinks."

I poked him in the chest. "You are impossible."

"That makes two of us." He let go and I hurried off to change, wondering if we'd get through the evening without a disaster. My only hope was Vida. If she'd recovered, I could rely on her to maintain civility.

It took only a few minutes to make myself reasonably presentable. The sheriff had our drinks on the counter. He'd also pulled out the dining room table in the alcove. "What do you put on this?" he asked.

"It's called a tablecloth," I said. "I'll get one from the hall closet."

He followed me. "You put on lipstick. Couldn't you wait?"

"It was automatic," I said. "You told me . . ."

I never finished. I was in his arms and he was kissing me with that familiar hunger. We fed off of each other, all our former restraints finally shattered. Something had to give or we'd sabotage the dinner party before the guests arrived.

Needing to breathe, we pulled away just enough so that I could speak. "Stop. Please."

"Right." Reluctantly, he let me go. "I'll wipe off the lipstick while you put more on." He sighed. "What would happen if I flat-out asked your damned brother what he's got in his freaking head?"

"Oh, please don't! This isn't an interrogation room."

"Too bad. That I can handle. Priests are a different deal." But the sheriff shrugged and went into the bathroom to get a tissue.

I took a tablecloth from the closet, grabbed a lipstick out of my purse, and applied a fresh coat of Crimson Snowbird.

"Hey," I said as Milo helped me put the cloth on the table, "Kip says one of your ski lodge perps is a famous snowboarder, Turk Durgan."

"He's an infamous asshole," Milo said. "So what?"

"Kip wants to interview him."

The sheriff's reaction surprised me. "Wait . . . I've heard of him. Only the first name, Todd, stuck." He made a face. "One of my kids has talked about him. Bran — he snowboards. Is this guy suing me?"

"If he sues you, he'll sue me. We're running a picture of Jack hauling him through your reception area."

Milo slammed his hand against the wall. "Emma! You're an idiot!"

"Hey — it's news."

"You take lousy pictures. It's probably a blur."

"I didn't take it. Kip did."

"Pull it."

"I can't. It's news."

He moved from the table, grabbing my shoulders. "Do it for me."

I shook my head. "That's censorship. You

274

can't expect me to knuckle under just because . . . just because."

He gave me a little shake. "The hell I can't. You and MacDuff didn't have permission. He must've come inside to take the damned thing." His eyes sparked with anger, though he'd lowered his voice. "Do what you have to, but don't run it. Does Jack know?"

"His back was turned," I said, my own anger rising up. First my reporter, now the sheriff. Whatever happened to freedom of the press? "Would you prefer we'd taken one of you collaring Mr. Suit?"

"Hell no!" Milo bellowed. "When was the last time I let you morons take a picture inside my office?"

"Could it be because you rarely do anything newsworthy except sit around on your dead butts drinking coffee and —"

Milo shook me. "Shut the hell up! I killed a man once for you, you little twit. Have you forgotten that? I sure as hell haven't!"

The doorbell rang. In fact, it may have rung several times. I thought my ears were ringing from Milo's shaking me. I groaned. "Oh, God! They're here!"

Milo dropped his hands. As I turned around, Adam and Ben entered. "Found my key," my son said — and grew sheepish.

"Uh . . . hi, Sheriff. How's everybody?"

I didn't know where to look. I was aware of Milo practically breathing down on the top of my head. It's a wonder my hair wasn't singed. "We were just . . . arguing about the public's right to know," I mumbled. "Get yourselves a drink." I tried to move out of the way, but stumbled over my own feet. The sheriff lifted me up off the floor and set me down none too gently in front of him so Adam could get into the kitchen.

Ben moved to where Milo and I were standing. "Good to see you, Sheriff," he said, putting out his hand. "Been fishing lately?"

Milo reached around me to shake hands. "No. I haven't had time."

I ducked down to escape being in between my self-righteous brother and my equally self-righteous lover. The handshake struck me as not unlike two boxers touching gloves before a bout. Maybe they'd end up killing each other before the evening was over.

Adam was getting a bottle of Henry Weinhard dark ale from the fridge. "Is one of those drinks on the counter for Uncle Ben?" he asked.

I avoided his gaze. "No, Milo and I haven't had time to drink them. Get your uncle what he wants." *Like a plastic bag over his head. Get two, and give the other one to the sheriff.* Where was Vida when I needed her?

"We dropped Shirley Bronsky at the courthouse," Adam said. "I guess Ed's going to be okay."

"Have you got any good news?" I snapped.

Adam stared at me. "What's wrong? You look kind of weird."

I put the French bread in the oven and checked the lasagna. I heard Milo and Ben talking as if they were civilized human beings. I had a flashback to their first meeting, fourteen years ago. After making a grisly discovery, the sheriff and the priest had gotten semi-plastered at Mugs Ahoy. They'd ended up driving me nuts then, too. Nothing had changed except for the lack of camaraderie between them now.

"It's been a weird day," I said. "How was the meeting with Marisa?"

"Good. She didn't ask if Uncle Ben wanted to date her."

"That's good, too," I said, smiling at Adam. "I've hardly seen you since you got here. I feel guilty."

He shrugged. "You're busy. You always took your job seriously."

Was that a reprimand? Why not? Add "maternal neglect" to my growing résumé of misdeeds. But there was nothing accusatory in Adam's brown eyes. The doorbell rang again. I heard Milo say he'd get it. At least he wasn't acting like a jerk. In fact, he was acting like the host. I didn't know if that was good or bad.

Adam was pouring Scotch-rocks for his uncle, who was greeting Vida and Leo. Milo entered the kitchen to collect his drink. "Vida's wearing a skunk on her head," he said, and went back to the living room.

"That I've got to see," Adam declared, taking Ben's Scotch with him and following Milo out of the kitchen.

I grabbed six plates before greeting Vida and Leo. Sure enough, the black-and-white fur creation on her head resembled a skunk.

"Give me those," Milo said, taking the plates out of my hands. "You'll probably drop them," he added under his breath.

Vida twirled around, showing off what apparently was a new dress. "Beth bought this at Nordstrom's," she said. "It was a Christmas gift."

The green and black taffeta with its pleated skirt suited her. "I like it," I said.

Leo grinned. "The Duchess looks like the real thing." He lowered his voice to a whisper. "And Adam looks more like his dad every day."

"Does he?" Not long ago, his comment would have evoked tears. But not now, with Milo calling my name.

"Emma — we're short one big fork."

I excused myself. "I forgot to empty the dishwasher," I said, fumbling in the silverware compartment. "Here."

"Got it," Milo said — and grabbed my rear before heading out of the kitchen. If he was still mad, he had a strange way of showing it.

Leo strolled in before I could take a sip of my own drink. "Dare I pour myself a wee dram?" he asked, nodding at the Scotch on the counter. "Vida would like a screwdriver."

"She would?" I said. "You're a bad influence, Walsh. I'll get the orange juice. Vodka's on the top shelf, glasses farther down to your left."

"I have been in your kitchen before," Leo said wryly. "But I never made it past the hall, otherwise known as first base."

I glared at him. "Don't you dare start in on me, Leo."

He laughed. "I'm just envious. Or would've been until lately."

I handed him the orange juice pitcher. "You're going to quit."

Leo blanched. "No. That is, not for a

while." He gave me his off-center smile. "I'll be sixty-two in May. I have to think about retirement."

I smiled, though it wasn't easy. "Vida and I figured as much."

"So she told me. I'd better deliver her adult beverage. You know what she's like when she hasn't had a drink in five or six years."

I picked up my own glass and some holiday napkins before going into the living room. I noticed that someone — probably Adam — had turned on the Christmas tree. Milo was building a fire. Vida was still wearing her skunk and sitting next to my son on the sofa. Leo had sat down in the smaller armchair by the tree. Ben was reclining in the easy chair where Milo usually sat when he wasn't on the sofa with me. I wondered if the priest and the sheriff had arm-wrestled each other for the rights to the chair. I parked myself on the floor by Adam.

"So flat in Ohio," Vida was saying to Ben. "How can people survive without mountains?"

"Beats me," Ben admitted. "Some Midwesterners don't like them. They get claustrophobia or feel menaced. Conversely, the endless vista of land that goes maybe thirty, forty miles soothes them."

"Maybe," Adam put in, "they'd like Alaska. Some days, like last week, you can't see anything at all."

Vida shuddered. "No! How do you know what people are doing?"

"Hard to get 'Scene' items, Vida," Leo remarked.

Milo had the fire going. He went out to the kitchen, leaving his drink on the mantel between two wax choirboys. What now, I thought — is he tossing the damned salad? And wished I couldn't think at all.

"Emma!" he yelled. "Your oven's on fire. Again."

"Oh!" I jumped up and would've knocked over my drink if Adam hadn't snatched it off the floor.

"Can I help?" my son asked.

"No," I said over my shoulder. "Evacuate, if necessary."

Sure enough, smoke was filling the kitchen. The sheriff had opened the back door. "Didn't you clean the damned thing after your last fit of pyromania?" he asked, obviously irked.

"Yes, but the turkey grease must've . . ." I started coughing as I squinted into the oven.

Milo slapped me on the back before pulling me out of the way. "The lasagna's safe on the counter," he said. "I'll get the bread.

Jesus, you'll burn this place down yet." He hauled out the two loaves and dropped them on the counter before closing the oven. "God, Emma, how have you survived all these years on your own?"

It was a fair question. "I don't know. Dumb luck, maybe."

He ran a finger down the bridge of my nose. "Put out the bread — and don't dump it on the skunk."

"What is it?" Ben asked, coming into the kitchen.

Milo shot my brother a sharp look. "This isn't what it looks like. I'm actually screwing the brains out of your sister." He picked up the lasagna pan and barged past both Ben and me.

"Oh, Ben!" I cried, torn between laughter and tears.

Before he could say anything, Vida leaned into the kitchen. "Kip's on the phone. He sounds upset." She handed me the receiver.

Ben sighed and returned to the living room. Milo announced that dinner was ready. The back door was still open and the smoke was dispersing. "Hi," I croaked into the phone. "What's the problem?"

"It's that Andrews guy," Kip said. "He's looking for Mitch. I played dumb, but he's coming to see you. Something's up and it sounds bad."

"For Mitch?"

"Yeah — maybe all of us. Be careful, Emma. This might get ugly."

And to think I thought it already had, but at least I didn't have to call the sheriff. Milo was putting the salad on the table. Ben was waiting to say grace. I sat down. My brother's prayer was mercifully brief — or that was my vague impression. All I could think of was Kip's warning about Charles Andrews's imminent arrival. I'd had no chance to warn Milo. When Adam handed me the salad bowl, I made an announcement.

"We're about to have an unexpected visitor."

"Who?" Vida asked, her eyes huge behind the big lenses. "Kip?"

"No," I said, with a swift glance at Milo, "a Seattle attorney named Andrews. He stopped first at the *Advocate*."

Vida looked as if she intended to vault across the table and accost me. "Who? Why? What for?"

"I've no idea," I admitted.

"Mom," Adam said, "are you keeping that salad all to yourself?"

"Uh . . . no." I all but shoved the bowl at Adam as the doorbell rang.

Milo stood up at the head of table. "Stay

put. This is my perp."

Vida gasped. "How did I miss that?" She shot Leo an accusing look. "I should never have let you take me home!"

"Is the sheriff armed?" my son asked, looking excited.

"I doubt it," I said.

Mr. Law Enforcement took his time opening the door. I assumed Charles G. Andrews would recognize the man who had arrested him a few hours earlier. But Milo wasn't in uniform. While there weren't many other six-foot five-inch, mid-fifties graying sandy-haired men in SnoCo, there were probably a half dozen within a block of Andrews's office in Seattle. I could see only the newcomer's dark overcoat and his hand from my vantage point, but the initial exchange between the two men seemed cordial. A moment later, Andrews stepped inside.

"Someone to see you, sweetheart," Milo said in a voice that didn't sound quite like his usual laconic tone. Nor had he ever called me "sweetheart" or any other term of endearment, unless I counted "dumbshit" and "pain in the ass."

Milo closed the door and ambled back to his place at the table. I stood up, discovering I was a trifle wobbly. "Thank you, darling," I said. "Don't let your dinner get cold."

Vida choked on her screwdriver. Leo patted her on the back. Ben and Adam frowned at each other. Seemingly unconcerned, the sheriff served himself more lasagna. Andrews's ice-cold blue eyes surveyed all of us. He was a broad six-footer with receding black hair and soft features that no doubt belied a sharp mind and sharper legal tactics.

"May we speak privately?" he inquired, not offering his hand.

"This *is* private," I said, "unless you prefer the carport."

Andrews didn't even blink. "Fine. I think on my feet in court."

He'd thrown down the gauntlet. For one fleeting moment, I wished Milo was wearing his uniform and my brother and my son had on their clerical garb. I even wished Vida hadn't finally removed the skunk from her head. "Why are you here, Mr. Andrews?"

"You know who I am," he said, looking smug.

"My production manager called me. Why are you intruding here?"

Andrews looked amused. "I want another

of your employees, Mitch Laskey. Is he here?"

"Do you see him?" I gestured at the table where my guests were pretending they were interested only in their food.

"If not here, where is he? He's not at home, either."

"I've no idea."

"That's a shame. Without your cooperation, it's likely that you won't be seeing him very soon."

"Oh?" I said calmly. His attitude had steeled my spine. "I didn't know you two were dating." I let my gaze travel from the top of his balding head to his expensive, if wet, wing tips. "Nice coat."

Somebody at the table snickered. Leo, I thought.

"You're very foolish," Andrews said, though his aplomb seemed slightly dented. "Laskey could be facing a prison sentence. By the way, I'm a married man with children."

"Did I ask? You're not my type. Why would Mitch be doing that?"

Andrews smiled sardonically. "How many charges would you like to hear? Since you won't help me, I'll hire someone who can. I've already wasted two days in this drab little town. Good night, Ms. Lord." He turned on his well-heeled heel and headed for the door.

"Well now!" Vida cried after I checked to make sure Andrews had closed the door all the way. "How dare he speak of Alpine like that?"

I sat down. "That's not the point. Why is Mitch in trouble?"

Milo was fingering his chin. "If he is and this S.O.B. is on his trail, why hasn't anybody notified me?"

Vida scowled at the sheriff. "Watch your language. Though I don't blame you. That man's intolerable. Did you really arrest him?"

"Yeah." Milo waved a hand in dismissal. "That had nothing to do with Laskey." He turned to me. "Where *is* Mitch?"

"He was still in Monroe this afternoon," I said. "Brenda was a wreck, so he was taking her somewhere to get help. For all I . . ." Something clicked in my brain. "Andrews was at their house when they were at the hospital. Now I know why that Escalade rang a bell. Kip saw it parked outside when he went to see Mitch and Brenda but apparently he told Alison he thought it belonged to the Laskeys."

Adam looked at Ben, who was sitting at the opposite end of the table. "Hey, this is a lot more exciting than hearing confessions."

Vida was aghast. "Surely not! You must hear outrageous things."

My brother shrugged. "Not after the first two years."

Milo got up, almost knocking over his chair. "I'd better check with Dustman in case this asshole shows up at headquarters."

"Language, Milo . . . ," Vida began, but he'd gone out to the carport.

Leo was serving himself more lasagna. "This has to tie in with Troy. Or does Mitch know what really happened to Jimmy Hoffa?"

"No," I said. "Mitch hadn't started on the Detroit paper when Hoffa disappeared. You're right about a connection with Troy. But how? The kid's back in prison, sick with pneumonia. It isn't as if Mitch helped him escape or harbored him when he was out."

Ben reached for more bread. "You sure of that?"

"What do you mean?"

"How did — Troy? — get out?"

I looked at Vida. "I don't know," I admitted. "Do you?"

"I left town soon after Mitch got the call," she said.

"Same with me," Leo said.

"And," I murmured, "I never thought to ask."

Milo returned. "Dustman said there's been no sign of Andrews." He sat back down and polished off his drink. "By the way," he said to me, "you can thank me for yanking that picture out of the paper."

"What?" I exploded so loudly that Adam jumped in his seat.

Milo shrugged. "Hey, Vida — toss me another piece of bread."

She complied. Annoyingly, the sheriff caught the slice with one big hand. I'd hoped he'd drop it and have to crawl around the floor where I could kick him. "Wait till I get you alone," I said so low no one else could hear, with Vida yapping about Andrews's denigration of her hometown.

"That," Milo said quietly, "is what *I'm* waiting for."

"Mom," Adam said, "are you okay? You look feverish."

"Why not?" I snapped. "Now I've got a reporter on the run."

"Hey, Sluggly," Ben said, "this Andrews may be blowing smoke."

" 'Sluggly'?" Milo said under his breath. "Jesus."

"He didn't come up here and spend two days blowing smoke, Stench," I retorted.

"This guy's high-end. I'll bet he's a criminal lawyer."

"Aren't they all," Leo mused.

"Now, now," Vida said, "my son-in-law in Tacoma is an attorney."

By a fortuitous stroke of luck, the talk turned to lawyer-related anecdotes. Ben recalled a black Delta bluesman named Poteet with a law degree from Vanderbilt. He never charged clients, impoverished or not. Years later, Ben learned Poteet wasn't a sharecropper's son as he claimed, but the scion of a wealthy Memphis banker.

After I'd served ice cream sundaes for dessert, we lingered at the table for another twenty minutes. Vida checked her watch and announced it was almost nine-thirty and she should be heading for home.

"It sounds as if we'll have another busy day tomorrow, post-deadline or not," she said, putting her skunk back on.

Leo agreed. They left together, though I assumed they'd arrived in separate cars. But Milo and Ben appeared to be settling in. I considered faking my own death. Instead, I went into the bathroom and called Kip.

"How's it going?" I asked, running the faucet and speaking quietly.

"So far, so good," Kip replied. "Did Andrews show up?"

"Yes, but he left pretty fast. What did he say about Mitch?"

"Andrews sounded as if Mitch was in some kind of trouble. Is he?"

I sighed. "If he is — and this jerk made it clear he could be — I don't know why. I'll bet that Escalade you saw at the Laskeys' house was Andrews's."

"Wow. Maybe it's a good thing Mitch wasn't there. I wonder if Andrews talked to Spence."

I'd forgotten Spence had also been at the Laskey house. "I should call him. Hey — you still have that Durgan pic on page one, right?"

"Uh . . . no." Kip sounded as if he were being strangled.

"Why not?"

"Dodge called." Kip paused. "He said it was a bad idea. He's at your place, right? I assumed you agreed. Dumping the photo is a good plan if I want to interview Turk. Henry Bardeen says he's still at the lodge."

Kip wasn't at fault. "You get a pass on this one, but *never* make a change like that again without consulting me first. The sheriff is not my boss."

"Are you mad?"

"Not at you," I said.

"Good. I was worried."

291

"Given the chance for a story on an Olympic snowboarder, I'll fold this time. Without Mitch, we need to fill space."

"Thanks. I hope we don't have to fill space with a story *about* Mitch instead of *by* him."

I agreed and rang off.

The Three Stooges were lolling around in the living room. Milo had reclaimed the big easy chair. Ben was in the side chair. Adam was on the sofa. They were all drinking something.

"We thought you'd died in the bathroom," Ben said, getting up. "I was ready to take a leak outside."

"Why not?" I muttered as he passed me on his way to the hall. "Dare I enter the kitchen or does it look like Omaha Beach after D-Day?"

"Hey," Adam said, "we're taking a break. The table's cleared."

"Vida did that," I said, and kept going. Milo and Adam resumed talking about fishing in Alaska.

The kitchen wasn't as big a mess as I'd feared, but I started emptying the dishwasher, which I hadn't had time to do before dinner. I was reloading it when I heard Ben come back into the living room. As I turned the washer on for another load, Milo joined me.

"I should head home," he said wistfully. "You okay?"

I was about to give him hell for pulling the photo, but I couldn't. Instead, I collapsed against him and didn't say anything.

"Hey," he said, mussing up my hair, "what's wrong?"

"I've never seen you play host before."

"I've had some practice," he said. "You've seen me cook on your barbecue. Unlike Mulehide, you didn't bitch every ten minutes for not testing the coals with my bare hands."

"I never think about you and Mulehide. As a couple, I mean."

"Neither do I." He gave my backside another squeeze. "I better go before I take you with me." He leaned down and lightly kissed my lips. "Damned good lasagna, by the way. Better than any box."

I followed him into the living room. Adam had put on some Christmas music. Ben looked as if he might nod off at any moment. Milo took his heavy jacket off the rack by the door.

"You leaving, Sheriff?" Adam asked, moving from the CD player.

"Yeah," Milo said. "Try to keep your mother from hurting herself."

Ben got to his feet. "I should go, too, or

morning Mass will be midmorning Mass."
He kissed my cheek. "Take it easy, Sluggly.
Dodge is right. You're always one step away
from going through a wall. No wonder you
need round-the-clock protection."

I kept my composure. "Drive safely,
Stench. In fact," I said to Ben, darting Milo
a look as he opened the door, "you should
drive behind Dodge so that he doesn't see
you're always one slip of the foot away from
replacing Durwood Parker as the most reckless driver in SnoCo."

Ben grunted. Milo left first, with my
brother not far behind.

"Well?" I said to Adam after I'd closed
the door behind them.

"Well what?" Adam asked, puzzled.

I flopped onto the sofa. "Did you have a
good time?"

Adam grinned. "I did. It's a hoot to see
how you live."

"It's usually calmer. I'd forgotten about
Vida's skunk. It's been ages since I've seen
it."

"Mrs. Runkel is awesome." My son
stretched out on his back by the hearth. The
fire was still going. Milo must have added
another log. The dishwasher vied with Perry
Como in the background. The lighted tree
lent a festive air. It was some time before

Adam spoke again.

"I like him," he said.

I'd been lost in thought. "Huh? Who?"

"Dodge. Who else?"

"Oh. That's right — you don't really know him, do you?"

"This is the first time I've been around him in years." Adam grinned. "When we first moved here, I thought he was one scary-looking dude. I decided then that I'd better behave and not have him bust me."

"I don't ever recall Milo as looking scary," I said casually.

"No." Adam had grown serious. "You wouldn't. You were probably too busy telling yourself he was a small-town hick."

I stared at my son. "Oh? Why? Because he's not like your dad?"

"Maybe. The biggest difference is that he's here — for you."

I nodded. "He always has been. Do you mind?"

Adam shrugged. "I hardly ever saw you and Dad together."

I'd never thought about that, but it was true. Adam had spent time with Tom. Tom had spent time with me. But we'd never been a family. The last occasion we'd all been together was when Tom was in a coffin. "Oh, Adam, that's so sad. You were cheated."

"So were you. So was Dad." He shrugged. "That's nobody's fault."

We were silent for a while before I spoke. "Ben is upset with me."

Adam rolled over to look at me. "Why?"

"He thinks I'm going to hell."

"With or without Dodge?"

"Oh, Adam . . . this is serious. You're a priest, too."

"I'm your son. I don't judge. I hand out penance and tell people to try harder. The 'try' part's the tough one, but that's what life's about."

"You don't think I'm a lost cause?"

"I told you, I don't judge. Do you feel lost?"

"Until your uncle tore into me, I was happy. I guess I still am. But I keep hearing him — and my conscience — giving me hell."

Adam sat up, wrapping his arms around his knees. "I don't know what to say. Are you and Dodge talking marriage?"

"Not yet." I paused, not sure how to explain to my son that I'd finally laid his father's ghost to rest. But I realized Adam saw Tom through realistic eyes. "I've always loved Milo, even when your dad was alive. I just didn't think I loved him . . . enough.

Then three weeks ago, I realized I did. I told your uncle about my feelings. When Milo came here Sunday night, I hadn't seen him since early December. There's been no time to make plans. He's gun-shy about marriage and I'm . . . not sure."

"Mom!" Adam rubbed his head. "Sure of *what?* You guys are a couple, like you've been together forever. I knew you'd had a fight when I opened the door, then you're nuzzling each other. Do it, make it legal."

"Milo was married in a Protestant church."

"So? Uncle Ben can't get you an annulment? He knows all kinds of people from here to the Vatican. What's wrong with him?"

I'd never considered Ben's network. "Why didn't he think of that?"

"Maybe he's got his own agenda."

"Like what?"

"It's not Ms. Foxx," Adam said. "He can deal with that stuff. Other women have hit on him. He's good-looking — for an uncle. Ask him."

I felt as if a great weight had been lifted. But it had been replaced by a smaller weight that was Ben. "Now I'll worry about him."

"He seemed chilly with you at first, but I thought he was just beat."

I smiled. "I did something right. You're the only grown-up in the Lord family."

"Don't flatter me. I might get vain."

"What are you going to do about your inheritance?"

"Put it in some kind of trust." Adam yawned. "That's up to Ms. Foxx. It's complicated. Except for her pass at Uncle Ben, she's smart."

"Yes, but as Vida would say, smarts don't equal common sense."

Adam grinned at me. "They sure don't, Mom."

I didn't argue.

TWELVE

The next morning, Adam again joined his uncle at the rectory. A weary Kip met me at the door. "How bad was it with Andrews last night?" I asked.

"He was a real jerk. I didn't know whether to punch him out or call the sheriff. That is," Kip amended, "one of the deputies. I knew Dodge was at your place."

Alison was shaking her head. "I'm glad I missed that. Who is this guy anyway?"

"That," I said, "is what I intend to find out first thing this morning."

Kip handed me a copy of our latest edition. "It looks fine, but I'll admit I was bleary-eyed by the time I finished. I probably tossed more overrun into the dumpster than usual before I could focus."

"Don't worry about that," I said, seeing Vida and Leo chatting in the middle of the newsroom. "Maybe we can relax a little today."

299

"A lovely dinner," she said in greeting, "despite that vile interloper. Leo and I were commenting on your excellent lasagna."

I tried not to stare at her red sweater with its Western Washington University emblem. She didn't miss my curious gaze.

"I bought this for Roger as a Christmas present," she said, tight-lipped. "He didn't care for it, and I won't let it go to waste."

"It's very . . . academic," I said. Despite Vida's big bust, I calculated that the sweater was too small for her grandson. And too academic.

"Great French doughnuts this morning," Leo said tactfully. "Good work, Vida. The Upper Crust only makes them once a week."

"I got there early," she said. "They usually run out shortly after eight." She sat down at her desk. "I must get a head start on my advice column. The letters simply poured in yesterday. So many family problems surfaced over Christmas. I shouldn't mention names, but Marlowe Whipp's parents went at it again at the retirement home. I thought we'd heard the last of that when Hector went into a coma last fall. Maybe it's too bad he came out of it on Halloween."

"Not a good week for postal employees," Leo commented, a French doughnut already in hand. "I suppose Marlowe will still be backed up on his mail route."

"We may have a substitute," Vida said. "His mother, Reba, had to be hospitalized after Hector tried to smother her with a fruitcake. That reminds me — I must call Bebe and find out if Roy's been released. I hope the medication Dr. Sung gave him helps."

Having heard far more than I needed to know about the always-combative senior Whipps, I poured coffee and grabbed a French doughnut. I had yet to peruse Vida's current column, not having had time during our hectic prepublication days. I turned immediately to "AdVIDAvice" — her title, which I didn't like much. The first letter was the one from Pastor Purebeck's wife. Vida's response was: "You are acting upon the flimsiest of suspicions. You indicate you have had a long and happy marriage. In the spirit of Christian charity, I advise you to dismiss any ugly thoughts and give your mate the benefit of the doubt. If you can't, ask your husband if you have reason to doubt him. If he's the kind, loving man you describe, he'll be honest. Do pray on this matter."

As always, Vida's common sense shone through in her answers. She'd pushed all the right buttons.

After skimming through the rest of the paper and not finding anything egregious, I focused on other things, mainly Mitch. I dialed his cell — and got his message. Frustrated, I did a search on Charles G. Andrews to see if any of his recent cases had made the *Seattle Times.* There were three, going back to late 2003 — he'd represented a builder who'd been sued by homeowners for shoddy construction, an investment broker who'd allegedly embezzled from a dozen elderly clients, and a surgeon accused of malpractice. Andrews settled the first, the second was on appeal, and the third was going to trial in February. I found no connection to Mitch.

Then inspiration struck from out of the past. On my *Oregonian* beat, I'd often had to cross-check names between different kinds of news categories. It wasn't usually necessary in Alpine, especially since I had Vida as a resource. I went back through the same time period searching for arrests. It took me an hour, but I hit pay dirt in the regional roundup. The builder's name was Carlton Madison. On June 10, 2004, Kiefer Madison, twenty-two, had been arrested on charges of attempting to steal a Cessna airplane from a hangar at Harvey Field in Snohomish. Jim McKay's name wasn't mentioned as the owner, but it had to be the same incident Melody had related to me.

A coincidence? Maybe, but there had to be a connection with Mitch and Andrews. Troy had escaped the first time on June 10 and was recaptured within forty-eight hours. Had he somehow been involved with Kiefer Madison? Were the two Madisons related? I put the would-be airplane thief's name into the *Times*'s search engine. There was no follow-up, given that the crime had been foiled and had occurred in SnoCo, not Seattle's home county, KingCo.

My last link to Seattle news sources had been Rolf Fisher when he worked for AP. Now I had to rely on Spence. His contacts had been vital during Milo's Bellevue crisis. Grudgingly, I dialed his number at KSKY.

"May I bring you lunch?" I asked.

He chuckled. "Are you tired of being mauled by the sheriff?"

"Don't make me beg. I may be onto something that could be a big story for us both. I'll go to Pie-in-the-Sky. What do you want?"

"That's a leading question." He paused. "Corned beef on Russian rye. Mustard, mayo, lettuce, and a dill pickle on the side."

"Got it," I said.

"Hey — who's this Andrews character?"

The question startled me. "Why do you ask?"

"He came to the station last night around eight. I'd seen him at Laskey's house on Monday, sitting in his Escalade as if on surveillance. I started walking to his car, but he took off. He caught me last night as I was leaving the station and asked if I knew where Laskey was. I said, *'No hablo inglés, señor. Soy un peón solamente aqui.'* He wasn't amused."

"No surprise. Your Spanish stinks. Did he say why he wanted to know about Mitch?"

"He insinuated that your reporter was in some kid of big trouble — mainly with him, as far as I could tell. Basically, he tried badgering me, but finally realized I was genuinely clueless."

"Same here."

"I checked Andrews out," Spence said. "A lone lawyer, offering hope to the awful unlawful. Office in One Union Square, with a ton of underlings. Chicago-born, Wisconsin undergrad degree, Northwestern University law school cum laude, blah-blah. High-profile cases keeping corporate and professional types out of the slammer. Well?"

"Those clients don't sound like Troy or Mitch."

"I wouldn't think so. Here comes my new kiddy engineer. He's late. Maybe the training wheels fell off of his console. See you later."

I dashed out to tell Vida my latest snippets of information.

"Interesting," she murmured. "But what does it all mean?"

"I don't know," I admitted, "but I'm doing some digging."

"Digging!" she exclaimed. "And you say those geo-whatever persons are involved? I should speak to Don Krogstad. I babysat him, you know. In fact, I have time to drive down to Index this morning. Would you like to come along?"

"Won't he be at work?" I asked.

"I'll call first." She picked up the phone and dialed.

"You have his number memorized?" I asked in astonishment.

She frowned at me. "Of course. Do you think I have time to look up every person I have to — "Dee? How are you? . . . Yes, company for the holidays — so lovely. . . . Is Don home? . . . No, no, don't bother him. . . . Goodbye."

"Ninny," she said after hanging up. "Don's taking this week off. He was outside doing something with wood. Let's go now. I have

305

to be back in time to meet Bebe Everson for lunch. Roy's reaction to his medication is still being evaluated, but be should be released later today. Oh — Shirley called. She's taking Ed home this morning. He was diagnosed as suffering from utter folly, an incurable condition for him."

"True," I agreed. "Maybe I should stay here. We're shorthanded."

"Nonsense! It *is* Wednesday. We'll manage."

As usual, Vida ruled. Five minutes later we were in Vida's Buick, crossing the Sky and heading for Highway 2. "You didn't tell Dee we were coming," I said suddenly. "Shouldn't you have mentioned that?"

"Dee chatters so. I had to shut her up so we could be on our way."

Traffic was heavier than usual, probably due to the holidays and the opening of the ski areas. Big patches of snow clung to the steep outcroppings on one side, while the river ran fast and gray on the other. We still made the seventeen-mile drive in good time. Turning off to go over the old plank bridge across the North Fork of the Sky, we entered the tiny town exactly at nine o'clock. The old-fashioned white church looked similar to St. Mildred's, though Father Den and a couple of parishioners had repainted the exterior brown with green trim. We passed Doolittle Park, which showcased an enormous saw that had been used to cut granite from the town wall, which was a popular site for rock-climbing aficionados — very skilled, very brave climbers. I shuddered at the mere idea.

Vida pulled up outside a modest two-story house. "Yes, Don's car is there, so is Dee's VW, and . . . now, who does that older pickup truck belong to? One of their children? They have two, both living elsewhere since graduating from college."

She led the way up the two steps to the front porch and rang the bell. There was no response. Vida peered through the lace curtain on the door's oval window. "I can't see . . . No, someone's moving . . ."

We waited almost a minute. Vida rang the bell again. Seconds later, a pleasant-looking middle-aged man I vaguely recognized opened the door. "Mrs. Runkel!" he exclaimed. "What a surprise. Dee told me you called, but I didn't know you were coming to see us. Darn. I can't ask you in. We're just taking down the tree and it's a mess. Dee would kill me. She's probably afraid you'd put it in your 'Scene' column."

Vida offered him her cheesy grin while putting a foot on the threshold. "Oh, Don, I don't mind a bit of disarray. We could come in the back way if you insist."

Don's laugh seemed forced. "The kitchen's even worse. Dee hasn't had time to straighten things up this morning." He was a solid man of six feet who somehow managed to edge just close enough to Vida that she had to back up on the porch. "Tell you what — we could drive down to Gold Bar for a cup of coffee. My treat."

Vida's smile had become fixed. "I don't think we should do that," she said. "Why don't you come outside and we can chat for a few moments? Oh — do you know Emma Lord, the *Advocate*'s editor?"

She might as well have said "Emma the Afterthought." I put out my hand. "Hi, Don. I've seen you in town."

"Nice to meet you," Don said, his smile strained. He turned to Vida. "I have to help Dee, but if you've got a quick question for me . . . ?"

"Very well." Her tone was brusque and the grin was gone. "I know Dee became ill when you found Gus's body in the cave. So distressing."

Don nodded. "I saw the ID of the body online. I never knew Gus well — Matt and Pete were more my age. That's a terrible thing."

"Of course," Vida agreed. "But I want you to think very hard. Do you recall anything — in the cave, or around it — that was at all peculiar?"

"Peculiar?" Don had managed to get onto the porch and close the door behind him. "No." He rubbed at the back of his balding head. "Wait. I forgot Dee told me Melody McKay called last night. Melody and Jim were with us. In all the excitement, one of them picked up a camera. Melody, I think. She thought it was theirs, but when they got home — in fact, just last night after Jim got back from one of his airplane treks — they realized they had two cameras, almost exactly alike. That's kind of odd, isn't it? Maybe you should call them."

"Yes," Vida said. "That's very odd indeed. Thank you, Don." She stalked off the porch.

Like a good little stooge, I followed her to the Buick.

"Well now!" she exclaimed. "Doesn't that beat all? First, Don won't let us in the house, and now duplicate cameras. Shall we go . . . where do these McKays live?"

"Maltby, ninety-minutes round-way from here. The sheriff can handle it."

Vida shot me an arch glance before starting the car. "I assume he still can handle more than you."

309

I ignored the barb. "He'll send a deputy. I'll call Melody right now. We wouldn't want to have her lock us out, would we?"

"That was intolerable." Vida sped over the old plank bridge so fast that the breaks squealed when she reached the arterial onto Highway 2. "And a lie. Don and Dee should've gotten their stories straight. While he was talking to us, she — or someone — turned on the Christmas tree lights. I could see them through that curtain. What on earth could they be hiding? Or should I say *who?*"

"That pickup looked familiar," I said.

"Yes," Vida agreed, slowing as we got behind an SUV with a Kansas license plate, "but there must be two dozen blue trucks like it in Alpine. I saw one at Cal's Chevron station when we left town." She smiled as we passed Baring. "I must say, I'll be glad when Buck moves to Alpine from Startup. I've gotten so used to this road I could drive it in my sleep."

I thought Vida was doing that now, virtually tailgating the Kansas vehicle. "Uh . . . Vida, aren't you a little . . . close?"

"Oh! They do have such handsome license plates with those wheat sheaves. I wanted a better look."

"So Buck really is buying a condo at Parc Pines?"

She nodded. "He put earnest money down just before he left. His house in Startup goes on the market after New Year's."

"That's nice. I'm glad for both of you."

"Much more convenient and will save on gas," she said. "Honestly, can't these people from flat country drive in the mountains? I'm going to pass them after this next turn."

She did, frightening me only half out of my wits. Highway 2 is not for the faint-hearted, no matter where they come from. We were still speculating — fruitlessly — when we got back to the office just before ten. I immediately called Melody McKay. Luckily, she answered.

"Yes, wasn't that a dumb stunt?" she said after I inquired about the camera. "It was lying by a log only a few feet away from our own gear. I must admit, I was agog about that body, so I picked it up and didn't notice it was a slightly different Canon model from ours. I never looked at it again until last night. Do you know who it belongs to?"

"Not really," I said. "I'm going to call the sheriff's office. They'll probably send someone to collect it. Will you be home today?"

She said she would. I thanked her, disconnected, and dialed Milo's number. Lori answered, saying he was on the phone, but she'd relay the message. He called me back five minutes later.

"If you didn't make such damned good lasagna, I wouldn't send one of my deputies to Maltby," he said. "Is this a hunch or what?"

"It could belong to Gus," I insisted.

"And laid there on the ground since last June? A hundred hikers could've gone through that area."

"Mrs. McKay said it was by a log. Maybe nobody could see it until they put their own stuff in the same place."

"This better be good," he warned. "By the way, I'm having lunch with Ben at the ski lodge coffee shop."

"Oh, no! Whose idea is that?"

"Mine. You won't talk."

"I haven't had a chance."

"I like going one-on-one with adversaries." He hung up.

Surely Milo and Ben would act like . . . Milo and Ben. I tried not to think about the confrontation. Instead, I wondered if the sheriff was humoring me about the camera. It was a pleasant, though unaccustomed, idea. To make sure the Maltby trip wouldn't waste time and money, I asked Alison to go through the classifieds from early June to find anyone had taken out an ad for a lost Canon.

"Sure," she said. "I don't think anybody's lost or found a camera since I've been here and this is the season when people use them."

"Maybe we'll get lucky," I said, retreating to my cubbyhole.

With Mitch AWOL, I used the time to brush up on the upcoming opening of Resthaven. The facility would provide rehab for addiction, therapy for the mentally ill, and recuperation for medical patients. The East Coast–based company that had bought the Bronskys' eyesore had done a good remodeling job, given what they'd had to work with. I was glad I'd tossed the editorial saying that a can of gasoline, some oily rags, and a match would be the best way to solve the problem.

Alison had found only one classified for a camera, but it wasn't a Canon. A little after eleven-thirty, I decided to update Vida. She was putting on her tweed coat. "You're leaving early for lunch?" I said.

She looked exasperated. "Yes, we're going to the ski lodge coffee shop. She's picking me up any moment."

An idea I'd had at the back of my mind surfaced. "Ask Bebe to find a pair of men's hiking boots Roy showed Amer Wasco. I don't have time to explain, but they might be important. Tell her to give them to you."

Vida narrowed her eyes at me. "Why?"

"Roy thought they were Mama's," I said hurriedly as I heard Alison greet someone in the front office. "Bebe can stop at her house —"

"Bebe!" Vida cried, looking beyond me. "How nice!"

Bebe Everson entered the newsroom. She was a small, dark-haired woman who skittered everywhere like a windup toy. When she ran down and stopped, she always seemed uncertain of where she was or how she'd gotten there. Her voice was high, thin, and staccato, adding to the illusion of her not being connected to the real world.

"Vida, Vida," she exclaimed. "And Emma. Surprise!"

Vida pursed her lips. "To find us at our jobs?"

"No, no," Bebe replied, unfazed. "To see you both."

"Hello, Bebe," I said, for lack of anything else. "Is Roy improving?"

She lifted her narrow shoulders and shrugged. "I think so. He's calmer. Poor Roy. He's right."

"About what?" Vida inquired, pulling on

her gloves.

Bebe wiggled her hands. "Not giving up. We need closure."

"I would think," Vida began, "that after sixteen —"

For once, *I* interrupted *her.* "That reminds me," I said. "I was talking to Amer Wasco yesterday about the hiking boots Roy showed him. My son lost a pair, so I thought they might be his." I caught Vida's irked stare. "They weren't his size, but I wondered where Roy found them."

Bebe's black button eyes widened in apparent surprise, as if I'd asked for the number to her bank account. "Oh, dear! I can't say."

"Can't," I said quietly, "or won't?"

"Can't," she said. "Roy fibbed."

I feigned shock. "Really? How so?"

Bebe swallowed hard. "He found Pike's old boots."

Vida's gaze had now turned to Bebe. "And . . . ?" she coaxed.

"He liked Pike."

"I liked Ike when he ran for president in the fifties," Vida said, "but I don't understand."

"Roy has Pike's boots, too. And he did get those at the dump. But the others came from the berry patch."

315

"You mean," I said, "on Mount Sawyer?"

Bebe nodded. "Roy gets tired of people making fun of him. About Mama, and searching, searching, searching for her where she picked berries. Not funny to him. Where else would she go with a bucket?"

"Yes." Vida checked her watch. "Come, it's getting on to noon."

I knew Vida would follow instructions, despite my vagueness. It might be a wild-goose chase, but she was game. Back in my cubbyhole, the phone rang. It was Adam asking if we could meet for lunch.

"I can't," I said ruefully. "I'm following a lead on Andrews."

"What kind of lead?" Adam sounded suspicious.

"Nothing dangerous," I assured him. "Really."

"Uncle Ben and Dodge are facing off at the ski lodge."

"I know. That *is* dangerous. Vida's eating there, too."

"Relax, Mom. Uncle Ben and Dodge are both civilized."

"They're both stubborn as mules and go by the book. Milo's is the law, your uncle's is Holy Writ."

"Hey — let them sort it out. You know Uncle Ben's running on fumes right now.

Cut him some slack."

"He could do the same for me," I said. "Got to go."

I arrived at KSKY as Spence wrapped up his fifteen-minute midday newscast that covered not only SkyCo but adjacent parts of SnoCo, KingCo, and over the pass in Chelan County.

He regarded me warily. "Why do I sense I'm being used?"

"You are. Isn't that the way we work?"

He nodded. "So it seems."

I removed our food from the bag with its PITS logo, an acronym I found off-putting for an eatery. "I never thanked you for what you did during the Bellevue standoff — and what you didn't do afterwards."

Spence shrugged. "You were my lifeline when I was sinking. As for Dodge's story, if it doesn't happen in Alpine, it doesn't happen."

We'd sat down at his desk in his small office. "Thanks anyway."

"So how might I help you?"

By the time I finished my Laskey-Madison theory, he'd eaten half his sandwich. "Who do you know that might fill in the blanks?"

Spence gazed into the booth where the student engineer manned the console. "A radio news producer, a TV reporter. I'll call this afternoon." He nibbled a potato chip. "It's worth a shot."

I checked the big clock in the booth. "It's almost time for your hour turn. I'll leave you in peace."

We both stood up. "Thanks for lunch," Spence said. "And the tip."

I shrugged. "I was up a stump."

"Hey — what are rivals for?" Spence said. "When we can't hinder, we help. Which reminds me, I've got something to show you." He opened a file drawer in his desk. "When my sister, Marsha, finished serving out Krogstad's term on the bench, she found some of his belongings in his chambers. She gave me this because she thought there might be a tie-in with the retired SkyCo VIPs I was working on for my weekly nostalgia segments."

Curious, I opened the small manila envelope. "It looks like letters or . . ." I unfolded a flimsy sheet of ecru stationery. "Poetry."

"I remembered the poems after our Everson bones chat." He shrugged. "I didn't know what to make of it when Marsha gave them to me, so I stuck them in a drawer. Maybe you can connect the dots."

"Okay, I'll try."

It seemed we all needed whatever help we could get.

THIRTEEN

Vida returned at one-twenty. "No boots," she said in disgust. "Bebe insisted she didn't have time in case they were discharging Roy. I told her I'd come by this evening or tomorrow and pick them up."

"That's okay," I said. "I may be nuts." I offered her my theory that maybe — just maybe — whoever left them had been in the company of Gus before he died.

She seemed ambiguous. "Well . . . it's possible. I did ask Bebe if she knew how long Roy had had them and she thought it was about six months. But if they were pricey and almost new, why would anyone leave such good boots? And what would they wear on their feet with a long trail back to where whoever it was parked?"

"People do strange things," I said. "Maybe the person had taken them off to rest at the trail's end. Maybe he got scared by a bear."

Vida allowed for that possibility, but

promised to retrieve them from Bebe.

Milo called at two o'clock. "Want to look at pictures with me?"

"Uh . . . sure. Where will we do this?"

"In my office. Door open. Dustman just brought in the camera."

"Oh! Sure, I'll be right there. I have to ask — how did lunch go?"

"It went. We can talk about that later. I'm working." To prove the point, he hung up on me.

I was there in five minutes. My arrival didn't seem to cause any undue looks or comments from Lori, Bill, or even Jack. I headed straight into the sheriff's lair.

He picked up the camera and frowned as I sat down. "This thing's complicated. Too bad the owner didn't leave instructions with it. Whoa — maybe it's easier than I thought." He peered at an image. "Huh. Take a look. Where is that?"

I stared at a shot that could have been anywhere around Alpine — or the Pacific Northwest. Conifers, ground cover, bare cliffs rising out of the frame. "I'm stumped," I admitted, handing the camera back.

He clicked off a dozen or more images. "Ah! I'll be damned!" Milo handed me the camera. "Look closer at the background."

Vine maples framed the scene. A trail cut

through an open expanse of ferns, salal, and vines. In the distance, I saw an outcropping of rock with more ferns, moss, and a clump of branches from fallen trees.

I looked helplessly at Milo. "What am I supposed to see?"

He pointed to the frame. "Those branches in the background didn't fall naturally. Somebody put them there. That's the cave where Gus was found. I'm betting it was done by the bastard who killed him."

I sucked in my breath. "You're sure?"

"You bet. It's near the creek where the dogs lost Myrtle's scent."

I felt stupid, but I'd never ventured that far up on Mount Sawyer. Milo had probably tramped all over that part of the area as a kid. It wasn't far from town. It wasn't even far from my little log house.

"Is this all?" I asked.

"No. I must've started this backwards. There's a whole slew of other shots. If only we could've lifted some prints off . . ." Milo peered at the next series of pictures. "Interesting, if not helpful. See for yourself."

More trail scenes, but from a different angle. "Maybe the same trail — and a stream. "Sawyer or Carroll Creek?" I asked.

"Carroll. Consider when these were taken, especially the ones closer to town, about four frames down."

"Alpine Falls," I said. "No snow, plenty of ground cover, so it's late spring, early summer. The clump of bright green leaves is Indian poke, not open all the way. My mother called it false hellebore."

"Right. Go past the next dozen shots of the bridge and the Sky."

"No people." I gave Milo a curious look. "Whoever took these was only interested in scenery. How far back did you go?"

"A couple dozen," he said. "Hand it over. Burl Creek area next."

I watched Milo load photo after photo, looking increasingly frustrated. "Damn! This thing's just a scenic tour. But why end at that cave?" He looked inquiringly at me. "You got it, don't you? I do, too."

I nodded. "Those pictures were taken by Gus, except the last few frames his killer took. That's why Pete asked if Dwight found a camera. Gus liked photography. Pete and Shari bought him a nice one. Whoever killed him," I said, with a sinking feeling, "stole the camera and took those last shots as . . . a trophy?"

"And the Laskey kid had a medal." Milo grimaced. "It doesn't make sense. If Troy killed Gus while he was at large for those two days in June, why? Or are we talking two different people?"

"Was Gus killed for his camera? Something about it bothers me."

"Me too." Milo fingered his chin. "Pete can tell me if this belonged to Gus. I'm going over there now."

"Can I go . . ."

He bagged the camera and stood up. "No, you can't. This isn't a tag-team match." He put on his jacket and came around the desk to where I'd stood up. "Where are the priests going to be tonight?"

"Adam will be with me," I said.

"I don't know what's tougher," he said quietly. "Not being with you or being with you when we can't . . ." He nudged me out of the line of sight and put his arms around me. "Don't worry, I won't mess up your face."

I clung to him, eyes shut, closing out everything but Milo.

"Oh, shit!" Jack cried. "Sorry, boss, didn't know you were . . . busy."

"Damn!" Milo bellowed, letting me go. He shot me a fierce look. "See what I mean? Beat it, Emma, before I deck Mullins again."

I forced a smile. "Thanks, Sheriff," I said. "Don't forget *Vida's Cupboard* with the priests tomorrow night."

Milo followed me out of his office. "I

won't miss it. I haven't heard her show since . . . the last time."

He lingered inside so I could escape by myself. "The last time" referred to the night we'd unleashed ourselves all over my living room floor. I was still thinking about a repeat when I reached the office. And stupidly realized I'd forgotten to tell Milo about the boots Roy had found near the cave on Mount Sawyer. Love was turning my brain to sawdust.

I finished researching Resthaven by three-fifteen, hoping Mitch would return for the complete coverage. I just hoped Mitch would return, period.

To Milo's chagrin, Pete had been uncertain about whether or not the camera was the one he'd bought for Gus. "The dumb-shit got it here in town," the sheriff explained on the phone, "but Gus wanted a lens that didn't work with that model, so they went to Monroe to get the right kind. Pete's going to look for the receipt."

I started to tell him about the boots, but he was interrupted by what sounded like Dwight delivering bad news. "Got an over-turned RV on 2," Milo said, and hung up.

Vida finished her current spate of advice-seeking letters and tromped into my office around three-thirty. Sitting in my surviving visitor's chair, she asked me to explain Amer Wasco's role in the hiking boots saga.

I related the cobbler's account. Vida accepted my odd notion without question. "I'll pick them up tomorrow," she said. "Maybe Billy can talk Milo into doing something with the boots. DNA, I assume. You're thinking Troy or Gus?"

"Neither, maybe. Those two sound too big for size nines."

"Hands and feet can fool you," she said. "Sizes are so iffy. I used to be a twelve in dresses." She shook her head and made her exit.

Ten minutes later, Sunny Rhodes timidly rapped on my doorjamb. "Emma," she said softly, "where's Leo?"

"The back shop, maybe," I said. "Can I help?"

She entered my cubbyhole, but didn't sit down. "It's a change in the Venison Inn ad. We're opening at six instead of seven on weekends as long as there's enough snow up at the pass."

I told her that was easily fixed and asked how her family was enjoying the holidays. I hadn't seen the VI's hostess lately. She worked evenings while her husband, Oren, tended bar.

"Fine," Sunny replied. "Davin's home

from Western for the holidays. I hear Roger is thinking of going there."

"He toured the campus over the Christmas holiday," I said.

"Roger visited last night." She glanced into the empty newsroom, making sure Vida wasn't in hearing range. "I'm so glad Davin was in Bellingham when Roger got into trouble. Roger seemed subdued, though typical in some ways. He wanted Davin to order a pizza, but our son hasn't eaten any since he almost swallowed that thing last June."

I'd forgotten about the incident. "Oh — the quarter in the topping?"

Sunny nodded. "Thank goodness Dr. Starr is such a good dentist. It wasn't a quarter, but something metal that broke his tooth."

"Yuck," I said. "Part of a utensil?"

"No, more like . . . jewelry. I told Davin he should save it in case someone lost it, but he told me he'd already thrown it out."

An odd thought came to me. "Do you recall what it looked like?"

Sunny shook her head. "I was too upset over Davin breaking his tooth. I'd better go. I still have Avon deliveries to make."

After Sunny left, I went to the back shop, where Kip and Leo were conferring. I inter-

rupted them to alert Kip about the over-
turned RV.

Vida reappeared a few minutes later. "I
just spoke with your brother about my
program," she said. "He wondered if we
might get together now to go over some of
the topics we should cover." She made a
face. "I suppose he doesn't think Presbyteri-
ans know anything about the Catholic
clergy. Very presumptuous, really. So little
difference between the major faiths in terms
of Christian goals."

"I suspect Ben is thinking more of geogra-
phy," I said. "St. Mary's Igloo, the Mississippi Delta, and Tuba City are a lot different than Alpine."

Vida gazed at the low ceiling. "Yes, but
that can't be helped. Perhaps you're right.
Ben did have some interesting tales to tell
last night. I enjoyed Adam's story about
whale blubber. Anyway, we're meeting at
the rectory at four. Am I leaving you in the
lurch?"

I thought about the poems Spence had
given me, but they could wait. I hadn't read
them yet. "Go ahead. I assume Mitch won't
be back, so tomorrow we'll have a staff
meeting and divvy up the workload. By the
way, did you see Milo and Ben at the ski
lodge coffee shop?"

Vida again looked at the ceiling, this time as if she could see through the roof and was seeking divine assistance. "Bebe was so aggravating. She insisted we sit behind a pillar for privacy. The only time I saw either Milo or Ben was when they came in — separately."

I shared Vida's disappointment, though I'd known all along that if she'd seen or heard anything that had gone on between my lover and my brother, she would've said so as soon as she got back from lunch. I'd have to wait for Milo — or Ben — to tell me about their confrontation.

Later, just as I was about to quit for the day, I called the rectory to see if Vida was still there. Mimi wearily informed me she was. "I don't understand why it's taking so long," she lamented. "Mrs. Runkel's show only lasts fifteen minutes."

I felt like saying that off the air, Vida could go on forever. But I didn't. My query had been answered satisfactorily. I called Milo and asked if he could meet for a quick drink at the Venison Inn.

"I can't," he said with regret. "I just got back from that RV mess at the pass. It's snowing further up. Three people hospitalized; one had to be airlifted to Harborview in Seattle. Some idiot biker cut off the RV just beyond milepost 63, and the driver lost control. The state patrol caught the biker just over the county line, so we're stuck with him here."

"Gosh, that's interesting," I said. "It almost sounds like news."

"Shut up. It'll be in the damned log." He hung up on me. Again.

I caught Kip at the door and gave him the latest from the sheriff's office. He could put it on our site from home after he got official word from any county employee who might not hang up on him. "You are now a reporter," I told him. "We'll discuss that more tomorrow."

"But I'm not a good writer," he protested.

"That hasn't stopped a lot of reporters I know," I said.

On the way home, I made a quick stop at the Grocery Basket to pick up cod for homemade fish and chips. I avoided running into anyone who might want to chat. I'd save my sociability for Adam and Ben.

My son arrived half an hour later. I asked him if his uncle was joining us. He told me Ben had been invited to dinner at the senior Bourgettes' home.

"They asked me, too," Adam said, between bites of raw cabbage I'd chopped for cole slaw, "but I figured I needed some

Mom time."

I was touched — and said so. "Speaking of sentiment, get the manila envelope out of my purse. I want you to see something."

Adam took a sip from the can of beer he'd opened. "Is it alive?"

"If it ticks, it's a bomb. I got the envelope from Fleetwood."

He retrieved it, sat down at the kitchen table, and removed the pages. "Fleetwood wrote you love poems?"

"Yes, and he always signs them 'Myrtle.' It's his real name."

"Funny, Mom . . ." Adam read for a moment. "Mushy mush. Who's Harold?"

"Our retired superior court judge, now in a nursing home."

"Who's Myrtle?"

"The judge's alleged girlfriend."

Adam sniffed the paper. "Lavender? No, more like musk ox."

"You've been in Alaska too long. It's jasmine."

"Hunh. This would've been steamy stuff — in *1888*."

"Is there a date? I didn't have time to see."

He thumbed through the flimsy pages. "Some are dated, some not, May to August, 1988. Why did Fleetwood give you these?"

Filling my deep-fry cooker with oil, I told

Adam about Myrtle. He was bemused. "What is this place? A dump site for spare body parts?"

"That's part of forest life. Lost hikers, skiers, campers, climbers. Animals. Avalanches, flash floods, falling trees. Meth labs discovered by the unwary. Hermits who dislike company. It's a good area to ditch a murder victim. KingCo figures there may be dozens of Ted Bundy's and the Green River Killer's victims who've never been found."

Adam shot me a curious glance. "And you worry about *me?*"

I laughed. "You have more room up there for bodies."

"That reminds me," Adam said, "I like your resident recluse's painting. What's he done lately?"

"No clue," I admitted, not knowing if Craig Laurentis was still alive and able to exercise his genius. "What about the poems?"

"Mostly love stuff except for the last page. Myrtle sounds like she's dumping Harold. Guilt. He had a wife."

I frowned. That sounded like a motive for murder.

We passed the rest of the evening quietly. Ben hadn't spoken to Adam about the lunch with Milo. My son thought his uncle brooded a bit afterwards, but had acted more like himself when Vida arrived. We went back to the Harold and Myrtle Show, which had caught Adam's fancy.

"How could she just disappear?" he mused aloud.

"It happens," I conceded, "but it *is* odd. Do you want to do some detective work with me tomorrow during my lunch hour?"

Adam was game. More than game, since he had a plan of his own that had nothing to do with Myrtle. "I'll go to the mall first and pick out a few of my *needs* as opposed to my *wants*."

My son was referring to an old maternal lecture. "On my credit card?"

Adam gave me a wide-eyed look. "You'd rather pay cash?"

My middle name being Sap, I simply sighed — and smiled. It was good to be a sap if it meant fulfilling my maternal *needs*.

FOURTEEN

Adam and I went to bed before eleven that night. I slept like a log until my son woke me up around five A.M. Bleary-eyed, I struggled to focus on him. "What's wrong?" I asked in a foggy voice.

"Don't panic," he said, his face illuminated by a strange light that seemed almost otherworldly. "The carport's on fire. I called 911. Come on, we'd better go outside."

"Oh, no!" I shrieked. "My car!"

"Never mind that, just move."

I threw off the covers and grabbed my bathrobe. I couldn't find my slippers. Then, as I realized Adam was holding some kind of flashlight, he beamed it on the blue slip-ons that were half-hidden under the bedspread. When we reached the living room, I could hear the sirens in the distance. I could also see an ominous orange glow in the front window beyond the Christmas tree.

"How could that happen?" I demanded as

Adam dragged me to the front door.

"No clue. Have you got anything out there that might explode?"

"I don't think so." I noticed he'd pulled a heavy sweater over his pajama bottoms and was wearing unlaced boots. "What woke you up?" I asked as we went out onto the front porch.

"I'm not sure," he said, "but I was thirsty, so I went into the kitchen to get a glass of water and saw the flames. The fire must've just started." He cocked his head. "It's a good thing I parked my rental further down the drive. The sirens sound like they're close."

"They come from the courthouse, so it only takes a few minutes." The rain had stopped, but everything around the house would still be wet. "This is awful! What would've happened if you weren't here?"

"Maybe Dodge would've been with you," he said matter-of-factly.

But Adam's comment suggested a sinister idea. "So we could both burn to a crisp?"

My son was startled. "You think this is some deliberate kind of thing?"

"I don't know. Here are the firefighters — and the medics. Damn!"

"Let's go inside. The living room should be safe." He took my arm.

"Wait," I said. "Can you take a picture?"

"Mom . . ."

"Please."

"Okay, go sit on the sofa and don't move. I'll get my camera."

I obeyed, trying to shut out the shouts of the firefighters and the sounds of the hoses. I'd left the front door open, knowing that one of the medics was bound to show up. Sure enough, just as Adam reappeared with his camera, Vic Thorstensen came inside.

"Emma! Are you all right?"

"Yes. Are your parents watching my fiasco?" I inquired, referring to Tilly and Erwin Thorstensen, who lived across the street.

"If they aren't now, they will be," he said cheerfully. "They're early risers. Any idea what caused your little inferno?"

I shook my head. "How's my car?"

"I didn't get too close," Vic said. "You're not in shock, are you?"

"How would I know?"

"Let me have a look." He opened his kit, but I waved a hand.

"Forget it. I'm fine. I'd just like to know how the fire got —" I stopped as Adam came back inside. "Well?"

"It's not too bad," my son said. "It didn't get to your car. As far as I can tell, it started with a bunch of papers by the woodpile next to the house. Some exterior log damage and maybe the carport roof. You're lucky you've got a concrete floor."

"Papers by the woodpile?" I said, puzzled.

"It had to be something like that," Adam said. "It wasn't spontaneous combustion." He frowned. "Come to think of it, there was an odd smell — like . . ." His voice trailed off. "I'm not sure what. Let me check with the firefighters. I think they've almost got it out."

Adam started out the front door — and nearly collided with Milo.

"Goddamn it, Emma," he bellowed, pushing past my son and almost stepping on Vic, "what now?"

"I didn't do anything!" I yelled. "I was sound asleep."

"Move it, Vic," Milo said. "And close that damned door. It's colder than a witch's tit in here." The sheriff plopped down beside me. He was wearing his uniform, but his shirt wasn't tucked in and he didn't have on his regulation hat. Obviously, he'd been in a rush to find out what kind of nitwit stunt I'd pulled this time. "Are you okay?" he asked in a more normal tone.

"Yes. Just upset."

He put an arm around me. "Beat it, Vic. I'm taking over now. Get your folks to make

336

you some coffee. They're out on their front porch."

"Yes, sir," Vic said. "Bye, Emma. Glad you're in good hands."

I pressed my face against Milo's chest. "I'm really not an imbecile."

He smoothed my tangled hair. "I know. That's what worries me."

I looked up at him. "What do you mean?"

"Wait until I finish talking to the firefighters. Mmm. You feel good. You always do." He kissed the top of my head.

"So do you, big guy."

"Hey, Mom," Adam called from the doorway. "One of the firemen wants to talk to you and the sheriff. Shall I tell him to come back later?"

Milo slackened his hold. I glared at my son. "Don't be a smartass. Plug in the coffeepot and show some respect for your elders."

Adam headed for the kitchen. Milo let go of me and stood up. "I want to take a look out there first. You're sure you're okay?"

"Yes. Yes, yes." I got off the sofa and poked him in the chest. "Do your sheriff bit. I'm not going anywhere."

"Good." He went out the door, making sure it was unlocked.

I joined Adam in the kitchen, where I

looked out the window into the carport. "I can't see much from here. Should I open the back door?"

"You better wait," Adam advised. "The fire was pretty close to it. They're probably showing that whole area to Dodge."

"I'd rather not see it," I said, taking mugs out of the cupboard. The clock on the stove read 5:33. "There's no point going back to bed."

"Probably not," Adam said — and smiled. "You and Dodge are kind of cute — for old people. I like seeing ol' Mom happy. I'm off the hook."

"What do you mean?"

Adam grew serious. "I feel guilty about not being around much. Now you've got someone to take care of you. Dad wasn't good at that."

"He had so many other people to take of." I leaned against the sink. "He lived in a world I was never part of. I used to long for an evening with him at the opera or the Top of the Mark. I envied Sandra, at least when she wasn't shoplifting at I. Magnin or undressing in Gump's display window. The social outings, the symphony, the ballet, the museums, baseball games . . . that Baghdad-by-the-Bay magic."

"Oh, he did that stuff," Adam said, "but

338

he didn't like it much. He told me he never stayed awake for more than fifteen minutes of any opera Sandra dragged him to."

I was astonished, being an opera lover myself. "He didn't?"

"It was all business," Adam said. "He was expected to do those things and Sandra made sure he did. Her money paid for his empire. Dad didn't like baseball. He was strictly a pro football fan."

"He didn't like baseball?" I was incredulous. "That's horrible!"

Adam shrugged. "Did you really know him?"

"I guess not," I said, reeling from my son's revelations. "We never had time to talk about much except newspapers, even from the start."

"Those he liked," Adam said. "All that other stuff was for show."

"Or for Sandra," I said bitterly.

"Both." Adam looked past me. "Coffee's almost ready, Sheriff."

"Good," Milo said from the kitchen doorway. "Bring it in the living room. Come on, Emma. Ernie Holt's here."

I knew only the name. Ernie was a relative newcomer, having moved from Oso in the late spring. He'd been the subject of Scott Chamoud's last personal profile story.

Before serving as a helicopter pilot in the Gulf War, Ernie was a smoke jumper for the Forest Service.

"Hi, Ms. Lord," Ernie said, holding out a grimy hand. "You look as if you survived your little scare."

" 'Scare' is right," I said. "Take a seat."

Milo waved at the armchair. "Go ahead." The sheriff sat down on the sofa with me. Adam remained in the kitchen, apparently waiting for the coffee to finish perking.

Ernie's angular face was all business. He had a dark buzz cut and the keen blue eyes I'd expect of a former chopper pilot. "The fire was started with some kind of accelerant, probably kerosene on newspapers. The logs were pretty dry, so it took off, but luckily didn't do much damage. You must've called in right after it started."

"My son called. You're saying this was set on purpose?"

"Probably," Ernie said. "A noise outside might've woke your son."

I looked at Milo, but he was staring straight ahead. The sheriff had reverted to type.

Ernie, however, was looking at me. "Do you have any enemies?"

"I run a newspaper," I said. "What more can I say?"

340

Ernie showed the barest hint of a smile. "I understand. But can you think of someone you've offended recently?"

Adam appeared with two mugs of coffee. He gave one to Milo and the other to Ernie. "I'll get ours, Mom. What about Mr. Andrews?"

"No," Milo said. "That's speculation. Andrews is not the type."

"Guess I'll stick to making coffee." Adam returned to the kitchen.

"Okay," Ernie said. "Anybody else?"

Milo reached inside his jacket, presumably to get his cigarettes, but apparently thought better of it while sitting across the room from a firefighter, and took out a roll of mints instead. "Look, Ernie," he said, "if it's arson, I step in now. I wanted Ms. Lord to hear from you how the fire started. Finish your coffee. You earned it. I'll keep you in the loop."

"I still have a report to fill out," Ernie said.

"Yes," Milo agreed, "and it'll come to me as well as to the county commissioners. This isn't the army. This is SkyCo."

"Okay." Ernie sipped from his mug and looked at the Christmas tree. "Those lights are kind of close to the branches. How long have you had your tree up, Ms. Lord?"

"Ms. Lord never turns on the lights," Milo

said before I could answer. "Ms. Lord lives in a very dark world."

"That's right," Adam put in as he entered the room and handed me my coffee. "My mother is a creature of the night."

Ernie drank more coffee before he stood up. "I guess I'm finished. Thank you, Ms. Lord. Thank you, Sheriff. Thank you . . ."

"Father Lord," I said. "My son's a priest."

"Right." Ernie gave the mug to Adam. "Thanks . . . Father." He left, looking bemused.

Milo shook his head. "Poor bastard. He spent too much time in that chopper."

I started to giggle. "Now somebody's trying to kill me!"

"Emma . . . ," Milo said.

"Mom . . . ," Adam said.

I sobered. "It's stupid. Who'd do that? Andrews wouldn't dirty his pudgy pink hands." I paused, hearing the fire truck pull away. "Well?"

Milo took out his cigarettes. "I've got some ideas of my own."

I got an ashtray from the end table. "Here. And give me one. How come you and Leo didn't light up last night?"

Milo made a face. "And have Vida yap at us? No thanks."

Adam had sat down in the armchair. "I

342

haven't seen you smoke in years, Mom. I thought you quit."

"I did. Often," I said, taking the cigarette Milo had lighted for me.

Adam looked askance at us. I turned back to the sheriff. "What ideas?"

He gazed at me through a haze of smoke. "You know better than to ask me that."

I did, but I remained curious. "Fine. Should I make breakfast?"

"Sure," Milo said.

"Pancakes?" Adam asked.

I sighed. "You're not saying Mass today with your uncle?"

"I wasn't going to," Adam said. "In fact, I'd decided to sleep in for once. But pancakes are a good trade-off."

Milo was standing up. "How long does it take to make pancakes?"

"Ten minutes," I said, also on my feet. "Have you got amnesia?"

"It's been three weeks since you made me pancakes. Did *you* forget my watch broke?" He hitched up his belt. He had lost weight during his Bellevue ordeal. "I'm going home to shower and change." He rubbed the stubble on his chin. "And shave. Take your time."

The sheriff left. "What," my son inquired, "was that 'three weeks' about? You already said you hadn't seen much of Dodge lately."

"Come in the kitchen and I'll give you the brief version," I said. "In fact, do you want to shower and shave, too?"

"No. I'd rather hear what happened. It sounds interesting."

"That," I said, leading the way into the kitchen, "is putting it mildly. I already told your uncle, but it didn't seem to move him to compassion for Milo or me."

While mixing pancake batter, I related the Bellevue standoff saga.

"That's horrific," Adam said when I'd finished. "You must've almost lost it while that went down on TV."

"I actually passed out at one point," I admitted.

"Were you alone?"

"No," I said. "Believe it or not, I was here with . . . oh, God!" I said under my breath as I heard a mellifluous voice call my name from the living room. Milo must have forgotten to lock the door behind him. "Speak of the devil. It's Fleetwood. Tell him I'm dead."

Adam left the kitchen. I heard him say good morning. I heard Spence ask for me. I heard Adam tell him I was dead. I heard Spence laugh. And then he was in the kitchen, obviously amused.

"You've looked better, but you're able to move," he said. "Is that pancake batter? A great favorite of mine."

"Go away. My son will eat all of it. He's one hungry priest."

"Ah!" Spence cried, offering Adam his hand. "I thought you'd dumped the brutal sheriff to take a young lover. How do you do, Father?"

Adam seemed reluctant to shake hands, but he gave in. "Hi. Nice to meet you." He turned to me. "I'm heading for the showers after all, Mom." He made a hasty exit. I didn't know if my son was chicken or afraid he might break Spence's nose.

Spence leaned against the fridge. "Thoughtless of you to have a fire before I woke up. Don't worry, I got it on our first newscast at six."

"You're a real jerk," I said. "I'm not putting it online. It'll be in the log, no name, just an address, and not until next week."

Spence's expression grew serious. "You're damned lucky, Emma. You really could be dead. What happened?"

"See for yourself," I said. "I haven't had the nerve to look yet."

He opened the door and went into the carport. "Come on. It's not too bad. Your car needs washing, though."

I gritted my teeth and joined him. The scorching on the cabin's logs was ugly. A lingering odor of kerosene hung on the cool morning air. The concrete floor was a mess of wet pulp, apparently from the paper that had helped start the fire. My car definitely needed a bath. It would've been nice if the firefighters had hosed it down before they left. Ashes covered part of the windshield and the hood. The fireplace wood had suffered the most, but it was going to be burned up eventually. I should be grateful that nothing worse had happened.

"How much of a deductible have you got?" Spence asked.

"It's either five hundred or a grand," I said. "I have to call Brendan Shaw."

Mr. Radio followed me back inside. "How do you think it started?"

"Ask the sheriff."

"No thanks." He took out one of his imported black cigarettes. "Anything new on Laskey?"

"Sadly, no."

He flicked ash in the sink. "Do I get pancakes?"

"Dodge is coming to breakfast."

"The sheriff and the priest." Spence inhaled and blew smoke rings. "If I stayed, what could possibly go wrong?"

346

I put two skillets on the stove. "My brother may stop by."

"Good Lord, woman, why not call in the Marines, too?"

"The Gulf War chopper pilot just left," I said, filling one skillet with rashers of bacon. Adam reappeared, giving Spence a curious glance.

Mr. Radio held up a hand. "I'm leaving, Father. Mother Lord has rejected my latest attempts to seduce her." Spence left, whistling.

"That guy's so phony I almost like him," Adam said. "You ever . . . ?"

"No!" I shook my head. "He's not a bad guy. Spence has carried some heavy baggage along the airwaves of life."

"Most do," Adam allowed. "Did Vida finish the orange juice?"

"She only had one drink." The phone rang. "Can you grab that?"

Adam shut the fridge before going to the living room. I couldn't hear a word over the clatter of freeing my griddle from the stove's drawer.

"Who was that?" I asked when he returned almost immediately.

"The sheriff canceled his pancakes," Adam said. "He's on the job."

"Oh." I looked at the stove's clock, which

displayed 6:44. "I wonder what's going on. And don't ask if I can wheedle it out of him. When it comes to his job, Milo is impervious to my charms."

"Is that why you guys fight and make up and fight and . . ."

"Can it. Just sit there and eat your pancakes."

He ate almost all of them. If the sheriff had shown up, I'd have ended up with toast. I asked my son what he ate in Alaska. He insisted he did just fine, but I envisioned him stalking a bear for breakfast or fishing ice floes for undersized pike.

My son said he'd drive me to work, then return to wash my car and clean the carport. Despite his stated relief that I finally had a man around to ensure I could — usually — walk and talk at the same time without incident, it felt nice to have Adam do something for ol' Mom.

Vida practically assaulted me when I came through the door. "Emma! How could I not know what happened until I turned on KSKY as I drove to work! Spencer said you had a fire!"

I glanced at my watch. It was eight-ten. "My chauffeur was late. He had to say his prayers."

"Your . . . oh! Adam, of course." Vida and

348

Alison exchanged quick glances. "How did the fire start? Spencer didn't state the cause."

"It's being investigated. We've got a busy day ahead. Who has the bakery run?" I'd forgotten, with Mitch out of the rotation.

"I do," Alison said. "I mean, I already did."

I smiled at her. "We're going to miss you."

"Maybe you won't have to," she said. "Ginny called a few minutes ago to say she was thinking about part-time. Between the two of us, we might be able to make that work. My classes are mornings only."

I considered my options. "That's a possibility. As you know, Amanda Hanson's my fallback person."

"Amanda's pregnant," Alison said.

"What?" I shrieked.

"I heard it last night," Alison said. "In fact, she only found out late yesterday. After trying so long, she thought it was a false —"

"Good grief!" Vida cried. "Why didn't Marje tell me?"

"Because her rear end hurts?" I suggested.

"She's lucky I don't make it worse," Vida muttered, standing in the doorway. "No excuse. Unless she tried to call me while I was out, but didn't leave a message. When?" she demanded of Alison.

"When?" Alison looked startled. "Oh —

349

the due date. Early July."

"Well now." Vida reflected briefly before going to her desk.

Leo came out of the back shop. "What's the commotion?"

"Amanda and Walt Hanson got the key to the parent trap," I said.

Leo raised his eyebrows. "You mean the kid Roger . . ."

I shook my head. "No. They did it on their own."

"You scared me," he murmured, heading into the newsroom.

I turned back to Alison. "No word from Mitch?"

She glumly shook her head. "Poor man."

Kip joined us, looking fresher than he had the previous morning. "That's awful about your fire. You want me to post it on the website?"

"No. At least not yet," I amended. "Let's wait for the official cause."

He nodded. "Then I'll clean up the mess out back. Our trash got trashed last night. There's stuff all over, almost to Railroad Avenue."

"Go for it," I said, heading toward Vida's desk.

"Here," I said, digging the manila envelope out of my purse. "When you get time, let me know what you make of these."

Vida pounced. "I have time now." She peeked into the envelope and sniffed. "Jasmine? My, my." Her eyebrows lifted as she carefully removed the fragile pages. "Poems? Harold? Myrtle? Well now!"

I left her to the task. Pouring coffee and selecting a maple bar, I went into my cubbyhole to fortify myself before doing Mitch's run to the sheriff's office. It wasn't quite eight-thirty, but it was now or never.

The rain had stopped and the clouds had lifted. I could see the crests of Mount Baldy on one side of the street and Mount Sawyer on the other. Yet the same wind sending the clouds away had a cold bite as it blew through the valley of the Sky. I walked faster, crossing Third.

"He's not here," Sam Heppner said with what sounded like uncustomary pleasure.

"Who?" I asked. "Dwight Gould?"

"He's not here, either," Sam said, reverting to his usual sour self.

Lori Cobb, however, was in place. I turned to her. "How are you?"

"Okay." She smiled wanly. "I sent Mrs. Runkel the details about Grandpa's funeral for your website. It's at the Baptist church tomorrow, one o'clock. Short notice, but it was hard to get the family to agree."

"She'll be there," I said. "I'll try to go, but we're shorthanded."

Bill Blatt, who had been on the phone, wished me good morning.

"Where is everybody?" I asked him.

Sam answered first. "Working," he said, looking down at me. "We're making up for lost time."

"Where did you lose it?" I asked innocently.

Sam glared at me. "According to the boss, we didn't do jack while he was in Bellevue holding his kid's hand. Serves him right for leaving Dwight in charge. It would've helped if Dodge had tended to business after he got back . . ."

Bill mercifully intervened. "Come on, Sam, Dwight has seniority. The boss made the right call. Don't bleed all over the citizenry."

Sam's allusion to Milo's defection on Monday afternoon rankled, but I refused to even look at him. Instead, I studied the log. No names of the juveniles in the Rudolph caper or The Pines burglary bust. "How come my fire isn't here?" I asked, addressing the question to Bill, who would at least be civil.

"Dodge hasn't seen Ernie Holt's report yet," Bill said. "You know the boss . . . I mean, you know how he works. Not logged until it's official."

"No problem," I said. "Deadline is past," I added, in case the deputies, like their boss, had forgotten. "I'm done here."

I made my exit, vowing that if I had to put up with any more guff from the deputies while Mitch was AWOL, I'd let Vida check the log.

As soon as I entered the newsroom, Vida waved the manila envelope at me. "I'm stunned. We must talk." She got up, not waiting for me to lead the way into my cubbyhole. "I confess I never took those rumors about Myrtle and the judge seriously. How did you get these?"

I explained about Spence's sister, Marsha. Vida was perplexed. "Why would she bother? I remember his retired-Alpiners series. I helped Spencer put it together. But there's no way he could have used these poems on the air without a scandal. There's more to it."

"What do you mean?"

"Marsha Foster-Klein's unsentimental," Vida explained. "Not the sort to save old love poems and pass them on to her brother without a reason. And the note Myrtle sent is ominous."

I nodded. "My reaction, too. I didn't know

Judge Krogstad. Is it possible he had a violent streak?"

Vida put her elbow on my desk and rested her forehead on her hand. "I shouldn't think so. In his prime, he was the most judicious of men — as well he should be. He barely made deadlines to hand down rulings. I never heard of him losing his temper in court despite ample provocation. The word describing him best is 'dispassionate.' "

"Except when it came to Myrtle," I noted.

Vida was dubious. "I can't imagine him in the throes of passion. Marsha wasn't here for much more than two years. I'm thinking bones, of course. She left around the turn of this century. I believe her last day on the bench was New Year's Eve, 1999. Now let me think . . ."

I always wondered how the machinations in Vida's head worked. I pictured tiny versions of her scampering all over Alpine, peeking in windows, poking in corners, picking up the phone, recalling every sight, sound, and sensibility along the way.

"Yes," she finally said. "That October, while you and Ben were in Italy, one of the Overholts found some bones when they were working in their pumpkin patch. The Eversons were all agog, but it turned out to be several cats, a litter perhaps. Marsha

354

probably heard about it because — being so close to Halloween and black cats — I put it in 'Scene.' "

I was puzzled. "So she'd wonder about Harold's connection to Myrtle? How would she know from a 'Scene' mention?"

"She wouldn't," Vida said. "I made no reference to Myrtle, but there was the usual buzz in town. Who knows what else Marsha might have found while taking Harold's place? Maybe she saved the poems because she had her own suspicions. In her position, especially since she was leaving town, she wouldn't want to get involved. Much better to hand them over to her brother, since he's in the media."

"And not tell him why?"

Vida shrugged. "Marsha is a brusque sort of person. She probably felt there was no need unless the whole situation resurfaced."

"And now it has," I murmured as my phone rang.

Vida left as I took the call. "Dodge is here," Adam said. "He won't let me wash your car."

"Why? Does he think you won't do a good job?"

"No, it's not that," Adam said. "He says it's evidence and he's impounding it. In fact, there it goes now."

"What?" I was flummoxed. "Did he say *anything?*"

"No. He told me to beat it. Then he and Gould did whatever."

"At least you can clean the carport."

"No, I can't. Dodge put crime-scene tape around it."

"Damn! He isn't about to cuff you, is he?"

"I don't think so. He just left."

I sighed. "I shouldn't be annoyed. He's doing his job. What are you going to do, or are you under house arrest?"

"I'm monitoring Jorge and the villagers. Hey — that sounds like a band. I'll alert you if Fleetwood stops by to do a remote for KSKY."

I hung up, but the phone rang again before I could get more coffee.

It was my nice neighbor, Viv Marsden. "Are you okay?" she asked. "I know your son's with you, so I didn't want to be a pest."

I assured her I was fine. "Thankfully, the damage was minimal. Something woke up Adam just after the fire started."

"That was lucky," Viv said. "I was questioned by the sheriff. So were the other neighbors. Dodge took our side of the street and one of his sourpuss deputies took the other."

"What did the sheriff quiz you about?"

"If we'd heard or seen anything odd," Viv said. "Val and I didn't wake up until we heard the sirens. I've talked to some of the other neighbors, but none of them were awake, either. I haven't seen the Nelsons since before Christmas. Is it true their younger kids were arrested for burglary?"

The grapevine was working efficiently. "Yes, at The Pines."

"Maybe Laverne and Doyle went out of town for Christmas. He's been unemployed since Jack Blackwell fired him from the mill."

Both men were at the bottom of my "Favorite Alpiners" list. Viv and I wished each other a better day and rang off.

My phone rang yet again. The voice was aggravatingly familiar. "You," Rolf Fisher said, "are an ungrateful wench. Could you not give me the courtesy of a *merci* in some form of communication?"

"Sorry," I said. "I've been busy. Thank you."

"That's it?"

"Isn't that what you wanted me to say?"

"It's not enough. Picture the Loire Valley in this beautiful, brumal season. Darkness falls on my quaint cottage among the barren trees. The mist settles on the starkly

357

withered grasses lining the riverbank."

"You're writing a book, aren't you?"

"Whatever I'm doing, I'm doing it without you." He sounded almost serious. "What's wrong, Emma? You can't bother to be polite?"

"I'm really busy. Ben and Adam are here. I apologize, Rolf. I'm . . ."

I looked up. The sheriff was leaning against the doorjamb. "Oh! Emergency! I have to hang up." I fumbled trying to disconnect — and dropped the phone on the desk.

Milo snatched the receiver. "Listen up, Fisher. If you ever call Emma again, I'll arrest you for harassment and throw away the key." He slammed the phone down and glared at me. "What was that about?"

"He called me," I said, in a pale imitation of my real voice. "I never thanked him for the gift basket. I forgot. You threw it out. Except for some cheese. And please stop glaring at me like that."

The sheriff straightened up. "Sorry." He looked sheepish. "I forgot I was the jealous type."

"Don't worry about it," I said, feeling more like me. "Rolf's a jerk. Tell me about my car, my carport, my . . . Why aren't you eating a bear claw?" Today's pastries included Milo's favorite.

"I already did while I was talking to Walsh."

"Have you had breakfast?"

"The bear claw *was* breakfast. I'll grab one more on my way out."

"Why are you here?"

"I guess I wanted to see if you were okay."

"I am. I'm tougher than I look."

"No, you're not." He sighed. "Don't ask about the fire, okay? I'm still working on it. I'll see you later." He wheeled around and left.

Ten minutes later, Alison brought my mail. "Late again," she said. "Marlowe Whipp says they're still backed up. Any news on Mr. Everson?"

I told her to ask Vida. I needed more coffee — and a nap. The early-morning drama and lack of sleep had caught up with me.

Leo met me in the newsroom. "Mitch called while you were on the phone," he said.

Vida looked up so fast that her red-and-blue-striped pillbox almost fell off. "What? Where is he? What did he say?" She seemed poised to vault across the space between her desk and Leo's.

"On the lam," he replied. "Brenda's in a bad way, so he's taking her someplace and didn't say where. He apologized for leaving us in the lurch. I told him to wait to talk to you, but he couldn't."

"What about Troy?" I asked.

"He's improving." Leo shrugged. "Now what?"

Vida had removed her hat. "Does he know about Andrews?"

Leo nodded. "A PI type checked the local motels. The manager where they were staying didn't cooperate and warned Mitch."

"That puts us in a bind," I murmured. "How are we for ads this coming week?"

Leo paused. "Over halfway to sixty-forty. All the post-holiday and pre-inventory sales help. Do I get to be Clark Kent or Jimmy Olsen?"

"Kip's already Jimmy," I said. "You're Clark. When you're not being Superadman. We'll survive. It's the long term that's dicey."

Leo grimaced. "Mitch is the best reporter we've had. An amoeba would've been better than Curtis Mayne, but still . . . where do we start?"

"Get more chairs and tell Kip we're having a staff meeting."

Leo went off to carry out his orders. Vida leaned toward me. "I'm taking on the sheriff's office. I have a source there, after all."

I cringed inwardly. Vida's florid style didn't fit hard news, but her dogged nosiness made up for her writing. If Kip could get Turk Durgan to cooperate, he could do a feature, maybe even another piece on how snowboarding had become the latest winter craze since the Salt Lake City Olympics. I'd keep tabs on Gus's remains. It took almost an hour to share our information. Vida was agog; Kip was thrilled; Leo was bemused; Alison volunteered to take up any slack that was left over; I was uneasy, hoping we hadn't seen the last of Mitch Laskey.

Adam agreed to pick me up at noon. He was fifteen minutes late.

"Where were you?" I demanded, getting into the car. "I'm freezing."

"In thirty-five-degree weather? You're a wuss, Mom. Try thirty-five below with a wind chill factor of minus fifty."

"No thanks. What have you been doing?"

"I went to the mall, finding sale items for you to buy me. Before that, I made us turkey sandwiches. Check the cooler on the backseat."

I looked over my shoulder. "Thanks," I said humbly, and dug out my credit card. "Use this. You can pick up your needs and even a couple of wants. The local merchants will honor it for you. Take a right on Front and then a quick left onto the Burl Creek Road."

"Thanks, Mom. You know I've never spent any of my inheritance on me. I never will."

"You amaze me," I said as we passed Old Mill Park, where Rudolph had returned. He seemed to be shivering in the chilling rain and wind.

"Where are we going?" Adam asked. "This part of town has changed since I sort of lived here during college breaks."

"Thanks to the community college, it's grown," I said. "A few new houses along this route, Spence's radio station — rebuilt since it was bombed — and of course the campus just ahead."

"Nice setting in the forest," Adam said as we went by KSKY and approached the college. "It looks like they've added some buildings."

"They have," I said. "The new fisheries classrooms open this spring. Slow down. We're almost there. Turn right on the gravel road."

He obeyed, stopping after fifty feet of the bumpy, crunchy ride. "What a dump."

"That's exactly what it is," I said. "The Eversons live next to it."

"In a dump?"

"No, they have a nice house." The last time I'd been here, Milo had found the Pikes dead in their old truck. He wouldn't let me look, which was just as well. The area near the river was much the same — just covered with a more recent layer of trash.

"Why are we here?" Adam asked after getting the cooler from the backseat and giving me my sandwich along with a bag of potato chips. "This is fun and all that, but as a tourist stop, it's kind of bleak."

"What would you say if I told you Myrtle's buried here?"

Adam took me seriously, but didn't speak until he'd taken a bite of sandwich. "I'd say you have a reason for thinking that. Is this county property?"

"Yes. There was a house here years ago, but it was torn down or abandoned. At some point, there was a property dispute. Myrtle claimed the adjacent land belonged to her. Judge Krogstad ruled otherwise. The land reverted to the county and people began using it for garbage."

I waited for Adam's reaction, which came after he swallowed some of his sandwich. "He killed her over the dispute? Or they became lovers while it was being sorted out?"

"The latter, I'm guessing. I doubt she wrote those poems to get a favorable ruling. Rejected love is a good motive for murder. If he did kill her, how fitting would it be for him to bury her body here?"

Adam nodded. "I haven't been a priest that long, but I've already run into some grim stuff." He shook his head. "What now?"

I paused to eat a potato chip. "It'll take sniffer dogs to find Myrtle — if she's here. When last seen, she was headed for home, where Roy and Bebe live now. In his few semilucid moments, Harold asks his son, Don, if she's come home. No one ever saw her again, so I doubt she ever left. The empty berry bucket she had with her when she called on her neighbor, Mrs. Roberson, was never found. No berries, either."

"So she never went after . . . what? Blackberries?"

"She may have started out to pick them in the area on Mount Sawyer where Gus's body was found. Milo went over his notes and Myrtle apparently got as far as the creek. The search dogs lost her scent at that point. Somebody may've stopped her."

Adam grimaced. "Harold?"

I shook my head. "I don't know. There are several ways it could've played out. Mrs.

Roberson was no Vida when it came to keeping tabs on her neighbors. Even now, the only full view of the Everson house is from what used to belong to the Robersons. If Harold showed up there, he wasn't spotted."

"What about Mrs. Krogstad?" Adam asked. "Was she jealous?"

"I've no idea," I admitted. "Whoever killed Myrtle would've had to carry her here and do some serious digging. Risky, too. But the judge was undoubtedly upset by her break-up note. I figure they quarreled and . . ." I shrugged. "It'd serve no purpose to charge him, but if Myrtle's remains were found, the family could finally stop searching."

"Nobody would have to know she was murdered," Adam said.

"So much time has passed that they probably couldn't tell. I wonder if Spence's sister sensed what happened. Marsha clerked for the judge. After he got gaga, she may've tried to discuss pending cases she had to take on. Maybe he let something slip. I can't think why else she'd keep the poems. If Myrtle was found, Spence would have a hot story."

"Let the almost dead bury their dead," he

murmured, finishing his sandwich. "Where to?"

"The newspaper," I said.

Adam reversed onto the road. "You'd share the story with Spence . . . Whoa!" He swerved as a vehicle raced past us. "Is that Dodge?"

"Yes. Skip my office," I said, seeing the red light flash as the Cherokee disappeared from view. "Take me to the sheriff."

FIFTEEN

As we drove along front street toward the sheriff's headquarters, I noticed that Milo's usual space was vacant. God help anyone who parked in it when he wasn't around. He'd arrest *me* if I did it.

But I was undaunted. "Pull in," I told Adam.

"Mom! It says, 'No Parking, Skykomish ___' "

"Do it."

"Jeez." Adam had overshot the space, so he had to back up before pulling in. "I'm not sitting here to get busted," he said as I opened the door. "You're on your own."

"I usually am." I exited the car without falling down.

"Oh, no," Sam said as I came through the door. "Who the hell pulled into Dodge's spot? That's a four-hundred-buck fine."

"Stick it, Sam, it was a dump-and-drive," I said, making sure Adam had reversed onto

Front. "What's going on?"

"Can't say." Sam looked smug as he strolled to the coffeemaker.

The only other person in sight was Lori, who offered me a kindly glance and leaned over the counter. "You better go, Emma."

"No," I said, sitting in one of the chairs by the entrance.

Lori turned, watching Sam disappear down the hall. "Really," she said earnestly. "You shouldn't be here. There's a big bust going down."

"Are you talking about Mrs. Runkel?"

Lori had lost her sense of humor. "No. I mean it."

Alarmed, I stood up. "Mitch Laskey?"

Lori shook her head. "Why would . . . Please, Emma."

I was torn. If something big was happening, I should be on the spot. But Lori wasn't fanciful or an alarmist. On the other hand, Spence might show up at any moment. Even if we were working on the same story angle, he'd gloat if he got the breaking news first.

I compromised. "Can I wait in the sheriff's office?"

Lori looked uneasy and paused, probably picturing the scenario. "Okay," she finally said, "but lock the door so nobody sees you.

I'll tell you when the coast is clear."

"Lori . . . Okay." I obeyed, locking the door behind me. A minute later, I unlocked it. I could still peek. There'd once been a window, but it'd been removed during the remodel and replaced with a skylight. Now that was also gone, because it had leaked. My watch said one-ten. I wandered to the sheriff's side of the desk. Prying was part of my job, but I refused to invade Milo's privacy. Still, I couldn't help seeing what was in plain sight on the legal-sized tablet he used for taking notes. He had decent, and, like the rest of him, big, handwriting: "paper frags"; "medal"; "JB"; "DK — wood"; "CGA — KingCo/SPD." The last entry was probably Charles G. Andrews. Milo must be checking on him through his KingCo and Seattle Police Department liaisons.

Except for the medal, I stopped guessing and moved back to the door. It was one-twenty. All was quiet. I felt antsy. After pacing and fussing for fifteen minutes, I heard raised voices. I tried to turn the lock — and couldn't. Maybe Lori hadn't locked it in the first place, but I had. Locks and keys were never my strong suit. Maybe the damned thing was stuck. Why hadn't I alerted Vida or Kip? We should get a photo taken outside instead of violating the sheriff's sacred premises. Maybe it wasn't too late. I dug out my cell and called Kip, who sounded confused.

"But if you're already there . . ."

"Just do it." After hanging up, I went to the door, but caught only occasional words, including barked orders from Milo. Then I heard a woman's voice — not Lori or Doe. A moment later, a baby cried. The sheriff was arresting infants? Visions of tiny pink or blue handcuffs danced in my head. The cries faded away. Five more minutes passed. I called Kip again. Alison answered. I asked if Kip was still gone. She said he'd never left. Vida was taking the pictures. I slumped against the door. "Where is she now?"

"Not back," Alison said. "Excuse me, Emma. The mayor's here."

Still leaning against the door, I stared at the ceiling. The noise had died down. Then I heard Milo cussing, followed by a shriek from Lori. The door opened, knocking me into the wall. The sheriff stalked on by, going to his desk and rummaging in a drawer while I winced in pain. *Maybe he won't see me,* I thought frantically.

But he did. "For chrissakes! What the hell are you doing?"

I couldn't speak. I was too humiliated.

And in pain. Milo would calm down, he'd haul me off the wall, he'd . . .

But he only shook his head, pocketed the cigarette pack he'd gotten out of the drawer, and strode past me. I was left to face Vida, who was just as stupefied as the sheriff had been.

"Emma! No wonder Milo is angry. What are you doing?"

I staggered over to the nearest chair and sat down. "My job," I said, grimacing. "What's happening?"

"If," she said severely, "you were doing your job, you wouldn't have to ask. Goodness, you look dreadful. Why are you in here?"

"Lori told me I shouldn't be, but I don't know why."

Vida sat in the other visitor's chair. "Lori followed Milo's orders."

"Huh?"

"The maple poachers' arrest," she said. "I took photos outside. Kip was coping with a computer problem. You know how he is when that happens. His brain only works on a tech level."

"And the poachers are . . . ?" I asked, not really caring at this point.

"Oh!" Vida clasped a hand to her unruly gray curls. "Your neighbors, the Nelsons —

371

Doyle and Laverne. And their eldest son, Luke."

"The Nelsons?" I echoed.

"I have no details, but Milo put it together after your fire."

"What did my fire have to do with it?"

"I don't know, except it was something he saw at the Nelson house when he was questioning the neighbors. Billy couldn't talk because he was responsible for bringing in Luke Nelson along with his wife, Sofia, and their baby, Chloe."

"What's Chloe being charged with?"

"Being too chubby for six months," Vida said. "Poor parenting skills. I don't think Sofia is under arrest, but she insisted on coming with Luke and they couldn't leave the baby." She glanced out through the door and stood up. "Here's Spencer. Yoo-hoo!"

"Oh, *please!*" I groaned. "I want to get out of here."

"I'll stay," Vida said, getting to her feet. "Hello, Spencer."

Mr. Radio kissed Vida's hand. "An unexpected surprise. Who's the waif with you? She looks like she was mauled by the resident bear."

"It was a door, jackass," I said, limping to collect my purse.

Vida simpered and withdrew her hand.

"Emma's accident-prone."

I got around Spence without stomping on his foot. Lori, Dustin, and Sam were conferring at the counter. I ignored them. It was all I could do to limp back to the *Advocate* as snowflakes drifted down.

Mayor Baugh had grown tired of waiting for me. I grabbed some bottled water from the stash under the coffee table. Rolling up my sweater sleeve, I saw a bruise on my left arm from where the sheriff's door had hit me. Vida returned just as I swallowed two Excedrin. I confronted her midway across the newsroom. "What's the charge against the Nelsons and why shouldn't I have been there?"

She slipped out of her tweed coat and sat down. "Dwight and Doe brought in the two younger Nelsons in connection with your fire. Billy thinks they set it in revenge for their arrest in the Pines burglaries. Living next door, they know you and Milo are . . . friends. He didn't want you there because he was afraid they might do something awful to you."

"Like hit me with a door?"

"Now, now. Milo didn't know you were in his office."

"How come those kids weren't already locked up?"

"Bail was posted on the burglary charge. The boys hid at home while their parents were away. Dwight and Doe just picked them up."

"So I missed all the excitement." I stared at Vida. "Who posted bail for them? They don't have any money."

"I've no idea," she retorted. "I was vexed because I couldn't take pictures of the younger Nelsons. The older one looks eighteen to me, though he insists he's not. I know the younger one is sixteen. Imagine leaving them unsupervised, especially at Christmas! And you'll never guess where Doyle and Laverne were found! With the Krogstads!"

"So they were hiding those crooks from us when we went there? Don't tell me the Krogstads are crooks?"

"They're family," Vida said. "Dee and Laverne are cousins. Dee's a weaver who also makes loom parts. Dee works with maple. She's been buying it — innocently, I hope — from Doyle Nelson. He and Laverne claimed their roof leaks, but I assume they were lying low. Perhaps they were afraid your artist saw them cutting the maples before he was shot. I suspect the Nelsons rarely read the *Advocate* and didn't know there wasn't any connection between

374

the poaching and the shooting."

I shook my head in dismay. "I hope they all serve time."

"Awkward, if so," Vida murmured. "You'll have to testify against them. No wonder poor Milo was so concerned."

"Poor Milo, my ass! He almost killed me. What about poor me?"

Vida shot me a disgusted look. "Emma, your language has become very coarse lately."

I held my head. "I'm frazzled. Too much has gone on . . ."

"Yes, yes," she said impatiently. "Too much indeed. The Cobbs, holding Alfred's funeral on New Year's Eve Day with such short notice! I can only imagine how long it'll take the Patricellis to figure out what to do about Gus. They'll probably wait until Matt gets here from Yakima."

"Matt?" I said stupidly.

"Yes, the eldest. I've told you about him. He's the banker."

I remembered Milo mentioning the eldest Patricelli brother. "Oh, right," I murmured as inspiration hit. "I'd better get to work."

"You should," Vida said, once again forgetting who ran the paper.

I immediately called Pete, asking for Matt's work number. He was in a rush, but had memorized the information. I dialed the Yakima Wells Fargo office and was transferred to Matt. I introduced myself and offered my condolences. Matt accepted graciously. Then I cut to the chase. "Along with the investigation concerning Gus, there's a second situation that I'm covering for the paper. Do you recall an accident with a young man and a Good Humor wagon a year ago around Labor Day?"

"Oh, that was terrible," Matt said dolefully. "A poor kid got hit and it turned out the Good Humor driver was a drug dealer. It happened only two blocks from the bank, and when I heard the sirens, I went out to see what was going on. Medics, cops, firefighters, and that poor little boy lying in the middle of the street. I said a whole rosary on the spot."

"Did you know the child?"

"No," Matt replied. "I heard later that the family was passing through on their way to Lake Coeur d'Alene. They stopped to get gas and the boy wanted to buy a comic book across the street. He ran between parked cars instead of using the crosswalk at the corner. It wasn't really the driver's fault, but the cops could see the guy was high."

"Was the boy badly injured?"

"That's the worst part. The driver wasn't

speeding, but the *Herald-Republic* had follow-up stories, saying the injury was freakish, leaving the boy paralyzed from the waist down. Maybe I should've said two rosaries."

"Did you ever find out the family's name?"

"It was in the paper, but I don't recall it. The dad was a lawyer from Seattle. I knew they had money — the family car was an Escalade."

Bingo! My hunch had paid off. "Very sad," I said somberly.

"Life's terrible." Matt's sigh was audible. "And Gus — how did he end up like he did? What went wrong?"

"I wish I knew," I said. "I'll see you at the funeral."

On that solemn note, I hung up and rushed out to tell Vida. "Check this out with the *Herald-Republic.* This has to be the link between Mitch and Andrews."

Vida studied the scrawled notes I'd made. "How clever of you to call Matt. Why didn't I think of that? Are you going to tell Milo?"

"I'll wait for confirmation," I said.

She nodded — and apparently didn't have the Yakima paper's number on file in her computerized brain. I left as she brought up the *Herald-Republic*'s site on her monitor.

Energized by my coup, I spent the next

few minutes trying to think up an editorial. Maybe I should beat the drums for Myron Cobb. Or not. We needed an infusion of fresh blood among the county commissioners. In the foreseeable future, the other two old duffers would either become completely incapacitated or join Alfred. I decided to urge any civic-minded — and sane — Alpiners to answer the call.

I'd written the lead when a smug Vida appeared in the doorway. "Ten-year-old Aaron Andrews, son of Charles and Olivia, Seattle."

"Ah!" But my elation faded. "Is Andrews after revenge? It can't be a lawsuit this far into the game. Besides, the Laskeys have no money."

"True," she agreed, "but at least we have a connection."

Vida headed for the back shop. The sheriff might still be dealing with the Nelson crime fest, so I decided to wait before telling him about the Laskey-Andrews link. But when the phone rang five minutes later, the voice on the other end belonged to Milo.

"Sorry about that door," he said, not sounding sorry at all.

"Give me a break. I'm up to my ears. I've got news for you."

"Skip it for now and listen up. I'm serious."

"Hey — you're not my keeper. Like you, I have a job to do."

"That doesn't mean putting yourself at risk. You never stop to consider consequences, you just do whatever pops into your head."

"Stop annoying me. I don't tell you how to do your job."

"The hell you don't. You've been doing it for fifteen years."

"I've saved your butt a couple of times, in case you've forgotten."

"I haven't done the same for you?"

"Back off. I don't need more lectures. You're not running my life."

The silence at the other end was ominous. "Okay. I'll stop. Maybe it's not worth it after all." He hung up.

I was crushed. Milo never did or said things lightly. I sat like a stone, numb of mind and body. Was I hexed? Was I doomed to self-destruct? Was Milo right and was I a real screwup?

I couldn't stay in my cubbyhole. My office, the news stories — the whole damned *Advocate,* which had been my life's work for fifteen years — suddenly was no comfort. I put on my jacket, got my purse, and fled through the empty newsroom. Alison was on the phone. I ran out onto the sidewalk. It was snowing harder and I'd forgotten I had no car. I trudged along Front Street in the opposite direction from Milo's office. At Fourth, I started up the hill to St. Mildred's rectory. The wind blew snow in my face, but I ignored it. Four blocks later, I was on Cedar, panting a bit, chilled down to my soul, and mulling what I'd say to Ben.

Mimi Barton let me in. "Is your brother expecting you?"

I shook my head. "It's a . . . whim."

Her homely, heart-shaped face was pained. "He's busy."

"Oh." We were in the hall of the old frame building that was connected to the church by a covered walkway. "I can wait."

Mimi's hands fluttered. "The meeting just started."

"Who's he got in there?" I demanded. "The archbishop?"

Mimi was shocked. "Can't you talk to him any time?"

"I'll wait in the church," I said. "Let me know when he's free."

She nodded, but added a caution. "It's cold in church."

Not as cold as it is inside of me. "I'll be fine." I left the rectory.

I went through the back door and knelt in the first row, staring at the crucifix above the altar. Instead of attempting to say a prayer, I kept staring. What should I say to God? *Hi, I'm a mess. But you know that. Done so many dumb things. Can't tell right from wrong. So why am I here? I can't ask for help, because what I want is wrong. Free will — bad idea. Humans like me can't handle it. Never mind. Sorry to bother you.*

I slid out of the pew, and, turning my back on the crucifix — in oh, so many ways — I felt as if even God couldn't help me. I left the way I'd come.

Sixteen

I didn't know what to do. Halfway between the church and the rectory, I stopped on the walkway, staring at the snow that was coming down harder. The parking lot was almost covered. It took me a moment to realize that the blue Audi next to Ben's rental belonged to Marisa. It had to be hers — nobody else in town owned a car like that.

I made up my mind and retraced my route to Cedar Street. Damn Marisa, damn Ben, damn Milo, damn everybody. The whole world was conspiring against me. Except my son. I reached the corner of Pine and Fourth, between Leo's apartment house and the Baptist church. Squinting through the snow, I called Adam.

"Can you rescue your mother?" I asked in a plaintive voice.

For once, there was no smart-mouthed remark from my son. He perceived my anguish. "What's wrong?"

"Everything. I'll be in front of the bank."

"I'm at Harvey's Hardware. Be right there."

"Wait," I said. "You're so close, come up Fourth. I'm on Pine, across from the Baptist church."

"No wonder you sound gloomy. Hang in there." He clicked off.

Three minutes later, Adam pulled up to the curb. I was shivering, though whether from cold or nerves, I wasn't sure.

"Mom," he said after I'd gotten in, "are you sick?"

"Not exactly," I said. "Take me home."

We didn't speak until we were inside. "The crime-scene tape's still up," I said, struggling to get out of my jacket.

"I know. Here," Adam said. "Let me give you a hand."

He managed to extricate me. I collapsed on the sofa. "I blew it."

Adam stared down at me. "Blew what?"

"Milo dumped me."

Adam sank down next to me. "How could he? What happened?"

"He's been hovering over me like a watchdog. I wanted him to back off. The sheriff and your uncle make me feel incompetent."

"Uncle Ben teases you. Hasn't he done that since you were two?"

I nodded halfheartedly. "I went to see him, but he's with Marisa."

Adam's jaw dropped. "What?"

"At the rectory. Maybe he's counseling her."

"My God, I hope so." Adam grew thoughtful. "I don't like this."

"Hey — what about your mother?"

Adam shook his head. "You're overreacting about Dodge. That guy can't survive without you. Have you forgotten counseling is *my* strong suit, not Uncle Ben's? I do it all the time in the village."

"Maybe you should try it on your uncle *and* Milo."

He stood up. "I'm serious. You don't know how vulnerable a priest can be in this situation — especially if the woman's a lawyer. I'm going to the rectory." Before I could stop him, he grabbed his parka from the back of the easy chair and was out the door.

Great, I thought. Adam had inherited his father's need to help everybody but Emma. I sat with my chin on my fist, thinking how fruitless it was to rely on anybody but myself. I hadn't raised a child on my own, held down a job on a big-city daily for almost twenty years, and run my own newspaper for another fifteen because I was inept.

I went into the kitchen. It was after four. I considered making a drink, but settled for Pepsi. Back in the living room, I forced myself to focus on something besides me. I wasn't ready to confide in Spence about the Laskey-Andrews connection, but I could tell him about my trip to the dump site with Adam.

"I'm not digging anything in the snow," he said after I pitched him my idea. "I might catch a cold and ruin my voice."

"That's not your job," I pointed out. "I wanted your reaction."

"The idea has merit," he allowed, "even Marsha's role in saving those poems. But why didn't she tell me her suspicions?"

"Hey — don't ask me about siblings," I said. "Maybe she's waiting for Myrtle to be found. She has no proof and she's a lawyer. By the way, did you air anything on my fire aftermath?"

"I missed the hour turn at two," he said. "Dodge was his old ornery self. How come? He was bearable for at least forty-eight hours."

"He's a real beast," I muttered. "Any word from your city sources?"

"You're off base on that hunch. Carlton Madison, builder of shoddy houses for gullible clients, and Kiefer Madison, would-be

385

plane thief, aren't related, not even the same race. Carlton has two daughters in college, and Kiefer is a high school dropout from Lake City with a rap sheet that includes dealing drugs. He's doing two-to-five at Monroe."

"Whoever Kiefer is, it's an uncanny co-incidence. His attempted plane theft was during the same time Troy was on the run. The airport employee, Rupert, said Kiefer was stealing the plane for a friend."

"You're thinking Troy?"

"Yes. His involvement with drugs goes back a couple of years. He and Kiefer might have had a connection before Monroe."

"You're reaching. Got to do a live commercial." He rang off.

I poured more Pepsi. Adding ice, I glanced into the empty carport. I wanted the crime-scene tape gone. I wanted my car. I wanted to strangle every man I knew. And I'd start with that jackass of a sheriff.

I stomped into the living room and dialed his number.

Lori answered. "Where's your idiot boss?" I demanded.

"Emma? Where are you?" Lori sounded agitated. "The sheriff's looking all over town for you. Mrs. Runkel's a wreck."

"I'm . . . home," I said.

"Thank goodness! I'll let everybody know." She rang off.

Stupefied, I fetched my purse from the sofa. Why hadn't Vida or Milo called me on my cell? I groped in my purse until I found the blasted thing. In my distress, I hadn't disconnected my ancient cell after calling Adam. Maybe I *was* an idiot. I tried to retrieve any messages, but got the low-battery signal. Frustrated, I threw the cell so hard it bounced off the front door. At first, I thought the impact had made the phone ring. But then it seemed to ring again. Trying to unscramble my brain, I opened the door.

"Goddamn it," Milo yelled, "where've you been?" He charged across the threshold and slammed the door behind him.

"Here," I said meekly.

He shook his head, snowflakes dropping from his jacket.

"How mad are you?" I asked.

"Damned mad," he barked.

I winced. "Stop snarling. You were so quiet and low-key when I first met you. What happened?"

"Life," he snapped, snatching off his hat and tossing it aside before taking me into his arms. "Don't ever do that again."

"What? Go home?" I said, my voice

muffled against his chest.

"You're going home with me."

I craned my neck to look up at him. "I can't."

"You have to. Adam can't stay here, either. Where is he?"

"He went to the rectory."

"I'll call and tell him to get his gear."

"What's going on?"

"First things first. Get your own stuff together." He'd taken out his cell. "What's the number at the rectory?"

I told him. He tapped it in. "Mimi? Dodge here. Give me Father Lord — either of them."

I was still standing in the middle of the room. Milo made a shooing motion with his free hand. I shooed myself off to pack whatever I needed for whatever reason for whatever was going on. It made no sense. The Nelson kids were locked up. So were their parents and older brother. What kind of danger could I — and Adam — possibly be in?

Milo was standing in the bedroom doorway. "Skip the evening gowns and furs. Just take enough for two days."

"Would you please tell me why I'm doing this?"

He drummed his fingers against the doorjamb. "I wish I knew. It's a good thing the Nelson kids are screwups. They did a lousy job and probably made enough noise to wake up Adam."

"How did you figure out it was them?"

"Quit dithering," he said as I tried to figure out which slacks to take with me. "It was a no-brainer. A bunch of last week's *Advocates* were stuffed under the logs. I saw those scraps in the carport and on your Honda. Kip mentioned somebody got into your dumpster last night, so Sam lifted prints off of it. They matched the ones we took of the Nelson kids after the burglaries. My first reaction was they'd set the fire as payback because they'd seen the Cherokee at your place so often and maybe they thought they could nail both of us. But I was wrong. They were hired to burn your place down."

I gaped at Milo. "*Hired?* That's absurd!"

He shrugged. "They convinced me. They're too dumb to make it up. They were contacted by phone. Sure, they might've invented that. But they didn't put two grand into a new account at the Bank of Alpine."

"Two grand?" I tossed a pair of shoes and my hair dryer into the overnight bag. "Those kids never saw that much money in their lives."

"Whoever it was posted their bail, too. You almost done there?"

"Yes!" I nudged Milo. "Move, big guy. I want my toothbrush."

Two minutes later, we were driving through heavy snow. I'd rescued my cell so I could charge it at Milo's. We drove the first few blocks in silence. The sheriff was focused on keeping the Cherokee on track. It was only when we turned onto the Icicle Creek Road that the enormity of what was happening hit me.

"My God!" I cried. "Is someone going to blow up my log house?"

"Don't worry," Milo said. "I've got Bill and Sam watching it."

"Then why can't I stay there?"

"Because you're safer with me." He turned in to the development. "I can't *not* keep you with me. Hell, I'd do the same for Vida. I think."

"Does she know where I am?"

"Better if she doesn't. Lori will tell her you're safe. Where were you? Why didn't you pick up? I tried to call three times."

"I forgot to turn off my cell after I called Adam to take me home. I have no car, you see."

Milo pulled up in his driveway. "Don't move. I'll get your satchel and then you.

This snow is really coming down."

"You sound kind of cheerful about that."

"Yeah." He opened his door. "We could be marooned for days."

I waited while he took the overnight bag inside. I had forgotten to bring boots. A moment later, he carried me into the house.

I buried my face against his chest. "I thought I'd lost you!"

Milo frowned at me. "Is *that* why you ran away from your office?"

"Uh-huh."

"Jesus." He stroked my hair. "Jesus." He took a deep breath. "I never thought you . . ." His voice broke.

I couldn't speak, either. We didn't need words.

If what had gone on before in early December had unleashed our inhibitions and broken down all barriers between us, the next hour was a gentle, leisurely journey, two travelers taking time to explore every nuance of the wonders along the way. I went to sleep curled up against him. He slept, too, though he was awake when I finally opened my eyes.

"Feel better?" he asked when he saw me looking at him.

"Mmm. If I were a cat, I'd purr."

He chuckled. "You did. Often."

"It's one way to *not* think someone wants to kill me."

"A damned good one," Milo murmured, nuzzling my shoulder before he lay back on the pillow. "No calls yet. And I didn't put my cell in the freezer this time. Yours is dead anyway."

I sat up just enough to realize I was suddenly cold. "Don't you have any heat in this place?"

"How much more heat do you want? Hey," he said, yanking at the blanket I'd pulled over my breasts. "Don't cover up the view."

I nestled down against him. "You've seen it often enough."

"Doesn't matter. It's like you with that hermit's painting. You never get tired of looking at it."

"You're . . ." I shook my head. "Oh, Milo, why would anyone try to kill me? Isn't that what this is about?"

"So it seems. Unless it's Adam."

I shuddered at the thought. "Who'd want to kill him?"

"A religious nut? Everybody must know he and Ben are in town."

"Then why aren't they being protected?"

"Because I don't want to sleep with them."

"Milo . . ."

He laughed. "Doe and Dustman are watching the rectory."

"Good grief," I said, "you'll run out of deputies."

"Then I'll call in the state patrol. I mean it."

"So we stay here and wait for something to happen?"

"Keeping you safe is the priority." He hugged me tighter. "The Nelson kids only know their contact as Mr. Hertz, so it'd help if you could think of something — anything — to give us a lead."

"Mr. Hertz? As in rental cars?"

"The kids didn't know. I doubt they can spell their own names."

"I don't know anyone who hates me. How about religious bigots?"

Milo adjusted the pillow behind his head. "Forty years ago, I could name dozens. I was still a kid during the Kennedy-Nixon presidential campaign. You wouldn't believe the crap I heard about what'd happen if Kennedy got elected — from the pope moving to the White House to burning Prots in the old Alpine Market parking lot. When JFK got killed, some dinks cheered. That breed's gone. People are more broad-minded since the college opened."

"Father Den, being black, and Dustin Fong, with his Chinese ancestry, helped pave the way. Vida tells tales about Protestant and Catholic animosity. So what went on with you and Ben at lunch?"

"Oh . . ." He grimaced. "Your brother's got a bug up his ass. Why," he asked, making a sweeping gesture with his free hand, "is this a sin?"

"We're not married."

"You know I don't like catch-and-release when I fish. I'd like it even less with you. We can fix that."

I stared at him. "Do you want to?"

"Do you?"

"I asked you first."

"Hell, yes. Didn't I ask you when you were in your dopey phase?"

"You didn't really ask," I said. "You sort of alluded to the idea."

He shrugged. "Okay, I was gun-shy after the divorce. That was a long time ago. This is now. So what's your answer?"

"Yes."

The sheriff looked stunned. "God. That was easy." He shook his head in apparent disbelief. "Hey, we're engaged. Is this still a sin?"

"Probably. I guess."

"Are you going to get all weepy about it?"

"No. Adam likes you."

"Can he marry us?"

"If you get your first marriage annulled. Didn't Ben explain that?"

"Ben kept going off track with theology and doctrine. He reminded me of suspects who talk all the way around the question so they can avoid a direct answer. All that does is piss me off."

I sighed. "That sounds like Ben. He's already pissed me off."

"How do you get an annulment?"

I covered my ears. "Stop. I can't cope with all this. Someone's trying to kill me, you want to marry me, I can't stay in my house, I have no car, my brother's mad at me — and you hit me with a door."

"I said I was sorry."

"You weren't. You thought it served me right."

"It did." He brushed strands of hair from my cheek. "You know the difference between me being an overbearing S.O.B. and giving a damn what happens to you?"

"I'm starting to find out," I said.

"You should. Who's taken care of Emma since you were . . . what? Twenty years old?"

I stared into those earnest hazel eyes. "Nobody. Except me."

He nodded. "Your parents got killed. Your

brother went off to be a priest. Cavanaugh walked on you. Then Adam stepped into Ben's shoes and he took off, too. You've spent your whole adult life on your own. That's okay, but that's enough. Nobody should do that forever. I had to figure that out for myself, too."

I shook my head. "You've had my back from the start."

"Well . . . I tried, but I wasn't too good at it in the beginning. I wasn't used to being needed. Mulehide and the kids made that clear to me."

I smiled weakly. "And I thought you were never introspective."

Milo grimaced. "I have my moments. Especially when I'm fishing."

I kissed his cheek. "You amaze me sometimes. Like now. But we have to get up and eat — and think. Please turn on the heat."

"God," he said, throwing off the covers and getting out of bed, "we get engaged and you're already nagging me. It's not that cold in here."

"Speak for yourself," I muttered.

Ten minutes later, I was scanning his fridge. "I should've brought leftovers. Do we really have to eat out of boxes?"

Milo was making drinks. "What kind of box do you like? Red, green, or blue?"

I grimaced. "How many Hungry Man dinners can you eat without brain damage?"

"How come you're wearing my bathrobe?"

"Mine was too bulky to pack."

"It's a good thing mine's short or you'd trip and break something. Make pancakes. I didn't get any this morning." He came up behind me. "You make this dump look good," he said, wrapping his arms around me and resting his chin on top of my head.

"Oh!" I exclaimed, turning my head just enough to look up at him. "Guess what? I found the link between Mitch and Andrews."

"The hell you did." Milo let go of me. "And . . . ?"

Having condensed the story for Vida, it took only a couple of minutes to tell Milo — and I added the Yakima paper's confirmation.

"The jerk's on a vendetta," he said when I finished. "He wants to go dad-on-dad with Mitch. Maybe it took him this long to find Laskey."

A phone rang, probably the landline, since it didn't sound like the sheriff's cell. He grabbed the receiver off the counter. "Yeah?" Milo took his cigarettes from his shirt pocket. "The package arrived safely." He shot me a quick look, the receiver under his chin, a cigarette in one hand and a lighter in the other. "No, it's empty. Good work with the motels. How about the traffic stops?"

I rummaged in the cupboards for pancake makings. No Bisquick, no Krusteaz, not even a bag of flour. Did Milo think I was a magician?

"How long does it take Andy to find out where the money came from? . . . Skip that . . . tell him to get his ass in gear. . . . Yeah, I will. . . . Just do it . . . notify those troopers. . . . Screw it, it's their job." Milo slammed the receiver down on its base. "What did those morons do when I wasn't here?"

I picked up my drink. "Might I ask what they're doing now?"

He sat down at the kitchen table, which was partially covered with unopened mail and magazines. "They checked the motels and the ski lodge for anybody suspicious. Just ordinary citizens, unless you count Turk Durgan, who's still at the lodge. The deputies are making traffic stops of all unknown vehicles. With this snow, there's not many. Chains are being required, so the state patrol's involved. Andy Cederberg is working on the electronic transfers into the Nelson kids' account — and who set it up in the first place." He shrugged. "That's it, for now."

I'd sat down, too, though I'd had to move an REI catalog off the chair to do it. "What's empty? What did you mean by a package?"

"You." He sipped some Scotch. "You don't know zip."

"Oh. The cupboard's got zip, too. You don't have flour?"

"Why would I? When was the last time I baked a cake?"

"No pancakes for you."

He offered me a cigarette. I accepted. "I've got hamburger in the freezer," he said. "What can you do with that?"

"Make hamburgers?"

"Sure." Milo frowned. "There has to be somebody out there who doesn't like you. If we rule out your priests as targets, this is personal."

"Are your deputies watching the *Advocate*?"

Milo nodded. "I've got Ron Bjornson keeping an eye on it."

Ron, whose other job was college security, worked part-time for the sheriff as a handyman. "I don't suppose you've got any potatoes."

"You mean that aren't frozen?" He shook his head.

"Frozen works." I went to the freezer. "I need an ice pick to . . ."

I recognized Milo's cell ring. Even before he spoke, I knew there was trouble. He got up and moved out of the kitchen. I was about to follow him, but decided that was a bad idea. Instead, I struggled to free a pound of hamburger, and after my fingers started turning numb, I dislodged half a bag of frozen fries. I'd turned the oven on when Milo came back to the kitchen. Judging from his expression, he was riled. I waited for him to take a swig of Scotch before asking what was wrong.

"Freaking Mulehide," he said in disgust.

"Oh!" Somehow I was relieved. "What now?"

"She wants me to send her and Tanya to Hawaii."

I laughed. Milo didn't. "Why," I said, "should you pay for that?"

"Because I'm here, not there. 'It's the least you can do,' " he said in a grating imitation of his ex's voice. "She sure picked a bad time to ask." He polished off his Scotch. "I told her I'd think about it."

I put my arms around his neck. "I don't want to go to Hawaii."

"Oh, Emma." He held me tight. "What the hell did I do right?"

400

"What you always do. You were persistent. Patient. Then you pounced."

He pulled away a bit. "Pounced?"

"Dumb word," I said. "We were always on guard. Scared. Afraid to really fall in love. Then we both let go. It changed everything."

He smiled. "I tried to treat you like . . . a lady. Mulehide was so cold you could've chilled beer on her butt. She acted like she was made of glass. She wasn't, even before she put on thirty pounds. You're kind of little." He circled my wrist with his thumb and index finger. "Itty-bitty bones. I was afraid you'd break."

The cell rang against my ear, since it was in his shirt pocket.

"Now what?" Milo growled, after letting me go and answering. "What does that mean?" he asked, getting a refill for his drink. "Run that by me again. . . . What about the post office? Somebody collects the mail." He checked his watch. "Right, it's after seven. Thanks, Andy."

I punched the microwave's defrost button for the hamburger and stubbed out my cigarette. "What?"

"The transfers were made from an account with a PO box in Kirkland," Milo said, sitting down again. "The box belongs to Main Cure, LLC. I thought Andy said 'manicure,' but he spelled it. He figures it's some quack medical outfit. Not listed in any directory he's checked."

I sat down, too. "There's lots of those alternative medicine places."

Milo stroked his long chin. "Andy's finding out if anybody at the post office knows who uses the box." He grew thoughtful. "You sure about Tom's kids being okay with Adam's inheritance?"

"They didn't want the responsibility. I heard later that although Tom's revised will was lost and his lawyer had been killed, there were people in the firm who'd take an oath that Tom made a new one."

"Do you hear from his kids?"

"No. I'm the stepmother who never was."

Milo put his hand on mine. "Just as well."

I nodded. "I still feel sorry for them, especially Kelsey. She seems to have some of Sandra's unbalanced chemistry."

Milo shook his head. "Parents can screw them up, even when it's not lousy genes." He stood up. "I'd better make rounds."

My eyes widened. "Where are you going?"

"Just around the house. Don't worry. I'll be armed."

But I did worry even as I made another foray into the freezer and found some frozen string beans. By the time the hamburger had thawed and the oven had reached four hundred degrees, the sheriff returned.

"Three inches out there and still coming down," he said, taking off his all-weather jacket. "No footprints. Relax."

"I need another drink, too," I said. "I'm shaky. Everything hit me when you went outside. How do we know if Adam and Ben are okay?"

"We'd know if they weren't. My deputies aren't total dopes."

"Who knows I'm here?"

"Dwight."

"Where does everybody think I am?"

"At the rectory with the priests."

"Where do the priests think I am?"

"With Dwight at headquarters."

I made a face. "That *would* be awful. Where are your prisoners?"

"In their cells. Evan Singer and Beth Rafferty are there, too," he said, referring to the 911 operators who usually worked in a back room.

"You've pulled out all the stops. That's scary. What," I asked, flipping a hamburger, "will I do about the paper? Can I charge my cell?"

"Sure, but don't use it tonight," he said, looking up from his copy of the *Advocate*. "You're incommunicado."

"Great. How can I help you if I can't make calls?"

"Unlike your home phone, which comes up as 'E. M. Lord,' your cell says '*Alpine Advocate.*' You want somebody to take a shot at Vida?"

"But I'd only call people I know."

"You might dial wrong. How often have you tried to call me when you were in a tizzy and ended up with the dry cleaners?"

"I never called the cleaners by mistake."

"Whatever. Your staff can cope. You've been away before." Milo was quiet as I removed the fries from the oven. "Nothing from Laskey?"

"Leo talked to him. They checked out of their motel. Brenda's a wreck, so they'll go where she can get help." I dished up the food.

"Why now?" Milo asked after eating some hamburger. "It shouldn't have taken a guy like Andrews all this time to track down Laskey, especially if he's got a PI on his tail. Something set him off."

"You're right," I agreed. "Christmas?"

Milo looked thoughtful as he ate some beans. "No. It's been what — at least one other Christmas since the accident? Andrews could've jumped on a plane, flown to Detroit, and kicked Laskey's ass then. Or he could've gone to Yakima for the hearing. I checked Troy's file this afternoon after everything cooled down. There were plenty of chances for Andrews to go after both Mitch and Troy. It's why now that bothers me."

"Oh!" I said, still wondering why my brain seemed to be sputtering. "That medal Troy had doesn't belong to Gus. Gus dropped his in some pizza sauce."

Milo paused with a forkful of hamburger halfway to his mouth. "No shit. Is this another one of your theories?"

"No," I shot back, and told him about Davin Rhodes and the pizza.

"That," he said, "is still a theory. But it's not a bad one. Verify it."

I looked at him blankly. "How? Mail him a letter?"

"Mullins can do it," he said begrudgingly. "He knows what he's talking about. He didn't let Rita see it, just to give her a bad time. I'll call him." Milo had polished off his dinner. He stood up and stretched before going into the other room.

I was still eating. The call took less than a minute. "You didn't move," he said. "Amazing. I guess I won't have to put a bell on you."

I gave him a dirty look. "Cut the crap and

call Monroe. Ask for a Samoan guard. He and Troy were tight. Find out about an older inmate who befriended Troy."

"Who's in charge here? We get engaged and you take over my house *and* job?"

"You asked me to help."

He sighed. "My contact list is in my workroom. I'll do it now."

Before he left the kitchen, I cleared the table and opened the dishwasher. "When was the last time you ran this?"

"How should I know? I don't wash boxes."

"I don't believe I'm in danger," I snapped. "You only brought me here because you want a cook, a housekeeper, and a hooker. If I had my boots, I'd walk home."

"You'd fall over your own feet and . . ." He stared in disbelief. "You didn't bring boots?"

"I forgot. You rushed me."

"I should keep you on a leash."

"Boots!" I cried. "I forgot that, too!" I grabbed Milo by his shirt and told him about the hiking boots that Roy had brought to Amer Wasco. "Vida's dropping them off at your office this evening. They're from REI. Being a co-op, they'd have a record of who bought them."

Milo looked pained. "I think I like it better when you forget stuff."

"I'm not done," I said sheepishly, before telling him about Kiefer Madison and the attempted airplane theft during the two days Troy had been at large the first time. "In fact, that moron Curtis Mayne didn't include the APB in his report of the log."

Milo grimaced. "The little jerk probably never checked it."

I didn't argue. "Anyway, Kiefer told security he was doing it for a friend, so maybe he was going to fly Troy to see Libby at Gonzaga."

"I think," the sheriff said wearily, "you've gone a theory too far." But he headed off to his workroom.

Knowing that Milo kept his personal area downstairs as orderly as the rest of the house was messy, I wasn't surprised to see him return in a little over five minutes.

"I called Monroe. The Samoan's there — Johnny Malifia. He'll get back to me. Let's finish our drinks in the living room and talk suspects."

We sat on the sofa. "You can't come up with an enemy around here," he said. "What about outsiders? That's why I asked about the Cavanaugh kids. You nixed them. Where else do we look?"

"I didn't make enemies in Portland. My beat was fairly tame."

"Too far back. So are the nuts with ties to Cavanaugh's killer. Damn it, Emma, you're usually pretty good at figuring things out. Can you pretend you're not involved and get your brain in gear? I have to be honest. I am — as you like to say — baffled."

"So am I."

He scowled at me. "See? You're part of the puzzle. You don't have perspective. It's why you walk into walls and trip over roots. You think outside of yourself. Your mind races all over the place. Focus on *you*."

I must have looked stupid. Milo removed his arm from around my shoulders and settled back against the sofa. "I'm not kidding. No more fun stuff for us." He grimaced. "Everything's off limits until you get your addled head working again. Mine too. You distract me."

I blinked, realizing I wasn't looking at my lover, but the sheriff. Milo, or whoever he was, was right. I had lost focus. So had he.

I glanced at my watch. It was just seven o'clock. I gasped. "Vida!" I cried. "Turn on the radio!"

Milo didn't move. "Uh . . . I don't think I can do that."

"What?" I shrieked. "Is it broken?"

He wouldn't look at me. "No. But the last time we listened to Vida's show . . ." He shook his head. "Do you want to drive me nuts?"

"Oh," I said. "I didn't think about that."

"Go ahead, turn it on in the bedroom and listen to your priests."

"No. I might turn on more than the radio."

He finally looked at me and laughed. "At least we're on the same page. We can get the tape from Fleetwood."

"I know what Adam and Ben will say," I said. "I've heard it before."

His cell rang. It was unusual for anyone in SkyCo to call during *Vida's Cupboard.* The sheriff got up and wandered into the dining room. His back was turned to me, so I could catch only a few words, which didn't mean a lot out of context.

"You're right," Milo said, coming back to the sofa but not sitting down. "The guard told me Troy got that medal from a girl at Gonzaga. Malifia thought it was a kiss-off gift."

"Why would a Jewish girl give a Jewish guy a medal? She — Libby — had a new boyfriend, despite not having been at Gonzaga very long. Why would she have a Catholic medal?"

"Do they hand them out to convert non-Catholics?"

"No. Catholic schools don't pressure

409

students. If Martin Luther showed up as a six-foot-ten-inch forward, they'd roll out the red carpet."

"Sounds like Troy should've thrown the medal back."

"What about Kiefer? And Gus?"

"Malifia said Troy and Kiefer barely knew each other. But Troy and Gus were fairly tight. The guard felt Gus was a good influence."

"That doesn't sound like Troy would want to kill him."

"Prison does strange things to people. When I was an MP in Nam, I realized how a few weeks in the stockade changed some guys' attitudes."

Milo rarely talked much about his tour of duty. I knew only that he'd been barely out of high school when he was drafted. "Did you become an MP because you knew you eventually wanted a career in law enforcement?"

"Hell, I didn't know what I wanted, but I figured there was less of a chance getting my butt shot off as an MP. I suppose I got an idea that stopping bad guys from doing bad stuff was a good thing to do. The one thing I did know back then was that I'd never be a logger — not much future in it, and I liked keeping my appendages. Logging's brutal."

I smiled. "It was a great choice. You're good at what you do."

Milo shot me an ironic glance. "Oh, yeah? Then how come I have to stash you here? A hotshot cop would've caught the bad guy by now."

"A hotshot journalist would've figured it out before the cop did." I stood up. "I'll clean your kitchen. I think better doing brainless jobs."

"If you say so. I'll watch a half-assed bowl game." He ambled over to his easy chair. "This Bowl Championship Series thing is bullshit."

I left the sheriff to his football. An hour later, I'd cleared off the counters and stacked everything on a shelf. I was about to start on the fridge when Milo entered the kitchen.

"Where's my stuff?" he asked in shock.

"On that shelf. I didn't throw anything out."

He studied what I'd moved. "Okay. It's all there. Mulehide tossed everything except my wallet."

His phone rang again. I headed for the bathroom. When I got back, Milo was in his easy chair. "Nina made Jack listen to Vida's show. Then they had to discuss it. Nina likes

411

discussions. When Jack called Davin, he was with Roger at Mugs Ahoy. The music was so loud the kid couldn't hear. It'd be just my luck for Roger to get wasted and run over somebody. I don't have enough deputies to bust the fat bastard."

"Will Davin call Jack later?"

"He'd better." Milo looked worried. "If this stuff about the girl and the medal is true, then I have to scratch Troy off as a murder suspect."

"Can the autopsy prove it was foul play?"

"Not necessarily. I have to go with my gut feeling. Troy didn't drop that camera." He glanced at his watch. "It's after ten. You've been up since five. Get some kip before you pass out."

I felt awkward. "Is the bed off limits?"

"Not for you."

"Oh, Milo, that's dumb. You can't sleep on your own sofa."

"I can't count how often I did that when I was married. The newer one's longer." He nodded at me. "Scoot. I still have work to do."

"You've been up almost as long as I have. What've you got to do?"

"Nothing big. Just go to bed."

Ten minutes later, I was undressed and under the covers. If this was what married life would be like, what was the point if I was sleeping alone?

SEVENTEEN

I'd never awakened in Milo's bed without him. I felt disoriented, but realized it was daylight. The clock we hadn't broken said it was nine-twenty. The sheriff was standing in the bedroom doorway.

"Just making sure you hadn't crawled out a window," he said.

"What's happening?"

"The snow stopped during the night, but we got over a foot," he replied. "Hungry?"

"I don't know yet. I'm not quite awake."

"Okay. I'm not going anywhere unless it's downstairs."

I showered and dressed, making myself semi-presentable. When I got to the kitchen, Milo was on his cell, looking disgruntled.

"Just do it," he said, and banged down the receiver.

"Do what?" I asked, wondering if Milo's home-brewed coffee was safe to drink.

"My deputies are morons." He stared off

414

into space. "Hell, it's not their fault. I've been playing nursemaid most of the month."

I felt guilty. "Why can't I go to work so you can, too?"

He drummed his fingers on the table. Apparently, he'd been making notes on the yellow legal-sized tablet in front of him. "In theory, I should be able to run this operation from here as well as I can from headquarters. In practice . . ." He shrugged. "That's different."

I poured coffee into a Seahawks mug and sat down. "I don't want you stuck being a nursemaid to me."

He heaved a sigh. "Damn it, Emma, I didn't mean you."

I shook my head. "You meant me, too, and you're right." I took a sip of coffee. It wasn't as bad as I'd feared. And it certainly was strong. Maybe it was the sheriff's hired help that didn't know how to brew coffee that didn't taste like dishwater or sink sludge. "I'm more hampered than you are. I can't even use my phone."

"I charged it," he said, not looking at me. "It's by the blender. Call Vida. She may run at the mouth, but she knows when to zip it. We got through the night alive, so maybe we can loosen up a bit."

"Gee, thanks," I snapped. "You're a peach."

"You're a pickle." He sighed again. "Jack didn't hear back from Davin Rhodes. He probably got too tanked with Roger to remember the call. I talked to Pete, asking him if Gus was wearing the medal the day he took off. He couldn't remember, and neither could Shari. Witnesses drive me nuts." Milo lighted a cigarette before loping past me as if I were another kitchen appliance.

Maybe I was. The floor needed a good scrubbing. I might take care of that after I ate something. But first I put bacon in a pan and forced my brain to work. Milo's coffee helped. If I hadn't been so upset, I might've climbed up the kitchen wall. Snatching my cell off the counter as if I were rescuing it from an acid bath, I called Vida. She practically screamed in my ear when she heard my voice. "You survived the night?"

I assured her I had, but didn't dare let on where I was.

"You sound odd," she said. "Is that because you spent the night with Milo?"

I leaned against the counter. It was a good thing Vida didn't want to kill me. At least not often. She could hunt me down if I sought refuge in a remote Amazon native village. "Why do you say that?" I asked.

"You think I didn't call your brother last night? Or check the sheriff's log this morning? He's not at work, you're not at the rectory — where else would you be? At least whatever you're doing, you're doing it behind closed doors. And closed drapes, I trust."

I stared at the kitchen floor. "It's not what you think," I said. "I wonder where Milo keeps a mop. If he has one."

"What on earth," Vida cried, "are you two doing with a *mop?*"

"Never mind," I said wearily, and went on to explain the sheriff's reaction to what I'd learned from Matt Patricelli about the Laskey-Andrews connection. She was reluctantly impressed by the sheriff's insight.

"You must have a good effect on him," she said grudgingly. "He usually has no imagination."

"That's unfair," I declared. "Milo speculates and thinks about possibilities, but on the job, he keeps all that to himself."

"He's very good at keeping it there," she said with a hint of sarcasm. "What comes to my mind is quite dreadful. I think the boy has died. Recently, too. Do you have your laptop with you?"

"I didn't bring it — or my boots. Milo didn't give me time to think."

She harrumphed. "I'll check the *Times* obits right away."

I should've thought of that myself. "Let me know. Oh — did you take those hiking boots to Bill?"

"Yes," she replied. "I didn't collect them until this morning. Roy's home, but the medication sedates him. I dropped the boots off with Billy on my way to work. I didn't have time last night because of my show. What did you think of it?"

"Well . . . it's hard for me to say," I hedged. "I mean, knowing Adam and Ben as well as I do, I knew what to expect."

"You really should have warned me," Vida said indignantly. "I don't know how much you could tell over the air, but it's a good thing Spencer was there to hit the delay button every time your brother used crude language. He's almost as foulmouthed as Milo."

I was literally speechless, having to cover my own mouth to keeping from laughing out loud.

"Emma?" Vida finally said. "Are you still there?"

"Yes," I finally said. "I can't speak for Ben. I mean, he's human."

"I cannot imagine Pastor Purebeck saying such things," she asserted. "Which is why I don't believe he's having an affair. He's not . . ."

"Human?" I broke in.

"Oh, hush! I must check those obits. Do take care."

I rescued my bacon and made some toast. Five minutes later, I was staring again at the kitchen floor when my phone rang. The sheriff hadn't told me I couldn't answer it, so I did.

"Mom," Adam said, "where are you?"

I hesitated, torn in several different directions, and opted for discretion. "I'm safe. Really."

"Uncle Ben and I've gone almost crazy worrying about you. When can we go back to your house? I left half my stuff there."

"That's up to the sheriff," I said. "Call him."

There was a pause before Adam spoke again. "Can't you ask him?"

"No."

He paused again. "This is too weird. Okay, I will." He rang off.

I was on my hands and knees scrubbing the floor when Milo reappeared. "Holy shit!" He stared at the floor. "What next, wallpaper?"

"You tracked snow and mud . . . skip it. I'm waiting to hear back from Vida. She thinks something horrible happened recently to Andrews's son and it set him off. She's starting with Seattle obits."

Milo nodded grimly. "For once, I won't argue with her. Something sure got to him." He refilled his coffee mug and started to turn away.

"Where are you going?" I asked.

"Back downstairs. I work better there. You're one hell of a distraction in a lot of ways. Why did you put on lipstick? Why didn't you smear your face with Crisco or something? Christ, but you're a pain in the ass." Shaking his head, he left.

Damn the man, he was so aggravating — but as usual, I couldn't stay mad. I was still tackling the kitchen floor when Vida called back. "I'm amazed," she declared. "I didn't have to look very far. The poor child's obit was in Sunday's *Times.* Aaron Andrews, born April 14, 1992, son of Charles and Olivia Andrews of Seattle, died December 24, 2004. The funeral is today at Epiphany Church."

"That's the Madrona/Denny-Blaine area," I said.

"Yes. Milo has a home computer, but he's never given me his personal email," she

420

added, sounding affronted.

"Uh . . ." I looked at the sheriff, who was back in the doorway, shaking his head in apparent dismay. "Any hint of how Aaron died?"

"It says 'after a long illness,' which often means cancer. I assume not in this case. Memorials to Children's Hospital."

"Nothing else of interest?"

"No, only survivors, immediate family, very impersonal."

"Then you don't need Milo's email," I said.

Hearing muffled voices at her end, I assumed she had a hand over the receiver. I ignored Milo and attacked a grease stain near the stove.

"Oh, dear!" Vida exclaimed into my ear. "Dwight just called. They got an APB for Mitch from KingCo. Does Milo know?"

"If he does, he hasn't —"

The sheriff bellowed my name. "Maybe he has." I rang off.

He gave himself a shake. "There's an ABP out on Mitch."

I nodded. "Vida just told me. She knows I'm here."

"She would." The sheriff threw up his hands. "See? When I'm not on the spot, Vida knows more about my job than I do."

"She probably does even when you are. Most people think she runs the newspaper — and she is now. Why is there an ABP on Mitch?"

"He's wanted for impeding an investigation," Milo said in disgust.

"You mean Troy's accident?"

"Who knows? The APB's statewide. I'm calling Yakima to see if they know anything. Maybe Andrews is pulling some heavy-duty strings. The kid's death must've unhinged him. That's damned rough." He took out his cell. "When did it happen?"

"Christmas Eve," I said.

"Christ." Milo had tapped in a number. "Hey, Dwight, I need Yakima County's number. . . . No, but I've met him. . . . Top drawer of my filing cabinet . . ." Milo looked at me and mouthed, "Blind as a bat." A moment later he jotted down the number and rang off. "I feel damned sorry for that Andrews bastard."

"Me too," I agreed. "You think a vehicular homicide charge?"

Milo rubbed the back of his head. "There's nothing about that in the APB. How could Andrews make a case now?"

"Because he's out of his mind with grief," I said.

Milo looked thoughtful. "That I get. If

Tanya had been killed and her fiancé hadn't offed himself, I'd have done it for him."

I nodded. "The quality of mercy is lacking in most parents. But if Aaron died on Friday, why was Andrews here Monday and Tuesday? Shouldn't he have been grieving and making arrangements with his family?"

"People grieve in strange ways. A guy like Andrews gets angry and lashes out. My guess is he came to get even with Laskey. It doesn't have to make sense. Didn't Kip see his Escalade at Mitch's house Monday night?"

"Spence saw it, too. Revenge is —" My phone rang. "It's Vida again," I said, seeing the *Advocate*'s number.

"Will that dunderhead of a sheriff let you talk to Kip?" she asked.

"I'll ask the dunderhead," I said, and posed the question to Milo.

"Hell, yes," he roared, adding, "and tell Vida to watch her big mouth."

"I heard that!" she cried. "How have you not killed each other? Here's Kip."

"Hey," Kip said excitedly, "Durgan's still at the ski lodge. Henry Bardeen's arranging an interview. Turns out that Turk's girlfriend works at the lodge and he's hanging out with her there."

"That's great," I said. "Are you going to

the lodge now?"

"Not until noon," Kip replied. "Libby's off until then."

"Libby?" I said.

"She works in the gift shop during the afternoons and at King Olav's in the evenings. Got to go, Leo needs some back-shop help."

Milo noticed the odd look on my face. "Now what?"

"Is my mind going?" I asked bleakly.

"You're supposed to be getting it back. Did you eat breakfast?"

"Yes. Call Henry Bardeen. Ask about his new hire, Libby or . . ." I paused, trying to recall the formal name of the waitress who'd served us at the dinner with Marisa. "Livna, I think. She's Durgan's girlfriend."

Milo's eyes sparked. "You think she's the one Troy was after?"

"It sounds crazy, but Vida had something about her in 'Scene.' What if Troy was trying to find her instead of his parents?"

"That's a stretch." But Milo shrugged. "Is Kip going to the lodge?"

"Yes, around noon."

He checked his watch. "It's ten-thirty. Tell him to get his butt up there now and talk to Henry. I'll send Dustman to make sure Libby isn't going anywhere." Milo made as if to muss my hair, but stopped. "Keep thinking," he said, heading out of the kitchen.

When I called Kip, he was still in the back shop, but I relayed the information to Vida. "Most interesting," she remarked.

After reminding Vida to make certain Kip asked about the medal, I wandered to the kitchen window. The clouds had lifted and the sky had brightened, but the view was snow and more snow. Milo knew every nook and cranny of my log cabin, but I felt like a stranger in his house.

I'd lost focus again, so I got back to cleaning the floor. After I finished, I wondered who'd chosen the much-scuffed and cracked Congoleum. If it had been Tricia, that was grounds for divorce.

I made more toast. I was munching on it when Milo came back into the kitchen. "Stop," I said. "Wipe your feet."

"I haven't been anywhere," he growled, and stared at the floor. "So, that's what it looks like."

"It's hideous," I said. "I shouldn't have bothered."

"Don't blame me," he retorted. "The only thing I bought for this place was my easy chair after Mulehide left. Oh — and the sofa and the bed. I got a king-sized because I didn't want the one she and Jake the Snake had been rolling around in." Milo poured himself half a mug of coffee. "We're out. Want to make some more?"

"Sure. When do I get to do the windows?"

He narrowed his eyes at me. "How's your brain?"

"Better." I found a can of coffee wedged between cereal boxes. Milo's kitchen system was a far cry from his work files. "Something eludes me, like a musical leitmotif. I don't know what it means."

Milo lit a cigarette and sat down. "You're out of my league. If it's not Waylon or Willie, forget it."

I plugged the coffeepot in and joined Milo at the table. "Hey, even Waylon and Willie had leitmotifs. It's just a theme, like 'Red-headed Stranger' or the 'Outlaw' thing or . . ." I frowned.

"What?"

I took a cigarette from the pack Milo had set on the table. "Can you light this for me without both of our brains exploding?"

He gave me a quirky smile. "Maybe."

"Thanks," I said after we managed not to bump heads while he held the lighter. "The camera, the shots Gus didn't take, his body being found where Myrtle was going berry-picking, but I don't think she did."

Milo scowled at me. "So where did she go?"

"Home." I stopped, but when I started again, I spoke very fast, giving him the same theory I'd tried out on Adam.

Milo slapped a hand to his forehead. "Jesus! Why did I ask you to think? You come up with . . ." He dropped his hand on the table. "Well . . . why not? She sure as hell isn't anyplace else."

"You don't think I'm nuts?"

His smiled wryly. "Yeah, you're nuts, but I've heard you come up with crazier stuff. I'd need cadaver dogs and a thaw. It'd be worth it to get that Everson bunch off my back. Maybe Roy could glue his brain back together. How we'd ever prove foul play or get evidence against the addled old judge is another matter."

"Good. I was afraid you'd laugh." I glanced at the floor to make sure it had dried. "Do you have any boots I could wear? Some of your daughters'? I need to clear my brain."

Milo shook his head. "I don't think so. Why do you want boots?"

"I'd like to go outside and breathe some fresh air."

"Stay put or I'll tie you to the sink."

"I hate you."

Milo shrugged. "No, you don't."

"Did Bill mention those hiking boots Vida dropped off?"

He nodded. "He'll check them out with REI when he gets around to it. They're kind of busy with some other stuff, like their jobs."

I leaned toward him. "Hey, aren't we looking for an X factor? You told me Gus was wearing sneakers. Troy was never on Mount Sawyer, where Roy found the blasted boots. We might get lucky."

Milo rested his chin on his hand and gazed at me broodingly. "What if whoever bought them wasn't an REI member? What if whoever it was paid cash? What if the boots were shoplifted? What if . . ." He put his hands on the table and leaned back in the chair. "Oh, hell, it's all we've got. At least it'll keep Vida off my back — and Bill's."

I smiled. "Good."

Milo was on his feet. "One thing, though," he said. "Why would Mr. X leave an expensive pair of almost new boots on Sawyer?"

I hadn't thought about that. "Uh . . . I don't know," I admitted.

"Think." His expression was droll. "By the way, the window cleaner's in the cupboard . . . somewhere." He grabbed his jacket and left.

He'd gone too far — as in *outside,* which I wasn't allowed to do. Furthermore, I loathed washing windows. I'd always paid one of our newspaper carriers to do that chore for me. The last time, Jim and Sherry Medved's son, Taylor, had done a good job until he was cleaning my picture window and a chipmunk bit him. Taylor had fled in terror. Given that his father was a vet, I figured the son wasn't destined to inherit Jim's practice.

I started in on the fridge, but except for a jar of mayo and some dill pickles past their prime, there was nothing to toss. In fact, there wasn't much in the fridge. That figured, given Milo's penchant for boxes.

I still had cabin fever. Putting on my jacket, I went down the hall to open the door and breathe mountain air. But the damned thing was locked from the outside. Frustrated, I stomped back through the hall in time to hear Vida call out to me from the porch. "Yoo-hoo, Emma! Where are you?"

"Wait," I shouted, going through the living room to let her in. "I'm a prisoner."

Vida, whose head was covered with something that looked like French Foreign Legion desert wear, tapped her fingers against her cheek. "So you are. But it's for

429

your own good."

"No, it's not," I said. "I could be protected just as well at my own house or the office. I'm going stir crazy."

"I could get your laptop — and your boots — if you give me your key," she said. "Speaking of boots, Billy just called to say Milo told him to trace the ones Bebe gave me. I thought you should know, men being so peculiar when it comes to conveying information. I was on my way to interview Maud Dodd at the retirement home when Billy called, so I thought I'd let you know in person. Besides," she added more softly, "I thought you might like company."

I smiled. "I do. I'm so frustrated. Shall I put on the teakettle?"

"I can't stay. Maud must be wondering where I am. She spent Christmas with her daughter and family in Denver, so I'm doing a brief article." She peered at me. "How are you two getting on?"

"Fine," I said.

Vida flipped a hand at the fabric hanging from the back of her hat. "You realize this is a preview of married life with Milo. Have you plans?"

"We got engaged. What more do you want?"

Vida's eyes widened. "Oh! You *are* serious

then. It's official?"

"I don't want anybody to know yet. I haven't told Adam — or Ben."

"I'm relieved. I thought you might dither. Shall I take your key?"

"No," I said. "I'd feel like I was giving up on getting out of here. Neither of us can think who poses such a threat. We're stymied."

"I never interfere," she stated. "But I warned you. It could be someone who's jealous, a thwarted soul who sees you two so openly in love and hates you for it." She patted my arm. "I'll be in touch."

"That," I said, somewhat shaken, "never occurred to us."

"It happens. Love is so akin to hate. Do be careful."

I was sorry to see her go, weird hat and all. More than that, I was sorry that I couldn't go with her.

EIGHTEEN

When Milo came to get fresh coffee twenty minutes later, I knew by his gloomy face that something was wrong. "Well?" I said, cleaning crumbs from the toaster.

"Mitch was picked up at Harborview fifteen minutes ago."

I gaped at him. "By the cops?"

He nodded. "I spent so much time with Tanya at Harborview that I got to know the hospital's security people. They called me after finding out Mitch lived here. He was at the psych ward with Brenda." Milo took his coffee to the table and sat down. "I haven't heard back from Yakima."

I sat down, too. "What can you do, besides talk to their sheriff?"

"That's what I'm working on," he growled. "Did you do a background check on Laskey before you hired him?"

I shook my head. "I was in a rush to replace the idiot I'd fired."

"Do you ever do a background check on anybody outside of Alpine? Leo? The good-looking guy . . . Scott? Or even Carla?"

From the way the sheriff was staring at me, I felt like the prime suspect. "No. Tom recommended Leo. Scott and Carla were U-Dub grads. So was Curtis, for that matter," I said heatedly. "A small-town weekly can't be picky. I can't afford to pay much more than subsistence wages. Mitch was like an answer to a prayer."

"Some prayer." Milo had poured coffee and lighted a cigarette, but he didn't offer me one. He got out his cell and dialed a number. "Dwight? I thought you went home. . . . Oh, damn, I forgot about Cobb's funeral. . . . I can't." He grimaced. "You're right. I'll be there. Meanwhile, run a background check on Mitch Laskey. . . . No, I'll ask." Milo looked at me. "What's his full name?"

"Oh . . ." My mind was blank. "It's not Mitch, I mean it's not Mitchell, it's a Jewish name and the only time I ever saw it was on his application. Damn it, Milo, I can't do anything trapped here!"

"You sure as hell can't." Telling Dwight he'd get back to him, Milo disconnected and looked as disgusted as I felt. "I have to go to Alfred Cobb's funeral at one o'clock.

Gould told me if I didn't show up, the county commissioners might cut our budget. God help me if I dissed one of those old farts, dead or just half-dead."

"You're going to leave?"

"They aren't holding the funeral in my freaking driveway." Milo angrily ground out his cigarette. "I won't stay for the reception. I wouldn't have time even if I was at my . . ."

"Say it! I'm a pain in the ass! God knows you've been telling me that for the last fifteen years!" I started out of the kitchen.

"Where the hell are you going?" Milo bellowed.

I whirled around to face him. "To get some air. I'm suffocating."

"You dumbshit! What have you got on your feet?"

"Shoes. What else?"

Milo looked almost apoplectic. "It's snowing again. Are you nuts?"

"Yes! I can't stay here another minute. I might as well have spent the night in one of your freaking jail cells."

"You are a piece of work. Get your ass back in the kitchen."

My chin was thrust out, quivering with rage. "Make me."

His expression changed. He looked amused. "That won't work this time. Nice try, though." He folded his arms and leaned against the door.

I covered my mouth and stared up at him. I was ashamed. He shrugged. "Adam called. He's more reasonable than you are."

My hand fell away. "I told him he was the only adult in the family."

"Maybe." He regarded me with concern. "Feel better?"

"I guess."

He sighed. "We'll both go to the damned funeral."

I gaped at him. "You're serious?"

Briefly, he looked conflicted, but shrugged. "Yeah, why not? There'll be a crowd there. How long for you to get dressed at your place?"

"Five minutes, tops."

"You're kidding." He grinned at me. "It took Mulehide half an hour just to find her damned shoes."

"Single moms have to work fast," I said, and blurted, "Menachem."

"What?"

"Mitch's real first name. His middle initial is M, not sure what for, but I recall thinking his initials were MML, as in two thousand fifty."

"When your brain works, it's in some really weird ways." Milo checked his watch.

"It's a little after noon. Be ready to take off at twelve-forty. Dustman should be reporting in from the lodge."

I was expecting to hear from Kip about his interview with Turk and Libby. I phoned the office, but Vida said she was the only staffer on hand. "I just got back from interviewing Maud, so I'm not taking lunch," she said. "I'll eat something at the funeral reception. I must shed those extra pounds. You and Milo have lost weight. Does he have food on hand? I can drop off my casserole leftovers. For such sturdy men, Ben and Adam don't have big appetites."

"They avoid the sin of gluttony," I said. "Milo and I have plenty to eat." I didn't add that most of it was in boxes, though even those would taste better than her casserole — boxes included. I was tempted to tell Vida that Milo and I were going to Alfred's funeral, but decided it was best to keep mum. I didn't want to waste time having her tell me why it was a bad idea. "Any word on Mitch?"

"No." She paused. "Oh, dear, here comes Rita Patricelli. Maybe she knows when Gus's funeral will be held. So many funerals this month! Al Driggers must be rolling in money. I'll talk to you later."

There was enough makeup in my purse to

get my face ready to go public. I was coping with my hair when my cell rang ten minutes later.

"You're right," Kip said excitedly. "It took a while to get anything out of Libby — real name, Livna Weinberg, and if we use it in the paper, she'll sue the socks off of us. The medal we found on Troy belongs to Turk, who'd left it wherever Libby was living. Troy flew into a rage and took it away from her when she told him to buzz off. Durgan's Catholic, spent two years at Gonzaga. He and Libby met at Mount Schweitzer in Idaho. He is awesome! I got terrific stuff from him, if you can help me write it. Pictures, too. I'm sure glad we didn't run the shot of him getting busted. He's buying a place at Leavenworth. Libby quit school to move here until he gets settled. Oh — Turk wants the medal back."

"He can probably have it. Good job. Yes, I'll help with the story."

"I can get another picture tomorrow when his new snowboard arrives," Kip said. "It's a Prior All-Mountain . . ."

Milo called my name. Again. "Excuse me, Kip, I have to dash."

"Is that Dodge?" he asked.

"It barks like him," I said. "Bye."

I went into the living room, but he wasn't

in sight. "Milo?" I called. He wasn't in the entryway. He wasn't in the hall. "Milo!" I yelled.

"I'm changing," he shouted from the bedroom. "Five minutes."

I unplugged the coffeepot and made sure the stove was off. Gathering up my meager belongings, I waited by the front door. The sheriff appeared, not in a suit, but in uniform. He saw my surprise and shot me a withering glance. "This is a county function. I have to be official. Hold this." He handed over his regulation hat, lifted me off the floor, and slung me over his shoulder. "Don't wiggle or breathe," he warned me. "This isn't as easy as I thought."

I held my breath, seeing a few footprints that were beginning to disappear as the new snow began to fall more heavily. The wind had come up, too, but we had to cover less than ten yards to reach the Cherokee, where Milo hastily dumped me into the passenger seat.

"Remind me not to try that stunt again," he said after getting behind the wheel. "You're a hell of a lot harder to haul around that way."

I was more out of breath than he was. "I'm dizzy. Honest to God, Milo, if somebody else doesn't kill us first, we'll do it ourselves."

"Right," he said, starting the SUV. "I keep forgetting we're not kids anymore. Hell, we're damned near eligible for senior discounts."

I leaned back in the seat. "I feel like it about now." It took me a few moments to get my bearings. We'd reached the Icicle Creek Road intersection and were passing the high school to get to Fir, which had been plowed. The new snow was beginning to stick, as it came down harder and faster with every block we passed.

Milo turned onto my street. "Heppner cleared your driveway while they were watching your house." He pulled up just short of the carport. "I'll wait for you here."

"With a stopwatch?"

"You bet." He looked at me sheepishly. "If I go inside, I might want to stick around. It does feel like home."

It was home to me, though when I walked through the back door, it seemed as if I'd been gone for several days instead of a few hours. I'd already figured out exactly what I'd wear — black dress with a high-necked shawl collar, boots with a two-inch heel, and black trench coat.

I was headed for the bedroom when I

439

heard the sound of breaking glass. Startled, I turned around and went into the living room. Seeing the Cherokee still in place, I opened the front door — and froze on the threshold.

The bright, white world was ripped apart by a wall of fire and a sound of fury. I reeled against the door that was being blown shut by the wind — or the explosion. Stunned, half-blinded by snow, half-crazy with dread, I tried to focus. It took me what seemed like forever to realize that the flaming mass just a few yards away was the Cherokee. An agonized scream tore out of my throat. I was paralyzed. My brain ceased to function. I had to get help, but I couldn't move. The wind kept whipping the snow into my face, though I wasn't cold. The heat from the fire was too intense, too close. I could smell something. Gasoline? Burning rubber? Melting metal? Finally I forced my feet to move — and slipped on the porch. Lying facedown, I felt a hand tug at my jacket.

"Get up!" The voice was hoarse, unrecognizable. I had no strength to respond. I was being dragged along on my stomach, flopping like a trout on the line. I realized I was being hauled inside, across the carpet, and into the hall between the bathroom and the bedrooms. At last, I summoned up whatever survival instincts I still possessed and found enough strength to struggle, flailing my arms and legs at the unseen assailant.

"Bitch!" The voice seemed to come from nowhere, but the hands that grabbed my arms and forced me onto my back were very real. I looked up and immediately recognized my attacker.

"I knew you'd show up eventually," Curtis Mayne exulted with the goofy grin I remembered all too well from his short stay as my reporter. He went straight for my throat with his bare hands.

I banged against the wall as Curtis fell on top of me. One of his hands pressed against my windpipe so hard that I could hardly breathe, let alone scream. His other hand was yanking at my slacks. "Bitch!" he shrieked again. "You and that fucking sheriff ruined me! He didn't believe I could murder somebody! I showed him! He can fry in hell! He wasn't the first and you're next! But before that, I'll make you pay!"

I felt my slacks rip from below the waistband to my knee. My left arm was pinioned between the hall linen drawers and my side. I tried to scratch at his face with my other hand, but he grabbed my wrist, jamming my arm between our upper torsos. He was struggling to get my jacket out of the way, yanking up my sweater and making some kind of animal growls low in his throat. Then Curtis began shrieking again, so loud that I thought my head would explode. My ears were ringing. I tried to move, but I was helpless under his weight, no longer able to fend him off. I couldn't even see. Had he covered my eyes? Had I fallen into some black void where I was beyond pain? Or was I beyond caring?

Suddenly I could breathe. The pressure was off my throat, even though Curtis still lay on top of me. He lifted his head just enough so that I could see his wretched face. His eyes were wide and his mouth was open. I was so traumatized that I must've blacked out for a few seconds. The next thing I knew, I no longer felt his weight. When I dared to open my eyes, Milo was kneeling beside me.

"You're safe," he said in a ragged voice before speaking into his cell. I caught only "ambulance," "backup," and "Doc."

Milo was still on his knees. He rested his forehead on one hand and took a deep breath. "Can you move?" he asked hoarsely. "I have to stay with the perp."

Dazedly, I saw Curtis twitching and whimpering on the floor a few feet away in my bedroom. One wrist was handcuffed to the leg of the bureau. The sheriff's King Cobra Magnum lay not far from my shoulder. I couldn't speak, let alone move. Milo glanced at the miserable mess that was Curtis before carrying me to the sofa. Wordlessly, he returned to the bedroom. I was still shaking all over when I heard the first of the sirens.

Jumbled thoughts raced through my chaotic brain. *The door. Locked? Deputies. Medics. How would they get in? Was I really alive? Had I imagined seeing Milo?*

"Ms. Lord!" Dustin Fong cried. "Are you okay?"

I'd never heard Dustin raise his voice before. I was vaguely aware of Jack Mullins and Sam Heppner on his heels. They both ran through the living room and disappeared. Dustin asked where he could find a blanket for me. I waved in the direction of Adam's room. The deputy left just as Tony Lynch and Del Amundson arrived with a gurney.

Del stopped on the threshold. "We're here for . . . ?" I motioned toward the hall. He told Tony to wait until he talked to the sheriff. A moment later, Del reappeared, beckoning to his partner to bring the gurney.

Dustin returned with a Hudson Bay blanket and carefully put it over me. "Can I get you something before Doc comes?" he asked.

"Doc?" I said, speaking for the first time.

Dustin nodded. "Dodge insists. He's really upset."

I groaned. "He's upset?" I flung an arm over my eyes and shuddered. "It's my fault." I hid my face against the sofa's back.

"Hey, Ms. Lord, don't, it's not . . ." He stopped.

I heard Milo close by. "Go ahead, Dustman, ride in the ambulance. I'm freed up. I handed my weapon over to Heppner."

"Yes, sir," Dustin said. "Bye, Ms. Lord. Take care."

I rolled onto my back. Milo knelt by the sofa, his hand on my head, his face buried on my breast. "Jesus," he said, muffled. "Jesus."

I flung an arm over his shoulders. "I thought you were dead. I didn't care if I died, too."

"Oh, Emma . . ." He lifted his head. "Damn, I don't deserve you."

I couldn't quite smile. "We deserve each other."

He just looked at me for so long that it seemed like I could see into his soul. "What happened?" I finally asked.

Milo took a deep breath. His voice was

still a bit ragged. "I saw fresh footprints, not touched by the new snow. I got out of the Cherokee and followed them. Then, just when I went through the carport, I heard glass breaking. It sounded like it came from the Cherokee. I'd never put my hat back on, and when I'd gotten out, I'd propped it on top of my seat. The perp threw the bomb in there. The next thing I knew, the whole damned thing exploded. I hit the ground."

I shuddered. "Curtis thought you were still in the car."

"I told you it was an amateur operation — thank God." He shook his head. "Anyway, I followed the footprints to your bedroom window. Curtis had jimmied it. I saw . . . You know what I saw in the hall." He touched my cheek. "It all happened in what? Not more than five minutes?"

"It seemed like forever." I took his hand and held it to my breast. "Your poor car."

"No big deal." Milo was beginning to sound more like himself. "I've been thinking about a new one. And I'm glad about the hat. I want to do away with those things. They make me look too damned tall."

"You'd look good to me in a dunce cap."

Milo smiled wryly. "I should get one for this case."

"Get two. I don't know why I never

thought about Curtis. I suppose I spent too much time trying to forget him."

"Main Cure," Milo muttered. "Curtis Mayne. Now it makes sense. Damn! I never heard back from Andy Cederberg about that PO box."

I didn't get a chance to respond. "Which one's the patient?" Doc Dewey inquired in a bemused voice as he entered the house with Vida at his heels like a hound dog on the scent.

"Goodness!" she cried. "Didn't I say they were both insane? Now see what a fine mess they've gotten themselves into. Oh — here comes the gurney. Who . . ." She sucked in her breath. "*Curtis?* No! I feel faint!"

Milo had looked up. So did I, just as Vida fell into the easy chair.

"Vida!" Doc cried. "Let me help you."

The sheriff got to his feet. "You take care of Vida, Doc. I'm getting a couple of stiff drinks for Emma and me."

"Bring two more," Doc called. "We're skipping Alf's funeral."

I realized Doc was wearing a dark suit and tie. I sat up, huddled under the blanket. Vida's head was between her knees while Doc hovered. Her hat was on the floor — not the desert number I'd seen in what seemed like another life, but a black froth of feathers and net.

"I'm fine," she declared waspishly, even though Doc was taking her pulse. "I'm merely stunned. Who would have guessed . . ."

"Hush," Doc said softly. "I'll take your blood pressure." He reached into his kit that he'd set down by the easy chair. Noticing Milo arrive with two drinks, Doc warned me not to take even a sip. "You're next, Emma." He turned back to Vida. "Roll up your sleeve, please."

"Oooh . . . such a fuss!"

Doc scowled at her. "Vida . . ."

Milo set our drinks on the end table. "I just talked to Bill. REI sold those boots to Curtis."

Vida's head shot up. "Billy?"

"Damn, Vida," Doc said, putting the cuff on her arm, "be still!"

"Mind your language . . . Ow! That's too tight!"

"I should've put it over your mouth," Doc muttered. "Remind me, Vida, the next time I get an emergency call just before a funeral starts, you aren't coming with me. You're not a nurse."

Milo had gone back to the kitchen. Doc finally got his reading. "You're almost normal," he said to Vida, shaking his head.

"You have the constitution of an ox."

"I should hope so," Vida retorted. "I was just shocked when I saw that crazy ninny on the gurney. Did he really cause all this trouble?"

I shrugged. "I guess so. He always wanted to be famous. Now he will be. Thank God there's a law to prevent him from profiting by a book he might write in prison. Assuming, of course, he doesn't die."

"He won't," Milo said, returning with the other drinks. "I shot him in the ass." He handed Vida what appeared to be a screwdriver. Like Milo, Doc drank Scotch. "Where do I put yours, Doc?"

"By that other chair. Don't sit too close to Emma. I have to check her out," Doc said. "In fact, you don't look so good, either."

"I'm fine now," Milo said. "Fifteen minutes ago, I wasn't so sure."

Doc put the cuff on my arm. "If you could aim your weapon exactly where you wanted to," he said to Milo, "you're probably in better shape than most people. But you know the aftershock can be rough."

"Right," Milo agreed, still standing. "It's not the first time."

I kept quiet while Doc examined me. "Your throat's bruised," he said. "This Curtis didn't inflict any other injuries that I can't see?"

I understood his discreet inquiry. "Milo shot him before he could do anything else."

Doc patted my arm. "All things considered, you'll be fine. I'll call in some prescriptions for you." He looked at Milo, who'd sat down next to me. "You take good care of her." It was a statement, not an order.

"I almost didn't," Milo said with remorse.

" 'Almost' doesn't count," Doc said, going over to the side chair. "You did what you had to. I'll drink to that." He raised his glass.

Fifteen minutes later, Doc and Vida left. They could still make the reception. I asked Milo if he should attend, too.

"Are you nuts?" He had his arm around me. "I'm not going anywhere. In fact, I can't. I'm on leave. I shot someone, remember?"

"Oh. Yes." I closed my eyes. "I can't even think."

"Don't." He kissed the top of my head. "My hands-off policy didn't work so well for either of us, did it?"

"It made sense at the time," I said, opening my eyes. "At least I remembered the damned boots and you took me seriously. But I'd rather not do it again. Maybe we could act like grown-ups. In public."

"Maybe." He tapped my chin. "You're beat. You need a nap."

"You look tired, too. How did you sleep on the sofa?"

Milo chuckled. "Damned little. I bought it after Mulehide left, so I never had to sleep on it. Besides, I was trying to think. Without you."

"Let's both . . ." I gasped. "Adam! Ben! Do they know?"

"Probably not. Do you really want to deal with them now?"

"I don't think I can," I admitted.

"I figured as much. I'll put you to bed." He grimaced. "You'll have to sleep in the spare room, though."

"Why?"

"That prick bled on your bedroom rug after I cuffed him. The room has to be processed. Doe and Jack can do that, but now we're shorthanded with the cemetery escort and my . . ." He shook his head. "Curtis caused a freaking mess. Bernie Shaw may want to kill both of us with all our insurance claims."

"Don't say that!" I cried.

Milo looked chagrined as he smoothed my hair. "But it's over."

450

I was able to smile. Finally. "Yes," I said, "it is."

Nineteen

It was almost dark when Adam and Ben showed up. I'd just awakened, having heard the arrival of Doe and Jack a few minutes earlier. The door to Adam's room remained closed, but I recognized the voices even if I couldn't make out what was being said.

The truth was I didn't care. I ached all over and still felt drained. Hungry, too, realizing I hadn't eaten since morning. My watch said it was five-ten. I'd slept for over three hours. The horror of what had happened overcame me. I didn't want to budge.

It was Adam who cautiously opened the door a few minutes later. He tiptoed into the room, apparently thinking I was still asleep. I called his name. "Mom!" he cried, hurrying to the bed. "How are you?"

"Wretched," I confessed as he took my hand. "I'm an idiot."

Gingerly, he sat on the edge of the bed. "Dodge told us what happened." His face was grave. "I don't know what to say."

"Don't say anything. I just need time to collect myself."

"No kidding." My son's expression was ironic. "Just from a bomb and a homicidal rapist nut? You should toughen up, Mom."

I felt as if I was smiling, but couldn't be sure. "Oh, Adam!"

He squeezed my hand. "Dodge had me pick up prescriptions for you on the way over. Tranqs and painkillers. You want a handful?"

"Just the painkillers. I'm hungry."

"You're not supposed to eat the painkillers, you're —"

Milo was in the doorway. "You're awake," he said.

"Yes." I smiled at him. "Dr. Lord is getting my meds."

Adam took his cue. "Be right back," he said, making way for Milo.

The sheriff came over to the bed, but remained standing. "I should've come inside with you."

I raised my head. "No! If you had, Curtis might've thrown the bomb in the house. It's my fault for not thinking of him. *He* was what kept eluding me. I'll bet the fire was meant for you, too. Maybe he'd seen your car at my house Tuesday night and thought you might be here again Wednesday. You said we might both be targets when we thought the Nelson kids acted on their own. I fired him, you humiliated him. After you booted him out of jail, he left town without coming back to the office. The Canon we use is the one he left behind. That's why the other camera kept bugging me."

"You must feel better. You can't seem to shut up."

I slumped back on the pillow. "Sorry."

He knelt on one knee. "Hey — it's fine. Damn it, I can't take care of you even when I'm taking care of you."

I touched his cheek. "I'm still alive. If not for you, I'd have been dead a long time ago. You've done everything including kill for me."

"You're worth it." He looked away. "Back then, I shot that perp not just for you, but for Honoria."

I was stunned. "No!"

He nodded. "She thanked me."

I couldn't help it. I was angry and hurt. "You never told me that!"

His hazel eyes shifted back to my face. "I knew you'd get mad."

"Did she thank you all the way from California?"

"She wrote me a note. Hell, the perp was

the guy who turned her into a cripple." Milo's color had darkened. "Why wouldn't she thank me? We'd gone together for three years. Are you still jealous of her?"

"Of course not! Was I ever?"

Milo ran a hand through his hair. "Jesus, you practically threw me out of the house when I finally told you I was seeing her. You and I weren't even dating back then."

"I was mad because I spent so much money on your damned lamb chops," I said, still angry. "Why would I be . . ." I lowered my head. "Okay, I was jealous. But I didn't know why."

"God, but you're slow." He frowned. "Anyway, she told me in the note she knew I'd always been in love with you."

"Oh." I bit my lip. "Oh, dear!" I covered my face with the sheet.

"Hey, Mom, here's . . . where is she?" Adam asked.

"Under the sheet," Milo said. "You got any *reasonable* pills from Doc? Your mother is the biggest pain in the ass I've ever met."

I peeked out in time to see Milo disappear. "Ignore him," I said. "He's the most aggravating man on planet Earth."

"You guys will be really happy together," Adam said, handing me a glass of water. "Who referees? Vida?"

"Just give me the damned Percocet or whatever."

"Here," Adam said. "Take two."

I obeyed. "What are Jack and Doe doing to my poor house?"

Adam glanced into the hall. "Doe's sweeping. Jack's watching."

"That sounds like the sheriff's staff. Can you fix me a sandwich? By the way, where's your uncle?"

Adam seemed uncomfortable. "He doesn't want to talk to you until you feel better."

"Tell him to get his butt in here right now. I mean it."

Adam surrendered. "Okay. What kind of sandwich?"

"Ham and Havarti."

A couple of minutes passed before Ben entered, looking bleak. "Hi." He gazed around the small room. "I should get a chair."

"Sit at the end of the bed," I said. "I'm short, remember?"

He sat. "How are you? I mean, all things considered."

"I'm alive, thanks to Milo."

"Don't rub it in." His eyes kept roaming the walls before settling on me. "I have my own confession to make." He sighed, though it didn't seem to relieve the tension in his stiff posture. "Is Adam more mature than I am? Maybe more than you, too?"

"Yes. I told him so."

"He is." Ben relaxed a little. "I was out of line. I gave you hell about Dodge because I never thought you'd get married. You and I seemed destined to be single. I had this idea that when we got old, we'd be together, like when we were kids. I'd retire around here, sub for absent priests, you'd sell the paper, we'd be back where we started, a damned nice thought."

I reached out to take my brother's hand. "Oh, Ben, I never guessed what you were thinking. Now I feel sad."

"Don't," he said, squeezing my fingers. "Hell, I can still hang out with you and Dodge. When you dropped your bombshell, I couldn't believe it. I figured it was a wild hair, like accepting Tom's proposal. But Tom was so unpredictable that I never took it seriously. I didn't know him very well, but you seemed nuts about him and I felt it'd be nice for Adam's parents to get married. I do know Dodge and I like him. In some ways, like his attitude toward you, he reminds me of me."

That had never occurred to me, not even when I'd lumped Milo and Ben together for making me feel like a clumsy idiot. "I had no idea!"

He uttered a small laugh. "No, Sluggly, you wouldn't. That's part of your charm, I guess. Here's your waiter with a sandwich."

Adam had also brought a can of Pepsi and a glass. "My tip's still at the mall. This looks like deep stuff here. Door open or closed?"

Ben shook his head. "Just keep out the riffraff. You included."

My son left. Ben slapped his hands on his knees. "That's pretty much it. I overreacted. Yes, I can try to get Dodge an annulment. It'll take time, though, and there are no certainties. Does he know that's a possibility?"

"He knows what an annulment is," I said, "no thanks to you for not mentioning it, but Adam did. There hasn't been time to explain everything to him. But we've waited fifteen years. What's another decade or so?"

"I mean in moral . . . Oh, shit, do what you want. Just don't do it in front of the courthouse. In fact," he went on, the idea apparently just occurring to him, "get married by a JP to give the appearance of legal wedlock."

"I don't think either of us gives a damn about that," I said. "When I get married, I'll do it in the Church."

"Think about it. You two lead public lives.

Too public, I'm told."

"You seemed unimpressed by what Milo and I have gone through this past month. Most people would've become unhinged. We got giddy."

Ben grimaced. "You sure as hell got everybody's attention. Maybe that helped set off your nut-job reporter." He put his hand on the one of mine that wasn't holding the sandwich. "Are you mad at me?"

"No. I can never stay mad at . . ." I stopped. "You're right. Am I marrying my awful brother?"

Ben stood up. "You could do worse. You can thank Adam for getting my head straight. Where did he get that? Must be from Tom."

"Hey — what about Marisa?"

Ben laughed. "She apologized. She swears it was the liquor."

"Maybe. She's no big drinker. But as Adam said, you're not bad-looking for an uncle — or a brother."

Milo had returned. "All clear," he said. "Your rug went to the cleaners. Doe and Jack just left."

He started to turn away, but Ben tapped his shoulder. "She's all yours," he said, and left the bedroom.

"What the hell did that mean?" Milo

asked, scratching behind his ear as he took Ben's place at the foot of the bed.

"It means he's okay with us. Did he say anything to you?"

"No. More about what happened and . . . You're not going to hell?"

"Not without you."

"You can explain that some other time. Still mad at me?"

I frowned. "About what?"

"Never mind." He chuckled. "Dr. Sung finished with Curtis about an hour ago. The little prick will be available for questioning later tonight, early tomorrow. I'm putting Dwight and Sam on it. They can play bad cop and bad cop. Dwight's back to being in charge."

"How long are you on suspension?"

"What day is it? I've lost track. Friday, right?"

I nodded absently — and realized it was December 31. "It's New Year's Eve!"

Milo grinned. "Hell of a way to spend it." He turned serious, that familiar yearning look in his eyes. "On the other hand, it's not over yet."

I smiled. "You didn't answer the question, big guy."

"Oh. Until Monday, unless the commissioners fire me for not showing up at Cobb's funeral. By the way, Bill figured out why Curtis ditched those boots. Our own lab's limited resources showed blood on them. I'll bet it belongs to Gus."

I let out a little gasp. "So he did kill poor Gus?"

"No guesses. I figure Curtis is going to sing like an opera star. He finally got center stage." Milo grew somber. "How do you really feel?"

"The pain pills are working. Can you hold me, just for a little bit?"

Milo made a face. "You've got cheese on your chest."

"Oh!" I flicked the small bit off onto the floor.

"You complain about *my* housekeeping?" But he stretched out next to me, and it didn't matter that I almost fell off the single bed. He put his arms around me and I knew I was safe.

We both went to sleep. I don't know how we didn't end up falling on the floor, but we were so exhausted that we never moved. When we woke up two hours later, the house was empty. Adam and Ben were both gone. If our phones had rung, we never heard them.

Milo insisted on carrying me to the sofa.

461

It was almost nine o'clock.

"Fleetwood was here while you were asleep this afternoon," Milo said, bringing me water for my second dose of Percocet. "I decked him."

"You didn't!"

He laughed. "No, but I threatened to if he ever told Vida we missed her show. He'll bring the tape tomorrow. Vida and Kip handled this mess on your site. She says Fleetwood did okay on the radio. I'd forgotten he'd almost been blown up when his station was bombed."

"That was when I saw his human side." I swallowed the pills. "Nothing on Mitch?"

Milo sat down next to me and shook his head. "The Yakima sheriff called back, but I wasn't available. Sam says my counterpart is as puzzled as I am. The good news is that there's no way Andrews can nail Laskey's kid on a vehicular homicide charge. The boy ran out into traffic. If Hitler had hit him, he'd get off, too. I figure Andrews is venting. I'll tap into my KingCo contacts Monday. The ones I dealt with in Bellevue were good cops. If his wife's doing better, I'll bet Mitch is back on the job next week."

"Really?"

He shrugged. "The Seattle cops let him go."

462

I punched Milo's arm. "You didn't mention that."

"I forgot." He grinned at me. "Even kind of beat-up, you're still a distraction. But Vida was right. Maybe we should act like grownups in public. It's been kind of fun, but it does call attention to us."

I nodded. "Maybe dangerous, too. But we've never been a secret in Alpine. Ever since we met, people have talked about whether we were sleeping together or whether we weren't."

Milo sighed. "Small-town mentality breeds that stuff. I didn't think we were that fascinating." He put an arm around me. "We're not in public now. How do you feel?"

I grabbed his free hand and put it against my cheek. "You tell me."

And so he did.

Milo was right about Curtis. The next morning, he sang like Placido Domingo. On the June day he'd missed checking in with the sheriff's office, he'd driven around the area, "getting acclimated to a primeval new world." He'd come across Gus, with his camera slung around his neck, walking by Cass Pond. Curious, he pulled over, wondering if he, too, was a journalist. They got to talking and Gus said he was going up to

463

Mount Sawyer in search of Myrtle. Curtis was intrigued, so they hiked the nearby trail together. Gus wasn't happy about having company and they got into a row inside the cave. Curtis said he didn't start it, but the situation deteriorated when he grabbed Gus's camera. Being bigger and stronger than Curtis, Gus had the advantage. But Curtis had his very sharp Camillus Boy Scout knife. He insisted he meant to stab Gus only enough to make him back off. His version was questionable. It was possible that Gus had bled out after Curtis bolted, taking a few pictures as he made sure his victim wasn't following him. Then he ditched the camera and returned to the office.

Later, when he'd confessed to a homicide he hadn't committed, Curtis figured he could use the experience to write a book. It hadn't taken me — or Milo — long to realize he was a total flake, but I was so involved with Tom's children, who allegedly wanted to buy the *Advocate,* that Curtis wasn't my priority. Even after his last stunt with the phony confession, I'd considered him delusional — but not mad as a hatter.

"He knew about the Nelson kids," Milo said, drinking coffee at my kitchen table after returning from the hospital, where he'd gone as an unofficial interested party. "Curtis knew a lot about you — and me, even though we weren't together much last summer." He paused, giving me a wry smile. "The grapevine was probably yakking about why we *weren't* sleeping together."

I nodded. "I wonder how long he'd been thinking about revenge. Ben suggested it might've been triggered by our public displays of affection, but I think this has been festering inside Curtis much longer. You were gone for three weeks, so he couldn't get both of us."

"That's the weird part," Milo said, looking chagrined. "Curtis went back to the Seattle area after he left Alpine. He grew up on the Eastside, but his parents had split up while he was in college. They'd set up some kind of trust for him, which is where he got the money for the Nelson kids. Maybe they knew he was weird — both Mom and Dad moved away, so there was no home to go to. If I can sort through all the bullshit, he bunked with whoever he knew with an empty couch in the Redmond, Kirkland, and Bellevue suburbs. He was always on the prowl for what he called a 'human horror story' — or some damned thing." Milo paused to light cigarettes for both of us and shot me a meaningful look. "Guess where

465

he found one."

I gasped. "Not . . . ?"

Milo nodded. "He saw me. That's when it's not good being tall."

I put my hand on his. "I never saw you on TV."

"No. I was with a bunch of other law enforcement types and they made damned sure the camcorders were kept off of us. Curtis hung out across the street with some of the other ghouls."

I shuddered. "And you never saw him."

He shook his head. "I was too focused on whether my daughter was about to be killed. I wouldn't have noticed a herd of buffalo in the cul-de-sac."

"Oh, Milo," I said, touching his hand. "No wonder we're nuts."

"Not as nuts as Curtis." He paused to puff on his cigarette. "That set him off, but the clincher was after he came up here and Gus's body was found. He got worried. We were the enemy and we had to go."

I closed my eyes for a moment. "Will there be a trial?"

"Plea bargain, maybe." He took my chin between his thumb and forefinger. "Hey, don't upset yourself over something that might never happen, okay?"

"I'll try not to. Really."

He leaned closer and kissed me lightly. "Good. Did I ever tell you you're cuter than a sandbox full of kittens?"

"I look more like bird crap," I said.

"Not to me. That was the first thing I thought when I met you." Milo stood up and went to the window, looking into the carport, where he'd parked my Honda after driving it back from headquarters. "The snow's stopped. The bomb didn't do much damage to your house — just more scorching. I've got to decide what kind of car to buy. The Nordby brothers are lending me a new Chevy Yukon."

"Is it red?"

He shook his head. "It's black. Looks like a damned hearse."

I got up awkwardly from the table. I was more stiff and sore than I'd been yesterday. It was time to take another pain pill. "Adam's staying at the rectory tomorrow. He and Ben are leaving right after Mass. They're coming for dinner tonight."

"Oh?" Milo turned around and leaned against the sink. "I'll leave you guys alone. I should go home anyway if I can borrow your car."

"You can," I said, moving closer and tugging at his shirtsleeve. "But you come to dinner, too. Things are different now. It's a whole new year. A whole new life for us."

Milo cradled my face in his hands. There was no wistful look in his eyes, only a steady calm that bespoke contentment. "You're right. I don't need to go home. I'm already there."

ABOUT THE AUTHOR

Mary Richardson Daheim started spinning stories before she could spell. Daheim has been a journalist, an editor, a public relations consultant, and a freelance writer, but fiction was always her medium of choice. In 1982 she launched a career that is now distinguished by more than fifty novels. In 2000, she won the Literary Achievement Award from the Pacific Northwest Writers Association. In October 2008 she was inducted into the University of Washington's Communications Hall of Fame. Daheim lives in her hometown of Seattle and is a direct descendant of residents of the real Alpine when it existed from the early twentieth century until it was abandoned in 1929. The Alpine/Emma Lord series has created renewed interest in the site, which was named a Washington State ghost town in July 2011.